Scripted

Scripted

FEARNE COTTON

MICHAEL JOSEPH

PENGUIN MICHAEL JOSEPH

UK | USA | Canada | Ireland | Australia
India | New Zealand | South Africa

Penguin Michael Joseph is part of the Penguin Random House group of companies
whose addresses can be found at global.penguinrandomhouse.com

First published 2024
001

Copyright © Fearne Cotton, 2024

The moral right of the author has been asserted

Set in 13.5/16pt Garamond MT Std
Typeset by Jouve (UK), Milton Keynes
Printed and bound in Great Britain by Clays Ltd, Elcograf S.p.A.

The authorized representative in the EEA is Penguin Random House Ireland,
Morrison Chambers, 32 Nassau Street, Dublin D02 YH68

A CIP catalogue record for this book is available from the British Library

HARDBACK ISBN: 978–0–241–67632–5
TRADE PAPERBACK ISBN: 978–0–241–67633–2

www.greenpenguin.co.uk

MIX
Paper | Supporting
responsible forestry
FSC® C018179

Penguin Random House is committed to a
sustainable future for our business, our readers
and our planet. This book is made from Forest
Stewardship Council® certified paper.

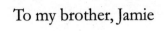

To my brother, Jamie

I

It was the worst summer Jade could remember. Although the late June sun sat lemony in the sky, the air was cool enough to bring goosebumps to the bare skin of her arms. It was the sort of summer's day that made her question why she lived in England.

Standing outside the main doors to her block of flats, she tied her brown unbrushed waist-length hair into a ponytail. She tapped her phone and opened the playlist 'Run Jade Run', letting the first track fill her whole head. But just as she was about to pick up into a jog, she heard a low voice cutting through the music from above.

Turning to look up to her fifties-style balcony, she saw Adam, his sleep-ruffled hair its usual mess of blonde and brown, leaning over the white iron railings, waving a set of keys and mouthing the word 'Jade!' theatrically.

Jade yanked out her earphones and stage-whispered back, '*What, Adam? What?!*'

'Your keys.' He held them aloft, pointing at them accusingly, his eyes squinting in the light. 'I'm not going to be here when you get back. I'm going for a coffee with Benny, then I'm meeting Tommo for a few beers later.'

'*Forfucksake,*' she muttered to herself as Adam lobbed the keys with a little too much punch in her direction.

'You really ought to invest in proper running gear at

some point,' he added once she'd caught them. 'You look like a teenage boy off to drink cider down the park.'

With that he turned quickly back inside, still in his boxer shorts, his arms wrapped around his bare torso. Jade looked down at her oversized, creased, tie-dye T-shirt. Then down to her legs and the grey tracksuit bottoms that sagged at the knee and ballooned at the ankle. She'd never seen the point in spending extortionate amounts on sleek, elaborately patterned leggings when she was more than comfortable in her favourite tracksuit bottoms. She stood motionless for three long seconds and felt the sting of his words.

Then she started to run. One foot in front of the other, as if each step further from the flat could distance her from her problems. Today she needed the hypnotic flow of water – so she headed for the river. She didn't want to think about Adam's reluctance to spend any decent amount of time with her, or his regular slights and put-downs. And she *really* didn't want to think back to their incredibly irritating conversation in bed last night. She winced and shook her head.

Picking up her pace, she could feel her hair splaying out like knotted tentacles behind her as gravity pulled her down the length of the hill. She let her legs pick up momentum and move in cyclones. Swinging her body, she took a right down River Lane, past the impossibly big houses with Georgian windows and trees sculpted into cones. She could see a glimmer ahead – early-morning sunbeams skipping across the grooves in the water. Her breathing and legs settled into an even rhythm, her heart matching the drumbeat in her ears.

The houses that lined the far bank of the river always piqued her curiosity, sending her into a fantasy world of people she didn't know. Her favourite was a small wooden house that she thought should be in the woods of Yosemite National Park. Jade could almost smell moss, smoke and cedar just looking at its porch and decking that overlooked the river. But, despite the meditative state she could slip into when running, Adam's words still rang in her head. When had it all started to go so wrong? More and more hairline cracks were appearing in their relationship. And still she found herself trying to replace her worries with memories of better times. Maybe everything would be OK. Maybe she could glue the cracks back together.

Letting her shoulders drop, Jade allowed her mind to meander back to the night they met. Sophie had dragged her to the opening of a new exhibition by an artist who painted rotting fruit using natural dye from the very fruits themselves. Jade had thought it sounded extremely pretentious, but they'd rushed straight from work in their paint-splattered overalls, and any excitement Jade had felt about the prospect of free wine and a night out had disappeared in the face of the preened and pampered fine-art crowd. Sophie had floated off to talk to an old friend from art school and Jade had stood awkwardly, feeling out of place and dishevelled, her eyes darting from the crowd to the ground.

She had noticed the veins that ran down the front of

his biceps first. Then, daring to glance up at his face, the naturally lighter streaks of hair that twisted messily through the darker shades beneath. He seemed to take up space without effort as he moved around the room, gesticulating as he spoke, his head thrown back with uninhibited laughter. Watching him made her aware of how tightly wound she felt. And, as the evening progressed, her body had gravitated towards his like a magnet. He had said something to her about her dungarees; she had made a quip about his spotless T-shirt.

Now she smiled, remembering the moments that evening when she had felt Adam's eyes on her, even when she wasn't looking at him; his half-smile when she stole a glance. Reminiscing about that first night felt like the recovery of something. A safety rope to better times.

From their first meeting she was hooked – and felt herself slowly unravelling at the seams. In those early days, Adam's confidence and breezy approach to life seemed to be the missing puzzle piece she so desperately needed. His self-assurance rubbed off on her like delicious aftershave. He had turned up when she was mostly made of tears and bowls of cereal for dinner. And she had raced into combining their lives, feeling she could at last breathe. But recently his unruffled demeanour, the space he took up, felt like a block of concrete dragging her down.

But she didn't want to be single at thirty-two. She didn't want to feel the surge of pain she knew was sitting just below one thin layer of skin. It would all be OK. It had to be OK.

Reaching Teddington Lock was a relief. She touched a tree with her fingertips as if to mark the halfway point, then turned on her heels to make her way home along the river path. Dodging dog-walkers and bedraggled parents pushing sleeping babies in buggies, she arrived back at the main road which led to her flat at the top of the hill.

Once she'd left the river behind her, the roar of car engines invaded the silence – and Jade lifted her gaze with mild dread. Jogging back up the hill felt like a battle with gravity. Her lungs pumped as she began her ascent, legs as heavy as steel. Finally she reached the small concrete stairway that ran alongside a row of luxury apartments that overlooked the Thames. It was her favourite view: the expanse of sky, the silky bend of the river that snaked through the trees.

Slowing to a walk, she gulped down cool air and stretched her arms above her head. As she took the first step, she looked down at the fluorescent trainers she knew Adam hated, and then to the random objects that littered the soil either side of the steps: a solitary rubber glove, which took on a sinister edge without its matching pair; a curled crisp packet; a decomposed apple core. She pushed each step away, her thighs twitching with fatigue. A crushed juice carton; a contorted, empty can of beer. So much litter hidden just out of view from the high-earners.

As her right foot hit the penultimate step, her eyes landed on a wad of paper. Compared to the rotting and crumpled litter strewn about, this stack of paper seemed pristine – untouched by human hand. She leaned in closer.

It looked like a script. Not that Jade had seen one since drama club at school. The font looked similar to that of a typewriter, with short stabs of text and names above each section. Shoving her phone into her sports bra, she wrapped the bottom of her baggy T-shirt around her fingers, pincered the sides of the stapled sheets, and picked it up.

Jade turned it over in her hands, inspecting it as if it were a fossil. Maybe a film star was staying in the adjacent apartments while on location. A couple of years ago, Brad Pitt had allegedly stayed down the road in Petersham while filming at Shepperton Studios – although she never did catch a glimpse of him, despite altering her run route to glide past his supposed rental twice a week. Maybe it was for a play? Richmond Theatre often showed small but acclaimed shows that had been touring nationally. Her mum, Sue, had once dragged her to watch Anton Du Beke's one-man show there. As a huge *Strictly* fan, Sue had worn a purple sequinned top to try and catch Anton's eye. At one point, Jade remembered with a grimace, her mother had even waved at him as he jived towards their side of the auditorium, spilling her plastic glass of wine all over Jade's lap. Jade had then excused herself to spend an inordinate amount of time in the bathroom.

Throwing a look over her shoulder to ensure she was alone, Jade started to read:

JADE

She froze. Scanning the page, she took in very little, but

tried to spot more mentions of her name. Her eyes jumped over every other word until they landed on:

ADAM

What? Her eyes ran back up to the top. Above the first line of script, headed with her own name, was a stage direction:

```
[Jade leans against the kitchen worktop. One of
the cupboard doors overhead is wonky, as the
top hinge is loose. Jade stares at the floor to
avoid eye contact with Adam.]
```

Jade's stomach lurched.

Her kitchen cupboard door – the one that stored her ever-growing assortment of mugs – was hanging by loose hinges.

Her eyes flicked to the next chunk of script. Under the stage directions were Jade's first lines of script:

```
                    JADE
      Adam, are you sure you need to go to
      LA? Aren't long-haul flights quite
      expensive?
```

Jade looked up from the page and dug her toes into the ground to steady herself. The trees around her spun.

Last night her boyfriend of three years had casually stated that he 'probably needed to go abroad for his next work project'. Now Jade finally allowed herself to think back to the irritation she had felt as he had nonchalantly mentioned it in bed, then rolled over to face away from her.

Adam's clothing line, Good2, had been in business for four years. Initially he had started the brand alongside his day job of styling for an established men's clothing line. But two years into creating Good2, Miley Cyrus had worn one of his T-shirts on a prime-time chat show in America, and, after a period of press interest and online hype, he had saved enough money to make the leap and quit his styling job. Although the brand still sold in Selfridges as well as on his own website, the yearly turnover had dropped – yet his lifestyle choices often didn't reflect it. A trip abroad in the midst of a period of low business felt excessive to say the least. Reckless, in fact. Adam's relaxed approach to anything remotely practical had once calmed Jade's nerves, but it now rattled her every bone. Whenever she questioned his rate of spending, he would simply blame their rent being too high. Last night, after his mention of a trip abroad, Jade had let her hand linger centimetres from the bedside lamp, while silence engulfed them both.

Jade blinked herself back into the present moment, letting the memory fade and her eyes focus on the page in her hands. The script continued with another stage direction:

```
[Adam leans against a wall where a brass clock
is hung. The clock reads 8:10pm and the weather
dial shows sun and cloud.]
```

The clock. This was Jade's clock – the most generous and well-thought-out gift presented to her on her thirtieth birthday by her godmother, Belinda. Each time a new weather front moved in, the mechanism would gently whirr and a little picture of a sun peeking out from a cloud, or raindrops, or even thunder and lightning would appear.

This script was a terrifyingly accurate look into a world that felt very much like Jade's. The names, the clock, the wonky cupboard . . . Her neck muscles tensed, and she noticed the uncomfortable stitch below her ribs for the first time since she'd left the house. She dared to read on.

ADAM

It's really important, babe. It's
the right scene. The right vibe. I
can't get that inspiration here.
It's so middle class. I can hardly
design an edgy top for young people
while walking around high-street
chains and the farmers market on a
Sunday. As much as I love popping
into Whole Foods, it's about as edgy
as a sponge.

Jade's eyes widened. Her large cup of pre-run coffee pulsed through her veins. She needed anchoring. Letting her thighs smack onto the step below, she sat down and read on.

Another stage direction:

[Jade keeps her head tilted down and her gaze on her feet.]

> JADE
>
> I just think that flights are, like, well over £500 to get there and back. Where would you stay?

> ADAM
>
> I don't know. With a friend.

> JADE
>
> You have friends in LA? Who?

> ADAM
>
> I don't know. People I've met over the years. I'll work it out.

> JADE
>
> So, you really need to go and do this?

> ADAM
>
> Babe, yes. I've told you. You want to see my brand expand, right? This is an important part of my creativity. I'm probably going to go next Tuesday.

[Jade continues to look at the floor and kicks
a clump of granola by her toes.]

                    ADAM
        It's an important trip. I'm sure
        flights won't be too bad.

                    JADE
        OK. It's just . . .

This was not a conversation that they'd had, but the
script bore an uncanny resemblance to a typical conversation between them – and not only because of the
storyline. It was as if the script was transcribed from her
mind. It was typical Adam, typical her. Adam making
light of a huge decision which impacted Jade; Jade
unable to find the right words. Her throat had become
the pit-stop for all the expletives she didn't dare shout,
the questions she was too scared to ask, the no's she
never felt brave enough to say.

   Jade closed her eyes and let her head flop back, face to
the sky, before her eyes flashed back down to the page.
She hoped to see more text under her name – questioning
Adam's trip, saying a vehement no, the right words to
wrap the conversation up tightly.

                    ADAM
        I'm probably going to stay in West
        Hollywood. There are some good
        flea markets there. I think they

call them Swap Meets or Meet Swaps
or something. I'm already feeling
inspired. I'm going to bring more of
a skater feel to the line, but only
subtly. It's still got to look
classy, clean, and continue with the
brand's core feel that I've
established.

                    JADE
Sounds good.

                    ADAM
Right, I'm having a bath and getting
an early one.

Jade gulped, freeing her fingers from her scrunched-up T-shirt as they fumbled to turn the page, the whole wad of paper falling to the ground. She grabbed at it, scooping it back up into her arms, then pinched at the pages and turned to continue reading, but there was nothing. The rest of the pages were blank. She tried again, working her way from the page she had just read and rubbing at it to ensure she hadn't missed anything. Nothing. Glaring white emptiness staring back at her. Heart racing, she rolled the pages into a tube and slid them down into the waistband of her joggers.

She walked home, her head spinning. One foot, the next foot, one more step, every now and then tapping the side of her waist to check the rolled-up script was still in place. As she approached the main door to their block of flats, her neighbour Mr Merry was leaving.

'Morning, Jade. Bit nippy out today, isn't it?' said Mr Merry as he tipped his flat cap towards her.

Mr Merry was indeed always merry – which had led to Adam secretly calling him 'Mr Men' behind his back. Always with endearment, as both Jade and Adam were very fond of their brief yet sunny corridor chats.

'Oh hi. Morning, Mr Men,' Jade blurted out. 'Er, er, Mr Merry, Mr MERRY,' she clarified. 'Have a lovely, lovely walk.'

Flustered, cheeks burning red, she rushed past him and ran up the stairs to her first-floor flat. She fumbled for the keys she'd shoved down her bra and ripped them out, scratching her chest as she did. Thrusting the key into the lock, she pushed through the door and fell to her knees in the hallway, pulled the paper from her joggers, and lay on her back staring at the ceiling.

What the hell was she going to do now? Call Sophie? Definitely not her mum, that would only create more drama. Maybe she should tell Adam – yet, somehow, that felt entirely wrong. Jade sat up and crossed her legs, letting her head hang towards the curled script on the floor. She was so consumed by the feeling of anxiety in her chest that it took her a whole minute to notice that Adam had walked mud across the carpet of the hallway on his way out.

Picking the script back up, she stared at the words and read them over and over. Who wrote this? How did they know such intimate details about her flat and relationship? She lay back on the floor, letting the adrenaline slide off her skin, leaving her numb and quiet.

2

Jade's thighs always went flamingo pink when she got out of the bath. It was one of the things Adam used to say he loved about her. He would call her his little dragon and rub her flaming thighs beneath her towel. Now, padding down the hallway from the bathroom, the script from this morning's run still playing on a loop in her mind, she couldn't remember the last time he had called her anything but 'Jade'. Before they met, she had simply felt ordinary, with her hazel eyes – not light enough to be green, not dark enough to be mysterious – and her brown hair – not rich and brunette but not sun-kissed either. Her body was not firm enough to be athletic, not soft enough to be voluptuous. She had always felt as if she were the midpoint to everything. Growing up next to her sister, Lily, only accentuated it. Yet Adam, for a brief time in the early days of their relationship, had made her feel far from average.

She sat on the end of their bed and let the sweat drip down her face onto her pink thighs. She didn't see the point in a bath or shower that was anything other than boiling. She wanted to feel like it was doing something – moving stuff on, sweating stuff out, burning off whatever she had picked up throughout her day. She closed her eyes and let the heat suck the last drops of adrenaline from her bones. It was still light outside, but the comfort of her bed pulled her nearer towards sleep.

When finally each limb was relaxed and her mind was losing its grip on the day, she heard a key in the door, then two heavy stomps on the doormat. Jade's body shot into an upright position.

'For fuck's sake, who's walked mud all over the carpet?' boomed Adam through the bedroom wall.

Jade wiped the sweat off her face with the towel. She hadn't been anticipating his return for hours, as a beer with Tommo almost exclusively ended with Adam crashing through the door at gone midnight, and it was only eight o'clock. She inhaled and said in a whispered hush, '*You! You walked mud over the carpet,*' then raced to put her knickers and a T-shirt on – the possibility of Adam feeling horny after a couple of beers was high, and she really wasn't in the mood.

'Hi, how come you're back?' Jade shouted. 'I thought you said you were out with Tommo?'

'Oh, he promised he would take his mum to the airport at five in the morning tomorrow so he didn't fancy a big one,' Adam shouted back nonchalantly.

'OK. I'm just out of the bath,' Jade said as she walked into the kitchen, where Adam was sitting on the counter with his shoes still on. She fixed her eyes on the texture of the worktops and tried to steer her brain away from the curled-up script in their bedroom. 'I was going to get a super-early night but we can just hang out if you fancy instead?' she asked, moving towards the corner of the counter below the wonky cupboard. Adam's eyes were on his phone, his fingers scrolling through Instagram, his mind lost in other people's lives. Jade's question was left hanging.

'Reckon you can fix this cupboard soon?' she continued. 'It's driving me mad. It's like playing a game of *Total Wipeout* every time I try and make a cup of tea.' She looked up at him, forcing a small laugh.

'Jade, I've been so busy. But I will, I will. I just haven't had a second. I'll get it done before I go away. Anyway, you're the handy, arty one, can't you do it?'

Jade swallowed, her throat sandpaper dry. Adam looked up at her for the first time.

'You look pretty. All flushed and pink.' One side of his mouth curled up, then his eyes drifted back down to his phone.

The unexpected compliment took the electricity out of her nerves. She gazed down at her bare pink legs and coyly crossed them, feeling her damp thighs stick together.

'I was chatting about the trip with Tommo. I'm thinking LA.' Adam kept his eyes on his phone.

'Adam, are you sure you need to go to LA? Aren't long-haul flights quite expensive?'

The words fell out of her mouth, each one landing quietly at Adam's feet. She noticed a clump of granola on the floor, and as she kicked it out of the way a wave of déjà vu hit her . . .

Adam continued to stare down at his phone, scrolling while answering her quiet question.

'It's really important, babe. It's the right scene. The

right vibe. I can't get that inspiration here. It's so middle class. I can hardly design an edgy top for young people while walking around high-street chains and the farmers market on a Sunday. As much as I love popping into Whole Foods, it's about as edgy as a sponge.'

That word. *Sponge.* Sponge. Why was that word kicking her in the gut? It was the line in the script! She replayed Adam's last sentence in her head and matched it with the script she had now almost memorised verbatim: *Whole Foods, sponge, farmers market.* She heard ringing in her right ear and leaned back to steady herself on the counter beneath the weather clock; glancing up, she could see the reflection of it in the window, the clouds moving in to cover the sun, the hands sitting at 8:10pm.

The urge to leave the room, or eat something very salty, or do both at the same time, moved Jade towards the snack cupboard. Crisps could annihilate thoughts one at a time. Thick peanut butter spread on crackers and stuck to the roof of her mouth could melt away worries. She lurched forward to grab a packet of Kettle chips, but something pulled her back to where she'd been stood beneath the clock and before she could process what was happening her mouth opened.

'I just think that flights are, like, well over £500 to get there and back. Where would you stay?'

She felt her pupils dilate. Those words. They belonged to her, but also to the page.

Adam kept his eyes locked on his phone screen. He pushed one trainer off with the other foot, letting dry mud shatter on the kitchen floor as it hit the deck. The next shoe followed. He didn't look up. 'I don't know. With a friend.'

The room took on a surreal form, like Jade was looking through a fish-eye lens.

'You have friends in LA? Who?'

Adam put his phone beside him on the counter and looked at Jade with a furrowed brow. 'I don't know. People I've met over the years. I'll work it out.'

He simply couldn't give a shit. She could see it in every muscle in his body. For every tight neck muscle Jade felt, he had one so relaxed it was almost falling off the bone. Even his hair looked chilled out; dark blonde streaks flopping carelessly over his eyes. Salt. She needed salt.

'So, you really need to go and do this?' she asked.

Adam jumped down from the counter and opened the snack cupboard, looked it up and down, then shut it again.

'Babe, yes. I've told you. You want to see my brand expand, right? This is an important part of my creativity. I'm probably going to go next Tuesday.'

Jade kicked the piece of granola harder this time. It ricocheted off the opposite cupboard and scattered. This small breakfast cluster seemed to take on a new meaning. Her world felt like it was scattering too – pieces moving in all directions, untethered, chaotic, no sense to any of it.

Adam walked out of the kitchen and towards the bathroom.

'It's an important trip. I'm sure flights won't be too bad,' he said over his shoulder. Then the bathroom door slammed shut.

Jade felt rage crystallise in her jaw. 'OK. It's just . . .'

The bath taps were now running fiercely. She was sure he could barely hear her.

She stared out the window. Why couldn't she say the words that were spinning around her head?

The bathroom door clicked open, breaking Jade's train of thought. Adam poked his head around the door.

'I'm probably going to stay in West Hollywood,' he said. 'There are some good flea markets there. I think they call them Swap Meets or Meet Swaps or something. I'm already feeling inspired. I'm going to bring more of a skater feel to the line, but only subtly. It's still got to look classy, clean, and continue with the brand's core feel that I've established.'

His usual move. Having to have the last word. His final manifesto to seal the deal and keep Jade silent. The words 'core' and 'feel' made her cringe.

Jade smiled and nodded her head. 'Sounds good.' Every ounce of energy drained from her.

Adam closed the door again and shouted above the noise of the running water, 'Right, I'm having a bath and getting an early one.'

Jade turned and slowly shuffled to the cupboard, her hand moving automatically towards the family-size bag of crisps. She shuffled back into the corner of the counter, beneath the clock. She was safe here. She knew how the counter felt on her back; the salt on her tongue; the numbness gradually moving up her body.

Slowly and without noticing, Jade's hand moved from packet to mouth, from packet to mouth, until her lips turned the colour of milk from the salt. She stopped when her fingers could feel only crumbs and grains of salt at the bottom of the bag. She needed to get into bed and somehow fall asleep before Adam clambered in. Her foot stomped on the bin peddle and she threw in the empty packet, then scurried to the sanctuary of her bedroom before the self-loathing kicked in.

What was going on? Was she being watched, spied on? Was somebody playing a trick on her? Her forehead pulsated with it all. She craved blankness and oblivion. No more talking tonight. No more thinking. Without bothering to clean her teeth, she slid under the covers and let her tongue pick the remnants of crisps out of her molars. She gave a deep sigh, letting her long damp hair press into the pillow. No more words.

3

The sound of the alarm clock centimetres from Jade's head made her chest heave. She sat up quickly, flapping her left arm to find the stop button. She knew she had exactly thirty seconds to grab her phone off the bedside cabinet before that alarm went off next. Desperately trying not to wake Adam, she slipped off the bed as if her body were lubricated. A slat beneath the mattress creaked and she froze. Adam turned on his side.

'Jade, seriously,' he said with closed eyes, 'I'm exhausted, can you try and not be so bloody noisy.' He rolled back over and pulled the duvet over to his side.

She watched his back muscles slide over his shoulder blades as a flush of foolishness blotted her cheeks. It had been five days since their stilted discussion about his trip. A whole five days of wondering if she had imagined the script and was losing her mind. True to his word, Adam had booked his LA flight for the following week. And each morning since, she had gone to her sock drawer where she was hiding the script and slipped it into her backpack to take to work. It would be inexplicable if it was discovered by Adam. But she also had the overwhelming compulsion to keep reading over the words to try and figure out what was going on. How had the exact script on the page predicted their conversation? It felt implausible. Impossible.

Within seconds the kettle was on, and minutes later warm strong coffee was sliding down her throat. Jade always left her work clothes in the bathroom so that she could shower and dress without waking Adam before she left the flat. Today she pulled her paint-splattered dungarees on, covered her long, unbrushed hair with her favourite purple hat, then, after putting on her Doc Martens, looked at herself in the hallway mirror and half smiled.

Outside, she hopped on her bike, and soon the cool morning air was skimming past her cheeks, blowing the stress away. Every day Jade felt grateful for her bike and the freedom and movement it gave her. It was pink, but not Barbie-pink; Jade always thought it was like the colour of the inside of a grapefruit. Even on days when she sat on her bike alongside rush-hour traffic, she'd be glad to be out in the world and pity those trapped in cars, sedentary and frustrated, their faces screwed up, necks craning to see what the hold-up was, then glancing down at hidden phones in laps as they tried to kill precious time.

The unseasonably bad weather had continued, and as she cycled down congested roads the grey clouds felt so low she could almost touch them. She had barely said two words to Adam since that night, choosing instead to stay at work late each day. He, meanwhile, had gone out most nights. The lack of communication had left her feeling empty.

A little before 8am, she reached the warehouse in Acton and slid the large wooden doors open to an already bustling scene. The speakers were blaring out nineties music and Lethabo, Sophie and Jackson were crouched down fixing strips of cloth to wooden boards. Lethabo, today in pink dungarees to match his hair, moved to the music as he worked, while Jackson crouched, long legs in tight black jeans pulled close to his chest, barely moving at all. They were yin and yang, Lethabo a dancing rainbow, his movements somewhere between a cat and Liza Minnelli. Jackson, meanwhile, was always dressed in black and barely moved all day, his long limbs only active when he had a paintbrush in hand.

Home. This truly felt like home to Jade. The smell of paint, irregular splodges of colour like birthmarks dotting the floor, her mates in full creative flow.

Sophie looked up, the nose ring hanging from her septum glinting in the overhead lighting. 'Morning, Jadey,' she chirped, waving with her free hand. Lethabo and Jackson echoed the good mornings while they carried on with the tasks at hand.

'Morning, gang. All good?' Jade raised her voice over the music.

Sophie stood up. 'Fancy a fag?' Knowing full well Jade didn't smoke, this daily joke was a ritual in their friendship. Jade lowered her eyebrows in fake disgust and followed her mate outside.

Jade had never felt so comfortable with another human. Prior to Sophie, she had never felt at ease hugging someone for more than two seconds; Sophie's average hug lasted at least five. They stood outside the large sliding doors, Sophie drawing in smoke from her roll-up, a ray of faint sunshine breaking through the clouds to illuminate their faces.

'You alright, mate?' Sophie said between drags.

'Mmm, I'm OK,' Jade said, chewing the side of her mouth.

Sophie cocked her head to one side. 'No you're not. What's going on?'

'I dunno, Soph. It's been a weird week.' She considered telling Sophie about the script, as she had the day before, and the day before that. She wanted to. She just wasn't sure how.

Sophie blew out a stream of smoke that flitted past her neat strawberry-blonde bob. 'Weird in what way?' Her lips curled back around her cigarette.

'Adam wants to go away again. Next Tuesday. You know, like last time, when he went to Morocco for an "inspiration trip"?' Jade rolled her eyes as she spoke.

'Oh yeah? That seems a bit extra. Why does he have to keep going away? Is his clothing line doing much at the moment?'

'I'm not sure. He constantly tells me it's on the up again, but all of these expensive trips abroad seem excessive. I also just get the feeling he has lost all respect for me, the way he talks to me, you know.'

'Have you spoken to him about it?' Sophie asked.

Jade scrunched her face up. 'Well, I sort of go to try and say something and then the words don't come out. I know that if I say what I'm really thinking it'll all be over. We'll have one big row and that'll be it.'

Sophie, playing devil's advocate, said, 'And how would you feel about that?'

Jade winced. 'Erm, sad, I guess, but also probably a little relieved if I'm honest.'

'Well, what's stopping you, mate? Seriously, Jade, you need to free yourself.'

'Yeah, but . . . well, for starters, who'll pay the other half of the rent?'

'Could you cover it for a month or two while you find a roommate? I'd move myself in if it wasn't for Shania Twain.'

'Oh Soph, I wish I wasn't allergic to cats. Shania would just have me sneezing and wheezing if we lived together.'

'I know. Shania doesn't want to make your life any harder, babe. Could you move in with your mum for a bit?'

Jade's face fell.

'Even if it were just for a short amount of time?'

'I don't know. It just seems too overwhelming to even contemplate. We've been together three years now. I guess I'm nervous of change. And all the hassle that would come with a break-up. Like him moving all his stuff out and—'

'—which would give you more space! So that one is a plus. Go on.' She rolled her freckled hand in a motion encouraging Jade to continue.

'Well, Mum would make my life so hard worrying about how I'll cope and what will become of me as a single woman in my thirties.'

It was Sophie's turn to roll her eyes. 'Oh come on, Jade. Your mum? She'll give you shit whatever. Also, we are not in the 1950s. Next . . .'

'Um, I have my sister's hellish wedding to go to in six weeks and I can't even imagine going alone.'

'*Mate*, I'll go with you. Next.'

'Well I—god, Soph, this sounds pathetic to say out loud, but I kind of hoped Adam was the one. I think because things ended so badly with Navi I wanted to prove to everyone and myself that I could make a relationship work.'

Jade's voice was a faint whisper as she landed on Navi's name. This was why she never mentioned him. A curdle of sorrow, shame and worry sat in her tummy.

Sophie leaned in and lowered her voice to match Jade's. 'Well, that's not entirely up to you, babe. You can't shoulder all of that pressure. It takes two to tango.' A spiral of smoke streamed up from Sophie's mouth. 'Also, Navi was yonks ago. That whole chapter of your life is in the past.' She smiled softly, her whole face like the sun.

'This might sound odd, Soph, and perhaps I'm saying this aloud for the first time, but I have this fear that because of how things ended with Navi . . . I'm now doomed *for ever.*' Jade overdramatised in an attempt to add humour to a situation she actually felt pretty miserable about.

'I don't think you're doomed, babe,' Sophie said, flicking the butt of her roll-up to the floor. 'If you think Adam is the one then maybe you just need to get that spark back? Do you need a good old shag-fest of a week-end away perhaps? Get you out of the monotony of living together in the flat? Maybe you need cocktails, Parisian views, and to wear anything that's not dungarees covered in paint.'

Jade shrugged her shoulders, letting them land heavily. Sophie put her arm around her. 'Come on, we've got woodchip to paint. This set ain't gonna make itself.'

She guided Jade back into the warehouse, her arm still draped over Jade's shoulder. Jade could smell the smoke caught on Sophie's baggy turquoise cardigan. Maybe she was right. Maybe these fears were just matters of the mind. Maybe she and Adam just needed to have some fun. She and Sophie bent down next to Lethabo and Jackson, picking up paintbrushes simultaneously.

The current job was a little less exciting than their last. Throughout May, the four of them had painted and created the set for a big new British comedy on Netflix. They'd got to spend most of the month on set while the show was being filmed. The director constantly wanted corridors painted different shades of yellow, then changed her mind to blue after the job was done. The work itself wasn't the most creative – but they got to meet Jack Whitehall and Morgana Robinson, who had Jade in fits of laughter in between takes.

This new project involved constructing the set for an escape room in East London, a Victorian sitting room with artefacts and movable props. There was lots of making ornate furniture from scratch and restoring old objects, but it was done mostly from the confines of their company's slightly damp warehouse. Today, Jade was due to continue making eighty faux leather-bound books that were empty inside. Some opened up into boxes where clues would be stored, and each had to be adorned with a book title and author along the spine. It was a long and slightly arduous task, during which Jade mainly worried about the onset of carpal tunnel. But she had not once felt bored in the seven years she had worked for Big Brush Set Design. When she went home every evening, the paint under her nails reminded her how design and creativity was part of her; sometimes she wondered if it was *all* of her.

'*Jade!*' Lethabo shouted over Baby D's 'Let Me Be Your Fantasy'.

Jade looked up and dropped her Stanley knife.

'Have you got any gold leaf? I'm trying to make this bloody clock look ornate and it's so fucking fiddly.' Lethabo threw his hands in the air dramatically, the smallest fingernail on each hand glittering candyfloss.

Jade stood up, stretched out her legs and replied, 'I'll get some for you, dearest,' with a fond smile. She interlaced her fingers and pushed them over her head to elongate her back. A satisfying pop and her shoulder seemingly went back to where it was anatomically supposed to sit.

The back room, a small space cordoned off by low plywood walls, was home to a trestle table that held their communal kettle, two tins of assorted biscuits, Sophie's roll-up papers, and a tiny fridge for milk. Directly in front of the makeshift kitchen were rows and rows of shelves packed with sheets of coloured paper, planks of every shade of wood, tins of varying tones of paint, brushes in every size and length, turps, bolts, old tin cans, a mannequin's leg, papier-mâché animal heads – an Aladdin's cave of craft. But Jade knew exactly where the gold leaf was. It was one of her favourite materials. The way it gently collapsed onto a surface, its surrender creating perfectly uneven flecks of light . . . it felt like magic every time she used it.

She bent down and tucked herself into one of the deep shelves, reaching for the back wall where the precious gold leaf was kept. But instead of feeling the soft, wispy sheets her fingers hit a solid pile of paper.

Lying flat, she stretched her body deeper into the shelves so her fingers could slide the paper towards her. She brought it out of the depths of the shadows and into the light. She froze, looking down at the confusing familiarity. The typeface, the spacing – and a name she knew.

4

The heady bass of the music from the warehouse seemed to fade away altogether. Peering down at the script in her hands, Jade became as still and silent as possible. How was this happening again? Her heart raced; her thoughts crashed against one another like cymbals.

'*Jade?*' Another call from Lethabo. 'You alright back there?'

'*Yup!* Give me a minute, Thabs, for Christ's sake,' Jade spluttered.

Her heart thumped. She looked down at the words on the page but felt too panicked to make sense of them.

She closed her eyes and breathed in, attempting to keep the fear at bay, then peered down at the script with her back pressed into the shelves.

LILY

'*Help*,' Jade said aloud to no one. The Adam situation was one thing, but Lily was almost always impossible. Jade felt a wave of dread just imagining what nightmarish words might sit beneath her sister's name.

Jade was due to visit her after work to discuss wedding looks. She could think of nothing worse. Happy in her dungarees and Doc Martens, she could only

31

hazard a guess at what pastel monstrosity Lily had in mind for her bridesmaid's dress. Not only did Jade feel resentment at having to go to *another* of Lily's weddings, she also felt pain at the idea of attending a wedding full stop after how things had ended with Navi. She sighed and let her eyes move to the dialogue on the page.

LILY

So, sis, I'm going to need you to
help me out here. I've envisaged an
archway for the ceremony and it's
very classic, very simple, but also
striking. I want it to be mainly
silk roses trailing up the archway
and then hanging silk ribbons with
those tiny fairy lights that you
can't really see until they're
turned on. You know I'm on a tight
budget, Birdy, so I'm going to need
you to do this as a favour, yeah?
I'm sure you'll find it fun and you
can ask those mates of yours . . .
Sophie and Labo.

Oh god. So many things. Why did she always get Lethabo's name wrong? And why did she still insist on using Jade's childhood nickname, Birdy? She was thirty-two, for crying out loud.

This new script was utterly accurate in ways that only

Jade would understand. Lily constantly asked for Jade's help and never returned the favour. Her demands got bigger and grander each time without ever thanking her or acknowledging her effort. Jade read on:

[Jade stands in Lily's kitchen stroking a grey cat.]

                    JADE
        Mmm, OK. Well, logistically I would
        have to build most of that on the
        morning of the wedding as the mar-
        quee is outside, right? If there is
        wind overnight, it would tear it
        down so how will I have time to get
        ready?

                    LILY
        Oh, there'll be time. I don't think
        it'll take you long. So, cool? Get
        the brief? Classic, cool, but also
        striking. Oh, wait. The dresses. I
        haven't even shown you your dress.

[Lily thrusts a tablet towards Jade with a Pinterest board open and five dresses lined up.]

                    JADE
        It's brown.

                    LILY

Yes. Brown was the colour to watch
for weddings in *Vogue* last month.
It's very chic and will complement
my dress perfectly.

                    JADE

Mmm. Right.

                    LILY

Birdy, I know you can deliver this
archway for me. If you don't do it
the whole vibe will be kind of off-
kilter. I've told Mum you're doing
it, and she's so relieved as it's one
less thing for her to worry about.

                    JADE

Yup. Cool.

Jade placed the script back on the shelf and momentarily
pressed her fingertips into her eyelids. After three long
seconds she opened her eyes, outlines of her fingertips
still imprinted on her vision. Everything about this conversation riled her. There was not a shred of her that
wanted to make a floral arch on the day of the wedding,
but even more irritating was the sense that her sister's
guilt-tripping was once again at play. It was so transparent. But a sudden sting of realisation pinched between
Jade's shoulder blades: she always *did* say yes in the end.

'Babes! Seriously, what are you doing back here?'

Jade snapped out of her daze.

'Sorry, Thabs, I was deciding whether to have a tea or a coffee,' she said faintly.

'In another time zone? You've been back here like ten minutes.'

'Soz, I'm on it. I think we're out of gold leaf anyway, so I need to call Colin,' she said uncomfortably.

'Oh no, he's going to blame me, I know it. It's always my bloody fault. He said he's coming in today anyway as he wants to check on our progress,' Lethabo said, mouth animatedly downturned.

'It's alright, I'll handle it. Leave it to me.' She smiled and walked towards the kettle. Lethabo slowly skulked away, a single footstep to every two beats of the song playing on the speakers.

What was this sick joke and who was playing it on her? She rewound her brain to all the people she could have possibly pissed off. The only person she could think of was one of her old school friends, Erica, who still held a grudge because Jade hadn't turned up to her thirtieth birthday – a banging headache had stopped her from going. But it was over two years ago and Erica wouldn't have access to this level of detail. Jade's temples pulsed. She clicked the kettle on and reached for the glass biscuit tin. Under the Jenga tower of custard creams sat one lonesome Bourbon. She dug deep and brought it to her lips with urgency. Two bites and it was gone, taking with it some of the sharpness she felt in her bones. The kettle hummed and gurgled while Jade stared at the coffee pot, motionless. Everything felt like a huge effort. Even the thought of constructing her usual instant coffee with one sugar felt overwhelming. She moved the empty mug away and rolled the script into a tube. Walking at pace to her backpack, she pushed the pages deep inside with the other script.

Back out in the warehouse, Jade sat down beside Jackson, feeling unplugged from everything going on around her.

'Hey, how are the books going?' Jackson looked up from beneath his floppy dark brown hair that fell over both eyes, making his work ten times more challenging. He wiped a paint-covered hand across his oversized black Ramones T-shirt, the new paint stain now leaving only 'The Ram'.

'What books?' Jade replied as she crouched on the floor, discombobulated both from the shock of the new script and from Jackson asking her a question. He rarely spoke, let alone asked Jade anything.

'The eighty-odd books you're in the middle of making.' Jackson spoke with almost a whisper, his shyness softening the edges of each word.

'Oh, shit, yeah. I mean, yeah, good, they're going good.'

'I'm not sure what's more boring, the books or this sodding clock that is taking me for ever,' said Lethabo, stretching out every syllable.

'God, this project is quite fiddly, isn't it?' said Sophie. 'I almost wish we were back on that Netflix set. I mean, the director drove me up the wall but at least we got to have a laugh with the actors, and the catering on set was excellent.'

'Oh, do you remember the coronation chicken baguettes? I could eat one of those right now,' Lethabo interjected.

'And proper coffee, not the instant stuff we have to deal with here. You can really tell how classy a place is by the state of its coffee,' Sophie said wistfully.

'Do you reckon Colin will bother coming in later? I desperately want to get out of here early and go and eat Mexican food and drink a margarita and not think about restoring faux-Victorian artefacts,' Lethabo said.

Sophie beamed. 'Oh, me too. Shall we? I know he said, but he never comes in on a Friday. I reckon we could finish just before 5pm and he would never know. We're in tomorrow morning anyway to finish up. I need a margarita.'

Jackson flicked his hair out of his eyes and said, 'I'm in.'

'Jade?'

'I have to go to my sister's,' Jade said miserably. 'It's bridesmaid-dress day. Please pray for me.'

'Just get her to text you a photo of it,' said Lethabo, wagging a finger in disapproval.

'She wants me to try it on and go through some other wedding details.'

'Isn't it mad how, because somebody chooses to get married, everybody else has to do so much. Awful hen do's and expensive wedding gifts that they've chosen for you to buy from John Lewis. I've never understood that.' Sophie shook her head.

'I know, and why are they so long?' Jade said. 'Why do you always get seated next to someone you don't know at lunch? Why is the day interrupted by a complicated photo shoot?' She had rejected most of these norms when planning her wedding with Navi.

'Whyyyyyyyyyy!' Lethabo howled like a werewolf to the moon.

'I can't be bothered with any of it. And the brides-maid's dress is *b-brown*,' Jade stuttered. Then she caught herself. She didn't actually know that the dress was brown; she hadn't seen it yet.

'Brown?' Lethabo spat, his face pulled back, creating several more chins.

'Well, I think they're brown. That's what I think she's planning. Anyway, I wish I could come tonight but have fun without me.' Jade hurriedly picked up her Stanley knife to signify the end of the conversation.

'Well, good luck, babe. Brown, bloody hell.' Lethabo sat shaking his head while clutching the Victorian clock face.

Suddenly the warehouse door slid on its tracks, sunlight flooding the space.

'Ladies!' Colin walked in with the swagger of Liam Gallagher, his bald head shining like a mirror ball in the overhead lighting. Jackson rolled his eyes at Jade. Lethabo and Sophie looked forlornly at one another.

'Jade. A word.' Colin motioned to the back room. Her

stomach churned. She pushed her body from the floor and reluctantly walked towards him.

Colin was a small man who always stood with his legs apart, as if anchoring himself against a strong wind. A light blue polo shirt with the Big Brush Set Design logo on the left side was his daily uniform, along with jeans – always dark blue – and brown boat-shoes that squeaked on the floor as he walked. He fiddled on his phone without looking up at Jade. 'Dog needs walking. Penny is dropping her off at midday. Alrighty?'

'I'm a bit behind on the escape room so I'm not sure I'll have time,' Jade meekly contested.

'Do it in your lunch-break, love.' He sauntered back to the warehouse floor with his phone to his ear. 'Yeah, Pen? Bring Doodles at midday. Got the walk covered. Ta,' he bellowed into his phone, barely letting his PA Penny reply before he hung up.

Jade watched him walk away. She slunk back to Sophie. 'Why does he only ever ask me?'

'Because he knows you'll do it, mate.' Sophie looked into Jade's eyes, her strawberry-blonde eyebrows raised.

Jade nodded. She felt powerless. 'At what point does trying to be a good person turn you into a pushover, Soph?'

'I think at the point of resentment,' Sophie mused. 'If you're happy to help someone then I think that's proper altruism, but if you're doing it because you think you should that usually leads to resentment, right?' Sophie was clearly figuring it out as she spoke.

'Well, I feel resentful. I wouldn't admit that to many people.'

'You know I'd never judge you,' Sophie said. 'Time to start saying no, Jadey.' Sophie grinned mischievously then looked back down to the gramophone she was painting.

The clock hands moved slowly, but eventually, after hours of intricate work on book spines and small Victorian wall-hangings, dog-walking, and the entire *Elton John Greatest Hits* album, they landed at 5pm. Lethabo, Jackson and Sophie grabbed their bags and made for the door, Colin having left the warehouse an hour before.

'Have fun. And a marg for me,' Jade called. The warehouse doors slid shut behind them and the silence was all-consuming. Jade had managed to keep all thoughts of the script on the peripheral for most of the day – she had busied herself with surface chat about Lethabo's new boyfriend and the new portrait exhibition Sophie was planning – but, now she was in solitude, every worry and thought was magnified. She got up quickly, rotating her head in semicircles to loosen the muscles, made her way over to her backpack and picked up her cycling helmet. As she locked up the big sliding doors and climbed onto her bike, she forced herself to find, in the midst of worry, a little nugget of hope. Hope that this script would be wrong.

5

Lily's house was the penultimate in a smart Victorian terrace. Jade looked up at the three-storey building and felt the beginnings of a familiar self-loathing. Seeing Lily's picture-perfect home, with its blooming window boxes, red-brick walls, white-lacquered windowsills and monochrome tiles leading to the front door made her feel like even more of a mess. It had been part of Lily's divorce settlement; a four-bedroom town house with a garden lawn so perfect it could be mistaken for carpet. Its Chelsea postcode was enviable – Lily's monthly council-tax bill was nearly as much as Jade's rent. Even so, Lily whined for ages after the settlement that the house wasn't big enough. Jade slowly walked up the chequered path, feeling as if she were shrinking the closer she got.

Before knocking on the door, she discreetly peered through the window into the front room. She could see her sister standing in front of a shelving unit, looking it up and down with a slight squint. As Jade watched, Lily reached for a blue vase displaying purple pampas grass and moved it down one shelf to sit next to a small pile of blue leather-bound books. She then moved a chunk of purple amethyst to the left a little and stood back, as if to admire the juxtaposition of the new and ancient.

Jade raised an eyebrow. The shelves sat directly behind Lily's desk-top computer, which was surrounded by mood boards of curated settings: soft pink tones and glossy tiles, bright mustard yellows and brown plush velvet. Jade watched as her sister smiled, her long black hair shimmying across her slender back.

Lily had mentioned to Jade by text that she had started her own interior design business. Jade wondered how long this new venture would last. Her sister changed her career path constantly – sometimes as often as every six months, depending on how little momentum was gained and how quickly her focus drifted. It was one of the things that Jade found most infuriating about her. Bored of one endeavour, she would quickly reach for a new hat, vernacular, Instagram account, and general persona. Her confidence in claiming to be an expert in any chosen field drove Jade to distraction, but Lily's relentless re-invention gained attention and praise from their parents, pushing Jade's long-standing dedication to her work into the shadows. They were different ends of a magnet, repelling each other when in close proximity.

Last summer Lily had started her own online cookery tutorials, showcasing her 'famous' vegan Wellington recipe on her YouTube channel one day, and tips and tricks on how to make the perfect omelette on another. Her Insta-gram account, @Lilyscookups, showcased overly curated shots of meals she had made but more than likely didn't eat afterwards. Jade once watched a live-stream cook-a-long, flinched every time Lily pronounced 'sauté' incorrectly, and vowed never to watch again. She could only assume that the visibly low online audience catalysed Lily's swift departure from YouTube.

Prior to this, Lily had taken up jewellery design – which lasted for ten months, until the lady she had hired to make her designs put her prices up, meaning Lily was losing money with each sale.

Before the jewellery, Lily had opened an online crystal shop, 'Quartz You Can', which sold a plethora of semi-precious stones at extortionate prices. She had created her own meanings for each and sold them with individual turquoise silk bags. On Instagram, Lily had made her life look serene and glamorous, surrounded by chunks of quartz, towers of green calcite and shards of black tourmaline. But after seven months of photographing herself holding crystals with colour-coordinated mani-cured nails for social media, she gave up. Each time, no matter how short-lived the endeavour, their mum, Sue, threw celebratory praise Lily's way and alerted all her friends to her latest business venture. Their dad, Tony, would squeeze Lily's shoulders and kiss her on the nose, growling 'Well done, princess' in his gravelly East End voice.

Jade turned away from the view of Lily, who was now taking photos of the shelves scattered with turquoise vases and lilac books, and stared at the light grey front door. Straightening her shoulders, she pushed her chest out, willing her body to start looking confident in the hope her mind would catch on to the idea. The doorbell chimed merrily, and shortly after she heard Lily padding barefoot towards her. Bracing herself for a hug, Jade forced a smile and chirped, 'Hiiiiii, Lily,' as the door swung open.

'Birdy, darling, come in! I'm just getting ready for my first flurry of online interior-design sessions. I'm basically going to be getting my clients to show me round their homes on Zoom, and then I'll advise them on colour palettes and general themes to follow.' Lily's delicate arms were moving wildly as she spoke, her purple cashmere sweater pulled down over her hands. This coquettish detail irritated Jade immensely. Her sister could flirt with a lamp-post. When she turned it on, her head would tip downwards, the odd strand of hair falling over her big dark eyes. Lily had been dying her hair jet black ever since their parents divorced. It was always worn long, poker-straight, and shone like wet tar. When she tied it in a ponytail, she looked like a horse from behind.

'Sounds great. What's your new company called?' asked Jade, trying to sound like she cared.

'Maison Lily,' Lily said with a heavy dose of drama.

'Maison?' Jade furrowed her brow.

'Yes. It's French.'

'I know it's French. It's just . . . you're not,' Jade said gingerly.

Lily's face remained jubilant.

'Shouldn't you pop your surname in there too?' Jade continued. 'Don't you have to be like Adele to just use your first name?'

'Well, I've already built up quite an online presence and it's too complicated to add my surname now, what with having to change it again when James and I marry.'

'Fair do's.' Jade shrugged, knowing that Lily's dedicated online following had most likely been bought.

'One day I'll sort out your flat. If you can afford me.' Lily's laughter echoed around the marble kitchen.

'My flat is fine.'

'Well, I don't do *fine*. I want each of my clients to really feel they've been left with some of my flare and style.'

'I like my own style.'

'There are just some things about design that you probably don't see that I do. For example, crockery says a lot about a person. I've noticed you have square cereal bowls?' Lily's words ascended in tone, as if she were asking a question.

'And . . .'

'They just don't say the right things about you, Birdy. They're – some would say – naff.'

'Sorry – what do square bowls say about me?'

'That you're, well . . . trying to be edgy, but missing the mark,' said Lily.

'I think you're looking into it a bit too deeply. They were cheap and they hold cereal and milk so seem to do the job.'

'Well as I said, *one day*, Birdy. Anyway, shall we chat le mariage?' Lily pushed her hair from her shoulder, an onyx waterfall cascading down her back, and turned on her heels. Jade looked blankly at her.

'Wedding, Jade. Wedding, obviously!' Lily barked.

The sisters walked into Lily's kitchen which had recently been refurbished. White slabs of marble shone in the overhead lighting, and brass doorknobs gleamed liked comets. Jade furrowed her brow, wondering how Lily was still eking out the divorce money. Lily's fiancé, James, worked in the City, so she imagined he earned well, but this renovation seemed excessive. She shuddered at the sight of the ostentatious brass taps and Shaker-style panelling. Scanning the kitchen, she wondered where her nieces' stuff was. For a house that contained a five- and seven-year-old there was a distinct lack of kid paraphernalia. She hopped her bum up on to the worktop.

'Jade, get off there. I've just had the worktops polished, for goodness' sake.' Lily put her sleeve-covered hands on her pinched waist and pushed her chest forward. Jade's eyes lingered on her pert boobs for a second too long, sure they'd been enhanced. She had never been courageous enough to ask.

Jade slipped off the worktop, desperately trying to keep her smile in place. 'Where are the girls? Not back from school yet?' she asked, bending down to gingerly stroke Lily's plush grey cat, Cumin, anticipating the sneezing fit she knew would come, who was acquired at the time of Lily's cooking tutorials.

'Stu picked them up for once. He's in the UK for a few days, so I suggested he actually sees his daughters before he jets off again.' Lily exhaled sharply, her sunny demeanour slipping with each breath.

Jade shrugged. 'Tell them hi from Aunty Jade.' She already felt drained from the effort it took to keep their conversation away from the wedding. Her brain raced as she attempted to remember the curled-up script she had found at work.

'So do you like the new kitchen? I've just taken some photographs of it for my new interiors website.'

'Greaaaaat.' Jade's smile waned.

'So, Birdy . . .'

Jade braced herself for the script, ready for the brown dress and the horrendous floral archway.

'James and I have booked our honeymoon.' Lily squealed the word 'moon', which gave Jade the same physical sensation as someone scraping nails down a blackboard.

'Wait, what?' Jade said, shocked and relieved simultaneously that this dialogue was totally off-script. 'Where? When? That's cool!' she added with genuine joy.

'Literally the day after the wedding – we cannot wait. Capri, Birdy! Ca-bloody-pri! I've always been so desperate to go there. There's this incredible hotel called the Capri Palace.' Lily rolled her r's like a purring cat. 'It's old-school glamour all the way. Loads of interiors inspiration for me too. The Italians know exactly what they're doing when it comes to décor. It's completely dreamlike and apparently they make the best white-peach bellinis in the world. I mean, get me there now.' She squealed again.

Jade winced. 'I thought you might be off to France,' she joked.

'What?' Lily looked genuinely puzzled.

'Never mind. It sounds amazing, Lils. Do they have, like, a kids' club or something? I mean it sounds so fancy.'

'Oh no, we're not taking the kids. Don't be mad. That's what I wanted to talk to you about tonight. I've already spoken to the girls about it and they can't wait. Ten days of your little nieces with you, Birds. You'll have such a great time with them. Saffron is particularly excited, but I know Jemima will enjoy the girlie time.' Lily scrunched her nose to emphasise the cuteness of it all.

The elation of this being a different conversation to the one Jade had anticipated instantly turned to shock. 'I . . . I . . . I mean— I have work. I would have to get them to school each morning and finish early enough to pick them up.'

Lily cut in. 'It'll be the school holidays by then, so no school, Birds.'

'Well, what am I supposed to do with them all day while I'm at work?' Jade said slowly.

'Birdy, come on. It's my once-in-a-lifetime honeymoon—'

'It'll be your second honeymoon, Lils,' Jade cut in.

'—and I've already told the girls and they're so excited to sleep over at your cool little teeny flat. It'll be such a novelty for them. You know Mum can't have the girls for *all* the reasons, and Dad is, well, just Dad, so you're my only hope here, Birds. Otherwise we simply won't be able to go.' Lily pouted her plump, glossed lips.

'What about Stu? He is their dad after all,' Jade spluttered, desperately looking for a way out.

'No, afraid not. He's on a work trip that week so isn't even in the country,' Lily said with a faux expression of sympathy.

The blood drained out of Jade's arms as they swung beside her. She felt the force of gravity pulling her to the ground. She wanted to slump on the cold marble tiles and pretend none of this was happening.

'OK.' A limp surrender came from a voice box that didn't have the confidence to say, 'No.'

'Oh, Birdy, I knew you would do the right thing,' Lily said matter-of-factly while removing Cumin from the worktop.

Jade's neck muscles tightened. 'I'll have to speak to Colin but I guess I can try and make it work.' Her face felt hot. Instant regret chomped at her ankles.

'Oh, I'm so excited and the girls will honestly be so super easy. You know they're total angels. *Anywayyy*, on to the actual wedding itself. So, Sis, I'm going to need you to help me out here. I've envisaged an archway for the ceremony and it's very classic, very simple, but also striking. I want it to be mainly silk roses trailing up the archway and then hanging silk ribbons with those tiny fairy lights that you can't really see until they're turned on. You know I'm on a tight budget, Birdy, so I'm going to need you to do this as a favour, yeah? I'm sure you'll find it fun and you can ask those mates of yours . . . Sophie and Labo.'

Jade jolted upright, her back suddenly poker-straight. No, oh no, *these* were the words from the script. But there was no way her sister could possibly dare to ask even more of her after dropping the honeymoon bomb-shell, was there? But, before she knew it, her reply fell out of her mouth like broken teeth.

'Mmm, OK. Well, logistically I would have to build most of that on the morning of the wedding as the marquee is outside, right? If there is wind overnight, it would tear it down so how will I have time to get ready?' She blinked in the silence after, trying to regain some control.

Lily wafted her hand in front of her as if she were swatting away a fly. 'Oh, there'll be time. I don't think it'll take you long. So, cool? Get the brief? Classic, cool, but also striking. Oh, wait. The dresses. I haven't even shown you your dress.' Lily's voice turned from stern to sing-song.

Lily grabbed a tablet off the worktop and shoved it towards Jade's pale face.

Jade looked up at Lily, and before she had time to think she felt the words fall from her lips: 'It's brown.'

At the same time a mental image flashed up of the bridesmaid's dress she had bought for Sophie. She had only wanted one bridesmaid and for her to be wearing something non-traditional. They had chosen a vintage sequined mini dress from Portobello Market. In the end she had given it to Sophie to keep as she didn't get to wear it down the aisle.

'Yes. Brown was the colour to watch for weddings in *Vogue* last month. It's very chic and will complement *my* dress perfectly.'

Jade swallowed and fully surrendered to this unfortunate shit-show, staring down at the shapeless brown silk dress on the screen.

'Mmm. Right.'

Lily carried on talking as if her audience were captivated.

'Birdy, I know you can deliver this archway for me. If you don't do it the whole vibe will be kind of off-kilter. I've told Mum you're doing it, and she's so relieved as it's one less thing for her to worry about.'

Jade shrugged. 'Yup. Cool.' She wondered what their mum could possibly have on her long list. It seemed Lily had it all covered.

'God, I haven't even offered you a tea or coffee. I have this amazing new coffee machine and also some incredible reishi mushroom coffee that I was gifted from one of my Instagram followers. Wanna try it?'

Jade put the tablet down and made for the kitchen door. 'I've really got to get going. I've got a lot on at work so I need to head home to crack on with some bits and bobs.'

Lily scrunched up her face. 'That sounds very generic. Sure you don't want to stay? I haven't even shown you my new mood boards. Now we're both working in the arts I think you'll really get a kick out of them.'

Jade inhaled sharply. 'No, Lily, I have to go. I'm going. I'm going home.' Little traces of anger escaped with pops and crackles in her voice.

'Well, suit yourself. I'll get back to working up this next design project, I guess. So much to do at the moment, especially with the new website.'

Jade could hear Lily carrying on with her torrent of boasting – without noticing that Jade had quietly left. She jogged out of the gate and turned right then leaned against a lamp-post to compose herself. She slapped her palm into her forehead, wondering how she had fallen into this trap.

'What is *actually* going on? Seriously, what *is* this?' She spoke to the sky, unsure who or what she was speaking to. She paused and waited for some kind of response, a gust of wind, bolt of lightning ... but nothing. Jade pushed her body weight away from the lamp-post and concentrated on putting one foot in front of the other back to her bike, which was chained to Lily's railings. She ducked out of eyeline while punching in the code to the lock. She couldn't face another word from her sister.

Climbing onto her bike, she thought about a full ten days of awful trampoline parks and early mornings full of sugary cereal and kids' TV shows blaring.

The floral archway.

The brown dress.

6

Today had been a good day. It had been a whole week since Jade had found the Lily script, and she'd had a whole four days of solitude in the flat. With Adam the other side of the Atlantic, the flat felt roomy without the omnipresent tension she had gotten used to.

The weather had been better, too. Blue patches of sky and a delicious warmth on her skin had allowed for optimism to creep in. Still, in these moments, when Jade was on the cusp of contentment, sometimes even joy, she would remember the conversation with her sister. Jade adored her nieces – but the thought of looking after them for ten whole days made panic rise in her chest. She wasn't even sure at this point whether it was possible with her job and general fondness of sanity. But she had time to solve it – weeks, in fact – so pushed the feelings down further.

After a long day of adding finishing touches to the Victorian props, Jade flopped down on her sofa and enjoyed the nothingness of being alone. The stillness of the room; the lack of a shower running, a phone ringing, or door slamming. Just silence, bar the odd hum of a bus moving sluggishly round the sharp bend outside the flat. From the sofa, she watched the handsome oak tree outside her window swaying gently in the breeze. She had no desire to fetch her phone from her backpack to check if Adam had called or messaged. She didn't want anything to interrupt this feeling of total stillness.

She looked around at her little world. A photograph of her and Sophie mid-cartwheel one sunburnt day on holiday in Spain sat atop the mantelpiece. The fireplace, empty of logs or indeed a fire, held a wooden boat she had bought on a trip to Dorset. Her eyes lingered on it and she made a mental note to visit her godmother Belinda and her husband Don soon. Dorset had, over the years, become a refuge, with Belinda's house a safe haven away from the drama of Jade's family – a roaring fire in their kitchen, the smell of cedar and smoke, thickly cut bread slathered in the saltiest butter. Adam hated the wooden boat and constantly told her it looked like it belonged to an elderly person who used to sail. He hated Dorset, too. Jade had attempted to get him to accompany her on a trip not long after they started dating but he insisted he was a city type and would go mad if faced with weak wi-fi and too many cows.

On the sofa next to her was a mountain of cushions. The collection had begun when Sophie had bought her a deep-green cushion the colour of the bottom of the ocean, dripping in beads that depicted a dragonfly. Jade had bought ten others since, all in rich jewel colours. Adam had made so little impact on this space over the last three years. He used one corner of their bedroom as a makeshift gym with some hand weights and a couple of kettle bells, but bar that his existence was untraceable to the human eye. It was her space, and her memories. It was perfect, and it was hers.

Yet she was constantly reminded that it wasn't *entirely* hers. This little flat, with its fifties iron-barred balcony, two shoebox bedrooms, and almost river views was one of many owned by Jade's dad. She wasn't even sure how many properties he now had. He claimed that they were more of a retirement hobby than a business, yet he still made Jade squirm by reminding her how lucky she was to live there.

Jade had spent a week on the sofa at her mum's one-bedroom cottage after her split with Navi, and it had felt like seven days too long. She had tentatively asked her dad about any empty flats, and he had reluctantly offered one up. Even though she paid the full amount of rent, he would mention her good fortune every time he set foot in the flat, when his Cockney lilt would reveal the working-class roots beneath the Gucci suit – *You're bloody lucky to have a dad with a spare flat going. I got you out of a right pickle there, didn't I?* Jade loved her dad, but she was sure it would be different if it was Lily living there. And she didn't dare react by stating that she paid full rent; her dad would have a one-liner ready to throw back that would cut the conversation dead. She had considered moving elsewhere but had grown so fond of it. In a way it had helped her heal after the break-up with Navi. Every time she walked through the front door she felt safe. The idea of moving again filled her with dread.

The moon looked bright through the gauze curtain – but the evening sky was still light enough to be called blue. Jade walked out to the small balcony and leaned on the railings, suddenly needing air. She craned her head round to the right to get a proper look at the waxing gibbous moon hovering above the river, white flecks lightly tiptoeing over the moss-coloured water.

A guttural screech below pierced the evening quiet, followed by a disturbing clatter. She looked down to see a trail of carrot peel and old teabags, and the tip of a bushy rust-coloured tail dash out of view. Foxes were constantly dismantling her food-disposal box, helped by the squirrels who had gnawed a hole in the top for easy access. The last thing Jade wanted to do was plod downstairs and hand-pick her way through rotting vegetables, but Rodney, whose flat was on the ground floor with a view of the bins, would not be happy if she left it until morning. Especially not after last week, when she had turned a blind eye and he had walked straight out of his flat into a sea of slimy peel.

Jade reluctantly walked back inside and into the kitchen to pick up her keys, grabbing her overflowing recycling bin on the way out.

Once outside, she knelt down by the trails of soft cucumber and half-eaten corn-on-the-cob. Gingerly picking up the gunky remains with her fingertips, she imagined Adam sitting by a pool in Los Angeles in one of the annoying linen shirts he only wore on holiday. She could picture him now, pretending to look busy on his phone, while actually on Instagram. She pulled her head back at the stench of the rotting food.

Next, she picked up the plastic bucket with the neatly

folded cardboard boxes and packages and started to slot them one by one into the recycling box. Jade found this incredibly satisfying. She took pride in having the neatest recycling box in her block of flats and prayed it counted for something. Taking two large delivery boxes, she folded them, then folded them smaller again and wedged them into the blue container. Her hand reached back to the bucket in a robotic rhythm. Flatten, slot, flatten, slot. She grabbed at the recycling container again – and this time picked up loose paper.

Her heart started to hammer as she registered what it was. She fell backwards from the squatted position she was in, losing her balance and landing painfully on one wrist. She needed to get into her flat. She clumsily poured the rest of the bucket's contents directly on top of the neatly folded items and ran inside, clutching the wad of paper to her chest.

Once inside, she threw the recycling bucket at the wall in the hallway and sprinted to the sofa, muttering *'No, no, no, not again'* to the empty flat. She felt like a fool – she had truly thought that she was free from this madness.

Was this Adam's doing? Who else would be able to access her recycling bin? Her teeth ground together and she looked down at the page, her hands trembling.

SUE

Jade's interactions with her mum were never easy. Never traumatic either, just tricky. She loved her mum

57

whole-heartedly, but had to walk into conversations with care. Sue was as unpredictable as her dad was predictable. Her dad's one-liners were solid and rehearsed, and he carried them around like a little bag of marbles, always ready to roll one out. Yet Sue changed like the tides. Her energy was always highly charged but could swing in either direction; a whirlwind of euphoria and misery, a Libra high on her own drama, constantly tipping the scales of emotion. And she offloaded any troublesome thoughts onto Jade, leaving her feeling heavy and cold as Sue's list of worries and woes spilled out of her within seconds. Brief platitudes from Jade would be knocked out of the way for a stream of depressing anecdotes and problems. And their conversations would always lead back to Jade's dad.

Then there was the drinking. It was never enough for any kind of label, yet every two weeks on the nose Jade knew she would get a slurry phone call. In these moments the heavy weight of parent and daughter role reversal made Jade's back hunch. She understood it. She knew her mum and dad's divorce all those years ago had hit Sue hard, and that Tony's happiness with his new wife, Jacquie, compounded it further. Wine had become her comforter, her quiet oblivion. But understanding it didn't make it any easier.

Jade glanced down at the paper in front of her – suddenly, strangely, wishing Adam were there so she could confess her secret of these mysterious and insanely creepy scripts. Maybe he would tell her she was going mad, or freak out and worry she was being stalked, or maybe he would laugh and change the subject quickly back to himself like he always did.

She quietly surrendered to whatever she was about to read.

[Sue is dressed in a tunic top and has a little too much blusher on.]

                    SUE
     Jade, you won't believe it. Pat is
     back on steroids again. It's a ter-
     rible shame as she was doing so well
     without them but the pain and swell-
     ing is back, so she's had to up them.
     Also, Caroline's daughter, remember
     Sarah?

Jade looked momentarily at the ceiling. Here we go, she thought. The list begins. She looked down at the script with one eyebrow raised.

                    JADE
     Yes, Mum, you mention her literally
     every time I see you.

                    SUE
     Well, she's dropped out of uni. She
     was having an awful time there.

Couldn't make friends, heightened
anxiety, hated being away from home.
Can you imagine, poor love, all that
way from home with no mates.

                    JADE
Well, yes, Mum, I went to uni.

                    SUE
It's awful. Wouldn't you help her
out? It's such a tough time for Caroline worrying about her all day and
night. Couldn't you ask Trevor . . . ?

                    JADE
Colin.

                    SUE
Colin, Trevor, all the same.
Couldn't you ask Colin if she could
come and help out?

                    JADE
Wait, what was she studying at uni?

                    SUE
Philosophy? Physics? Psychology?
Something like that . . .

JADE

Mum, those subjects are drastically
different and none of them include
any art or design whatsoever.

SUE

Oh, but couldn't she just come and
make tea or something?

JADE

We make our own tea.

SUE

Or sweep up, or fetch tins of paint?

JADE

It doesn't really work like
that, Mum.

SUE

Oh well, I'm sure you can think of
something. Shall we have a glass of
wine? It's just been so stressful
that I think I need a relaxer.

JADE

I don't have any wine here. You know
I can't stand it. Gin yes, wine no.

SUE

Oh well, gin will have to do I suppose. What is it, Gordon's? Please
say Tanqueray.

Blank pages followed the scripted part, just like the other two she had previously found.

It was all harmless enough – just the usual quota of low-level stress from listening to the ongoing list of problems her mum had clung on to that week. Jade felt a little less freaked out by this script, and instead found herself a little curious as to what it was showing her. To see her own words written down felt surreal. These scripts illustrated the dynamics in her life with clarity, the power-play visible, her lack of confidence glaringly obvious. She wondered why she hadn't noticed it herself before now.

She also found it puzzling that she had found this script so late in the day. Previously the scripted scenes had unfurled within the same day, but it was almost 8:30pm and she certainly wasn't planning to go to her mum's house this late. Shoving the script under the sofa, she stood up with an urgent desire for a cool drink. She got as far as the doorway, then turned back. A thought entered her head at lightning speed. Reaching under the sofa to grab the script, she ran her fingers over the dialogue.

Tippex. She must have some in her art cupboard. Maybe she could change the wording. Kindly ask her mum about her drinking, as she'd been trying to for so long, and suggest she try and stop or get help of some kind?

A small blue wooden cupboard sat in the corner of the front room precariously rammed with pyramids of paint pots, jam jars of buttons and beads, old mugs holding multiple paintbrushes, and stacks of different-textured paper.

Jade pulled out tins of paint, placing them on the wooden floor next to her, scanning the back of the cupboard. There were some old erasers, a few discarded knitting needles – yet no Tippex. She reached for a tube of thick white paint instead, and held it up in a quiet moment of triumph. Grabbing a thin paintbrush, she left the contents of the cupboard spilling out onto the floor.

She laid out the script on her small two-seater dining table, examining the wording like a detective piecing together clues. Dipping the thin paintbrush directly into the tube of paint, she hovered the brush above the paper, working out which part to erase first.

But as she lowered the brush onto the first line of dialogue the buzzer rang, startling her. Jade dropped the paintbrush directly onto the table, her heart racing. She couldn't remember the last time someone had turned up at her flat at night unannounced. She pressed down the intercom button to talk – realising who the mystery guest was before the voice even answered.

7

'Hello, who is it?' she asked, knowing who would reply.

'It's your mother! Just swinging by, Jadey,' Sue declared, as if Jade should have known of her arrival.

Every muscle in Jade's body tightened, her toes gripping the ground. Her early night was slipping through her fingers, and she didn't feel prepared to white-knuckle her way through another of these scripted encounters.

'Oh, hi Mum, I'll just buzz you up.'

Jade dashed to the small entrance hall and looked at her face in the mirror, knowing her mum would comment on her bedraggled appearance. She fluffed her hair and waited to hear her mum's footsteps.

She heard her silver bracelets before the footsteps. Sue wore ten or so silver hoops piled up on both wrists, acting as armour against the outside world. Jade was sure she must sleep in them too. Jade clicked the latch on the door, and it swung open with Sue's bangled arm.

'Daarrrling!' she cried, her middle-class vowels drawn out with drama.

'Hi – I wasn't expecting you, Mum.'

'Jadey, I just had a feeling I should come. My sixth sense was telling me you're not OK. I literally could feel a pulsating in my third eye.' Sue pressed the space between her own eyebrows with force. A small red mark appeared as she removed her middle finger.

'Mum, I'm fine. I'm literally fine.'

Sue pushed past Jade, her long blonde plait, laced with strands of grey, swinging as she walked. A silk scarf was knotted at the end of the plait, making it look twice as long. Sue's clothes were a subtle hangover from the 1970s when she had been a teen stomping the King's Road, yet they were usually paired with something jarringly modern. Today she wore a tunic top which Jade assumed by its snug fit was from the long-closed-down Alkasura, Sue's favourite boutique in her youth. It was paired with black loose-fitting harem pants and a pair of purple Nike Air Max.

'It's bloody hot up here, Jadey. I could never live this high up. I need earthing, darling. For my toes to be amongst Mother Nature's soil.'

'I'm on the first floor, Mum.'

Sue sashayed into the kitchen, her plait moving in the opposite direction to her body. She always had accessories dangling from her: scarves, belts, bangles, long necklaces, all swinging as she moved. 'Oh, you do look tired. That baggy old T-shirt isn't helping,' she said without even looking back. 'You know I've told you before – for the fifteen years I was married to your father, I always made an effort with my clothing.'

'*And look where that got you*,' Jade muttered under her breath, knowing her mother was far enough out of earshot.

'Darling, let me do your washing-up, for god's sake.

65

There's a pile the size of Everest here,' she went on, her large quartz necklace dangling dangerously close to the pile of dirty dishes.

'Mum, I'll do it. I have a dishwasher. I'm just waiting for the other load to finish.'

Sue ignored her and started passionately squirting washing-up liquid over the mound of plates and glasses.

'So, what's going on? Where's Adam?' Sue pushed her bangles a little further up her arms as she plunged them into the bubbles in the sink.

'He's had to go away for business.'

'*Business?!* Darling, I don't think that printing out a few T-shirts constitutes business. Now, I may not be your father's biggest fan, but he worked to get all he has from very humble beginnings. I was there at the start of it and watched him build his portfolio from nothing and now look, he's practically got his own empire. Lucky for Jacquie that she didn't have to deal with his moods and absence as he built his company. She's simply reaping all the rewards now. Heard they're on holiday in Lake Como currently. It's alright for some.' Sue flared her nostrils.

'Do you want a tea, Mum?'

Jade turned the kettle on before the answer came, hoping the break in conversation would allow for a positive change in theme. Sue carried on frantically washing plates and placing them with a little too much force onto the sideboard, and was practically shouting over the noise of the kettle when she said:

'Jade, you won't believe it. Pat is back on steroids again. It's a terrible shame as she was doing so well without them, but the pain and swelling is back, so she's had to up them. Also, Caroline's daughter, remember Sarah?'

Oh god, here it was, the script. Thinking back to the open white paint and paper laid out on the table, Jade felt a surge of adrenaline. She needed to hide it as soon as possible. The script would be inexplicable if her mum were to move into the front room. Jade walked backwards out of the kitchen doorway.

'Yes, Mum, you mention her literally every time I see you.' Her brain was on autopilot, not even attempting to fight the words that were exiting her mouth.

'Well, she's dropped out of uni. She was having an awful time there. Couldn't make friends, heightened anxiety, hated being away from home. Can you imagine, poor love, all that way from home with no mates.'

Jade gathered the script, white paint and brush and chucked them into the open art cupboard, slamming the door quickly before skipping back into the kitchen feeling the relief written on her face. 'Well, yes, Mum, I went to uni.'

Sue had barely noticed her daughter's momentary absence and continued with her stream of consciousness.

'It's awful. Wouldn't you help her out? It's such a tough time for Caroline worrying about her all day and night. Couldn't you ask Trevor . . .'

'Colin,' Jade said, rolling her eyes.

'Colin, Trevor, all the same. Couldn't you ask Colin if she could come and help out?'

This time, Jade attempted to muster up new words.

Ones that were not on the script. Fresh, autonomous words. She opened her mouth – and her throat felt like it was constricting. Silence. A void where the words should be. Sue looked up and nodded with her brows raised as if to say, 'Go on.'

Jade gave in, letting the script unfurl from her lips: 'Wait, what was she studying at uni?'

Sue looked back at the dirty dishes and wafted one soapy hand in the air, a smash of bangles clanging. 'Philosophy? Physics? Psychology? Something like that.'

Jade looked over her shoulder to ensure she had tidied away all evidence of the script. 'Mum, those subjects are drastically different and none of them include any art or design whatsoever.'

Starting to sound ever so slightly irritated, Sue replied, 'Oh, but couldn't she just come and make tea or something?'

Jade attempted a new line of dialogue again, remembering the rough outlines of the script. She wondered if just agreeing to help would close this conversation off so she could then thank her mum for unexpectedly turning up, and then gently usher her out the door so she could continue with her peaceful, moonlit evening. Yet the other half of her brain wanted to challenge the script even more, and change the course of the conversation altogether.

Again, nothing. Not even a squeak. It was as if her brain and voice box had severed all relations. She bit down on her lip and let the script once again take over.

'We make our own tea.'

Sue, ignoring her daughter, continued in her stream of thought: 'Or sweep up, or fetch tins of paint.'

Resting against the worktop, Jade replied, 'It doesn't really work like that, Mum.'

Sue's blushered cheeks now looked cherry-red from the exertion of washing up. 'Oh well, I'm sure you can think of something. Shall we have a glass of wine? It's just been so stressful that I think I need a relaxer.'

This was the part of the script that Jade desperately wanted control over. She didn't want her quiet evening interrupted by alcohol and endless chat and questioning about where Adam was.

'I don't have any wine here. You know I can't stand it. Gin yes, wine no.'

Sue placed the last clean plate on the worktop and dried her hands on a tea towel.

'Oh well, gin will have to do, I suppose. What is it, Gordon's? Please say Tanqueray.'

Relieved she had come to the end of the script, Jade let her shoulders drop. 'Mum, I never normally drink at home. I just like to relax after work by watching trash TV or by having a nice bath. I'm going to stick to my tea.'

Sue grabbed a clean glass out of the cupboard and turned quickly towards Jade, 'Oh, darling, don't be a spoil-sport. It's no fun drinking on your own. I should know. It's ever so lonely in my little cottage. Just one for Mummy? Go on, I'll put lots of ice in. It'll barely count.' Sue's mascara-caked eyelashes fluttered slightly.

Jade had already pressed down on the kettle button,

and its steam now filled the kitchen followed by its low grumblings. 'Oh, Mum, I'm just not really in the mood, I have work tomorrow and . . . oh, bloody hell, OK, just a tiny, tiny one.'

'There we go, darling. Perfect. Coming up. You go and put your feet up in the front room and I'll bring it in. We can have a good old gossip.'

Jade retrieved a near full bottle of gin from a cupboard above the fridge, left it on the counter and then sloped off to the front room, mentally saying a sweet goodbye to her evening of perfect isolation. She sat cross-legged, her bare feet tucked under her thighs, cursing the script quietly under her breath. Next time, she would act more quickly. She jumped up and dug her phone out of her backpack and wrote in her notes *Buy Tippex* as her mum came strutting into the room, ice clinking in the glasses.

'Here you go, darling. Drink up. As I said, I would have preferred wine, but this will do. Oh, it's lovely and cold. Cucumber would have made a great addition but next time, eh?' She sat down beside Jade, each of her accessories landing a second after she did.

Jade turned to her and said softly, 'Well, yes, if you tell me you're coming it would help. You only live five minutes down the road. Just tell me next time, Mum.'

Sue curled her lips down theatrically. 'Oh well, if I'm not wanted I can always go and have a crisp white wine at the Roebuck on the hill, darling.'

'No, Mum, I didn't mean that, it's fine,' Jade said with a sigh.

Sue instantly brightened. 'So where shall we start? Did I tell you Lily has a brand-new interior design company now? It seems to be doing ever so well.'

Jade kept her head down, looking at the gin she really didn't want. 'She doesn't actually have any clients, you do know that, right?'

Sue took a deep swig of gin, smacking her bright pink lips together. 'Oh, darling, don't be so hard on her. She's starting all over again and she's created a lovely website. Have you seen it? It looks very professional.'

Jade let her lips touch the ice-cold gin, but didn't sip. 'Well, you kind of need more than a nice website to make money from it, and you sort of also need to know how to actually do the job, but hey, it hasn't stopped Lils before.'

She knew her words were loaded with years of pent-up frustration at her parents' pandering to Lily, but she couldn't stop herself.

She had always felt partly responsible for the dynamics at play today. Jade's self-sufficiency had allowed her mum and dad's attention to engulf Lily. Sue and Tony's marriage had ended explosively when Jade was ten and Lily was thirteen. Jade's understanding of what was going on was limited but the atmosphere in the house made her feel a dark-blue sadness. She missed her dad's big presence and feared her mum's mood swings, but after a couple of months the sadness had turned into a feeling of numbing indifference. Her fondness of solitude, in her room with her pens and paint and coloured sheets of paper, led to her being slightly forgotten about.

Even now she wasn't sure whether it was because she was extremely mature for ten, or if her young mind simply couldn't process the pain. Looking back, even then she'd sensed that her parents separating was the right thing for them. She'd kept her head down in her pen box and dealt with the big life changes internally.

Lily's reaction to the divorce was loud, visible and chaotic. Jade first noticed her sister's outpouring of pain when she went to clean her teeth one evening and the sink was splashed with black dye. Sue had cried again, wailing the words *gold hair* and *gone* and *my golden princess*. Not long after, black leather jackets replaced Snoopy sweatshirts and the smell of cigarettes wafted from Lily's room across the hallway to Jade's. There were parties on Friday nights when Sue had gone to the pub with her friends – teenage boys with long black fringes swept to one side, covering an eye, swigging bottles of cider on the stairwell and Green Day blaring from a speaker. Jade would hide in her room and draw pictures of woodland owls and bright red toadstools until her right arm ached. Then Sue would come home, and there would be shouting and tears. There was shoplifting black nail varnish from the local chemist, multiple nights where Lily would head into central London and not come back until the morning, Sue a crumple of anxiety at the kitchen counter, staring at the clock. Then, at sixteen, Lily was expelled from school. A cycle of absences, missed exams and smoking in the car park had given the school little option. Sue blamed herself, and Tony blamed Sue, and the only thing they seemed to have in common was a shared focus on keeping Lily from going off the rails again. The dynamics forged in Jade's childhood had seemingly been set in stone. Lily the cherished rebel – and Jade the quiet peace-maker.

'You know she's asked me to have the girls when she's off on her honeymoon?' Jade said through gritted teeth.

'Oh, darling, well done you, they'll love that.'

'No, I can't. It's going to be a nightmare juggling work while they're on their school holidays. God knows how I'll make it work.'

Sue raised her eyebrows and swigged a mouthful of gin, pink lipstick left on the rim of the glass.

'I love the girls, but I'm not sure I can even get the holiday. Colin is so tight with time off.'

Sue took another gulp that nearly emptied her glass. 'Oh, they'll love sleeping at Aunty Jade's little flat. How fun. So wonderful for Lily too. She'll need a nice holiday after all the prep for the wedding.'

'Nobody has forced her to get married. Again! Is there any way you could have the girls for a bit of that ten days? It would help me out so much.' Even saying the word 'married' out loud made Jade feel light-headed. The word hung in the air as she thought back to her own cancelled plans. She wondered if her mum's mind had wandered back to that painful time too.

Sue finished off her drink and got up to refill it, her long plait swaying as she waltzed into the kitchen. She shouted back, 'Darling, you know that's not possible. I have so much on this summer. I'm going to be redecorating the cottage at some stage, I have my tai chi class

73

once a week, and I'm thinking of going on a little week-end retreat in Cornwall after the wedding to replenish my body after all the stress of it.'

Jade looked to the ceiling and mouthed *'FUUUCK!'* Sue walked in and caught the tail end of Jade's blasphemous mime.

'You OK, darling?'

'Yup, yup, fine. Just a bit tired,' Jade said, squeezing out a forced yawn.

'Well, I can go home if you like. I only popped in to see how you are.'

Jade smiled. 'Erm, well, I am pretty tired and I have a long day tomorrow.'

'OK, I'll just have one more for the road.'

8

A bus hummed past the window, stirring Jade from sleep. Her eyes felt like they had been stuck together with glue. The blinds were open, and she was lying awkwardly on the sofa. Disorientated, she pushed herself up onto her elbows as the room came into focus. Next to her sat a full glass of untouched gin and her phone. A dressing gown was draped over her as a blanket. Piecing together the puzzle of the last twelve hours, she assumed she must have drifted off at some point last night while her mum was over. Sue's 'one for the road' had turned into two, then three, and more chatting that incrementally became looser by the sip. She remembered seeing her mum's arm movements gathering speed and size as she spoke, as if conducting an orchestra.

The conversation had, unsurprisingly, ended up circling around Tony and Jacquie. It was painfully inevitable. The memories were now slowly coming back to Jade, along with a dose of gratitude that she had chosen not to drink any of the gin. She recalled her mum's slurred words as they'd meandered around Jacquie's good fortune and the photos she had posted on Facebook from their Italian holiday. These inevitable digs at her stepmother made Jade squirm. She always remained silent, as she had a good relationship with Jacquie, but nodded along so her mum felt supported. Jade had mentally switched off as Sue's words became punchier and louder and had allowed herself to slide down the sofa and curl up in the foetal position. She wasn't sure at what point she had dozed off, but her mum had clearly gotten the hint and draped a dressing gown over her before exiting.

Her phone screen was too bright as she squinted to see that the time was only 5:30am.

Mum. Are you OK? J X she typed, her eyes still blurred.

Although Sue only lived five minutes down the road, it was a treacherous walk in the dark – either through a meadow of cows that skimmed the Thames or down a very steep dark hill with little street lighting. Theirs was a rare pocket of London that slept in the dark at night. Imagining Sue drunkenly staggering home through unpopulated areas made Jade shudder.

An unread message sat below the one she had just typed to her mum. Adam. It had been sent six hours ago while Jade had been sleeping, when he would have been enjoying a late Los Angeles palm-tree-lined afternoon. When Jade tapped the message, a photo filled her screen of his legs stretched out on a sun lounger. The colourful and out-of-character espadrilles that covered Adam's feet were new to Jade. That was it, though. No actual message, not even a selfie, or heart emoji, or text asking how she was, just an obnoxious photo of his legs, and questionable shoes. She wondered again what was keeping her in this relationship. Three years ago, when they had just started dating and things felt hot and breathless, with no appetite for food, and butterflies in the middle of the day, she could easily have overlooked patterned, slip-on espadrilles. She was too under his spell, too intertwined in his toned limbs, too distracted by the V-shaped scar above his right eyebrow. Now these new shoes seemed emblematic; a loud warning sign that he was happy without her, in his colourful shoes, in colourful LA, with people she didn't know. She couldn't even be bothered to reply. She needed to clear her head from the jumbled thoughts and worries about her mum, the impending wedding, and approaching Colin about time off work.

Automatically, she opened Instagram and began scrolling through the endless carousel of slithers of other people's lives. Videos of kittens cuddling up to baby ducklings, followed by pictures of Lethabo's night out with his new boyfriend, were the ultimate distraction from having to worry about whether her relationship was salvageable. She stopped on a recent post from her sister. Lily had posted an arty shot of her work desk with a mood board, a mug of yellow turmeric latte which Jade had never seen her drink before, an expensive-looking pen and some fabric swatches. Underneath the photo it read: *Prepping for another busy day at Maison Lily. Helping create mood, comfort and sophistication in homes and workspaces. Head to my website for inspo and all the latest news from the world of Maison Lily.*

'*The world of Maison Lily*,' Jade snorted. Sue had commented: *Well done darling. All the hard work has paid off*, followed by several clapping-hand emojis.

Jade kept scrolling through photos of friends on nights out and celebrities whose real lives she knew nothing about, as if the more she consumed the less empty she would feel. She was on autopilot, thumb moving swiftly over the screen, barely taking in the images flashing up, when she stopped on an image that felt familiar.

The photo showed outstretched legs, blurred palm trees in the background, the turquoise of a pool . . . and patterned espadrilles. The picture she had been sent in the middle of the night was a regurgitated Instagram photo; meaningless, flippant and impersonal. She used two fingers to zoom in on the terrible shoes, irritation twitching through her. They were even worse close up – an ocean design with an orange sunset painted over the arch of each shoe. She tapped the photo and several tags popped up – seemingly all names of people, none she recognised: @Jam01 @Robsta_underwood @AC1990 @Bowmanjason3 @TammyC. Jade clicked on Tammy's profile, now caught up in a vortex of detective work and intrigue.

The Tetris grid of photos that appeared showed a symmetrical face framed by long caramel-coloured hair, an elegant nose, and chocolate-coloured eyes. She looked otherworldly, untouchable. Skimpy dresses showed bronzed, bare shoulders and bra-less boobs that sat perky to the sky. A wave of self-loathing pushed Jade deeper into the sofa as she compared her own baggy T-shirt, pale arms that hadn't seen far-flung sunshine in a long time, and broad shoulders, to this picture of honey-toned perfection. Clicking on her own profile, Jade studied herself. The full grin with a twisted incisor to the right of her front teeth, paint-splattered dungarees, arms flung with gusto around Sophie's shoulders; her and Lethabo having tea in the sun; a pot of brushes dripping with gold paint; her pale feet with unvarnished toenails at the edge of a stream. There was nothing posed or polished about Jade's curation of photos. She wondered whether that was a good thing or not, and clicked back onto Tammy's profile. For every toothy grin on Jade's page there was a filtered, creamy shot of Tammy's smooth face. The subconscious need to compare herself to this stranger would end badly, she knew that much. The guaranteed deflation was only minutes away, she could feel it, yet she couldn't stop herself from studying Tammy's face. Zooming in to her plump lips, impossibly white teeth, eyes framed with a fan of thick lashes. Once, Sophie had told her not to watch *Luther* when she was alone in the flat. She knew she shouldn't but couldn't stop herself from bingeing three episodes back-to-back. She didn't sleep for a week. Staring at Tammy's face felt like watching *Luther*: she knew it was a terrible idea.

The most recent photo displayed Tammy by a shimmering pool, mouth pouted, holding what looked like a strawberry daiquiri. The picture sat without words below it; a girl seemingly confident enough not to waste her time writing any explanation of her whereabouts or thoughts. She tapped the photo, which revealed the same five names tagged – including Adam's.

Jade threw her phone on the floor and kicked off the clammy dressing gown that was draped over her knees, committing not to look on social media for the rest of the day. Sloping to the kitchen, she started to tidy away her mum's debris from last night. The bottle of gin, now half-empty, two large tonic bottles lying on their sides, a glass with the dregs of strong-smelling alcohol.

Unbidden, the image of Tammy flashed back up in her mind: the tiny dress, the caramel legs, the cherry-stained pout. Insecurity started to rise from her chest. It was a feeling she was used to – comparing herself to Tammy merely highlighted the self-doubt that had sat under her skin since childhood, born out of comparison to Lily.

She knew this thought pattern had to stop. She needed air. The summer sky was already powder blue and she knew the river would be quiet. She slipped on the striped baggy shorts that had become her warmer weather running attire, and a sports bra, then slung the T-shirt she had been wearing all night back on. Tying her trainers tightly, she pushed through the front door and immediately started to run down the stairs so as not to talk herself out of leaving the flat.

It was early enough for the streets to be eerily quiet; only a large ginger cat strolled the pavement and a pigeon cooed overhead. The curve of the river caught the light on its bend. From the top of the hill, Jade could see miles of river below and let her eyes follow its shape. Right foot, left foot, she let her soles stomp out the self-loathing. Allowing her breathing to quieten the brain chatter, she reached the bottom of the hill and made her way down the lane to the water's edge. Without stopping she swung left, to be greeted by the solitude of the river's path.

A single swan gracefully glided on the water's surface, the air still and unbroken by human voice. She took in the wooden house with its moss-covered edges, the neat row of boats bobbing, the moon still happily in the summer sky.

9

Friday's child is loving and giving. The words circled Jade's mind. Her mum had always recited the nursery rhyme when she was a kid and reminded her she was a Friday's child. The commitment followed her around long before she could grasp what it meant. She would share her toys with Lily, let kids at school take her pens straight out of her pencil case, and now seemingly everyone took what they needed. Giving generously, whether it be her time, energy or possessions, felt intrinsic to who Jade was, but she was beginning to question, at what cost? Lily was born on a Monday. Lily would beam as Sue recited the first line of the poem, grasping Lily's heart-shaped face. *Monday's child is fair of face,* she would coo in a sing-song trill. Jade would stare at Lily's delicate chin, her button nose and high cheekbones, wondering what it all meant. For as long as she could remember, Jade was a Friday and Lily was a Monday.

Jade pushed down on the pedals of her bike, feeling the muscles contract in her thighs from her run earlier that morning. Stopping at a red light, she could feel her phone vibrating in her backpack and prayed it was her mum calling, but didn't have time to find out. The lights turned green, and the cars and other bicycles around her lurched forward with urgency. Reminding herself that this had happened before, many times, allowed her a small chink of peace. Her mum was no doubt sleeping off a gin-infused hangover.

Battling through the Saturday morning traffic, her mind jumped from worry for her mum to the script she had found in the recycling bin. She wondered if telling Sophie would make her feel lighter and less full of dread. She had tried so hard to override the script, but each spoken word had matched the scripted text exactly. Sophie's calm, grounded logic could surely help her make sense of this craziness. She let her bike weave in swooping S shapes along the last stretch of road, then, after chaining her bike to the railings, she fumbled in her bag's depths to trace her phone. The screen lit up with three missed calls from her dad. Wondering why he was calling on a Saturday morning, she called her voicemail box on speakerphone.

She heard the automated voice chirp: '*You have one new message.*' Then her dad's gruff voice broke through. 'Jadey, it's Dad. You must be asleep still.'

Her dad's assumption that she would be asleep and not on her way to work riled her immensely.

'I'm . . . *we're* . . . in Italy. Bloody lovely. Anyway, I'll be quick. I'm calling because Jacs has booked the restaurant for Lily's rehearsal dinner. She pulled some strings and got us into Scalini's on the thirteenth of August. Jacquie's sorted it all out so drop her a text to let us know you can come. Alright, Jadey, gotta run.'

Scalini's was her dad's favourite restaurant. It offered old-school Italian glamour and theatrical banter, with white-jacketed Italian waiters and framed photos of famous people who had been to the restaurant on every wall. Jade shook her head incredulously. Of course Lily had tasked their dad and Jacquie to sort out the rehearsal dinner. It was also utterly typical that Lily would be stretching out the wedding furore as much as humanly possible. She opened her diary and punched in 'Scalini's' and a weary face emoji.

She knew she would need a robust force-field around her to deal with all of her family members being in one room. She couldn't remember the last time her mum and Jacquie had crossed paths. Jade constantly walked the tightrope of feeling fond of Jacquie but loyal to her mum. Jacquie had always made an effort with Jade, bringing her home small trinkets from her travels – a blue beaded necklace from Mexico, an ornate mask from Venice, even a large ceramic fruit bowl adorned with painted lemons from Positano. In fact, Jacquie had always made it quite obvious that she preferred Jade's company to Lily's, which Jade greatly appreciated. But to ensure her mum stayed as sane and sober as possible, Jade kept mentions of Jacquie to a minimum.

'Jade!'

Vinnie the delivery man was balancing a tower of packages and holding them out in Jade's direction. He was a regular at the warehouse, given the steady stream of deliveries of paint and materials.

'Hey, Vinnie. How ya doing?'

'Well, apart from England getting knocked out of the Euros, I'm alright.'

'Oh, sorry about that, mate.'

Vinnie shrugged. 'It was a rough one. I shouldn't have even bothered watching,' he said, passing Jade the large box and four smaller packages balanced on top.

'Well, I hope your day improves, Vinnie,' Jade said, resting her chin on the top package to keep the precarious pile from toppling.

'Gotta see the ex-wife tonight, so probably not,' he said with an eye roll.

She laughed. Vinnie was an expert in small talk and always managed to finish their short conversation with a punchline. Jade imagined that he left every beneficiary of his parcels with a smile on their face.

She turned to walk into the warehouse. As she pushed the sliding doors across with her boot, paint fumes enveloped her – the smell so familiar these days that it barely registered. Inside, Lethabo was spray-painting a large cardboard tree trunk. His canary-yellow boiler suit moved with his body as his painted nails – today the colour of egg yolk – caught in the overhead lighting. Bob Marley was playing over the hiss of Lethabo's spray, while Jackson was crouched on the floor to Jade's left, cutting sizeable squares of black card with a Stanley knife, his long legs in skinny jeans curled into his chest as if he were folded in half.

Jade let the smile sit on her face as she took it all in. The chaos, noise, smell of paint, colours splashed on the floor and hands, always made her feel safe. She craned her neck to scan the entirety of the warehouse and sighed with relief that there was no sign of Colin.

'Morning, babe. I'm feeling super summery today, so

I've whacked some Bob on,' Lethabo said as he moved his shoulders to the beat while gracefully wafting the spray can in the direction of the tree.

'Good!' Jade shouted back, still trying not to lose her balance with the tower of parcels. 'You look like a ray of actual sunshine, Thabs.'

Jackson looked up from beneath his floppy hair and nodded at Jade.

'Morning, Jackson,' she added. Without responding he carried on carefully cutting with his Stanley knife.

Jade slipped behind the wall which separated the warehouse and back room, where Sophie was rolling a cigarette.

'Morning, Soph,' Jade said, clumsily dropping the parcels onto the worktop.

'Morning, mate, how are you?'

'Yeah, I'm alright. Dad's just asked me to a ghastly rehearsal dinner for Lily's wedding, where I'll undoubtedly have to endure a potent mix of family members who do not get along. Bar that, I'm good. You?'

Sophie licked the cigarette paper and then put it behind her ear, the end poking out from the side of her bob. 'I'm good. Oh, babe, I forgot to ask you – do you want to have a really amazing night out with me?'

Jade opened the largest parcel, addressed to Colin, on the counter and pulled out a large pack of coloured card. 'Err . . . yes!'

Sophie bit her bottom lip and fiddled momentarily with her nose ring, then asked, 'Guess who I have tickets to see?'

'I don't know?' Jade said, lifting multiple packs of card out of the parcel. When Sophie still hadn't replied, she added, 'Just bloody tell me, Soph.'

'It begins with K and ends in *"They're-so-good-and-also-fit"*.'

Jade looked down at one of the smaller packages that was, strangely, addressed to her. She loved how her name looked when written out. Each word four letters: Jade Shaw. Neat, even, precise. She rarely got packages delivered to the warehouse unless she had been tempted to shop for clothes online, but she couldn't remember the last new piece of clothing she had bought.

The label on the envelope was printed in black ink. She tore the package open.

'Soph, just tell me who you have tickets for.'

'*Kings. Of. Leon!*' Sophie said. 'Jade, I have two tickets. Next Saturday. You down?'

Jade stared down at the contents of the smaller package in her hands.

'Jade. Did you hear me? Kings of Leon! The actual Kings of bloody Leon.'

'Yeah, yeah, I'll come,' Jade muttered in an uncertain tone.

'I thought you'd be a bit more excited. Aren't you obsessed with the drummer?'

'Yes, no, no, sorry, yes, yes I am.'

Jade placed the wad of paper from the smaller package on the counter. 'Sophie, can I tell you something?' she said, her eyes still fixed on the paper.

'Oh god, what? You're not pregnant, are you?' Sophie

scrunched her nose up, creasing her freckles into new constellations.

'Oh god, no. No. It's a flat no. No, this is weirder than that. So, so weird. I'm not sure how to even explain what I'm about to say. You'll never believe it. But look,' she said, thrusting the paper under Sophie's nose.

Sophie looked at the script. 'I don't get it. What is it?'

'I wish I knew, Soph. They keep turning up. Scripts. It's so stressful. This is the fourth one I've found so far. It was delivered by Vinnie in an envelope, but I've found one in a bush when I was out running, one in my recycling bin, even one on the shelves here.' Jade pointed towards the stock area accusingly. She lowered her voice to a hushed whisper and forced herself to slow down. 'They're scripts of my life, but bits that haven't happened yet. The whole thing is freaking me out. What is going on? Please don't tell anyone – I'm so confused by it all.'

Sophie's eyes were wide, her irises sitting in pools of bright white. 'What the hell. What do you mean?' she said, matching Jade's hushed tones.

Jade pressed her fingertips into her cheeks and shook her head. 'I don't know but it keeps happening. I find the script and then that exact scenario unfolds later that day.'

Sophie leaned forward so her forehead was nearly touching Jade's. 'Babe, this is mental. What are you talking about?'

'I know. I told you, it's almost impossible to explain. Look, let's read this one and you'll see.' Jade held the script between them. 'Oh god, it's a scene with Lily again. The last one was so irritating and accurate. Look,' Jade said, pointing at her name followed by her sister's, 'it's all there, and I'm due to go to her house tonight as she wants to run me through my nieces' bedtime routine ahead of her honeymoon in a month's time so I know what I'm doing.'

Forgetting to whisper, Sophie said, 'You've got your nieces staying the whole time Lily is on her honeymoon? What a piss-take.'

'I know, I know, she always does this to me, but look – that's beside the point. Whatever is in this script will unfurl later, whether I like it or not. It's like I have no control over my own mouth when I'm faced with the scene.' Jade framed the word 'scene' with quotation-mark fingers, mocking the new cinematic hell she found herself in.

'Bloody hell, babe. This is weird.' Sophie shook her head slowly. 'Weirder than when you drunkenly con-fessed to having fantasies about Alan Sugar.'

'That was a phase.' Jade wafted the comment away with her hand. 'Soph, what is going on? Do you think I'm being stalked?'

'You're not being stalked, Jade. If someone out there had such accurate psychic abilities, they wouldn't be using them to make your life hell. They'd be on *Britain's Got Talent*, or working on a cruise ship somewhere making loads of money.'

'Well then . . . what? Why? It's so freaky.'

Sophie looked up to the ceiling pensively. 'Have you tried changing the wording?'

'I thought of that last night, but then my mum showed up without warning so I didn't get the chance.'

Sophie turned on her heels, her scuffed-up Vans squeaking with the velocity. 'Well, try it now! There's Tippex here somewhere. I bought a bulk load when we were working on that festival installation last year as it dried super flaky and matt and was perfect for the chalky mountains I was making out of papier mâché . . .' Sophie was on the floor on her knees, her legs poking out of the shelving, her upper body tunnelling through paper and paint. She finally emerged with her strawberry-blonde bob in disarray and her roll-up missing from behind her ear. 'Got it!'

'Do you think it'll work?' Jade asked despondently.

'Well, I don't know. I mean this is all bloody bonkers, but it's worth a go. What do you want to change the first line to?'

Both Jade and Sophie peered down at the script, hair falling over their faces, creating a curtain of privacy around them.

```
[Lily is in the hallway looking at Jade, who
has just removed her cycling helmet.]



                    LILY
     Birdy, we'll run through the routine
     in a bit as it's quite detailed and
     I really want the kids to have some
     familiarity while we're away. Do you
```

want a green tea? Or I have some
charcoal-infused water?

Sophie tilted her head up to Jade's face. 'Birdy? Who's
Birdy?'

Jade shook her head. 'Me, she's called me it since I
was a tiny kid. Beyond annoying.' They swivelled their
heads back down to the page.

> JADE
>
> No, no, I'm fine, just a normal
> water please. Can I talk to you
> about Mum? I'm a bit worried about
> her drinking again.

> LILY
>
> Oh, don't be so dramatic. She's let-
> ting off steam. She has a lot of
> stress in her life.

> JADE
>
> Like what?

> LILY
>
> Well, you know, Dad.

> JADE
>
> They've been divorced for over
> twenty years, Lils.

                         LILY

Birds, that's very short-sighted of
you. It's been ever so hard for Mum
over the years. Anyway, enough about
all that. I'm so excited — next
weekend James and I are off for our
respective hen and stag do's.

                         JADE

Oh, cool.

                         LILY

Obviously my friends are very busy
people so pinning down a single
weekend for both James and I and
our friends has been like arranging Glastonbury. So much planning
and coordinating. James is off with
his pals to play golf in Portugal
and of course my hen do is a very
holistic affair. The last thing I
want is an alcohol bloat for the
big day.

                         JADE

Yeah, terrible.

                         LILY

I'm on a pre-wedding detox so the
hen is at Dukes. With Dad being a

member, he's gotten us a discount on
rooms and spa treatments. It will be
such a dreamy weekend in the
countryside.

> JADE

Sounds great.

> LILY

Now, I know you hate that sort of
thing so didn't want to make it awkward by inviting you, only for you
to have to come up with an excuse to
get out of it, so—

> JADE

Well, it actually sounds rather—

> LILY

So, I was thinking that you could
have the girls for a night next
weekend so they can get used to your
flat— *Dad's* flat.

> JADE

My flat. I pay full rent.

> LILY

—and you can practise putting them
to bed.

                    JADE

Practise? Don't you just put them in
a bed?

                    LILY

It's not really that simple, Birdy.
There's a routine that helps them
relax and unwind from the day.

                    JADE

Wait, I'm out next Saturday night.
Sophie asked me to a gig, so I can't,
I'm afraid. Can't you ask Mum?

                    LILY

You know I can't. It's too much for
her. She'll let them stay up super
late watching TV and not feed them
properly.

                    JADE

Dad?

                    LILY

Obviously not. He's never in the
country for a start. Oh, come on,
Jade! It's a huge deal, and if you
can't look after the girls we can't
really go, and it's taken so much
planning.

<pre>
                    JADE
     I can't, Lils.

                    LILY
     Well, I'm not sure what I'm going to
     do, then. We'll have to cancel the
     hen altogether, I suppose.
</pre>

Sophie looked up from the page with eyes as wide as the moon. 'Jade, this is unreal. Is this how she talks to you normally? The manipulation!'

Jade nodded slowly. 'This is the *most* accurate portrayal of our relationship, Soph. It's so depressing.'

'You cannot let her do this to you, Jade. The gig. *The gig.*' Sophie's voice rose higher with every word.

They both looked back down at the script.

<pre>
                    JADE
     Oh for fuck's sake, I'll do it.
</pre>

'No, babe. No, no, no.' Sophie stomped her feet on the concrete floor like a child.

'Shhh, Soph. Keep it down. This cannot be discussed outside of these three walls,' Jade hissed, pointing to the missing fourth wall that led directly out to the warehouse floor. 'You have no idea how powerful my sister is. She is terrifying.' Sophie blew air out of her mouth while shaking her head, and peered back down at the page.

Oh, the girls will be thrilled. What
an adventure for them. I've already
kind of told them and they were very
excited.

'Do you always give in so easily to her demands, babe?'
Sophie's voice was gentler this time.

'You try dealing with her. She's like Medusa. She pulls
you in. I can't be bothered with saying no and facing the
stress and relentless guilt-trips about it for weeks afterwards. It's just not worth my while.'

Sophie stepped back, picking up the Tippex. 'We.
Must. Sort. This. You and I are going to this Kings of
Leon gig, no matter what. You are going to be there,
with a cider in your hand, screaming at the drummer
while I dance wildly, holding gaze with Caleb. Got it?'

Jade nodded. 'It's worth a go, I guess. Tippex over my
answer when Lily asks me to baby-sit Saturday. I'll go
find a marker pen.'

Sophie removed the brush from the oversized pot of
Tippex and leaned in carefully, as if inspecting an archae-
ological site. She dabbed gently on each word, making
sure not to go over any other text.

'Done!' she called out to Jade.

Jade dashed back holding a fine marker pen. 'OK,
what do I write?'

Sophie stopped blowing the Tippex dry. 'Er, how
about "NO!"'

'I have to come up with a valid excuse, surely?'

'Why?'

'Well, that's kind of in keeping with our dynamic, I guess. I can't turn up to her house a completely different person.'

Sophie shrugged.

Jade leaned in with her pen and made her first mark over the Tippex. 'Well, I'll soften that "no" around the edges a little, perhaps. How about: "I'm afraid I can't on Saturday, Lils. I've already got something in the diary. I'm sorry but I really can't change my plans"?'

'OK. Definitely too polite if you ask me, but whatever you think will work. What about the part where she throws guilt your way? You have to find a way to not catch the guilt,' Sophie pleaded. Jade's pen hovered over the next line, but before she could add anything more—

'Ladies!' a voice boomed from the main warehouse.

IO

'Shit. Colin,' Jade whispered, stuffing the script back into its envelope as Colin's footsteps grew nearer.

'Morning, Colin,' they chimed together, sounding as innocent as possible. He swaggered round the dividing wall as Jade hid the envelope behind the tins of biscuits.

'What are you girls doing back here? I don't pay you to make tea and have a mothers meeting.'

'Mothers meeting?' Sophie said. 'We don't have kids and that's a pretty sexist—'

'We've got a lot on today, ladies,' Colin cut in. 'Let's snap to it.' He turned to leave, then said: 'Jade. A word.'

She looked at him with dread in her stomach. 'Yup?'

'Dry-cleaning needs picking up. Nice new suit. Got curry all down it the other night, didn't I? Be a good girl and go grab it for me at lunchtime.'

She wanted to scream in his face, tell him to go and get his own curry-sodden, ill-fitting suit and that she was not a *good girl*, she was a grown woman who was competent in saying no. Her head spun. She struggled to breathe in the air around her.

'I'm a bit snowed under today, Colin,' she said, barely moving her mouth.

'Yeah, you'll find the time.' He was already walking

towards the main door of the warehouse to leave. 'Penny said she left all my dry-cleaning tabs on my desk,' he said without turning back.

'What a knob,' Sophie snarled. 'Why did you say yes?'

'I didn't! I said I was snowed under and then he told me to do it anyway.' Jade looked at her feet. The bang of the sliding doors shutting echoed through the warehouse.

'Right, we have changes to make, my friend. I'm so sick of this good girl shit. This idea that we have to be *the good girl*. That we are being difficult if we don't go along with what people want of us, or that we are arseholes if we stand up for ourselves. I think every woman feels it to a degree, whether we like it or not. But I don't want to be a good girl; I want to be a complex woman who changes her mind and says no and gets things wrong but picks herself up again and sometimes does weird things that she can't explain and doesn't say sorry when really she means *You're in my way*. We have to sort this out for the next generation, Jadey. No more good girl shit, OK?'

Sophie's cheeks were pink with exertion. Jade clapped slowly.

'God I love you, Soph.'

'We've got this. Let's get back to the script with your sister, and whatever you do, *do not* get his dry-cleaning later,' Sophie said, fishing the envelope out from its hiding place and flicking to the correct page.

'He'll bollock me, though. It's easier just to do it.'

'Right, fine, park Colin and his curried suit for now, let's focus on Lily, because you are coming to this gig, OK, mate?' Sophie looked directly into Jade's eyes.

'I find this so hard, Soph. I'm such a fixer. I can't bear people attempting to make me feel bad. I always give in. How do you do this? What the hell do I say to Lily that sounds final and confident?'

'How about, "I'm so sorry but I can't help out this time. I'll be letting someone else down if I cancel this late in the day"?' Sophie said, pointing at herself and grinning broadly.

'Yeah, that works, I guess. It's reasonable and fair. OK, here goes . . .' Jade carefully touched the marker onto the Tippexed area of the script and wrote: *I'm so sorry, I can't help out this time. I'll be letting someone else down if I cancel this late in the day.*

Jade stood back with head tilted, squinting at the page in front of her.

'Guys! Are you going to help us out today or not? Bloody hell.' Jade and Sophie jumped. Lethabo was standing behind them with his arms folded and both eyebrows raised.

'Alright, Thabs!' Sophie gasped. 'Yes, yes, I was just helping Jade with some . . . important documents.'

Jade quickly scooped up the script, trying not to smudge the yet-to-dry ink.

'Mmm, OK,' Lethabo said conspiratorially, 'I don't know what you're up to but these trees aren't going to paint themselves.' He turned on one foot and strutted back to the main warehouse floor.

'One sec, Thabs,' Sophie called after him. 'Let me just have a quick rollie and I'll be there.'

Jade realised she had been holding her breath for the

last thirty seconds. She took a gulp of air, tapped the newly penned wording to check it was dry, and then carefully rolled it up and placed it in her backpack. She could only pray that she had found a solution to how the day would play out.

Just then her phone pinged.

I'm fine Jadey, what r u worrying about? Just woke up. Needed bit of a lie in. Love Mum X

Jade sighed, feeling a familiar cocktail of relief and frustration. She flicked the kettle on, dropped a teabag into the cup and leaned on the worktop waiting for the water to boil. Thinking about the script, she let her mind focus on her sister. Tonight, everything was going to change.

Tonight, she would take back control.

11

A familiar dread crept across Jade's shoulders as she chained her bike to the metal post, its pinkness jarring against the grey and monochrome of Lily's house. She wondered how her sister had the ability to make her feel like this. She had felt so determined when Sophie waved her off from the warehouse, but with each footstep towards the door she felt the confidence drain out of her body.

The rain had made way for a perfect July sky: bright blue without a blemish of cloud. A light blue butterfly danced in her path. She mentally made a note to look up the significance of blue butterflies after the visit to her sister, but for now she decided it was some kind of messenger of hope.

She straightened her spine as she approached Lily's front door, pulling back her shoulders. *'I can do this, I can do this. I am an adult in charge of my own life,'* she quietly muttered under her breath while looking to the sky.

'Birdy!' Lily almost screeched, flinging open the door. 'Come in. Gosh, I've been so busy with my new business that I completely lost track of time.' Jade took in her sister's silhouette – the skin-tight grey workout leggings and minuscule sports bra, the ripple of abs below – and sucked in her tummy.

'James is doing bathtime tonight, such a sterling step-dad. I'll get him and the girls to come and say hi in a minute, but I won't disturb them in the midst of it all. Why are you dressed like that? Did you come straight from work?'

Jade ignored the question, her eyes fixed on her sister. 'Wow. When did you do that?'

Lily flicked her newly chopped hair, letting each glossy strand fall between her fingers. 'It's called a French bob. I thought it would be *chic* for the wedding. What do you think?'

Jade's grin widened. 'Yeah, it's, er, chic.' Her fingers moved through her own long hair that fell over her shoulders in matted tendrils, showing the signs of her bike ride. She hadn't had it cut in over a year and the ends were starting to split.

Lily looked at herself in the hallway mirror, smoothing down the sides of her neat bob, unconsciously pouting as she did so. 'Birdy, you will have your nails done before my wedding, right? I can't have a bridesmaid with paint-covered hands and bitten-down nails.'

Jade looked down at her hands. She loved seeing the workday's imprint on her skin; the dots of bright yellow and deep red caught in the creases. She nodded and gulped as Lily continued, 'Birdy, we'll run through the routine in a bit as it's quite detailed and I really want the kids to have some familiarity while we're away. Do you want a green tea? Or I have some charcoal-infused water?' As she spoke she glanced at her moving reflection as they walked to the kitchen.

Jade knew what was coming next. Her fingers dug into her palms. She mentally said to herself *I can do this, I can do this.*

'No, no, I'm fine, just a normal water please. Can I talk to you about Mum? I'm a bit worried about her drinking again.' The script flowed from her mouth.

Lily furrowed her brow as she reached into the cupboard to get a glass for Jade. 'Oh, don't be so dramatic. She's letting off steam. She has a lot of stress in her life.'

Jade tried to look calmer than she felt. Small droplets of sweat began to gather in the middle of her back. She twisted her arm behind her to wipe it with her T-shirt.

'Like what?'

Lily waved her hands about as if swatting a fly away. This was a habit of hers that irritated Jade to the core. She could pooh-pooh an idea or statement without even speaking a word. 'Well, you know, Dad.'

Jade took the glass of water that Lily was holding out to her. The glass was deep purple, Moroccan-looking.

'They've been divorced for over twenty years, Lils.'

She steadied herself, knowing the doctored part of the script was nearing.

'Birds, that's very short-sighted of you. It's been ever so hard for Mum over the years. Anyway, enough about all that. I'm so excited – next weekend James and I are off for our respective hen and stag do's.'

Jade kept her eyes on the kitchen floor-tiles, examining the grouting to try and steady her nerves. She gulped. 'Oh, cool.'

'Obviously my friends are very busy people so pinning down a single weekend for both James and I and our friends has been like arranging Glastonbury. So much planning and coordinating. James is off with his pals to play golf in Portugal and of course my hen do is a very holistic affair. The last thing I want is an alcohol bloat for the big day.'

Jade shifted from foot to foot. 'Yeah, terrible.'

'I'm on a pre-wedding detox so the hen is at Dukes. With Dad being a member, he's gotten us a discount on rooms and spa treatments. It will be such a dreamy weekend in the countryside.'

Jade hated Dukes. Nestled in a wooded area on the outskirts of a Cotswolds village, the private members club and hotel attracted Londoners who needed time out from the bustle but with close proximity to other Londoners. Her dad and Jacquie had arranged many a birthday lunch there over the years, and every time Jade felt like a fish out of water as she sat amongst a tribe of wealthy Londoners in gilets and pristine wellies.

'Sounds great.' Jade heard her own voice echo around the marble kitchen.

'Now, I know you hate that sort of thing so didn't want to make it awkward by inviting you, only for you to have to come up with an excuse to get out of it, so—'

'Well, it actually sounds rather—' Jade interjected.

'So, I was thinking that you could have the girls for a night this weekend so they can get used to your flat—*Dad's* flat.' Lily corrected herself, then smiled as if she were doing Jade a favour.

Jade tried to sound breezy in her response: '*My* flat. I pay full rent.'

'—and you can practise putting them to bed.'

Jade pictured a force-field springing up around her. What was it Sophie said? *She should not catch the guilt.*

'Practise? Don't you just put them in a bed?' Jade said, her voice wobbling a little.

'It's not really that simple, Birdy. There's a routine that helps them relax and unwind from the day.' Lily was uninterested in Jade's protest, picking up her phone and scrolling while talking.

Jade made sure not to look into her sister's eyes while she said the next words. This was where she needed the most focus. This was where she would sound definite and confident. This was where she would say 'No.'

'Wait, I'm out next Saturday night. Sophie asked me to a gig, so I can't, I'm afraid. Can't you ask Mum?'

Jade started to tail off towards the end of the sentence. Why hadn't her mouth formed the words that she had penned with black ink atop the Tippexed parts of the script? She was supposed to firmly state that she couldn't.

Before she could try again, her sister jumped in.

'You know I can't. It's too much for her. She'll let them stay up super late watching TV and not feed them properly.'

Jade's confidence further dwindled, and she felt her shoulders sloping towards the newly tiled kitchen floor.

'Dad?' she almost whispered, starting to give up hope.

'Obviously not. He's never in the country for a start.

Oh, come on, Jade! It's a huge deal, and if you can't look after the girls we can't really go, and it's taken so much planning.' Lily looked up and grinned with her large, very straight teeth on display, like a wolf out to get its prey.

Again, only a whisper left Jade's lips: 'I can't, Lils.'

Lily looked disgruntled but remained confident, 'Well, I'm not sure what I'm going to do, then. We'll have to cancel the hen altogether, I suppose.'

This was Jade's last chance. To rectify this conversation so she could go to the gig with Sophie, but also to prove to herself that she had control over her own voice and life. Steadying her breath, she visualised the wording on the reworked script. She could see it now, written in her neatest handwriting. Black ink. Powerful, permanent black ink.

'Oh for fuck's sake, I'll do it.'

Jade let her head roll back in disappointment. Why wasn't this working? The room rotated as control slipped through her fingers like soap.

Lily, still grinning with her teeth on show, almost sang in jubilation, 'Oh, the girls will be thrilled. What an adventure for them. I've already kind of told them and they were very excited.'

'Well, I'd better dash,' Jade said weakly. 'I've got . . . oh, it doesn't matter, I've just got to go.'

'But you haven't even said goodnight to the girls; they're just upstairs with James getting ready for bed. And we haven't been through the routine. I need to talk you through which books the girls like to have read to them at bedtime and which soundscape to use on their white-noise machine. Sometimes they like the ocean sound, but I've just read a blog on brown noise which is supposedly the best for sleep.' Lily looked suddenly flustered, her thin arms flapping like a distressed bird.

'Just email me,' Jade said, grabbing her cycling helmet and moving swiftly towards the front door. 'Bye!' The door slammed.

12

Jade had never been happier to see her front door. Leaning against the wall in the hallway of her flat, she scrambled for her phone in her bag. She punched in Sophie's name and pressed call.

'Hi, mate. How did it go? Are we going to the Kings of Leon or are we going to the Kings of Leon?'

'Soph, *I* am *not* going to the Kings of Leon. That was a total mess.' Jade dragged herself along the hallway and slumped into the armchair in her front room. The blue sky had turned Turkish Delight pink and only a single lamp illuminated the room, throwing shadows of Jade, the armchair and the piles of books next to her on the walls.

'What! Why? How? We changed the wording. I don't get it?'

'I don't either, Soph. I'm so down about it. I feel like I'm spiralling out of control. I feel like a puppet. Someone else is pulling the strings and I'm dancing about blurting out these empty words without communicating what I really need to say.'

Sophie went silent for a moment. Jade could feel Sophie's mind whirring and imagined her taking a long, delicious drag of her roll-up.

'Mate. This is just a thought. I'm reading a book at the

moment about the law of attraction. It's so interesting. I swear it works. You have to focus on what you want, but really *believe* it. Dreaming or wishing isn't enough. It must come from a place where you truly believe you deserve the best. How long have we known each other now? Six, seven years? In those six-odd years I've seen how beautifully empathetic you are, how helpful you are to others, how generous you are, but I'm not sure I've seen you giving the same to yourself. You're so hard on yourself.'

One tiny tear formed in Jade's left eye, the unexpected wave of kindness breaking down her defences. She couldn't remember the last time she had cried. It was like Sophie had unlocked tears that had been just below the surface.

'Do you *believe* you deserve to go to this gig on Saturday night with me? Do you really believe your time is as important as your sister's?' Sophie's voice grew punchier.

Jade looked up to the ceiling; it was textured with an eighties design that looked like somebody had pushed plaster around with a wide paintbrush.

She sighed. 'I don't know, Soph. I'm not sure any more. Sometimes I don't think I know much at all. I feel lost. Lost in other people's drama, lost in other people's lives and expectations of me. Sometimes I'm not sure what I want.'

'Of course you do. If anything, these—' Sophie searched for the right words '—unexplainable scripts are showing you exactly what you *don't* want. By a process of elimination, you can see exactly what you do want. I'm no therapist but just from seeing the script earlier I can see that fear is holding you back. I'm pretty sure you want to feel free from certain situations. Maybe even people.'

Sophie let silence hang in the air. Jade knew she meant Adam.

Sophie continued, 'But, my god, babe, you're a gift! You are pure joy. I'm so lucky I get to be your mate. Why can't you see how brilliant you are?'

Jade laughed, small tears mixing with saliva as they swam past her lips. 'I don't know? I guess I'm not sure I believe I am?' Jade wiped a stream of snot running from her nose.

'How can you not see what I see? A talented artist, an amazing friend, caring daughter, helpful sister. Beautiful, funny – especially when drunk on cider. Jade, you need to start seeing this and believing it. This isn't just about you not being able to come to the gig on Saturday – although I am super pissed off at your sister about that – this is about you being able to shine as brightly as you should in life. It's about you making decisions that work for *you*, not taking on responsibilities that aren't your own. You deserve that, babe.'

Jade felt another tear reach her lips, its salt stinging where she had been biting at the plumpness. 'I know. I feel so far from it, but I know.' She wound her long hair around her index finger for comfort.

'Right. Count me in as your official cheerleader. I am here to remind you every day how bloody brilliant you are. I will remind you until you tell Lily to stick it and are sick to death of me, OK?'

Jade laughed and used both sleeves to wipe her damp cheeks. 'I love you, Soph.'

'I love you too, mate,' Sophie replied gently.

Jade hung up and watched her phone fade back to black. Placing it beside her, she sat tracing her shadow on the wall with her eyes. Her shadow, in her flat, in her life. It was *her* life. How had she forgotten this? She wasn't a bit part in her sister's life, or the supporting role in her mum and dad's life. Yet she had always felt dragged along by other people's currents. As Lily's teenage rebellion had taken up more time and space in Jade's childhood, she'd often felt as if someone had rubbed her out of her own life. She imagined a sketch pad with grey lines depicting her bedroom, with her sitting on the bed, then a rubber slowly blurring her out of the scene.

Her phone pinged and 'Adam' popped up on the screen. She didn't feel quite ready for his arrival back to the flat. His absence had given her headspace and peace that she felt in every cell in her body. She picked up her phone with trepidation, expecting to see another photo of a palm tree or green juice perched elegantly by a turquoise pool.

Instead, a text read: Hey, landing Thursday at midday. Can u get me from Heathrow? A x

A dull numbness engulfed her body, reading his short sharp text. After three years together, the familiarity had diluted platitudes or pleasantries. Their relationship had mutated into a dysfunctional friendship. Mates that occupied the same space but lived separately. Tammy's photo had been mentally plaguing her and at times she failed to squash the despairing comparison. Maybe if she made more effort, wore her dungarees less and silk dresses more, or cut her hair, or made her lips look all bouncy and wet like Tammy's, or stayed out late once in a while . . . She wondered if she needed to change to make this work.

She lethargically typed back: I'll be at work then. See you when I'm back about 5:30/6. Safe flight. X

She hesitated just before sending the message, changed it to read *Safe flight, baby* to soften things, and hit send.

She then googled an online florist and chose a bunch of dusty peach flowers to match Sophie's strawberry-blonde hair. Sophie's pep talk was still fresh in her head. The words made sense to her but felt almost impossible to action. Did she believe she deserved better? Currently she wasn't so sure.

Dear Sophie. I'm bloody lucky to have you. Love Jade.

She requested next-day delivery and then turned her phone off. It was too late to cook. Crumpets and jam would be quick, she thought, grabbing them from the bread bin. They were two days past their sell-by date. Still, she shoved them in the toaster, and watched the orange bars glow.

13

'What year did Christina Aguilera release "Genie in a Bottle"?'

'What?' Sophie looked at Lethabo, who was grinning and nodding at her.

'What year did Christina Aguilera release "Genie in a Bottle"?'

'I don't know. Why?' Sophie licked a Rizla paper.

'Jade?' Lethabo motioned to her.

'Sorry, what's going on?' Jade stood with a large pot of paint in her arms.

'Guess. Just guess.' Lethabo flapped his arms.

'Er, 1997?' Sophie tucked her roll-up behind her ear.

'Eh-eh.' Lethabo mimicked the noise of a disqualification buzzer.

'1998?' Jade guessed.

'God, you two. Don't you know anything about pop music?'

'My mind is kind of elsewhere, Thabs,' Jade retorted.

'1999! The last year of truly decent pop music. I got the answer right in the pub quiz at the Windmill last night.'

'Oh well done, babe,' Sophie said, making for the door.

'Didn't win, though. Some jokers called the Agatha Quizties won.'

'Shame,' said Jade and patted him on the shoulder.

'Those things will kill you, babe. I keep telling you this,' Lethabo said, pointing accusingly at Sophie's roll-up as she closed the large warehouse door behind her.

'Let me enjoy myself, Thabs,' Sophie shouted back through the small crack in the door, sunlight streaming in to create a slice of gold on the concrete floor.

Since Vinnie had delivered the last script, and anticipating Adam's imminent arrival, Jade had felt edgy. She had moved around the warehouse slowly, vigilantly looking out for wads of paper. She hadn't found a script, but assumed she would before he landed, so a new paranoia constantly followed in her shadow. A plastic bag on the pavement would send shivers up her spine. A pile of white T-shirts in her drawer had made her heart leap. Her anxiety was at fever pitch.

What had Sophie said? *She had to believe that she deserved better.* Although she felt consumed with frustration towards Adam a lot of the time, she still felt blindsided by silly, inconsequential worries about being single – like going to Lily's wedding on her own and dealing with spiders in the flat without an accomplice. And alongside the worries, rose-tinted nostalgia papered over the gaping cracks. Maybe they were just going through a blip. Perhaps absence would have made the heart grow fonder. She'd suggest they take long strolls down the river on Sundays, and maybe have a picnic dinner with prosecco in plastic cups one weekday evening . . . as she plotted, her eyes scanned the room.

'You looking for something, Jade?' Jackson quietly

asked, his dark hair covering his face as he kept his eyes on the sign he was painting.

'No, no, I'm . . . just figuring out what I'm going to work on next I guess.' She attempted to sound breezy.

Jackson wiped a splodge of orange paint from his finger onto his oversized Nirvana T-shirt. 'You can help me with this sign? It's for Pukkelpop.'

'Pukkelpop is the best festival name ever.' Jade repeated the name, enjoying each sound. 'Didn't you go last year?'

'Yup. The Belgians are good at festivals.' Jackson's hair restricted any eye contact with Jade. 'They want all of the signposts to look traditional, almost circus-like. I'm doing "Toilets This Way", but you could do "ATM This Way" if you like?' Jackson said without looking up.

'Sure.' Jade had learned to sign-write from one of her dad's four brothers, Uncle Pete, who had run his own sign-writing company for years. He could move his hand across a sign, paintbrush in hand, with such elegance it was almost hypnotic. He had taught her how to hold brushes with long sweeping ends to create swooping letters. His hands were always caked in paint, embedded in the creases of his calloused skin. His jumpers would be dotted with it too, his hair permanently ruffled, and work boots his only footwear. Growing up, Lily's snobbish remarks about Uncle Pete had only ever made Jade fonder of him. Pete and Jade spoke a language that Lily didn't understand; one of paint colours and brush strokes. Lily would often fake a yawn to interrupt a conversation and laugh like a small child to switch attention back to herself. But Jade hadn't cared. They had paint, and Lily didn't.

Picking up a long paintbrush, she sidled up to Jackson, who was hunch-backed over a long trestle table, knowing each stroke would distract her from the noise in her head. Scooping her hair, she knotted it on top of her head and secured it with a velvet scrunchie.

'You going to see the Kings of Leon with Soph at the weekend?' Jackson muttered, filling the silence.

'No, nope, sadly I must look after my nieces. I mean, I'm not sad about seeing my nieces, I just desperately wanted to go,' Jade replied.

'Can't what's-his-face look after them?' Jackson never remembered Adam's name, which to Jade seemed utterly deliberate. She remembered the first time they'd met, outside the warehouse when Adam had come to meet her after work. Watching them try to navigate a conversation was like viewing a hummingbird interacting with a gorilla. Adam had been loud and brash and had attempted a kind of bro-hug which Jackson had misinterpreted as a handshake Their bodies had clumsily clashed together, sending Jackson's wiry frame crashing into the wall behind him.

'You mean Adam? Ha, no I don't think he'd be up for it. He's arriving back from LA at lunchtime, so he'll be tired and on a different time zone altogether. I actually haven't let him know about my nieces coming to stay yet. Sort of dreading telling him, to be honest.'

Jackson peered up through his hair and slowly raised one eyebrow.

'I know, I know. It's not going to go down well. Anyway, I don't want to think about it. What colour shall I paint this sign? How about orange for the font?'

Jackson silently carried on working without answering Jade. She busied herself dipping her brush into pools of orange, keeping her eyes on the work.

The day moved by mechanically and slowly. Jade and Jackson fell into comfortable pockets of silence as they worked. At five-thirty, Jade picked up her cycling helmet and walked to the door, feeling relieved she had made it through the day without any unsolicited fortune-telling. Perhaps it was a good sign that she was walking into her first conversation with Adam after his time in LA without a looming pre-written dialogue. That meant things would go well tonight, surely?

Outside, the blue sky was electric and the air a warm hum. This summer had been a constant cycle of one or two sun-kissed days followed by a week of rain, so she took in every inch of the cloudless horizon. Arriving back at the flat, she smoothed down her hair that had been bunched under her cycle helmet, pinched her cheeks into flushed blooms and practised a gentle smile. She had to make things good again, it was the right thing to do. She put the key in the door and slowly pushed it open, feeling a mix of nervous butterflies and anxious anticipation.

The door hit a stop, leaving only a small gap. Jade squeezed her face through the gap between the door and the frame. She looked down and saw Adam's open suitcase lodged between the door and wall, clothes spilling out of the open case, socks in knots and those awful shoes she had seen a photo of lying atop the crumpled clothes.

'*Adam!* Adam, I can't get in,' she shouted.

She could faintly hear the shower on in the bathroom.

'Adam!' She pushed the door again. Using her right foot, she kicked at the case, and it started to dislodge. With one almighty thump of her foot, she sent the case flying, balled-up socks and T-shirts exploding in every direction. She leapt over the mound of clothes and now empty case and bent down to tidy them.

'Hey, it's me. I'm home,' she cooed in Adam's direction. The shower thundered without a response. She picked up the newly purchased LA shoes and examined them with a downturned mouth. Sprinkles of sand cascaded out onto the floor. She neatly folded some T-shirts she didn't recognise and bent down to put his toothbrush back in his toiletries bag.

A small rectangle of glossy paper flew from under the bag and onto the floor. She picked it up and turned it over to reveal four photo-booth pictures. The photos were in black and white, and as she looked closer the faces came into focus. Adam was sitting, mouth wide, hair flung back, laughing, his straight teeth gleaming. Then a second face. Round cheeks, neat dimples marking each one, thick dark hair perfectly spilling onto her shoulders and his. Their bodies were close and it took Jade a few seconds to realise the woman's bare thighs were touching Adam's legs as she sat on his lap, her black dress clinging to every curve of her outline.

A queasiness punched Jade in the gut. She stood up, the blood in her head pounding and the adrenaline in her chest pulsating.

'*Adam*. ADAM. What is this?' Her hand was shaking as she pressed the photos up against the shower glass. Adam squinted under the water. Pulling the photos away, Jade used her hand to wipe the steam from the outside of the glass and then forcefully splatted the photographs back in his line of vision.

'What. Is. This?' she repeated, adrenaline spiking in her throat.

Adam turned the shower off, his eyes closed, shampoo still bubbling below his eyebrows. 'Oh, that's a nice welcome home,' he said. 'What are you on about?'

'THIS! This in my hands. What. IS. THIS?'

'Pass me a towel, I can't bloody see. Why are you screaming at me? I literally only got in an hour ago as my flight was delayed. What is up with you?'

Jade stood motionless, her arms still pressing the photos into the glass like she might be able to smash through to where he was standing. Adam staggered out of the shower, arms out in front of him like a zombie, reaching blindly for the towel rail. He grabbed at a towel and wiped his face and the shampoo out of his eyes.

'Hey, babe. I missed you. What's up?' Each word soft and breezy.

'What's up? You tell me. Who the hell is this? Is this "Tammy C"?'

Adam stepped back, tying his towel around his waist and putting his hands on his hips. 'Tammy C?' he spluttered through a short laugh. 'Tammy is a vintage buyer out there that I've been working with. That's not Tammy. I mean, Tammy was there. We were at this brilliant new members club called Six Forty, which is a key place for the LA fashion set. Great networking. How do you know Tammy?'

Adam wasn't taking a breath between thoughts, so Jade leapt in: '*Know her*? I don't *know her*.' Her words tumbled out of her tense mouth. 'And *networking*? This doesn't look like networking to me. Who is she, and why is she on your lap?'

As Jade's momentum and anger dissipated with each word she started to wonder if she really felt that bothered at all. She couldn't tell whether the initial rage was about the mystery girl on Adam's lap, or frustration at herself for thinking they could make a go of it. Maybe this was all utterly unfixable.

Adam leaned against the edge of the windowsill casually. 'Babe, there's nothing to worry about. The girl in the photo is Tammy's little sister and she was a bit pissed. There was a photo booth, and we were all messing about taking photos in there. You know what these booths are like; the stools are tiny. So I jumped in and she had to kind of sit on my lap to get in the photo. That's why we're laughing. It's nothing, seriously.'

Jade let her hands fall by her side in surrender. To continue this argument was futile. She knew how Adam operated. He wasn't about to back down or tell her the truth, and she really didn't have the energy to continue the conversation. She slowly walked out of the room, head and arms heavy, eyes fixed on the floor. Adam carried on drying himself in the bathroom nonchalantly.

'Jade, honestly, it's nothing,' he called out in an ambivalent tone.

The windows were open in the front room and the curtains billowed in the breeze, moving like waves against the wall. Jade sat and stared at them. She could hear him pulling on clothes and moving to the kitchen, the kettle rumbling and a mug landing on the sideboard.

'Anyway,' he shouted through, 'I've got something planned for us this weekend so we can spend some proper time together.' Jade's eyes widened. She played with her top lip as she mustered the courage to break the news.

'Adam. The thing is . . . I can't do much this weekend.' Her muffled words, spoken through her fingers, landed gently in the kitchen. Adam poked his head round into the front room.

'What, why? You're not working, are you? I haven't seen you in days.' Adam spoke accusingly, as if his absence were Jade's doing. She felt a swell of anger in the pit of her stomach.

'You haven't seen me because you chose to go to LA.' She felt her neck reddening in raspberry blotches. 'I can't do anything this weekend because we've got Lily's kids staying. Lily and James are off on their hen and stag do's, so I said I'd help out.'

Adam shook his head and sucked his cheeks in. 'Erm, I don't think so. You haven't discussed this with me. I've only been back in the country for five seconds.'

'You've only been back for five seconds because *you* chose to go away.'

Adam threw his arms in the air, bashing his right shoulder on the door frame clumsily. 'I'm so bored of this, Jade. I'm super jetlagged and have been non-stop out in LA; this is the last thing I need. I'll be staying with Benny this weekend. I'm not putting up with early wake-ups and kids' TV blaring all weekend. Fuck that.' With this, he turned on his heels back into the kitchen and plucked his keys from the counter.

'Where are you going? You've only just got in,' Jade stammered. Adam turned back and leaned his body towards Jade.

'Out!'

The door slammed shut and Jade was left with silence, an upturned suitcase and the terrible espadrille shoes staring at her menacingly from the hallway.

She got up and kicked the shoes against the wall, picked up the photos from the floor, and ripped them into tiny fragments. Throwing the shards of glossy paper into the air behind her, she walked out onto the balcony and took a deep breath. Adam, in a new striped linen shirt, was now a distant blob on the hill. She sat down cross-legged on the floor, shaking her head in disbelief at the explosive drama of the last half an hour.

She felt foolish for kidding herself that she could salvage their relationship. Ironically, her attempts to protect herself from the heartache of breaking up were proving to be just as painful. There was no going back. She had to let her heart fall into tiny pieces.

She searched for the words that she knew she should have spoken: *It's over, Adam*, letting them leave her mouth quietly and fall to the floor beside her.

'It's over.'

She said it out loud, then a little louder, the muscles in her neck spasming. Why weren't the words there when she needed them? Picking herself up off the floor, she walked into the kitchen with purpose. She reached for the cupboard above the fridge and pulled out a bottle of vodka. An image of her mum flashed up like a picture from an eighties View-Master toy. She shook it out of her mind and poured an inch of vodka into a tumbler. Opening the fridge, she was met with a sorry lack of mixers – or really anything at all. A wave of shame made her feel light-headed. She pulled a half-full bottle of orange juice out of the fridge door and poured it over the vodka. She swigged it back, wincing at the bitterness and lumpy strings of orange.

A text pinged in the next room, breaking Jade's trance. Trudging back, she found her phone glowing with unread messages. She ran her eyes over the names: Dad, Lily, Sophie. She decided to start with the most dreaded and work backwards.

Hey Birdy, so all set for this weekend? The girls are so pumped. I'll drop them at 4pm after the school run tomorrow. x Lils

The forced pleasantries made Jade wince. She reread the timings; four o'clock on Friday afternoon? She was certain that Lily had only said for her to have the girls on Saturday night. She sighed heavily, then fired off a short text to Colin. Possible to leave early tomorrow? I have a doctor's appointment at 4pm.].

Crackles of stress coursed through her chest. She swiped her phone to get back to her messages.

Hey Jadey. Still good for the rehearsal dinner next month, Jacs said she hasn't heard from you? Is Adam coming? Jacquie needs to know for numbers. Dad x

At this point Jade didn't know or care if Adam was coming for dinner, or home later on that evening. She punched back a simple 'Yes'. Another bitter swig of vodka blurred the edges where stress had taken hold. The emptiness brought relief but also a void which needed filling. She swiped across her screen to activate Instagram, even though deep down she knew it would only make her feel worse. She located Adam's page and the photo of the ghastly shoes, and clicked then on @TammyC.

Scrolling through Tammy's endless stream of perfectly curated photos of vintage bomber jackets, fruit-laden smoothie bowls and a small, overly manicured snow-white dog, Jade's eyes darted from square to square looking for Tammy's little sister. Her eyes landed on an image of five women together, a bouquet of tanned legs appearing from the end of skin-tight dresses; shiny cheekbones, soft almond-coloured clothes, honey-coloured skin and rich dark hair – a human crème caramel. Bringing two fingers to the screen, she zoomed in close to examine Tammy's sister, taking in every millimetre of beauty. This time she noticed her eyes were emerald green and her teeth impossibly white and straight; proper LA teeth. Jade ran her tongue over her own, feeling every dip and groove, and let it linger on her twisted tooth. Tammy's sister was wearing a loose-fitting pair of beige trousers and a bra top that tied in a knot below her breasts. Jade glanced down at her dirty work jeans and Debbie Harry hoodie that had a hole in the side where she relentlessly pulled at it to cover her bum. She hovered her finger over the sister and clicked the tag that appeared over her face: JaneyC. Tammy, Janey; you could barely say them aloud without sounding like you were flirting. Having clicked on Janey's tag, she was taken to a locked profile. Her investigation was halted before it had even started. Frustrated and a little inebriated from the bitter vodka, she resisted the urge to click 'Follow'.

Jade picked at the skin around her thumb, the shame of this private, failed investigation burning through her chest. She stormed into the kitchen and swung open the fridge door with a little too much vigour. She stood staring at the bare shelves, the empty fridge. Pulling a box of cornflakes out of the cupboard, she poured milk over them and sat up on the kitchen counter. The sound of her teeth crunching on the cereal filled her head as she monotonously spooned heaps into her mouth.

14

The weather had turned again, and so had Jade's mood. The steel-grey sky looked incongruous above the lush summer oak trees that lined the street. Colin had bought her white lie about the doctor's appointment and OK'd her early departure, on the condition that she promised to pick up a birthday gift for his wife in her lunch-break the following week. She had nodded with gritted teeth.

Each foot pushing aggressively on her bike pedals, she gathered momentum up the last leg of the hill. She reached her flat just as Lily was pulling up in her car.

'Aunty Jade!' Jemima screeched from her open window. Jade waved back theatrically, hoping to mask her fear of the coming days.

'Hey, Birds. Well, they're all set for you. Just remember: not too much TV, bath before bed to calm them down, Saffy doesn't like sausages, but Jammy loves them, and don't give them too much sugar, especially on Sunday before you hand them back to me. OK? Bedtime routine all outlined in my email yesterday. You've looked at it, right?'

Jade, still panting from the steep incline, nodded and smiled with a tense jaw. 'Come on, girls.' Jade chained up her bike and waved her nieces over. Lily opened the boot and produced two huge holdalls and a giant cuddly tiger, followed by two scooters.

'Oh, bloody hell, sis, they're only staying two nights.'

Lily sharply turned her head. 'Jade, you have no idea how much stuff kids need. You'll get it one day.' She raced back into the car. Winding down the window she shouted, 'Love you, my little hot cross buns.' Her foot hit the pedal, and her car screeched away from the pavement.

Choosing to ignore Lily's condescending tone, Jade gathered the bags, threw both scooters over her shoulder, and ushered the girls towards the main door of the flats, her neighbour Mr Merry emerging in a flat cap and light blue shirt at the exact moment the girls were about to push through to the hallway.

'Oh, hello there. Who have we got here, then?' he said cheerfully, his cheeks pink and bursting with a huge grin.

'Hello, Mr Merry. These are my nieces, who will be staying this weekend.'

Mr Merry leaned towards the girls and patted Saffron on the head. 'Oh, how lovely. You will be good for your Aunty Jade, won't you, girls?' Both girls looked at him accusingly without saying a word.

'I'm sure they will, Mr Merry.' Jade nodded to the girls to walk through the door, her heavy load feeling more of a burden by the second.

'Did I tell you I'm off to walk the new trail at Kew Gardens?' Mr Merry continued. A scooter was slipping from Jade's shoulder. She bounced on her heels to try and edge it back up to the crook of her neck.

'No, no, you didn't mention that Mr Merry.'

His smile broadened to an impossible width. 'Oh well, I must tell you, I'm so very excited about it all. It's a delightful chance to walk around Kew off the beaten track and learn about the history of many of the trees there.'

Jade shuffled from foot to foot, trying to keep the bags and scooters balanced. 'Oh wow. Marvellous. You must tell me how it all goes.' The effort to speak and hold the contents of her nieces' lives in her arms was causing her voice to strain.

Mr Merry looked off into the distance with dreamy eyes. 'Jade, I think it's going to be a very special day. I might even take my old watercolours and paint one of the grand sycamores.'

Jade nodded, frantically biting down on her lip. 'Oh yes, you must. Anyway, I'd better get these girls . . .'

Mr Merry, still looking at an imaginary horizon, continued, 'I used to be very good in my day, you know. Fields. They were my speciality. Especially in spring when all the rapeseed flowers bloomed. All that delicious yellow to get lost in.'

The giant cuddly tiger fell to the floor. Jade used her foot to bring it nearer to her body.

'Oh, sounds great, Mr Merry. But—'

'I must dig out a painting or two and show you next time I see you. Anyway, I'd better let you get on. Don't want to hold you up with these two whippersnappers needing their tea, no doubt. Bye bye, ladies.' Mr Merry chuckled to himself as he waddled away.

'*Bloody hell*,' Jade muttered under her breath, bending down to scoop up the tiger. 'Right, girls, takeaway pizza for dinner?' Jade pushed the front door open, noticing Adam was yet to clear away his suitcase and clothes.

'Mum said we're not allowed takeaways, Aunty Jade. They're full of salt.' Jemima, the older of the two girls, looked at Jade disapprovingly, her neat bob – newly cut to match Lily's – swinging as she spoke.

Jade dropped the bags, tiger and scooters haphazardly on the hallway floor. 'Well, I'm in charge this weekend, so let's not worry about the salt, eh.'

Saffron looked around with squinted eyes. With her thumb in her mouth, she scrutinised the flat. 'Where are we sleeping?' she asked, without taking her thumb from her mouth.

Jade motioned to the first door on the right. 'Here, this is our guestroom. It's got a double bed for you to get super cosy in.'

Jemima looked up at Jade with her bulbous blue eyes. 'Haven't I got my own bed? I'm nearly eight, you know. I don't really like sharing a bed.'

A smattering of panic ran down Jade's spine. 'Well, you can always sleep on the sofa and then Saffy can have the bed?'

Jemima's eyes widened. 'The sofa? I don't think I'd like that very much. It'll be so itchy. Saffron can go on the sofa.'

Saffron took her thumb out of her mouth, making a suction noise like a plug coming out of a sink. 'I'm not schleeping in a sofa.'

Jemima bent down to look into her little sister's eyes. 'Not *in* the sofa, *on* the sofa, and yes you are.'

Saffron gritted her teeth. 'No, I'm NOT!' she cried, her foot stomping loudly on the floor.

'Yes, you ARE!' Jemima retorted.

'NO I AM NOT!' Saffron screamed back.

Jade closed her eyes and inhaled deeply. *Don't think about the Kings of Leon gig, don't think about the Kings of Leon gig*, she repeated mentally.

'Girls, girls, I'll tell you what. *I'll* sleep on the sofa, then you have a bed each. Capeesh? She paused, motionless, instantly regretting her suggestion.

'What does capeesh mean, Aunty Jade?' Saffron twirled her blonde hair in loops around a finger, thumb firmly back in her mouth.

Jade sighed. 'It doesn't matter. Come on, let's get you that pizza.'

Both girls settled down on the sofa and Jade put a kids' TV show on that featured talking pugs.

'Where's the man, Aunty Jade?' Jemima said without looking away from the TV.

'Man?' Jade said while trying to download a food delivery app. She rarely used them as they felt like an expensive luxury she couldn't justify. Selecting two margherita pizzas, some garlic bread and a pasta dish for herself, she looked up at Jemima.

'You know, the man that's always here.'

Jade laughed. 'You mean my boyfriend Adam. He's, er . . . he's, well . . . he's also at a sleepover tonight, but at his friend Benny's house. So it's just us three. A proper girls' weekend.'

Saffron removed her thumb from her mouth again

and looked at Jade. 'Oh, I like him. Can you make him come back? He always swings us about and does silly voices.'

Jade added her payment details into the food order and took a deep breath. 'Well, Missy,' she strained in a terrible American accent, 'Aunty Jade is great at silly voices too.' She cringed at her own desperation.

'That was bad,' Jemima retorted.

Jade tried to block out the pugs singing on the TV show and continued to fend off a relentless stream of questions from her nieces until the buzzer rang. The food had arrived terrifyingly quickly, which Jade was grateful for. The pizza was consumed without any further mention of salt.

15

After Jade had let the girls eat on the sofa – watching crust crumbs fall from their mouths onto the beige fabric with a combination of resignation and dismay – she stood up and said, 'Righto, gals, time for bed.'

Both girls stood up with their hands on their hips.

'NO! We want a midnight feast.'

The TV blared out in the background; an erratic theme tune engulfing Jade's head. She strained to think straight.

'Well . . . I was thinking we could go to Kew Gardens tomorrow for a day out, so we really should get some sleep.' This was a plan Jade hadn't thought through at all but her subconscious must have clung on to Mr Merry's earlier mention of Kew. 'The weather is going to be better tomorrow so we can go and explore in all the conservatories and try and find the elusive chameleon that lives in the Princess of Wales one. What do you say?' Jade smiled broadly, hoping and praying she could get them in bed quickly.

'What's eloooolive mean?' Saffron lisped.

'Hard to find, I guess,' Jade said, slightly flustered.

'Well, if he is hard to find how are we going to find him?' Jemima replied in a sulk. Her mouth remained open with accusation, revealing a missing front tooth.

'That's the adventure of it. Now come on, let's get that giant tiger and you guys to bed.'

Both girls eventually settled into their respective beds and, after an hour of shouting goodnight to each other from across the corridor, fell into blissful silence. Jade, who was sitting in the hallway at Saffron's request, back against the wall, let her head hang down to her chest in victory. Exhausted, she picked herself up off the floor and walked to the bathroom. The last week had been so busy at work that she hadn't properly prepared for this weekend of childcare, and she definitely hadn't planned for one of the girls to be snug in her bed with her pillows and duvet.

She grabbed her dressing gown from the bathroom door and her winter puffer coat from the hallway cupboard. Rolling the coat into a cylindrical clump, she stuffed it into one end of the sofa and draped her dressing gown across it.

She stood back with her lips curled. Her makeshift bed for the next two nights looked utterly uninviting. Torturous in fact. Lying down and covering herself with the robe, she prayed sleep would come, promising a god she wasn't sure she believed in that she would be the best aunty ever if she could get a solid eight hours.

Car engines grumbled outside the front window; happy voices left the Chinese takeaway across the road; the main door of the flats slammed shut. After tossing from one side to the other and rearranging her head on the pillow multiple times, she gently slipped into a hazy sleep at midnight, stirring only when she heard the odd plane humming overhead.

'AUNTY JADE, I'm hungry.'

Jade felt a sharp poke in her ribs. 'What the fuck?' She sat up disorientated.

'You said a bad word. I'm going to tell Mummy you said the F-word.'

Jade rubbed her eyes, trying to shake the discombobulated feeling of being woken from a deep sleep. 'Oh, sorry, Saff. I didn't know where the hell I was then or what was going on.'

Jemima followed her little sister and proceeded to jump on top of Jade – a blur of pastel pyjamas and dishevelled hair moving at speed. Jade tapped her phone's screen and saw a shocking number six peering back at her.

'Do you two normally wake up this early?'

Jemima and Saffron didn't answer – they were too busy giggling and jumping on Jade's crumpled body, which contorted as small feet hit ribs and the round of her tummy.

'Morning, Jammy. Did you sleep well, little one?' Jade added, trying to cultivate a tone that sounded happy and carefree while her eyes refused to fully open.

'Not really. The bed is a bit weird.' Jemima bounced on her knees on the sofa, causing Jade's whole body to jolt up and down. Jade heard a vertebra crack and swung her legs out from the makeshift blanket.

'Oh well, that's a shame. What can I get you ladies for brekkie?'

Now Saffron started bouncing vigorously. 'Pancakes. We want pancakes!'

Standing up and stretching her arms above her head, Jade replied, 'Well, I don't have the stuff for pancakes, but how about I pop to the bakery to get some chocolate croissants. They make such huge fluffy ones at the bakery on the hill?'

'Can we stay here and watch TV while you go and get them?' Jemima pleaded.

'No, Jammy, you've got to come with me I'm afraid. You can pop your onesies on, it'll only take five minutes.' Both girls slumped their shoulders and reluctantly turned to the hallway to find their onesies in the bedrooms.

Croissants eaten and onesies swapped for clothes, the girls lined up at the front door, waiting eagerly for Jade.

'Aunty Jade, can we go now?' Saffron called, jumping up and down impatiently, blonde waves spiralling in different directions.

'Coming, coming. I'm just packing some snacks and water for our adventure.' A bead of sweat gathered above Jade's lip as she threw packets of crisps into a backpack and pulled her trainers on.

'Can we play games on our tablets on the train to Kew, Aunty Jade?'

'No girls, we're going to chat and watch the world go by instead.'

'That is sooo boring,' Jemima moaned. 'Mum always lets us on our screens at the weekends so she can do Pilates with her online trainer.'

'Well, I'm not doing Pilates, Jam. We're going to have a cool train journey to Kew. We can . . . play I spy.'

'I spy? That is sooo rubbish. Saffron doesn't even know which letters words start with,' Jemima moaned.

'Yes, I do. R for rubbish.'

Jade ushered them out towards the street.

At Kew, powder-blue delphiniums stood to attention alongside blush-pink, bobbing roses. Jade breathed in the colours of the gardens and exhaled, letting her shoulders drop and wondered how long they had been up around her ears.

The last time she had visited Kew had been with Adam over two years ago. She had excitedly suggested a day trip there as he had never been, and she had spent many sunny days there as a kid, so knew it well. Looking back, she could see how, even in the early days, she was desperate to feel close to him. The more he went out with Benny and Tommo, the more he dismissed her in conversation, the more she wanted to climb into his skin. She remembered that she had hoped he would feel the same level of comfort from Kew Gardens that she had as a kid. That maybe he could, by osmosis, feel some of that simple, delicious nostalgia, and they could share that experience; halve it, so it was half hers and half his. He had moaned for most of the walk round. It had been a cold day, and he hadn't worn enough layers. He hadn't liked the close air in the conservatory, nor understood the magnificence of the tall pine trees, or the comfort of a warm scone in the café. 'Granny food,' he had quipped.

'Girls, this way,' Jade commanded, weaving in and out of parents pushing buggies and an elderly couple with linked arms. Swans sat in the shade under the big oak tree, and bright orange koi carp swam close to the surface in the big pond.

They made their way down the central path of the gardens, pink echinacea lined up like soldiers either side. A teenager's bright white backpack slumped by a wooden bench made Jade lurch, her eyes still in the habit of turning any white objects into a wad of menacing paper. She exhaled. She had enough on her plate this weekend without having to navigate another script.

The Princess of Wales Conservatory stood glorious against the verdant backdrop, its jagged glass roof piercing the blue sky above. Jade loved opening the large glass doors to the cool, dry desert air where the cactus lived. The fragrant smell transported her to parts of the world she had not set foot in. She breathed it all in.

'Let's go find this pesky chameleon, eh?'

The girls dashed towards the indoor pond, where giant lily pads splayed across the water's surface.

'Girls, did you know they have a record-breaking lily pad in this pond?' Jade had seen the post about it on Instagram the week before.

'What does record-breaking mean? What's a record?' Saffron asked.

'It means it's the biggest in the world.' Jade took in the green rippling surface of lily-pad skin stretched across the water.

'Our mum is called Lily,' Saffron slurped.

'Well, I know that, Saffy. She's my sister.'

'Is Mum record-breaking?'

'In her own way, Saff.'

The heat was almost uncomfortable in this section of the conservatory, the moist air enveloping Jade's skin, her tie-dye T-shirt sticking to her back. She kept her eyes on the girls as they darted past other families. 'Girls, don't run off. I need to see you at all times.' It felt surreal hearing these words leave her mouth; the unfamiliar sound of responsibility. 'Otherwise my sister will kill me,' she added to herself.

'Oh, it's a nightmare with kids in here, isn't it,' said a neat woman dressed in a Breton top.

'Yeah. It's pretty intense. I mean, they're not my kids so I'm not used to it.'

The lady scrunched up her nose and looked at Jade with uncertainty.

'Oh, I mean I know them. They're my nieces. I just normally don't have them for a whole day. Ha.' She laughed nervously as the woman turned and walked away.

Jade wondered why she had worn a long-sleeved T-shirt. Even moving her eyes to look for her nieces created perspiration on her forehead. 'Girls, girls, wait up!' Jemima and Saffron were peering into the pond, watching a shadowy shape move beneath the surface. 'Wow, well, we got lucky today,' Jade said, placing her hands on her hips triumphantly. 'That is the elusive catfish.'

'I thought the chameleon was eloolive,' said Saffron, looking confused.

'Well, they are both a little shy usually, but we can already tick this big guy off our list.' Jade leaned over the low metal railings to get a better look at the elegant fish gliding through the water, whiskers splayed out in fans.

'I wanna see the chameleon, Aunty Jade. Make it come out.' Jemima pulled on Jade's T-shirt. Jade pushed her sleeves up and wiped her damp forehead.

'Well, I can't make any promises but let's head over to this really leafy area as I've seen him lurking in there before.' The girls dashed off and peered underneath large tropical leaves. Cocoa pods swung overhead, and pink bougainvillea hung from the ceiling in fluffy clumps. Jade craned to look up to the rafters, not wanting to miss out on a single dose of colour.

'Aunty Jade, look – I think I can see its tail. Quick, quick.' Jemima crouched down by a bright green rubber tree, its leaves so shiny it looked like it was made of plastic.

'Look, look!' Saffron bounced on her toes.

Jade's eyes moved slowly over the plethora of green ahead of her, desperately searching for a camouflaged tail.

'Aunty Jade, look, there, there.' Jemima pointed in the direction of a small spiky tail poking out from beneath the oversized leaves.

'Aunty Jade!' Saffron poked Jade in the back.

Jade couldn't respond. She remained frozen in a crouched position, eyes fixed on one spot to the right of her. Amongst an aloe vera plant she could see the corner of a stack of paper.

16

Everything around Jade moved in slow motion. Saffron and Jemima's voices were muffled into background noise; a sharp ringing in her ears threw her off balance. The scripts had previously shown up in places Jade visited regularly: her running route, the warehouse, her recycling. She hadn't been to Kew Gardens in years and she hadn't told a soul about her last-minute plans. Pins and needles prickled across her scalp. The shock made her feel dizzy. She put one hand to the floor to steady her balance.

Her phone beeped. She snapped out of her trance and reached for it. Hey babe. Hope it's going ok with the girls. I'll miss you so much tonight. Love you. Soph

She had almost forgotten she would be missing the buzz and sweat and euphoria of the gig. She replied: Surviving. Just. Will miss you and the gig. Send pics. Love you back. X

She pushed the phone deep into her pocket and quickly whipped the wad of paper from under the aloe plant and into her backpack. She would look at it later.

'Come on, girls. We better go grab a scone from the nice café before we go home.'

'What? No! We can only see his tail. We need him to

come out so we can see him properly,' demanded Jemima, her bob swinging as she punched out her words.

'Another time. Come on, girls.'

'No. I'm not moving.' Jemima stood indignantly, statue-still.

The woman in the Breton top walked by slowly, side-eyeing Jade. Jade grinned with squinted eyes and turned back to the girls.

'Come on, Saff and Jam,' she whispered through gritted teeth.

'I do not want to. I don't even like scones,' Jemima said a little too loudly. The woman peered back over her shoulder with a patronising look. Her own kids sat peacefully in a double buggy, eating shiny apples. Jade smiled back at her again, this time with teeth showing. 'How about a chocolate muffin? An ice cream? A doughnut. You can have whatever you want.'

'Yes please,' Saffron replied.

'Yes to which bit?'

'All of them.' Jemima smiled victoriously.

'OK. I guess, that's . . . OK. Let's go.'

Saffron and Jemima sprinted to the café and picked out giant muffins, doughnuts and orange juice in the self-service area. Jade sloped behind with one hand on her backpack, feeling for the new script.

'Can I have a cappuccino please? With a double shot.' Her mouth watered at the thought. They found a nearby table covered in other people's coffee cups and half-eaten sandwiches. Saffron and Jemima ripped into their muffins, crumbs spilling over the Formica tabletop. Jade placed her backpack next to her on the bench and slid the paper out, the familiar font staring back at her. Her stomach flipped. By now she knew what to expect but that didn't negate the wave of anxiety each fresh script brought.

[Jade leans against the wall in the hallway, her face looking up to the ceiling.]

Oh, a really great start to this one, Jade thought.

                    JADE
        Do you just think your life is more
        important than mine?

                    LILY
        What are you on about?

                    JADE
        Can you not see . . . ? You don't get
        it, you never have. It's like my own
        life is invisible to you.

                    LILY
        I'm not sure what you're talking
        about, Birdy. Has something hap-
        pened? You seem different.

                    JADE
        I'm not really up for talking.

Oh god, well I'm not sure what's
going on here but I'm going to give
you some space, as you clearly need
it. I'll see you soon.

[Jade shakes her head. Lily exits without
looking back, her black bob swinging chirpily.]

Jade took a large swig of her coffee. It burned the back
of her throat as she swallowed it down. She stared at the
words, unable to make sense of them. She wondered
what could possibly warrant such a showdown. A wave
of dread enveloped her. Yet maybe this was her chance
to say what she really felt in the gaps. No matter what
was about to cause this near confrontation, there were
spaces for her to say what she really wanted.

What *did* she want to say? She would have to work
that out later – but as she jumped up from the bench,
she felt buoyed. This script felt like a turning point; a
seminal moment where she might just be one step closer
to slaying the dragon. She would tell Lily that she
wouldn't be bossed about or manipulated any more. The
words would come. They had to.

'Righto, little ladies. Let's get back to the flat for
some screentime,' she announced, her voice chirpy and
light.

'Can you buy me a new game on my tablet, Aunty
Jade?' Saffron looked up at her with a moustache of
blueberry muffin crumbs.

'I'm not sure I can, sweetie, as I imagine it's your mummy's credit card that's linked up to it.'

'Oh, come on. Just one new game. There's this kitten one I want.'

'Saffy, if I could, I would, but I can't.'

'Mean!' Saffy said this looking directly into Jade's eyes.

'Mean? You think I'm mean?'

Saffron crossed her arms and looked away.

'We'll get the game,' Jade caved.

Back at the flat the girls threw Jade's dressing gown and puffer coat from the sofa and sat cross-legged, their faces illuminated from the glow of the screens that were just inches from their faces. Jade sank into the peace, the odd ping or digital fanfare from the tablets the only noise to break it.

The rest of the day was a blur of TV shows, pesto pasta and drawn-out refusals to go to bed. Jade had already decided that Sunday morning would be a very low-key affair in the flat, with a movie and more croissants from the bakery. She would tidy the whirlwind of mess the girls had created once Lily had collected them at lunchtime, then sink into silence and blissful solitude. She fell onto the sofa, ready for slumber in her makeshift bed, knowing she was nearly there; almost at the finish line of this never-ending weekend. Her body felt as if it were almost vibrating with tiredness, a fatigue that felt as physical as it did emotional. She thought about the latest script and wondered when it would slip off the page and into her real life. A sense of urgency and – for once – a wish for time to spool forward to the moment she saw her sister made it particularly hard to drift off to sleep.

'Morning, Aunty Jade. I'm hungry.'

Jade opened her eyes and Saffron's face came into focus a mere five centimetres from her nose.

'Ooh bloody hell. Morning, Saff,' Jade croaked.

'That's a naughty word too, but I won't tell Mummy about that one.'

'Thanks.' Jade hauled herself up to a seated position and kissed Saffron on the nose. The lower backache from another night on the sofa was overshadowed by a feeling of pride. She had given her nieces a good weekend and made some special memories. Surely that was worth missing a gig with your best mate for.

Looking down at her phone, she saw six messages from Sophie. She clicked on the first. Screaming and whooping filled her ears, accompanied by a jittery shot of an out-of-focus stage. Jade half smiled; half happy, half jealous.

'What's that? Can I watch?' Saffron peered down at Jade's screen.

'It's just a gig I was meant—'

'Why are the men all sweaty?'

'I guess it's hot in there, and they're having a good time.'

'I'm glad I'm not a man. I don't want to sweat when I'm having a good time.' Saffron scrunched up her nose in disgust.

'Well, there's some brilliant female bands that probably sweat just as much on stage. Do you know Wet Leg?'

'Wet Leg? Ew!'

'Wait, that was a bad example. That's not why they're called Wet Leg,' Jade said, flustered and tired.

Saffron jumped up and bounced on the sofa. Jade's body jolted uncomfortably. 'Wet Leg. Wet sweaty Leg. Wet Leg!' Saffron squealed.

'What about . . . Billie Eilish? Or Florence and the Machine? Or FKA Twigs. I'm pretty sure they all sweat.'

'Who? Mummy only listens to this weird music that sounds like you're underwater.'

Jade knew exactly what Saffron was referring to. Since her crystal phase, Lily had been partial to meditation music that usually featured a cooing whale or trickling waterfall. She thought back to Lily the teenager; the leather jackets, the smell of thick smoke and Juicy Fruit chewing gum, the loud guitar music blaring from her bedroom. 'Well, your mum used to love rock music. Loud, loud rock music.'

'No, she didn't.'

'OK.' Jade had run out of steam.

The next message was a photo of the lead singer leaning into the mic, sweat glazing his face. The text simply said 'So fit!!!!!!' Jade swiped through a series of photos and videos, each one making her sink a little more into the sofa. She texted Sophie back: Happy hangover babe. Love you, with a love-heart emoji, before sleepily dragging her body off the sofa.

'Shall I put the telly on for you, Saff?'

'Yes, gimme gimme gimme.' Saffron reached her tiny hands out towards the remote.

'Search for something to watch while I make breakfast.' Jade sloped to the kitchen, the thought of coffee keeping her body upright.

The girls watched *Sing 2* twice, Jade not anticipating how quickly a kids' movie would pass by. She thoroughly enjoyed the first viewing, yet began to tire of the pig constantly singing on the second.

'Right, we'd better pack your bags before Mummy and James come to get you.' Jade walked towards her bedroom to find every conceivable surface now covered in fluorescent toys: cuddly tigers, LOL dolls and pastel-coloured fluffy slippers littered the room. She air-punched as she passed the clock on the kitchen wall; she only had around thirty minutes until her nieces were collected and she could get into her own bed and rest. Dutifully she folded their clothes into piles, placed all their toys back into their small holdalls, and gathered their tooth- and hairbrushes from the bathroom. Leaving the bags by the front door, she joined her nieces in the front room to sit and wait for Lily.

'When is Mummy here? Can we stay longer? I want to watch *Encanto* now.'

'Oh Saffy, next time we can watch it. Remember, you're staying with me when Mummy is on her honeymoon.' Jade allowed an image of her sister to form in her mind. Lily in a white bikini holding a bellini by a shimmering pool, Jade pushing her in gleefully.

Drumming her fingers on the side of the sofa, Jade

glanced down at her phone. It was now 1:30pm. In Jade's world lunchtime was 1pm, yet she knew in Lily's it could be anything between 1 and 3pm. Lily's time-keeping had always been bad, except when it came to something she herself had organised. Jade thought back to her own thirtieth birthday, which had been a small springtime picnic by the river. Lily, clearly not deeming it an import-ant occasion, had turned up an hour before it finished. Yet she had managed to drop the girls off this weekend with an unusual amount of timely precision. Unlocking her phone, Jade clicked on her sister's name, only to hear a constant trill of ringing with no answer.

She sent a message: **What time you getting the girls? They're all ready to go.** The message was delivered but remained unread.

Jade walked into the kitchen and turned the kettle on, taking deliberate deep breaths, attempting to keep the anger at bay.

'Aunty Jade, can we watch *Encanto*?'

'Yes, yes. Just coming.' Abandoning her tea-making, Jade walked back into the front room.

'£15.99? For a kids' film?' Jade stepped back in shock.

'Pleeease. Please. Please. It's our total favourite.'

'Oh, surely there's something good and free on here. What about *The Lion King*?'

'That is so old,' Jemima protested.

'Or . . . *Honey, I Shrunk the Kids*?'

'What?' Jemima looked at Jade accusingly.

'Oh, blimmin' hell. OK, OK. Give me the remote.' Jade punched in her code to pay for the film.

Pretending to watch, Jade began to plot her revenge on her sister. Arguments played out in her head with bitter words tossed about freely. She might even bring up the thirtieth birthday picnic if things got particularly out of hand.

An hour passed by, then another. Jade paced around the flat, catching her tired reflection in the hallway mirror. She was still wearing yesterday's tie-dye T-shirt, and her jogging bottoms were losing the elastic around the waist, so sagged at the top of her thighs. More phone calls and text messages went unanswered. A small portion of worry set in, but not enough to negate Jade's fury.

At 6pm Jade called her mum.

'Mum, have you heard from Lily?'

'Oh, darling. How are you? I haven't heard from you in weeks.'

'I spoke to you on Monday, Mum. Have you spoken to Lils?'

'No, darling, why?'

'I've had the girls all weekend. She was supposed to collect them at lunchtime, and she is still not here.'

'Ooh, don't worry, darling, she'll be there soon, I'm sure.'

'Well, I'm *not* sure, that's why I'm calling you. Can you have the girls at yours? I have loads to sort out before work tomorrow.'

'Oh, darling, I'm sorry, I can't. I'm not home, I'm on Tagg's Island with Bill. He invited me onto his house-boat for the night. We've been having such a good chat about the old days. We've been laughing our heads off, thinking of all the fun times we had back in the day on the King's Road and our little trips to Ibiza before I met your dad. We're about to get the photo albums out.'

'Great. Well, have fun. I'd better go.'

'Oh, darling, don't be like that.'

'Like what? I need to go,' Jade snapped back.

'Well, I'm sure it'll all be fine in the end. Just pop a movie on and—'

'I've done that, three times. Thanks, Mum, bye.'

Jade hung up and threw her phone across the kitchen counter vigorously. *'Fuck, fuck, fuck.'*

'I heard that even from in here, Aunty Jade, I'm going to tell Mum . . .'

'I know, I know, I'm sorry.'

17

Opening the fridge, Jade stared at the empty shelves.

'Saffy, Jammy, as a treat we are going to have a cereal dinner, OK? I do it all the time.' She strained to sound chirpier than she felt.

'Can I have Coco Pops?'

'I only have cornflakes or porridge, I'm afraid.'

'That's so boring,' Jemima shouted from the sofa.

'*Tough tits*,' Jade whispered to herself. 'Well, it's all I've got,' she yelled back through a tense jaw.

'Cornflakes, then. With lots of honey on, please,' Jemima confirmed. 'Mum says I'm only allowed oat milk. Do you have that?'

'Yes,' Jade lied. 'Coming up.' Pouring regular milk on the cornflakes, she placed two bowls on a tray and carried them into Jemima and Saffron.

'Yum. This tastes so much like real milk.' Jemima spoke through a mouthful of cereal.

'It's good, isn't it.' Jade smiled at this tiny one-up on her sister. It was 8pm and her texts remained unanswered. The sun was dipping, throwing amber light onto the walls, and the girls had barely moved all day, watching movie after movie. Jade wondered how long she could keep her nieces awake for and if it was futile to assume Lily would turn up eventually.

Jemima and Saffron had both sunk down and were lying on the sofa, a head on each armrest, eyelids heavy and movement reduced to the odd yawn. They would have to stay another night. As the realisation dawned, her mind jumped back to the script she had found the day before, words that previously hadn't made sense now coming to life with a brand-new, garish clarity. She had initially felt proud that she had confronted her sister about her dismissive ways in the script, yet now it all seemed rather flimsy and pathetic on her part. Her sister had encroached on her time and freedom and caused her so much stress. Surely she could find punchier words that taught Lily a lesson once and for all. She could summon loads of them now; a torrent of expletives and carefully constructed, cutting one-liners.

'Right, girls. It seems you are going to be staying another night with Aunty Jade. So let's get you in your PJs.'

'I want to go home, though. I miss Cumin.' Saffron's eyes widened and glistened.

'I know, and I'm sure Cumin misses you too, but the good thing about cats is that they are very forgiving.'

'I don't want to sleep in your lumpy bed again, Aunty Jade.' Jemima stuck her bottom lip out in protest, her bobbed hair now matted on one side from lying on the arm of the sofa all day.

'Well, let me plump up the pillows extra fluffy for you. It'll be like sleeping on marshmallows. Come on, you two. Teeth-cleaning time.'

Both girls sleepily unfolded their crumpled limbs and slumped towards the bathroom.

Once they were settled into their beds, Jade walked to the kitchen, feeling she had aged dramatically in the space of two days. Picking up her phone, she clicked on the letter A to locate a name she knew would be no use at all. But she was desperate. So desperate.

'Hey. I'm having a slight emergency. When were you planning on coming back to the flat?'

'Hey. I can't really hear you. I'm in the pub,' Adam shouted above the background noise of Richmond upon Thames on a sunny Sunday evening.

'Well, it would be great if you could come home first thing tomorrow morning. I have to go to work and for some reason Lily hasn't turned up to pick the girls up. Can you just wait in the flat with them until she arrives, or nip them to school?'

'Er, no, Jade. I've got stuff to sort for the new collection. I'm heading into Soho first thing.' Adam's sentences were peppered with short silences that lacked truth.

'Do you *have to*, though? I HAVE to be at work at a certain time, otherwise Colin will sack me. Do you *have to* like that?'

'Well, this collection isn't going to design itself. I'm sure Lily will be over soon. Just chill.'

Jade stretched her mouth out into a silent scream. *Chill*, how could she chill when everyone around her seemed so bloody irresponsible? She hung up without saying goodbye.

'Aunty Jade, I can't schleep,' Saffron shouted from the bedroom, thumb firmly in mouth.

'Coming, Saff.'

154

Jade climbed into bed next to Saffron's tiny body, her dainty floral pyjamas splattered in hot chocolate from that morning.

'Hey, little one,' Jade said in a whispered voice, 'what's going on in that little head of yours?'

'I want Mummy. Where is she?'

'I know. It's hard when we miss people. Sometimes it can make us feel a bit lonely.'

Jade stroked Saffron's freckled nose. Saffron's big green eyes were staring up at her. She knew those feelings. She remembered the uncertainty of her own childhood with way too much clarity. Not knowing where her dad was or feeling confused by her mum's tears and angry outbursts. She would stare up at the glow-in-the-dark star stickers on her ceiling, wishing she could drift off to sleep. Looking at Saffron's wide glistening eyes brought it all back.

'You know, we're never really alone. Think of all the people you love. Can you count them all?' Jade whispered, closely nuzzled into Saffron's ear. Saffron began sticking her little fingers up in the air while mentally counting. Her thumb stayed in her mouth as she used the remaining fingers to count to nine.

'I think nine including Cumin.'

'Wow, that's a lot of people, Saffy. I think I probably have about the same. Now even when you're not with those people, and cats, they're never far away, as their love lives in here.' Jade tapped Saffron's heart. 'All of that love, times nine, lives in there. Can you feel it?'

Saffron nodded and her eyelids slowly closed and opened again as she fought sleep.

'So, as you drift off to sleep, think about Cumin and all the people you love and how they live in your heart. Feel your heart beating and know that with each beat those lucky nine people are with you. Listen to it now. Can you hear it? Thud-thud, thud-thud.'

Saffron nodded, more slowly this time.

'Thud-thud, thud-thud, thud-thud.' Jade tapped her own heart as she whispered the beat. 'It'll keep beating like that all night as you're sleeping, reminding you of all the love in there. Thud-thud, thud-thud, thud-thud.' Jade looked down and saw that Saffron's thumb was half hanging out of her mouth and her eyelids were closed.

She slipped out of the bed quietly and carefully, and made her way to the sofa with her puffer coat pillow for a third night.

Her phone pinged. Picking it up expecting to see Lily's name, her face fell at the sight of Colin's. Wife's gift you need to pick up tomorrow. Nice undies. Pref red. 34D and medium bottoms. Expensive ones. Ta. Jade shuddered and screwed up her face.

It was time to practise saying no.

18

The sharp trill of Jade's phone alarm interrupted a dream where she was being chased by an ever-changing entity. A dark grey blur of smoke that morphed into her sister, then Colin, and moved like a charging rhino. She picked up her phone and saw it was exactly 7am. With still no text from her sister, her mind oscillated between sitting tight and waiting for her, or taking the girls to school so she could get to the warehouse. A thick fog rolled in over Jade's thoughts. Rather than committing to a conclusion, she found her index finger moving to the Instagram icon on her phone. The sweet numbness of scrolling through photos felt a lot easier than working out what to do next.

She flicked past images of Sophie, strawberry-blonde hair swinging in every direction at the Kings of Leon gig; an inspirational quote from Brené Brown; a video of a cat falling in a bath of water; before landing on the latest post from Lily. Posted at eleven o'clock the night before. Jade used the back of her hand to wipe her heavy eyelids, then let the photo come into focus.

Lily's black hair shone like an eel in the depths of the sea. She sat with her legs crossed, eyes closed, a vision of utter serenity, with the caption *Having a magical time on my holistic hen – #Hen #Holistic #Holistichen #Meditation #Notlongnow.*

A hot rage burned in Jade's cheeks. Her hands started to shake. The ignored texts, the blanked phone calls – yet an Instagram post before midnight. It would have been impossible for Lily to post the photo without seeing the pile-up of missed calls. Jade clenched her jaw, pushed the dressing gown off her torso and stomped to the kitchen. As the kettle boiled, she hastily made a plan. She would wake the girls up, take them to school on the bus, get the bus back and then race to work on her bike, blaming a punctured tyre for her lateness. It wouldn't be fair on the girls if they missed school. It was the right thing to do. She would deal with Lily later.

The puzzle pieces slotted into place as she thought back to the script. She tried to remember each word she had seen, the gaps where she could speak freely. Once at work she would study it and work out how to tell her sister how she really felt.

As the kettle whistled and chugged steam, she went back for a second look at her sister's photo. The serene look on Lily's unblemished face made Jade shake. Wanting more evidence, she searched for the names of Lily's old school mates that she knew would be present.

First up, Sinead. She had constantly been at their mum's house when Jade was a teenager. Sinead O'Brien. Bingo. She clicked through. Sinead hadn't posted anything on her Instagram grid so Jade clicked on the photo icon to look at her stories. The first picture to ping up was one of Sinead, Cathy, Sarita and Lily, all with white fluffy robes on, pouting to camera. Cathy and Sarita were also Lily's friends from school. Big balloon letters stretched across the photo reading SPA DAY.

The next photo was a long lunch table – the aforementioned friends with the addition of three women Jade didn't know. Jade assumed they were mums from Saffron and Jemima's school.

Next was a video, the camera shaky and slightly out of focus. There was loud music and Sinead's free hand was holding a shot of tequila out in front of the phone. The next video saw Lily throwing her head back, the clear liquid from a shot glass slipping past her plump lips. Jade's eyes widened. What on earth was this? Things were looking decidedly un-holistic. The next video clip showed two men standing either side of Lily, who was sitting on a dining room chair as if it were a throne. The man to her right looked like Peter Andre in the nineties: oiled six-pack, greasy hair flopping in his face, a bow tie swinging from his neck as he gyrated. To Lily's left stood a man-mountain with his leg up on the arm of Lily's chair, his crotch mere inches from her face, which was contorted in a confusing mix of utter pleasure at the attention and disgust that this was slightly off-brand for her.

Jade knew that if Lily found out Sinead had posted these videos she would flip out. She must have been drunk enough to not notice or care in the moment. Jade shook her head. Just when she thought her sister couldn't surprise her any more, she had managed it. Drumming her fingers on the kitchen worktop, she wondered whether to use this fresh information as ammunition for when her sister eventually turned up, or if it was smarter to save it for another time.

Looking at the clock on the kitchen wall, the weather forecast looked fair, with the picture of a yellow sun peeking out from the side of two small grey clouds. But time was ticking. What time did kids even start school?

'Girls!' she called. 'Time to wake up. Time for school.' Jade thought it was strange that on Saturday and Sunday, Saffron and Jemima had woken at six, but today, when they all needed to be out of the flat, they were still asleep at seven like tired mice. Jade tiptoed into their rooms in turn, gently kissed both girls on the forehead, and one by one carried them out of bed and onto the sofa.

'Aunty Jade, I'm tired.'

'I know, Jam, but we've got to get you to school.' She raced into her room and pulled on some tracksuit bottoms and a baggy polka-dot T-shirt.

'Come on, we'll grab a croissant on the way.'

Jemima came running out of the front room with a cuddly panda clutched to her chest. 'We don't have school today.'

'It's Monday, so I'm afraid you do, little lady.' Jade pulled a brush through her long hair; it caught in knots at the back of her head.

'But we don't have school uniforms, Aunty Jade. Can we just have the day off?'

Jade bit her lip; she hadn't anticipated school uniforms, school bags, packed lunches . . .

She dropped to her knees at the front door where the bags were still lined up for the girls' collection. Opening

Jemima's bag to locate some clean clothes, she attempted to work out how she would explain the lack of uniform to their teachers. She could say her washing machine had broken, or that there had been an emergency, so she had had to take over parenting duties for her sister. She then contemplated telling the teachers the truth. She dug through food-soiled pyjamas and more soft toys to scavenge for something passable. As she pulled hoodies and onesies out of the bag, she spotted neatly folded clothes at the bottom of Jemima's bag.

A grey pinafore dress, white shirt, small black Mary Jane shoes.

'Oh, would you look at that. Mummy has kindly packed your school uniforms. That's lucky.' Jade's jaw tightened again as she thought back to Lily saying she would see her Sunday for pick-up. She remembered where she was standing, the exact wording. Another move from her sister to dodge responsibility and burden Jade. She had gotten away with it for so many years now that Lily didn't think twice about twisting the truth to get what she wanted.

'Do you normally have packed lunches? Or do you have cooked lunch at school?' Jade asked, still reeling from the pre-planned extra night away. She dug through Saffron's bag to find another neatly folded school uniform and pair of small black shiny shoes.

Saffron walked over to Jade with a puffy, tired face and hugged her. 'We have packed lunches, Aunty Jade. Can you make me a jam sandwich with Pom-Bear crisps and a chocolate biscuit?'

Jade mentally pictured her fridge and its distinct emptiness. 'We'll have to get something from the bakery.'

The bus was packed and sweaty, condensation lining the windows, and Jade's wallet was now fifteen pounds in deficit due to two overpriced baguettes. It was 7:35am, and Jade's blood felt laced with adrenaline. If she were to make it to work anywhere near on time she needed this morning to run exceptionally smoothly.

They squished into a row of seats, their knees knocking together. Jade rubbed her eyes and tried to breathe through the stress. She texted her sister again: I'm taking the girls to school. Where the hell are you? I'm late for work.

Arriving at the school, Jade looked about at the parents rushing in looking like they knew what they were doing. Feeling like a paint-splattered fish out of water in her tracksuit bottoms and garish T-shirt, she followed her nieces into their respective classrooms.

It was 8:05am. Jade was going to be seriously late for work. Colin normally strolled in thirty or so minutes after the rest of them, but you could never be too sure. After a cordial chat in her most responsible voice with both teachers, Jade sprinted out of the school gates and onto the bus back to her flat. She fired a text to Sophie: Babe, I'm having a mare of a morning. I'm gonna be so late. Can you stall for me?] x

The bus stopped halfway up Richmond Hill. It was 8:20am. Split-leaping off the bus, Jade started to pick up pace towards her flat. Her thighs ached as her body struggled to come to terms with a vigorous sprint this early. As she reached the main door to the flat, Mr Merry slowly walked out, a huge smile spreading across his face. It was 8:25am.

'Morning, Miss Shaw,' Mr Merry announced, tipping his cap towards her.

'Morning, Mr Merry. I'm terribly late.' Jade pushed her bedraggled hair from her face, thick strands stuck to the sweat on her forehead.

'Oh dear, one of those mornings, is it?' Mr Merry stopped, squarely blocking the entrance to the flats.

'Well, yes, you could say that,' Jade panted and grinned.

'You know, I meant to tell you when I saw you last week, I'm thinking of having a little picnic down at Terrace Gardens for my birthday. I won't say how old but it's a big one.' Mr Merry laughed through the last part of his sentence, red cheeks wobbling with each syllable.

'Sounds great, I'll be there.' Jade moved closer to Mr Merry, signalling that she was keen to get through the doors.

'An official invite will be posted through your letter-box imminently, Miss Shaw. I might also boldly ask everyone to bring a little something. A small contribution, if you will, for a buffet-style luncheon.' Mr Merry's grin grew impossibly large.

'Yes, yes, I can do that. Do you mind if I just . . .' Jade pointed at the double doors.

'I have heard you make an awfully good banana bread.' Mr Merry's eyes widened at the thought.

'Yup, yup. A birthday banana bread is no trouble at all.' It was 8:30am.

'The Hawthorns at Flat 12 have already suggested a tuna quiche, which sounds ever so exotic.'

Jade bobbed up and down on the spot anxiously. 'Mmm, yum. Mr Merry, I'm ever so la—'

'As well as Carrie, who has offered to bring Pimms and lemonade and all the accoutrements. Ever so kind.'

Jade nodded manically.

'Anyway, dear, I'd best not hold you up. I'm sure you've got a lot on today.' Mr Merry seemed to move away from the door in slow motion, allowing Jade to sprint past. 'Bye bye, dear.'

Jade waved as she pushed through the double doors, stumbling on the first step and falling awkwardly on her hand. 'Shitting shit.' She wiped the sweat from her forehead. Her phone pinged. Mate. Colin is in already. What shall I say? x

Jade pushed through her front door and held down the microphone icon on her screen to leave a voice-note for Sophie, her words breathless and rushed. 'Err, just tell him . . . my bike has a puncture. I'm en route. Or something. Thanks, babe.'

She grabbed her cycling helmet and sprinted back down to her bike. Mr Merry was still out at the front, this time talking with Rodney.

'Oh, one more thing, Miss Shaw. If the weather is bad we'll have a contingency plan. I'm working on all the finer details now.'

Jade pushed down on the pedals and moved away from the pavement. 'Sounds great, Mr Merry,' she shouted back over her shoulder as she whizzed down the hill.

It was 9:20am by the time she arrived at the warehouse, after cycling to Acton in record time, her T-shirt clinging to her back with perspiration. She was going to kill her sister. Pulling back the large wooden doors, she breathed in the familiar fumes of paint and turps. Sophie was carrying a large sheet of plywood across the room, the usual roll-up behind her ear.

'Are you OK?' she whispered.

Jade flapped the bottom of her T-shirt to air herself, still trying to catch her breath.

'Nightmare, *nightmare* morning. The headlines are: I never want kids and my sister is a gigantic bitch.'

Sophie put the plywood down on the ground. 'Come here, mate. You need a hug.'

Jade stepped back. 'I'm so sweaty, Soph, but I'm grateful for the sentiment. Where's Colin?'

'Last time I saw him he was in the stockroom shouting at some suppliers down the phone.'

'OK. Here we go.' Jade prepared herself for one of two possible outcomes. If Colin was in one of his good moods, he would potentially make a snide remark about young people today and move on. If he was in a bad mood, he would go very, very quiet. Jade was not sure she had the bandwidth for either. She exhaled deeply, pulled her shoulders back and wiped the sweat off her top lip. Pulling her mouth into a forced smile, she approached her boss.

'Colin, I'm so sorry I'm late. Typical, it's the day you're in early. I'm literally the most punctual person on the planet. I just had a disastrous morning with a

punctured tyre on my bike. It will not happen again.'
Jade mimed riding a bike as she spoke and instantly
regretted it. Colin turned around slowly and locked
eyes with Jade.

'I'm not happy, Jade.'

'I know, I know. It won't happen again.'

Colin looked away and started surveying the shelves
of the stockroom. 'I can't run a business with a team
that's not willing to put the effort in.' He spoke quietly, a
cold edge to his words.

'Oh, I always put maximum effort in. This was a one-
off mishap.'

'You're all easily replaceable.' Colin occupied himself
putting sheets of card into neat piles.

'I love my job so much. This won't happen again,'
Jade pleaded, trying to sound assertive, but her voice
wobbled in spite of herself.

Colin remained static, without a verbal or physical
reaction to Jade's words. After an uncomfortable pause
he said, 'Don't forget the wife's birthday gift at lunchtime. I need it bought and wrapped by tomorrow.'

'I, er, the thing is, Colin, I've been thinking about this.'
Jade nervously twisted the silver ring on her index finger.
'I don't believe it's appropriate for me to be buying your
wife's . . . knickers. It seems, er, a little too intimate.' Jade
looked away, eyes flitting anywhere but in the direction
of her boss. He turned slowly.

'Don't be daft. She won't mind. Remember, saucy red
ones,' he said, sounding much more jovial now.

'I . . . I feel uncomfortable with this arrangement.'

'You'll get over it. Penny will leave my work credit card on my desk.'

'Isn't this something Penny could do, as she's your PA?'

'Course not. She's far too busy for things like that. Right, I'm off for a lunch with some of the honchos at Sky. Remember, I need it wrapped too.'

He walked with purpose, leaving Jade little opportunity to argue any further. Stress mounted in her head, a pressure that bore down on her temples. Shuffling back into the main warehouse, she joined Sophie leaning over a long trestle table, and rested on her elbows. Sophie mouthed, 'What's going on?'

Jade shrugged her shoulders and tried not to think about the red knickers.

19

Jade glugged water from a pint glass in the back room. Her whole body felt dehydrated. She wondered when she had last drunk anything at all. She hadn't even had a coffee yet.

A new commission occupied conversation in the warehouse: a kids' TV arts and crafts show that started filming in two months. The brief was to create a multi-coloured set complete with giant scissors and paint palette. Weaving through paint pots that scattered the floor, Jade walked over to Sophie and quietly sighed. 'Want to work with me on the palette, babe?' Sophie asked. Jade nodded and looked for instruction. It was now a matter of hours before she would face Lily, and a whirlpool of dread laced with excitement spun in her belly. She ran over the words in her head from the script she had found at Kew Gardens. Since her sister's extended hen party and lies, it all made so much more sense. The time had come. She couldn't sit in the shadows convivially nodding *Yes* but really meaning *No* any more.

Sophie leaned into Jade so their shoulders were touching. Jade could smell the smoke and paint on Sophie's T-shirt. 'I'll get this out of the way as I know you're having a shit one today, *but* the gig was a banger. I swear Caleb looked directly into my eyes at one point. Oh, and my flowers. Mate, you're the sweetest.' She squeezed Jade's arm. Jade smiled, feeling the relief of thinking about something other than her sister. 'Anyway, what's going on with you?' Sophie talked in hushed tones so Lethabo and Jackson wouldn't hear. Jade picked up a bucket of plaster and began using her hands to make giant swirls to create the effect of paint around the edge of the three-metre-long palette.

'My sister is unreal. I literally have no words,' she said, matching Sophie's hushed tones.

Lethabo turned the speakers up so Self Esteem's voice filled the huge space, and sang along, his voice booming without inhibition, bouncing off the breeze-block walls.

'Why, babe? What now? Is she still pretending to be an interior designer?'

'Oh yes, course she is, but the latest drama isn't related to any of that. I had my nieces this weekend and she was supposed to pick them up Sunday lunchtime, but she didn't. I have been calling and texting and she isn't responding.'

Sophie's mouth was slowly parting to an open-mouthed gawp. 'Aren't you worried about her? Might something have happened?'

'Oh no. Definitely not. Last night at 11pm she was posting photos of herself sat in a bloody lotus position. Then I checked her mate's Instagram account, and they were all pissed up, caressing oiled strippers. I'm incandescent with rage.'

'Shit. Why would she ignore your calls? Also, strippers? That's not very Lily.'

'I know. It's all bonkers. She's ignoring me because she is incredibly entitled. She believes her life is much more important than my tiny existence. I'm so sick of it. I actually found another script this weekend too.' She lowered her voice to an even quieter whisper, so she was almost inaudible.

'And . . . ?' Sophie leaned in even closer so Jade could hear her breathing, desperate to hear more.

'It was a strange sort of argument between me and Lily. At the time I didn't understand it as I had no idea she would be late and ignore my calls. It was along the lines of me telling her I felt she had no regard for my life.'

'Well, that's good.'

'Yeah, although the script did not include me telling her that she is utterly clueless and entitled and has been her entire life. I wanna let loose and say exactly how I am feeling.'

'Right. Get the Tippex out, babe. It's going to work this time – I can feel it.' Sophie clicked a finger to the sky.

'Soph, in the chaos of this morning, I've bloody left it at the flat.'

'Shit.'

'I'll do it when I get home later. Do you really think it's worth trying again?'

'*Yes*,' Sophie hissed. 'You have to. You know what they say: if at first you don't succeed, try and try again – so your sister stops taking the piss.' Sophie's light eyebrows rose as she continued, 'Remember what I said on the phone, Jadey: you have to believe in yourself. Believe that you deserve better and believe that you have the right to create boundaries with people. *Especially* people like Lily who will try and cross any boundary you set.' Sophie's eyes were fixed on Jade's. 'I know I sound like a budget version of Oprah Winfrey, but it's true. You can do it, Jadey. Set that boundary firmly.'

'I know, Soph. I feel it. Today I actually do feel I deserve better than this. To be ignored after looking after her kids all weekend while she farted around on a yoga mat and necked tequila really is the final straw. I just need the confidence to say how I feel when I see her. My throat almost constricts when I'm in her presence.'

'Do you know when that will be?'

'No, she's still not texted. I have no clue if she's even picking up the girls from school later. It's a total joke.'

'She sounds pretty irresponsible to me.'

'She is, but she masks it with this light, breezy air that most people fall for. If she walked in here now she would be so lovely to everyone. She'd flit around this warehouse like a shiny-haired fairy, and everyone would fall for her charms, but if she wanted something from you – that's when she switches. She is ruthless when it comes to getting what she wants.'

'Right. While we're working today, you need to really hone in on that feeling of deserving better. Remember how marvellous you are, my friend. Then dash home after work, take the Tippex with you, and rewrite that script.'

Jade nodded and carried on swirling the plaster in big loops on the wooden surface.

Lethabo changed the music and put on a nineties pop mix. 'Right, we need to lift the mood, you two. Stop bloody whispering and let's get vibey.'

Jackson remained statue-still behind them, delicately painting the handles of a giant pair of scissors.

'I will never not love All Saints,' Lethabo shouted above the music.

'Hey, have you got a tooth gem, Thabs?' Sophie stood up for closer inspection.

'Yup. They're back, babe.' He grinned widely, curling his top lip up to reveal the gem perched on his incisor.

'That is the most nineties accessory I've ever seen. You'll be wearing jelly shoes next.'

Lethabo grimaced. 'That's a step too far, Soph. Even for me.'

The morning passed accompanied by nineties music and Lethabo's commentary on each track, as they worked together on painting a giant plywood can of spray paint. Eventually Jackson stood up from the base of the giant can and stretched out his wiry frame, his spindly arms unfurling from his black clothing like an octopus. Jade looked at the clock on the warehouse wall and felt a jolt of panic. She dashed to her backpack and pulled out her phone, googling Saffron and Jemima's school and pick-up time, and noticed she had four missed calls from Lily. She clenched her teeth and then pressed call to ring her back. Lily answered after two rings.

'Oh, *now* you're picking up, Birdy. I've tried calling four times in the last hour,' Lily said with force.

Jade stumbled backwards and tried to find a response.

'Lily, I'm at work. I have an actual job. I'm not sat by my phone all day. AND – where the hell have you been?' Jade's hand holding the phone started to shake, her cheeks burning hot.

'What do you mean, where have I been? How are the girls? I miss my babies.' Lily's cadence was steady and confident. Jade paused in total confusion.

'Wait, what? You were meant to pick them up on Sunday.'

'No, no, we said Monday, Birds. Anyway, I'm just in the car on the way home. The weekend was such a dream. I feel cleansed, physically, emotionally and spiritually. James is going to collect the girls from school, and I'll come to yours and get their bags. Five o'clock OK?'

Jade swallowed. Her throat was burning. She gritted her teeth. 'Can it be five-thirty? I don't finish until five.'

'Well, it's not ideal but I guess I can make that work. See you then, Birdy!' Lily sang her goodbye gleefully then promptly hung up.

'Arrrgh.' Jade shook her arms out as if they were on fire.

She had experienced this feeling so many times over the years. A feeling of being completely squashed by Lily until she barely existed; a single splodge of pulp where there should be a whole juicy piece of fruit. An image flashed up in her head of her eleven-year-old self playing Connect 4 with her godmother in Dorset. She had been shipped out to stay with Belinda and Don the weekend after Lily had been expelled. Belinda was the most calming presence imaginable – but Jade felt rattled that she hadn't been told what was going on.

She was regularly sent to her godmother's so that her mum could be one-on-one with Lily. Sue would pack Jade an overnight backpack and a cloth bag with her pens and sketchbooks, and Belinda would valiantly drive all the way from Wool to London to collect Jade and let her listen to pop songs on a CD on their drive back. Now, as an adult, she could appreciate how much Belinda had put into the friendship with her mother. They had met working at a department store on Sloane Square as teens in the seventies, when Sue would get the bus from her parents' house in Battersea, and Belinda would do the same from Clapham. Sue had loved Fleetwood Mac, whereas Belinda was more into the ethereal Pink Floyd, but despite their musical differences they had fallen into a deep friendship and stomped the King's Road in bell-bottom flares and velvet plunging tops. They had been side by side ever since, navigating marriage, parenthood and life's unexpected twists and turns, only geography now causing a distance in their friendship.

Jade thought back to her own teenage years and the weekends in Dorset, where Belinda had settled after her marriage to Don. How nobody had really asked how she was doing amid all the disruption of her childhood. The focus was always on Lily: how she was, pre-empting another explosive moment or act of rebellion. At the time, Jade had felt sorry for Lily, and found great comfort in her weekends with Belinda – but as the years passed without much change, Jade started to understand that her sister would perhaps never have self-awareness or be accountable for her part in it all. All these years later, Jade had huge empathy for Lily the teenager, who perhaps lacked wisdom and life experience. But Lily in her mid-thirties acting in the same way seemed tiresome and just plain rude. Of course, Lily had never asked Jade how their childhood had affected her – she was simply used to being the one that mattered.

Sophie marched over to Jade, who was frozen to the spot.

'What? Was that your sister?'

'She is Satan. Honestly, she has no limits. She just completely ignored my questions about where she'd been, papered over it and then lied. I could scream.'

'Right. You need to get home and work on that rewrite of the script, quick. You've got to try again – but really mean it this time.' Sophie shook Jade's shoulders.

'She said she's going to come and get the girls' bags at five-thirty. It's cutting it fine.'

'Well, you'll need to cycle like you're in the Tour de France and beat her to your flat.'

Jade burst through the flat door at 5:25pm, her thighs pulsating from the speed at which she made it home. Adam was lying on his side on the sofa watching *Ozark*, a beer in hand.

'Oh, you're back.' Jade froze, taking in the scene.

'Yeah, been in Soho all day sourcing fabric, I'm pretty whacked.' Adam didn't bother to look up at Jade.

'You're whacked?'

'Yeah, I am,' he said without looking away from the TV.

'Lily's coming over in a minute, so I just need to sort something out quickly.' The words raced from her mouth.

Adam didn't respond. Jade rushed into the bedroom and to her bedside cupboard where she had stashed the latest script. The sweat on her face felt suffocating. She stumbled to her knees and pulled out the script.

'Shit, shit, Tippex.' She stuffed the script back and sprinted into the hallway to retrieve it from her backpack.

'You alright, Usain Bolt?' Adam said from his reclined position on the sofa, a casual sarcasm drenching each word.

'Yes, I just need to do something quickly.'

Sliding onto her knees and gaining a small carpet burn in the process, Jade flung open the bedside cupboard for a second time. Flattening out the rolled-up script and rolling it in a counter direction, she attempted to lay it out on the floor. She needed to replace the timid scripted wording with something punchy. She recalled the anger she had felt earlier: the image of her sister's glistening hair and yoga leggings stretched over her svelte crossed legs on Instagram; Colin reprimanding her; racing around town on the bus. In the stress of it all she had completely forgotten to get Colin's wife's birthday underwear. She threw her head back and breathed deeply. She would deal with the fallout from that tomorrow.

She looked at the page and wondered which words could hold all that rage. The new dialogue had to be enough to stop Lily from treating her like this again. She wanted to usher in a new Jade, the Jade with boundaries and confidence and words that left her mouth clearly and without her neck burning red. She would tell her sister that her behaviour was entitled and that she had no empathy for others. She would tell her that she was unable to have the girls during Lily's honeymoon and that if she were going to ask for favours, she needed to be respectful of other people's time. The delivery would be calm, yet confident and laced with conviction. There would be no pauses, no wobbles in her voice, or gaps for the blame or guilt to creep in. It would be watertight. She held up the Tippex wand like she was about to cast a spell, ready to change this future conversation for the better.

The intercom interjected, the shrill buzz of it making her body jolt.

'Oh, no, no, no,' Jade wailed like a baby. 'Ads, don't answer the door, I'm not ready,' she shouted.

'I've already buzzed her up. Why do you need to get ready?' Adam said nonchalantly while walking to the front door to let her in.

Jade paused, Tippex wand a centimetre above the page. She considered rushing out a new sentence to replace the current one, but feared that could make the situation worse without proper thought. Her brain buffered like a stalling computer.

'Hi, Adam?' she heard Lily say from the hallway, her drawn-out annunciation already expressing a lack of remorse or urgency. 'How was Los Angeles?'

Jade squirmed at hearing Lily pronounce Los Angeles with an American lilt.

'Yeah, very productive. Got loads done. I'm really excited about the next collection. Made some great contacts too.'

Jade rolled her eyes from the bedroom. She surrendered, put the Tippex lid back on and slowly walked to her fate in the hallway. Her sister was standing, neck craned to the ceiling; a cashmere black tracksuit encased her tiny frame.

'You really need to sort these textured ceilings out. They're god-awful.'

Adam walked back into the front room and flopped back onto his side, leaving Jade and Lily alone in the hallway.

'Ceilings? Well, yeah, I hate them but Dad won't—' Jade stopped, catching herself over-explaining and totally off the topic she needed to focus on. The muscles in her face felt as if they were made of cement. In vast contrast, Lily's face looked rested and well slept; no sign of a hangover, no black circles under her eyes from a wild night with strippers. She had had eyelash extensions again, Jade could tell. They always made her sister blink slower than normal.

Lily smiled at Jade, her lips glossed like a toffee apple. She filled the silence: 'Ahhh, that was just what I needed. I so rarely get a break from all the juggling I do. The masseuse at Dukes was sensational. The best ever.' She sighed peacefully, pushing strands of black hair behind her ear.

Jade felt drained before the conversation had even begun.

'So you just had massages and did yoga?' Jade lifted one eyebrow as she pressed further, wanting to see any signs of discomfort as her sister lied her way through their chat.

'Well, not just massages and yoga. We did some meditating, long country walks, and perhaps this is too much info, but I did opt for a colonic too.' Lily ran her hands across her flat stomach.

'Wow. Wow.' Jade bit her lip and nodded, failing to muster up any further line of questioning, bemused by how her sister could lie without even flinching.

'Where were you on Sunday? I specifically remember you telling me that you would collect the girls after lunch. I had work today. I was late and my boss was not happy about it.' Jade clenched her fists and steadied herself.

'No, no, I remember telling you it would be a weekend trip, Birdy. The whole schedule had been planned months in advance. There is no way we could have gotten through it in a single day.' Lily's voice was dismissive and firm. 'And I packed uniforms for the girls for today. I wouldn't have done that if I were picking them up Sunday, Birds . . .' She trailed off with a light laugh.

'I remember it clearly, Lily. You said Sunday lunchtime.'

'Nope.'

Jade remained focused. 'I was calling you all day Sunday, well into the evening, and you didn't pick up once.' Her voice wobbled.

'We were in the countryside, Birds, terrible reception,

179

and, also, I didn't want the girls to hear my voice. They might have gotten upset.'

'You posted a picture on Instagram on Sunday evening, so you had wi-fi,' Jade threw back, curious to see how her sister handled the evidence.

'Yes, we could get on to the wi-fi but we had literally no phone reception.'

'I called you on WhatsApp, though.'

'Oh, I must have missed it. As I said, we had a lot to get through. Anyway, stop being so dramatic. I'm here to collect their stuff now. The girls are with James. Everyone is OK, so just calm down.' Each word drenched in a patronising tone.

Adam reappeared in the hallway. 'Yeah, Jade, give your sister a break. It's great she had some time away from the kids to relax this weekend.' He leaned one arm on the wooden door frame.

Jade swallowed the rage building in her throat. 'Are you really jumping in to get involved in this, Adam? You weren't even bloody here all weekend.' Adam raised his eyebrows and again backed out into the lounge. She breathed deeply to try and steady her nerves and trembling hands. The wall felt cool as she pressed her back into it, the script's dialogue hanging in the air between them. There was always a numbness that set in before the script tumbled out of her mouth. She was used to it now. It was what she imagined being in space felt like; a gigantic separation from anything remotely real. She looked up at the textured ceiling. The words rose up, swelling in her mouth, then liberated themselves without consent.

'Do you just think your life is more important than mine?'

There it was. The words were shaky and lacked punch.

Lily threw her hands up, each manicured nail perfectly almond-shaped. 'What are you on about?' she said sharply, defensiveness spiking each word.

Water filled Jade's mouth, as if she had bitten into a slice of lemon. The words crept out, slowly and nervously.

'Can you not see . . . ? You don't get it, you never have. It's like my own life is invisible to you.'

Jade kept her eyes on her sister's. Lily was good at playing the game. It was her trump card in any altercation or disagreement. She could twist words and circumstances like she was wringing out a wet cloth. Her mood, stance and facial expressions could change in a millisecond, leaving the victim confused and questioning themselves.

'I'm not sure what you're talking about, Birdy. Has something happened? You seem different.'

With each word, Lily's smile grew – a smile that reeked of fake concern. Jade had seen this face so many times over the years. It was reserved for moments of pure manipulation. As Lily's black hair swung above her shoulders, Jade imagined her as a crow. Midnight black, pointed nose, beady eyes. Jade turned and walked into the kitchen with her head down. She was tired.

'I'm not really up for talking.'

Lily elevated her breeziness to new levels. 'Oh god, well I'm not sure what's going on here but I'm going to give you some space, as you clearly need it. I'll see you soon.'

Jade was nestled into the corner of the kitchen, cuddling her own arms tightly. She looked up at the weather clock. Small grey clouds had moved in over the sun.

'*Not even a thank you?*' Jade whispered, almost to herself. Lily's footsteps could be heard on the steps outside the door. The crow had left the building.

Jade stood in a puddle of her own silence. Adam walked in with heavy feet and turned the kettle on.

'Thought Lily's looking really well. Love her new hair,' he said casually.

'Really, Adam? That's the takeaway from my sister's flying visit? She looks rested because she's just been chilling out all weekend with a colonic pipe stuck up her arse while I've been looking after her kids.'

'Jealousy is an ugly trait, Jade.' He paused. 'You should think about cutting your hair off like your sister. Yours looks so straggly at the moment.' He picked up a mug and moved towards the kettle.

'Can you just give me some space, please,' Jade said sternly. Adam poured hot water over his teabag deliberately slowly and backed out to the front room without answering. The stress clung to Jade's skin. Her sister's toxicity seemed to remain in the air inside the flat. She now understood why Sophie kept bundles of sage in her kitchen drawers. The desire to smoke out her sister's unwanted energy was overwhelming.

She opened the window above the sink and hoped the bad vibes would exit accordingly. Staring at a small plump robin on a phone wire outside the window, she cursed herself for allowing her sister to come out on top again. She had waltzed away triumphant, getting what she wanted with zero accountability. And once again, Jade knew she had crumbled under the pressure of the moment. The pride she had initially felt when discovering this new script, knowing she would usher her sister from her flat, had well and truly dissipated. When spoken aloud, the words had made such little impact. She stood motionless and watched the robin fly off into the dusty grey sky.

20

'Pass the salt, bubs.'

Lethabo stretched his arm across the wooden bench towards Sophie.

'I think the chips are better at the White Swan, personally,' Sophie remarked, squinting as she faced the sun.

'What are you? The chip expert of West London, babes?' Lethabo pouted.

'I just know my chips,' she shrugged, popping one into her mouth. The sky was baby blue, and the sun felt warm on their backs. A break in the bad weather had prompted a visit to a pub garden, with Lethabo reminding them all that the sun wouldn't last, and they'd better make the most of it. It had been a long week for Jackson, Lethabo, Sophie and Jade, and their paint-splattered clothes signified to others that they were in a pack – a pack that needed to let off steam and talk about life outside of the warehouse.

They had worked with pace and focus to meet the deadline for the kids' TV show and had felt a collective sense of achievement as they shipped the giant props off to the studio. Jade had found herself in such a flow that the impending doom of finding scripts had faded into background noise. It had been nearly three weeks since she had found the last one at Kew, which had given her more space to think, more time to ruminate on what it all meant. Not much had changed between her and Adam. Jade had been racing to bed as early as she could each night, avoiding conversation or physical touch. The void between them was growing to a point of no return. She knew it couldn't go on much longer.

'Oh, this is more like it.' Lethabo stretched his arms up towards the sun-bleached sky. Sophie pushed a large bowl of chips towards Jade.

'Am I too old to be eating chips in a pub garden after work, guys?' Jade looked into the eyes of her three workmates.

'Who's too old for chips?' Sophie countered. 'They're just potatoes, really.'

'Shouldn't I be at home making an asparagus risotto or something?'

Jackson grimaced and quietly replied, 'I hate risotto, it's so . . . claggy. I hate that it sticks to the roof of your mouth.' This was the most Jackson had said all day, his first beer loosening his shyness.

'OK, shepherd's pie, then?' Jade quickly interjected.

'Babe, you're only three years older than me and two years older than Jackson and Thabs. It's fine to be eating chips in the pub. Unless you would rather be at home cooking claggy rice?'

Jade shook her head vehemently at Sophie. 'No, that's the thing. I would way rather be here with you lot eating the second-best chips in West London, I just worry that, at *thirty-two*—' Jade whispered her age for dramatic effect '—I'm supposed to be doing something else.'

Sophie leaned on her elbows, popping another chip into her mouth. 'Why? Because loads of other people choose to settle down in their thirties? Jadey, you've got to do what makes you happy. I see you at work every day, and when you're creating you're in your bliss. That's what happiness is all about, not following some weird socio-norm narrative.'

Jade smiled broadly. Creativity had always been her escape; an escape from her thoughts, the drama of her childhood. Most of her happiest childhood memories were based at her desk in her bedroom. Her pens lying neatly in a Tupperware, her pencils fastidiously sharpened in a Snoopy mug. Four sketchbooks piled next to a plastic flower in a pot that held a guitar and danced when you waved your hand in front of it. She would lose herself in sketching cartoons, drawing her school friends' portraits, and making small roses out of tissue paper. She could block out the noise of her mum crying or shouting at her dad down the phone, her sister's self-prophesied drama; her mind would be lost in making. That feeling had never left. Her fine arts degree at Newcastle had allowed her to dive into her passion and push her own creative boundaries even further. Today, the shelves in the warehouse, stocked with their rainbow-coloured card, piles of plywood, thick-bristled brushes sitting in turps, offered the same escape: from her sister's manipulation, Adam's antics, and worrying whether she was too old to be eating chips for dinner.

'*And*, if you *were* indoors eating shitty rice, you wouldn't be with us, and what is more gorgeous than us? Nothing, that's what.' Lethabo stood up and curtsied. 'Now, who wants a vodka?' Three hands shot up as Lethabo walked with purpose to the bar.

'Can I ask a weird question, Soph?'

Sophie leaned in again. 'Obviously. I love weird. Go.'

Jackson shuffled in his seat. 'Should I leave?'

'No, no, you're all good, Jackson. I just need help in understanding a word that I hear batted about a lot. I know what the word means literally but don't truly understand the word, if you get me?'

'Which is . . . ?' Sophie said, nodding.

'Boundaries,' Jade said apprehensively. 'I just don't understand them. I clearly have none as Adam has no respect for me, my sister treats me like a member of staff, my mum disregards most of my concerns, and my dad . . .' Jade tailed off. Jackson sat up straight and pushed his long brown hair from his eyes. Jade went on, 'The other week Colin asked me to get his wife underwear for her birthday. We all know that is totally wrong. I genuinely forgot to get them and he gave me such a bollocking. I sort of just stood there and took it, and then went out that morning and bought this hideous red lacy number for his wife.'

Sophie laughed out loud. 'I know I'm not supposed to be laughing but that is hilarious, and grim. What were they like?'

'Oh god, do you really want the details? I chose really naff lacy ones with bows on the side. He loved them, which made it even worse. I still feel sick about it.'

187

'He's using his power completely inappropriately, Jade,' Jackson said very seriously. 'I feel compelled to discuss it with him next week.'

'What? Really?' Jade looked shocked.

'I'm not comfortable with a man I work for abusing his power like that. Colin aside, I have some other thoughts,' Jackson continued quietly. 'You can't be the victim, Jade.'

Sophie, who had a chip in her hand an inch from her mouth, froze and looked at him. Jade fixed her eyes on his. Both were shocked at Jackson's contribution.

'You have to decide how you're going to react to each of these people. They aren't in control of you. That's the first step in creating good, healthy boundaries.' Jackson was on a roll, his delivery steady, quiet, loving, controlled. 'It's for *you* to decide how much of them you let into your life. You decide on how their words will land with you. You decide how much head space they will take up.'

Jade nodded, a small smile on her face.

'Then you learn to say no. You practise saying no without any emotion rolled into it. You say it unambivalently: it's a flat "No". You don't need to follow this up with an explanation or apology, it's simply a no, all on its own. No.'

'Yesss, Jackson,' Sophie whooped. '"No" is a full sentence.'

He continued, 'The next step is maybe the hardest part. You have to sit with the reaction to that "No" and not let it bother you. Don't let other people's tantrums or protest rattle you. You aren't here to please everyone.

You are not here to fix everyone. If you say no to someone and they don't like it, that is their issue and not yours. You have set a boundary by telling them what you are capable of and what you are not capable of. It's on your terms. By nature, you're a good person so there will be moments when you will naturally want to say yes, but there will also be moments when you feel the no at your core. You'll know the difference. You say the emotionless "No", then you walk away peacefully, knowing that the aftermath of that is theirs and not yours. Think of it like a small but sturdy fence around your own energy source, mental health and happiness.'

Jackson picked up his beer and took a small sip. Jade and Sophie sat, eyes wide, marvelling at Jackson's unexpected flow of wisdom.

'Well, fuck me, Jackson, you kept that all a bit quiet, didn't you, mate?' Sophie said, folding her arms.

'Jackson, thank you.' Jade was smiling at him. 'Thank you for that. I get it. I totally get it. I suppose I hadn't realised how much I was allowing all of this to happen.' She spoke slowly, letting the realisation settle.

Jackson nodded, his hair flopping over one eye.

'I think I'm going to find the aftermath a bit tricky. I'm such a guilt harvester.'

'You'll get there. It's just practice.' Jackson took another sip of his drink without looking up.

'You're like my very own pocket Eckhart Tolle,' Jade chortled.

Jackson smiled with one side of his mouth and shrugged. 'Just basic stuff, Jade,' he said softly.

Jade laughed; it couldn't feel any further from basic to her. 'Well, thank you anyway.' Jade knew she needed to start putting up some small but sturdy fences, and quickly.

'Oh my god, sorry, my babes,' Lethabo said, balancing four vodkas on a plastic tray. 'It's bloody bonkers in there tonight. Sun comes out and every man and his dog finds the nearest pub garden.'

Each of them took a vodka and held it up into the blue July sky.

'To boundaries,' said Jade.

'To boundaries!' they chimed, Lethabo chinking his glass with confusion written on his face.

Jade was glad that she had stopped at two vodkas. Despite the temptation her three slightly intoxicated friends had offered, she remembered the last time she had drunk a third, then fourth, which had led to her leaving her bike chained up at the pub overnight and an expensive cab ride home.

'Bye, you beauties,' Lethabo sang as he swung round a nearby lamp-post, his arms outstretched like the wings of a bird.

'Bye, Thabs,' Jade whispered into the warm evening air. Jumping on her bike, she cycled through the busy streets of Acton, swerving wobbly-legged pedestrians who were aimlessly walking out into the road after one too many. As she approached Chiswick, she decided to take a different route home, not quite ready for her evening to end. She needed more time to allow Jackson's words to percolate. Maybe she did have much more control over the story of her life than she believed. Maybe she could start saying no.

A ten-minute cycle led her to Kew Green. As she cut along one side of the grass, she slowed to take in the charm of the houses that lined it, with their pastel front doors and wrought-iron balconies. It felt like cycling through a film set. Swerving off down a small lane that led her directly to the river, she let her bike's momentum carry her until, hopping off, she transitioned into a slow walk along the river path. She let her eyes land on the hypnotic navy-blue water of the Thames.

After Jackson's pep-talk something inside of her had shifted. It was humbling to realise that she didn't have to feel like a victim to those around her. Being malleable and accommodating had been her normal for far too long and she felt ready to shed that skin, but how? Where would this rousing confidence come from? Would it just show up when she needed it like an unexpected lifeboat in a storm? Or would she have to find it deep within her? Where did it live? In her heart, amongst the red, the love, the broken parts of her? In her head, amongst the constant chatter, over-thinking and big dreams? She let her mind wander as she watched the water ripple in silky grooves.

A flock of geese flew noisily overhead, twenty or so elegant silhouettes, wings stretched out, moving in perfect unison. She let her gaze follow their arrow-shaped formation as an idea fell into her head: Dorset. A trip to stay with her godmother had never felt more necessary.

She needed the air, the space, the candlelight, Belinda's warmth, the waves.

Picking up pace, she jumped back on her bike and cycled the rest of the river path with purpose. More geese flew overhead, with more noise this time, their screeches making the air crackle with excitement.

The flat was cloaked in silence. Jade gently padded into the hallway. The air smelt of spice, tinged with the sourness of booze. Walking into the kitchen, Jade saw several half-eaten containers from a takeaway meal, splashes of bright orange and yellow on the work surfaces, two empty bottles of beer.

Normally, irritation would have led her to clear the debris away, almost wanting to make a point, but tonight she turned slowly, knowing it wouldn't be her problem in the morning. Peering into the front room, she saw Adam asleep on the sofa fully clothed, his trainers still on and his mouth slightly parted. She crept into their bedroom to pack.

Belinda would be asleep by now; she would text her in the morning. She knew that even the most last-minute arrival would be welcomed – Belinda was constantly reminding Jade she could turn up any time of day or night. She rarely left Dorset, but Jade knew that even if by a small chance she wasn't home there was the lodge in the garden, which was normally left unlocked. The small, cosy, wood-lined cabin that sat nestled amongst apple trees and crawling ivy, with fairy lights lining each window, was always ready for visitors.

She quietly packed a small backpack with an assortment

of clothing options and her swimming costume, then left it by the door covered with her coat in case Adam woke and saw it in the night. Then she set an alarm for 6am and booked a train ticket online. Colin was the only obstruction. He had already threatened to sack her after her recent lateness. But she had heard this threat before, and she knew it was worth taking the risk. Colin wouldn't be able to replace Jade quickly and without uproar from Sophie, Lethabo and Jackson.

Opening her email, she thought back to Jackson's words. This email would not be full of apology and self-deprecating statements; it would be confident and clear. Forming these sentences felt utterly alien. She deleted the word 'sorry' several times before forming a message that felt ready to send. There were no white lies or profuse apologies; just an honest email stating that she needed a short break and wouldn't be in on Monday. She hadn't taken any time off for over six months – when she had gone with Adam to Amsterdam, as there were some vintage shops he wanted to scope out. She had imagined the trip would be romantic and reckless; late-night tipsy rambling through canal lanes, holding hands and laughing. It had in fact been a rainy few days where she ended up sitting alone outside countless shops, eating waffles. This weekend away was overdue and she was only asking for one day off. Imagining the salt on her skin and the sound of the tide pulling pebbles on the beach out to sea, she pressed send, then slipped silently into bed.

*

Adam had got into bed next to her in the middle of the night. She vaguely remembered him pushing her over to her side with an elbow. She had placed her phone under her pillow, so when the alarm shrilled at 6am she quickly silenced it. Slipping out of bed, she felt a pang of excitement for her secret adventure. Knowing she was only hours from the silence and refuge of Belinda's house, with a big distance from the madness of the scripts, she let a small smile creep onto her face. The smell of Adam's takeaway still lingered in the air, the wonky stack of containers lying sticky and pungent on the kitchen counter.

Pinging a short message to her godmother, who she suspected would already be up eating her usual marmalade on toast, she grabbed her belongings as quietly as possible. Tiptoeing out of the door and closing it with the lightest touch, she made her way down the stairs.

'Morning, Miss Shaw!'

Jade jumped back, her eyes moving from a sleepy squint to saucers.

'Oh, Mr Merry, you shocked me. You're up early,' she whispered, still concerned by the possibility of Adam waking and discovering her shady exit.

Mr Merry closed the door to his flat behind him and moved out into the corridor. 'Up with the lark, Miss Shaw. I like to walk to the river at this time of the morning in the summer months. It's ever so peaceful.'

Jade smiled and kept walking towards the exit to the street.

'Oh, Miss Shaw. I wondered if you had given any

more thought to my birthday plans? No obligation whatsoever but if you did fancy contributing to the birthday buffet it would be marvellous.'

Jade pushed the main doors open and looked back over her shoulder.

'Do let me know, when you can, which genre of culinary delights you are proposing to offer. I've made somewhat of a spreadsheet to ensure we don't end up with too many quiches and too little cake, you see.' Mr Merry chuckled loudly. Jade felt panic rise as Mr Merry's laugh boomed through the hallway. 'It's my first ever spreadsheet. My nephew Phillip showed me the correct . . . what's the word . . . software. It was actually ever so fun.'

Jade stepped out onto the street, eager to get to the station.

'As I said previously, most flat-dwellers in our block are contributing. Jane in Flat 5 is keen to make an Eton Mess and the Richards family are whipping up a—'

Jade turned back to face Mr Merry.

'Mr Merry, I won't be able to make your birthday lunch. Life is a little . . . hectic at the moment. I really hope you have a gorgeous time, though. Do save me a slice of quiche.' She spoke with fondness, a softness that let him down gently. His eyes sparkled and he smiled, tilting his head towards Jade.

'Understood, Miss Shaw, I know how very busy you are.'

Jade realised she was holding her breath. She liked Mr Merry very much but knew committing herself to his plan would overwhelm her. Her sister's rehearsal dinner loomed, and the wedding, which still gave her chills, was creeping up too. Deciding to respond with honesty felt terrifying but she also realised deep down that Mr Merry, the sweetest man, deserved honesty rather than resentment on the day of his birthday. She chose not to feel guilty.

She leaned in and gave him a hug. His body remained rigid, unsure how to reciprocate. Jade turned and pushed through the double doors, the early-morning birdsong engulfing her. She waved at Mr Merry and walked away with a lightness that only rejecting guilt could offer.

As Jade jogged down the road, she felt an unfamiliar pride. It felt like a miracle that she had been honest and chosen what was right for her, and no one had died. Mr Merry hadn't wept or shouted or called her a selfish cow, and the world was still spinning. How novel, she thought.

Her phone vibrated in the pocket of her jeans. Oh what a treat. Don't forget your swimmers. B x

Curtains were drawn and shop doors closed. She had forgotten how much she loved this time of day. The birds sang without inhibition, signalling a new, blank page. She picked up her pace. The sea was calling.

'Belinda, I'm here, I just got into Wool station.' Jade heaved her over-stuffed backpack onto her back and stepped onto the deserted platform, holding her phone to her ear. The air already felt cleaner.

'Oh, darling, I can't wait to see you. I'll be pulling into

the car park in five mins. You'll see me. I'll be the old bird dressed in green.'

Jade laughed. She had loved adding to her godmother's green obsession over the years. One Christmas, she had given her a glass jar full of just the green Quality Streets, which she had hand-plucked out of a huge tub. This time she came gift-less, which felt uncomfortable, but she knew Belinda wouldn't mind one bit.

'Jadey! Oh, darling, it's been too long. Come here.' Belinda held Jade's face, her green nails sparkling in the morning sun.

'You don't mind, do you? Sorry to have only texted last minute. I just felt the urge to get down here and see you guys.' They walked towards Belinda's dark green Land Rover, splattered with tyre-flung mud.

'Darling, what have I told you? You are welcome here any time you want. There's only so much Don and I can say to each other these days. God, I love the man, but nearly forty years together does leave the conversation bank a little empty at times.'

Jade breathed in Belinda's strong rose perfume. This rich, exotic oil Belinda wore, combined with the unpolluted Dorset air, made Jade's shoulders drop.

'How is your mum, darling?' Belinda asked as she pulled out of the car park.

Jade sighed. 'Err, she's . . . you know – Mum. I'm never quite sure how she is.'

Belinda kept her eyes on the road, lush green fields closing in on either side.

'In the forty years I've been friends with your mother

it's certainly always interesting. She has a huge heart and a lot of love to give – but that makes the pain extra heavy. I'm not sure she has ever found the right coping mechanism to deal with a heart that big.'

Jade looked out of the window; blue sky sat neatly above the never-ending green of the farmland, the two colours perfectly complementing each other.

'Well, her coping mechanism is still wine, sadly.' Jade paused as she watched a large kite glide, wings open and graceful. 'I worry about her.'

Belinda quickly glanced towards Jade. 'I know, I do too, darling. We'll get her sorted, I promise. In the meantime, let's focus on you. What do you need? What does the sea need to heal while you're here?'

Jade's throat tightened; a sudden swell of sadness moved through her. Belinda's genuine kindness made her want to cry uncontrollably.

'I'm a bit confused about life if I'm honest.'

Belinda turned onto the dirt track that led to the house. A thirty-second drive through a canopy of trees brought them to a circular driveway with an island of grass in the middle. As the house came into view, with its handsome thatched roof and gothic windows, a huge grin broke out on Jade's face. Belinda pulled up outside the large green door and hopped out with the agility of a twenty-year-old.

'Well, I'd better get the kettle on, then.'

22

Walking through Belinda's front door was a coming home of sorts. The cool of the flagstone floor, the smell of wood smoke from the fireplace, the incense that was always burning, and the fresh bread in the kitchen were a sensory concoction that equalled a feeling of safety and made Jade feel like a kid again. Her head already felt a little clearer. It was like the feeling she got when a plane broke through the clouds on take-off; nothing but blue sky, with the world and its problems below a layer of white a long way down.

Jade walked past the almost floor-to-ceiling framed film posters that lined the hallway walls. She had seen most of them, all indie films that Belinda had directed in the eighties.

'Hey, Don.' Jade walked into the kitchen where Don stood by the racing-green Aga, cup of tea in hand.

'Oh, Jade, hello. Welcome, welcome. How have you been?' Don was tall and lithe, with impeccable posture. His hair, snow-white, was pushed over to one side and his tanned face was creased with kindness.

'I'm good. So, so happy to be here. Thank you for having me to stay.'

Don pulled out a wooden chair from the small kitchen

200

table which was scattered with papers, crumbed bread-boards and empty teacups.

'Don, you could have tidied up a little bit while I was collecting Jade from the station. Deary me, sorry, Jade. Sit, darling, sit.'

Don took this as his cue to leave Jade and Belinda to catch up. 'I'll be in the garden if you need me, ladies.' He walked out through the kitchen door to a small patio that was surrounded by bird-feeders of all shapes and sizes. Beyond the patio the garden stretched out into neat green lawns that transitioned into woodland. Flowers threw colour from every direction.

'So, darling, tell me,' Belinda said as she made tea and passed an open packet of biscuits to Jade.

She slid one out of the tube and took a bite. 'I'm not sure where to start. I just know I need to make some changes.'

Belinda nodded with her eyes closed. 'Well, I'm here for you. Just tell me what is troubling you in your own time.'

Water filled Jade's eyes; the armour she wore back in her real life started to fall away.

'Which part of your life needs a shake-up, darling?'

'Parts plural,' Jade corrected with a teary chuckle.

'OK, *parts*,' Belinda clarified warmly.

'The first part is the relationship part. I feel stuck.'

Belinda sipped her tea. 'Why do you feel stuck? What is keeping you in it?'

'I guess I'm a bit scared.'

'What of, my love?' Belinda tilted her head to one side.

'I'm not even sure any more. Perhaps that I will regret it?'

'Is that true, though, darling? Would you really regret it?'

'Probably not. Perhaps I'm scared because I'm thirty-two and I feel I'm supposed to be settling down at this point.' She shrugged, not quite believing her own words.

'Thirty-two?' Belinda raised one eyebrow, her shimmering green eye shadow creasing at the edges. 'You're a baby! There is so much time and no rules at all. Rules are boring, and there to be broken. When I met Don my mother told me I would have to give up my dreams of working in film as I should attend to his needs. All very old-fashioned. I took great pleasure in dismantling all those patriarchal rules. I married the man I loved, and I also continued to climb the ladder at work, following the dreams I was not prepared to let go of. It was a juggle with the boys. I might have missed some of their school concerts as I was always in an edit suite, I might have been socially shunned at the school gates by mums who went for tea after the drop-off, but darling, I don't like rules. I have always done things my way. You must do your life *your* way.'

'What do you think of Adam?' Jade took another bite of her biscuit, intrigued to hear Belinda's take on him.

'Well, darling, I've only met him a handful of times as he's so averse to the countryside! It's not really for me to say. But what I will stress is that you, my god-daughter, deserve the best. So, if you don't feel like he is the best – the best *for you* – then you must make a decision.'

'I think my past is holding me back and stopping me

from making a decision. I wonder if I'm cursed, having broken things off with Navi. I mean, we were so close to the wedding day and it was *me* who decided to bail. I don't think I've forgiven myself. How can I trust my instinct this time?'

'I have always so admired your ability to follow your gut, darling. Navi was a good bloke, but you knew it wasn't right. What would have been worse – you calling things off before the day, or going through with the marriage and then having to go through a messy divorce? You did the right thing.'

'I think I'm just a little superstitious. Because *I* broke it off, I now feel like I'm undeserving of love, or like my love life is cursed – so I shouldn't rock the boat with the relationship I do have.'

'Darling, you're not cursed. You're simply not used to putting yourself first.' Belinda gave Jade a knowing look. An expression that nodded to her sister's teenage truancy, her mum's drinking, her dad's pandering to Lily. Belinda was one of the few people who really understood Jade's family dynamics.

'Ending things with Navi was perhaps the first time you got the chance to prioritise yourself, so no wonder it felt so traumatic. But look, that was years ago now. You were young. We rush into things. That's what being young is for. Forgive yourself. Let yourself live.'

Jade nodded while playing with the silver ring on her index finger.

'I think I'm just putting it off. I can't be bothered with the admin of a break-up. Adam will protest as he has a comfy life in my flat. Then we might have to go through the awkward part where he still lives there but we're not together, or even talking.'

Belinda shook her head vehemently. 'Darling, it's your flat. If you tell him it's over, he goes. He's a big boy. He'll have to pack his stuff while you're at work and respect-fully leave.'

'Do you think?'

'I don't think, I *know*.' Belinda rearranged the grey bun of hair on her head and pushed a green jewelled pin through the top.

'I guess I just need to bite the bullet.'

'That's the spirit.' Belinda slammed her hand down on the wooden table. The teacups rattled in their saucers.

'Wasn't I supposed to have had this sort of epiphany when I turned thirty? I'm a bit late to be rethinking everything. Or maybe I'm just having a midlife crisis way too early.'

'Oh, you're definitely not having a midlife crisis. This is just you coming into your power. It's exciting.' Belinda beamed.

'Exciting?'

'Yes! You're seeing very clearly how powerful you are. That's a scary prospect when the concept is so new to you, but really it's the most exciting thing in the world. It's time to start living, my darling.'

'Yup, I want to feel like I'm really living. More fun, more boundaries.'

'Well, we don't need to use new-fangled words like *boundaries*, darling – you just need to tell people no from time to time. You must also learn that it is not your job to shoulder other people's . . . mind my French . . . *shit*. Other people's mess is not yours to tidy up. And yes, more fun. Lots of it.'

'Yup, I've certainly shouldered a lot of Lily's shit over the years. Speaking of French, she's called her interiors company Maison Lily.'

'It's a phase. It'll pass. Concentrate on your path, darling.'

'Her phases are *trés* annoying.'

'I know.' Belinda laughed. 'And your father? What's your relationship like with him these days?'

'Well, I probably need to have an honest chat with him down the line. He doesn't have much interest in what I do. It's all eyes on Lily. But he also constantly highlights that I live in one of his properties. I pay full-whack rent, you know. Not a discount in sight. When he brings it up I feel like screaming.'

'Well, maybe you do need to scream.' Belinda's green bangles jangled as she passionately waved her arms around. 'Go to the sea and scream. Scream it back into nature. Nature can handle it. It can turn any stress or negativity into power.'

Jade rested into the back of her chair. 'I'm so glad I'm here, Belinda.'

'And I'm glad you're here, too. Now – let's get your bag to your room and get you to the sea.'

Jade knew where she would be sleeping: the green room, with its dark green walls and bedspread patterned with ivy. It had a gothic window with an arched top that looked out to the garden and nearby rose bushes. It had once been Belinda's son Sasha's room, before he moved to Bath.

Jade flopped down onto the bed. The silence of the countryside was unnerving and always took her a few days to acclimatise to. In her flat, the hum of buses, chatter from school parents across the road and planes overhead blended into a white noise she was used to. The soundscape of Belinda's home was so very different. Birds chirped, the odd pheasant screeched, but there were no cars, or planes, or chatter; just complete silence.

Jade pulled all her clothes off quickly, letting the energy of London fall from her body with them. She pulled on her black swimsuit, and then her shorts and baggy T-shirt. There was always a basket of green striped towels by Belinda's front door, ready to lure you to the coastline – and she didn't want to waste any time getting to the beach.

'I'm headed to Lulworth, Belinda. See you a little later,' Jade called once she was back downstairs, stuffing a striped towel, her phone and wallet into a canvas bag that was hanging on a nearby hook.

'Enjoy, darling. Lullers is looking beautiful at the moment.'

Jade grinned and raced out the door, turning left into the garden and clambering over the wooden fence that kept the sheep out. A few hundred metres ahead, the sheep field merged with a dirt track that Jade meandered down to reach the village. The wind shook the nearby trees, their leaves clapping together like a chorus of applause. A steel-coloured mountain of cloud loomed on the horizon like a warning; the weather this summer had remained as unpredictable as her life had felt. The sea was almost in sight, her nostrils picking up the salt before her eyes reached the blue.

She walked past the row of holiday cottages that lined the road and descended the shallow hill towards the main beach car park. Children held ice creams in pastel colours, piled high and precariously balanced. Parents lugged huge beach bags of buckets and spades, sun lotion and stripy wind-breakers. Jade loved how changeable weather rarely deterred the British from visiting the seaside. She marvelled at how many holiday-goers were heading for the beach, optimistically wearing swimsuits and flip-flops. She passed the Lulworth Cove Inn, with its brightly coloured exterior wall depicting the cove in vibrant blues and greens; the Doll's House café, painted in a delicious chalky turquoise, selling fudge and seaside paraphernalia; a small garden backing on to one of the holiday cottages, where tall sunflowers proudly stretched towards the sun; all the colours of Dorset. Everything felt more vibrant and vivid than back home. Her thoughts became less cluttered as she concentrated on her senses: the salt air on her skin; happy voices coming from every direction; the smell of fudge and seaweed.

The sea came into view. Milky-green swirls of water moved gently, gathering momentum further out towards the mouth of the cove. The perfect circle of the coastline held tourists carefully in its curvature. Walking down the concrete slipway, Jade reached the beach, her feet moving from solid ground to unpredictable pebbles, each foot making a delicious crunch on the shore's surface. She followed the cove round to the left, where a huge white rocky wall of cliff loomed to her side, eventually breaking into rolling green grass on top.

Stopping for a moment to breathe it all in, she thought about how this scene never changed. It was always waiting for her, a film set stuck in time, too robust to change with the passing years. She turned out to face the sea as she crunched step by step down the smooth pebbles. The waves were dragging the silky stones out to sea then purging them back to shore with each lick. The noise was hypnotic and soothing. Several small fishing boats sat anchored in the middle of the bay. Jade fixed her eyes on one, which bobbed in the centre of the cove. It swayed lightly, its blue body weathered to a beautiful hue of summer sky. A bunch of bright orange buoys sat tied at the back of the boat, far enough away to be mistaken for a jolly collection of balloons.

She felt her calves burning as she plodded over the moving stones. She passed small groups on towels and fold-away chairs, chatting and smiling, faces towards the water. Dogs bounded in and out of the gentle surf, euphorically shaking the excess water at nearby spectators. The slow fifteen-minute walk around the pebbled bay was worth it for the small break of sand at the cove's edge.

Jade slipped her trainers off and let her toes sink into the soft mustard-coloured sand. Slipping her shorts and T-shirt off, she moved quickly towards the clear water, knowing that if she gave it too much thought she would procrastinate and chicken out. The sky overhead, now charcoal in places, had stolen all the warmth from the sea.

She sharply inhaled as her feet entered the freezing water, her toes gripping at the slippery stones below. One day, she would invest in rubber shoes, she thought. Striding with purpose, her mind went blank, only able to concentrate on moving forwards and submerging further. She panted short sharp breaths of air out of her lungs as she plunged into the cold up to her waist.

'*Three, two, one,*' she whispered, and then pushed out with a quick, almost comical breaststroke into deeper water. The tingling started to dissipate, and the numbness relaxed into a cool silky state of calm. Lifting her face to the sky, small droplets of rain began to fall onto her skin.

Jade realised she hadn't thought much about Adam, or her sister, or whether Colin would sack her. Her problems felt like they lived in London with the lights, and noise, and bustle. She looked out to the cove's mouth, where the pond-like stillness transitioned into bigger waves and boat sails littered the horizon. Those boats could go anywhere. They could sail to the Isle of Wight, maybe even France. Their freedom made Jade's skin tingle.

'*Dear sea, can you help me out?*' She flipped over onto her back to float, her waist-length hair moving behind her in the water like tentacles.

'*Dear sea,*' she whispered again, barely moving her mouth in case the families picnicking on the nearby shore saw her talking to herself and thought she was out of her mind.

'I want to feel more in control of my life. Where do I start? I'm willing to listen if you have any answers, or signs.' Jade thought back to a YouTube video she had watched with Sophie in their lunch-break a few months ago of Gabrielle Bernstein talking about signs. Jade hadn't asked for one since watching the video, as she wasn't sure she believed it would work, but now seemed as good a time as any to give it a go. She remembered Gabrielle looking into the camera with her big almond eyes, telling a tale of asking for a butterfly to guide her in the right direction. 'I don't mind what the sign is, just . . . a sign of sorts so I know where to start?'

A kite glided overhead, its wings intuitively catching air pockets as it swooped in perfect semicircles. She smiled, watching its ease, and wished she felt as free as the bird did. Was that the sign? Probably just a bird flying, she thought. Waves moved underneath Jade's body, her back gently bending and moving with each curve. She felt each vertebra move with the sea, each bit of her body surrendering to where the waves wanted to take her. Undulating, irregular, a rhythm without a steady beat. She let her body relax further as bigger raindrops now fell from the low clouds above. She turned back onto her front, swam towards the beach, and plodded out of the water.

'You're brave!' hollered a nearby dog-walker wearing a bright yellow raincoat, the hood pulled over his head as the rain now lashed down. 'It's cold in there today. And in this rain! Good on you.'

Jade smiled towards the man and his cocker spaniel. 'Thanks! It wasn't so bad,' she called back. 'You just have to get over the initial period of shock.' Her wet hair clung to her back as she navigated the discomfort of the pebbles on the soles of her feet. Maybe she *was* brave, she thought.

The dog-walker nodded back, a thumb held aloft. 'Well done!'

Jade sat on the small patch of sand and let the cool rain bring goosebumps to her skin. Maybe life was like that too. Perhaps you had to sit through excruciating, uncomfortable moments to move into a new phase of life. If she could bear the initial freeze of the water, then maybe she could endure a little pain in her actual life too. Making changes would mean discomfort – and maybe that wasn't so bad after all.

Her hands ran through the wet sand, scattered with pebbles, the odd shell, and the glimmer of sea glass – bright green smooth-edged jewels amongst the neutral tones of the beach. Tiny fragments of bold, bright happiness. She picked up a small round of sea glass and held it to the light: its story unknown; its beauty heightened by its time at sea. She placed it in the pocket of her shorts and patted it safe.

23

Jade ducked into the pub by the beach car park. She had changed from her swimsuit into her shorts and T-shirt on the beach under one of Belinda's stripy towels, but her clothes were now wet through from the rain.

'Good afternoon.' A waitress with cropped red hair beamed in Jade's direction. 'How can I help you?'

'Table for one, please.' Jade forced a smile. 'I'm just going to try and dry off in the bathroom first.'

'Toilets to the back left. Then you'll have the small table by the window.' She pointed to one of the few remaining empty tables for two that overlooked the path to the cove.

'Thanks.' Jade made her way to the bathrooms and caught sight of herself in the mirror. Her hair was slicked to her head and her T-shirt was nearly transparent with rain. She stood under the hand dryer and warmed her skin. She managed to dry the front of her hair and most of the moisture from her T-shirt before heading back out to the packed pub. Jade settled down on the padded chair by the sliding glass doors, grateful to be inside.

The waitress returned, placing a wooden clipboard with a menu attached onto the table. 'The specials today are sea bass with tomato sauce and black olive tapenade or a vegetarian linguine – otherwise, here's our usual menu. I'll be back in a tick.'

'Thank you.'

She wondered whether it would be embarrassing to just order a large bowl of chunky chips, as the sea had made her crave the salty stodginess. But her thoughts were interrupted when she picked up the clipboard and a thin sheaf of papers slipped out from under the menu, landing on her lap.

She looked down at the paper but didn't move. The font, the layout, her name staring back at her. Goose-bumps shot up her arms.

She had come to Dorset to escape the drama of her life and the relentless appearance of these scripts – how could this be happening? Placing the clipboard on the table, she peered down at the paper on her lap, trying not to look too suspicious.

```
[Scalini's, Chelsea. Jade is sitting at a large
oval table with Tony, Jacquie, Lily, James,
Adam and Sue, all dressed in smart-casual
outfits.]
```

Scalini's? Lily's rehearsal dinner wasn't for another two weeks, and these scripts seemed to turn up just a day or two before the real-life scene. She bit her lip and carried on reading.

```
[Jacquie sips a glass of red wine.]
```

                    JACQUIE

Well, it'll be handy come September, as Tony and I are off to
Brazil. It's part work trip, as
there are some properties we're
going to look at—

                    SUE

We? Is it a joint business now?

                    JACQUIE

Oh, you know what I mean. *We'll*
look, *Tony* will do the business
part.

[Sue rolls her eyes to the ceiling.]

                    JACQUIE

Then we're off to stay at
an eco-lodge an hour outside of
Rio. We're trying to learn as much
as we can about sustainable living
as it's a smart business move
to convert as many of our,
sorry, *Tony's* properties going
forward.

[Jacquie directs the last part of her sentence
to Sue.]

```
    Sounds lovely.

[Sue is slurring her words.]
```

Jade grimaced, recognising that this was already a messy scene. She wondered how far through dinner this chat was, but feared her mum's potential intoxication from numerous glasses of wine was a recipe for dinner-party disaster. Jade clenched her fist under the table.

'Are you ready to order? What can I get you?' The waitress's voice snapped Jade back to the present. Sitting up abruptly, she pushed the script further under the table.

'Did I mention the specials? We have a vegetarian linguine or a sea bass with olive tapenade.'

Jade's brain whirred. She hadn't even looked at the menu but needed to get out of the pub quickly to examine this fresh nightmare on paper. 'Er, yes, that one.'

'Sorry? What would you like?'

'The, er, pasta one.'

'The linguine, of course. Can I get you a glass of wine, perhaps?'

'No, no, I'm fine, thank you. Just a tap water. Thanks.'

Jade's mouth felt unbelievably dry. Paranoia began to set in. Was everyone looking at her, as she imagined? She looked to the left and right, scanning families playing Uno, couples clinking glasses of rosé, checking to see if all eyes really were on her.

                         LILY

Oh, that sounds fab. I once stayed
at the Fasano Hotel in Rio. It was
divine. I was working on a project
there in my days as a party organiser. The manager is called Fabian
and is quite literally FAB. You must
pop in.

                         SUE

Oh darling, you did know how to put
on a great party. You really were
the best event organiser out there.

Jade laughed out loud. The couple on the next table
looked over, then back to their drinks. Lily had piggy-
backed on her mate Cleo's business for all of four
months. Cleo had been running Hi-Light Events for a
decade at this point. It was the perfect job for Lily; free
champagne, glamour and the glitterati, and Cleo's fas-
tidious organising to hide behind when she felt out of
her depth. Their mum always over-praised Lily, as the
outward expression of most of her jobs was dispropor-
tionately lavish and loud in comparison to the actual
work involved.

                        TONY

Yeah, Lils, we've been there. Think
I met Fabian when we were over for
the carnival one February. We've got

                         216

a lot of work to do out there,
though. Not too much of a holiday,
Jacs. Got to keep working hard to
expand the portfolio. These properties won't buy themselves.

Jade could hear her dad's Cockney twang when pro-
nouncing Fabian's name. This was becoming a very
predictable conversation, where he tried to one-up who-
ever had just spoken. Jade imagined her dad's eyes
landing on her as he delivered his last line.

                    ADAM
      I've heard the scene is pretty good
      out there at the moment, fashion-
      wise. I might have to swing by at
      some point and do a recce.

                    TONY
      You don't really swing by, matey.
      It's a long old flight and not a
      cheap one. If you're going to be
      supporting my daughter here you
      might want to recce nearer to home.

                    ADAM
      With all due respect, Tony, all
      businesses have to start out strug-
      gling somewhat, with optimistic,
      confident projections for the

future. Putting in the work now
means big rewards down the line.

[Tony takes a sip of red wine.]

                    TONY
Been there, matey, got the T-shirt.
But let me tell you, I wasn't dashing off to Rio in the early days. I
was working twelve- to fifteen-hour
days. Rio comes later.

[Tony winks at Adam.]

                    ADAM
Times have changed, Tony.

[Tony ignores Adam.]

                    TONY
Another bottle, please.

[Tony barely looks over his shoulder to the
waiter.]

                    LILY
My interiors business is really
taking off, talking of business,
Dad. I've had tons of bookings for
online consultations and a few

prospective clients wanting full
renovations.

                    TONY
Lovely, darling, well done.

                    LILY
It's a lot of work but it's really
taking off.

                    JACQUIE
Oh, how brilliant. You'll have to help
us do a few of our properties up.

                    SUE
Tony's properties up.

                    JACQUIE
What's your point, Sue? I've been
with Tony for twelve years now. It's
really none of your business.

                    LILY
Mum, maybe make that your last glass
of wine.

                    JACQUIE
Yes, if you could, Sue. You've
already done a whole bottle and
we're only on our starters.

ADAM

Go easy on her, guys. It can't be
easy for Sue.

TONY

Pipe down, matey. Leave this one to
the adults.

ADAM

I'm thirty-three, Tony.

JACQUIE

This is all getting unnecessarily
tense. Aren't we meant to be celebrating Lily and James tonight,
guys?

LILY

Yes, yes we are.

TONY

We are celebrating you, Lils. Raise
a glass for my princess and James.

JACQUIE

Can we slow down on the wine,
though, everyone. This is clearly
not a cheap restaurant so to have
brazenly drunk a whole bottle
already is thoughtless, Sue.

                    SUE

Well, it's also *clearly* not your
money, Jacquie, so it shouldn't
bother you too much.

                  JACQUIE

Well, you would know, Sue. That
lovely cottage you live in didn't
buy itself, did it?

                    SUE

No, it didn't. That lovely cottage
is what you get after putting up
with *that* for twenty years.

[Sue points in Tony's direction.]

                   LILY

Mum, Dad's work ethic, which I've
been lucky enough to inherit, has
paid off in your favour.

                  JAMES

Jacquie has got a point, though. Do
you think you have a drink problem,
Sue?

                   ADAM

James, you've been part of this
family for all of two minutes, I

                    221

don't think you should be getting
involved here.

                    JACQUIE
This is a joke. I worked so hard
trying to organise a wonderful
dinner for Lily, and look at you
all. It's embarrassing.

'One pasta special for you, and one tap water. If you need anything else just shout.'

Jade looked up at the waitress with wide eyes. Her red hair looked like it was on fire as she stood under a ceiling spotlight. She placed the pasta dish in front of Jade.

'Enjoy your meal.'

'You too,' Jade replied.

You too? Her mind was still trying to process the new script. Her cheeks flushed red.

She sat back in her chair, shaking her head. This script was a nightmare. It was no surprise to her that she didn't feature at all. In moments of chaos and confrontation, Jade would usually go mute, as if all her words were caught in her throat. She had been in situations like this so many times with her family. Her frustration would build up inside like a pressure cooker – watching everyone's egos collide. She usually imagined herself screaming or roaring like a lion, but in reality she would sit there frozen and silent.

Jade swigged her water and stuck a fork forcefully into her pasta. She slowly chewed and leaned back in her chair again. For the first time since these strange scripts had entered her life, she felt almost grateful. The first few had brought absolute dread, but now she could see that they were showing her where she needed to speak up. They were acting as lighthouses to better days.

Twisting several strands of pasta onto her fork, she gazed down at the script. Why had she found this one so early? Maybe she wasn't meant to find it so soon. Yet the accuracy and timing of the previous scripts were undeniable. She ate unconsciously, and within minutes her plate was empty, her brain elsewhere, picturing the future dinner with bright lucidity. She waved her hands cheerily in the direction of the bar. 'Can I get the bill, please' she mouthed, while miming a signature. She wondered why people still did that. Within moments, the bill was paid and two humbug mints were left on a small silver tray in front of her. She popped them in her pocket, her shorts still damp from the downpour, the fabric clinging to the softness of her thighs. Rolling the script into a tube, she stood up, shoved it up her T-shirt and headed for the door.

Walking out of the pub, Jade's skin prickled. The rain was now lighter, a mist of seawater mixed into the fine rain that fell on a diagonal. She turned right and made her way up the hill. Thick swathes of dark grey cloud sat clumsily on the horizon, looming over the green hills. They were moving overhead at a visible pace, so Jade started to move her feet with more urgency. She pumped her arms as she trudged up the hill towards the house. Jade's fast walk transitioned into a jog as the droplets grew in size and frequency, and she longed for the warmth of Belinda's kitchen. A fresh earthy scent kicked up from the ground as she was rained on for the second time that day.

24

As Belinda and Don's house with its golden thatched roof came into view, the wi-fi kicked in and Jade's phone came to life. She rummaged for it in her bag. Two messages from Sophie, who had sent photos of Portobello Market, a favourite weekend haunt for them both, a missed call from her mum, and a text from Jacquie: Jade. Change of plan. Dad and I have to nip to Dubai in a couple of weeks' time as some properties have come up for grabs that we're keen to see. The only date everyone else can do for the rehearsal dinner is tomorrow night. James's dad can't fly in from Spain but has said to carry on regardless. So just our lot. Luckily the restaurant could accommodate us all too. I managed to pull a few strings. So see you tomorrow, Jadey, 7pm Scalini's. Love Jacs.

Jade's heart sank. The script's timing was impeccable, drawing Jade nearer to a future she now knew too much about. Could she blame trains and say she was stuck in Dorset? How much shit would her dad give her if she was a no-show? She stopped walking and stood on the wet grass, letting the rain pound down on her. She looked up at the grey underbelly of the clouds and mouthed *Why?*, then slowly sloped into the house and grabbed a fresh towel on her way in. Taking off her sodden T-shirt, she wrapped herself in the dry towel and headed towards a whistling kettle in the kitchen. She hung the T-shirt on the back of a chair near the open fire and let the warmth lick at her skin.

'A fire at this time of year. Who would have thought it, Belinda?'

'Oh, you're back, darling. How was it? It really is the worst summer ever.' Belinda was in her green dressing gown and matching moss-coloured slippers.

'It was gorgeous. As it always is.'

'What's wrong, darling? You look a bit . . . grey, like the clouds.'

'I'm going to have to head back to London tomorrow. Dad's changed the date of Lily's rehearsal dinner as he has to go abroad. I'm guessing Lily has had to go with it as Dad will be paying for this extravagant meal.'

'Oh, darling, I understand. I know that Lily wouldn't take it too well if you were absent.'

'No, she wouldn't. And Mum would give me hell too. I'd better head back in the morning.'

'Maybe it's all a sign that you need to get back to your life and start telling people no, darling.' Belinda took her glasses from her head and positioned them on her nose.

'Yup. Guess so.'

Jade thought back to the script she was too nervous to tell Belinda about.

'All you can do is what you feel is right. Tell Lils congrats, and give your mum a squeeze from her old pal, won't you?'

'Sure. I'd better go pack and jump online to see if I can get a train first thing tomorrow.'

Jade folded the few items of clothing she had taken with her and popped them into her backpack. Staring at her phone, she found that she didn't have the energy to call her mum back and hear the predictable moans about having to see Jacquie; she would do it tomorrow. She was still holding her phone when Adam's name popped up with a message. **Where the hell are you?** Jade clicked through to reply quickly, feeling a knot of guilt in her tummy. She once again retrieved Sophie's words from the depths of her memory bank: *Don't catch the guilt.*

Popped to Dorset to see Belinda but am headed home tomorrow. The urge to apologise felt overwhelming but she kept the message short and concise.

Three dots immediately appeared as Adam typed back his response.

Well thanks for telling me. Do you think I'm psychic or something? Pretty selfish move on your part.

Jade's stomach twisted. She sat, fingers hovering over the keys, unsure of which one to press.

I didn't want to wake you this morning. I was going to text you but the reception on the train was bad. She pressed send, then instantly regretted over-explaining her motives.

Whatever.

The rain pelting on the roof had started to subside, and the sound of early evening pulled Jade towards rest. Owls hooted in echoes in distant trees, and light winds swirled and tapped the window frames. She lay on her back staring at the ceiling. Her mind flashed up pictures. Adam in LA, the girl on his lap – what was her name? Jamie? Jacey? Janey? Janey, that was it. Lily's shiny hair, her dad on a flight to somewhere hot. Her body sank into the duvet and she pictured what she needed to do to set herself free.

25

A thin strip of sunlight danced on the wall opposite the bed, the strobe of amber broken by the swaying shadows of branches. Jade's eyes were half open, her eyelids heavy with sleep. Everything was silent, bar the light tapping of rain on the window. She stretched her arms above her head and enjoyed the suspension between sleep and a new day; the nothingness before the torrent of thoughts started up again.

She lowered her arms and spotted the script, still curled at the edges from being rolled up, and slightly damp from the rain. She turned her phone on. It was 8:00am.

'Bugger,' she muttered. She had thirty minutes until her train back to London. She dressed hurriedly, grabbed her things and skipped lightly downstairs, where she could smell coffee brewing. She found Belinda and Don at the kitchen table.

'I'm off, then,' she said in a disappointed tone.

'Oh, darling. Coffee for the road?' Belinda stood, her emerald kaftan moving gently round her body.

'I'd better not. I don't want to miss my train.'

'Tell you what, I'll pour you one in a mug for the car journey to the station.'

'Are you sure you don't mind dropping me? I can always get a cab.'

'Darling, you've more chance catching a space shuttle round here.' Belinda slipped on a pair of wellies. 'Come on. Here's your coffee. Don, say goodbye to Jade.'

Belinda passed her a steaming mug of coffee and Don tilted his head and raised his mug as if to say cheers.

They fell into a comfortable silence once in the car. The windscreen wipers glided over sheets of rain, like ticking hands on a clock. Jade gazed out of the window, not quite ready to leave the tranquillity of the country-side. The field to the left was covered in sunflowers, all with their heads facing down. They looked almost ashamed, perhaps embarrassed that the sun hadn't come out for them.

'Those sunflowers look sad,' Jade whispered. Each stalk was bent at an acute angle just below the flower, a lifeless neck leading to a forlorn head, face to the ground.

'They are, darling. They need the sun. They revel in the heat and light. They're so full of personality, aren't they?'

Jade craned her neck as the car sped past the field. She couldn't take her eyes off the sunflowers. She wasn't sure when her own light had begun to fade, but being by the sea had made her realise that in the last year it had felt so dim that at times it was barely traceable. She knew she could easily blame Adam for her low self-esteem, or her sister for disregarding her existence, her mum for caus-ing moments of stress, her dad for favouring Lily, but she was starting to see that it was up to her to emerge from their shadows. The image of the forlorn sunflow-ers stayed firmly in Jade's mind as she waved Belinda goodbye from the train platform. She felt the shape of the curled-up script in her backpack and tilted her face up towards the sky.

From the train window the sea looked like grey slate, but a small patch of blue was peeking through the clouds. A moment of bright blue hope. Jade laid her head back on the seat and let the seascape rush by.

Her phone beeped.

Where are you?

Adam was awake.

Told you, I'm headed back today. Just on the train now.

His text flew back: There's no food at the flat.

Jade bit down on her tongue then typed: Go to the shops then.

Adam responded: I've got loads on at work, got a Zoom meeting in an hour. Don't you normally do a shop on a Friday?

Jade looked out at the clear line where the grey of the sea met the lighter grey of the sky and wondered why she was putting up with this shit.

Did Jacquie text you about Lily's dinner? she replied, ignoring his previous moan.

Yeah, I've had to move a work thing, annoyingly. I'll be there though.

Of course he would, thought Jade. He wasn't one to pass on an expensive dining experience in one of London's best restaurants, all paid for by her dad. Her eyes rolled in an arc.

She was also pretty sure Adam hadn't had to move a work 'thing' on a Sunday night. She texted back a solitary 'x' and looked back at the coastline rushing by. Droplets of rain slid down the windowpane. A stillness set in. She could sense a small portion of sadness as the end of a chapter loomed, but she could also feel a surge of confidence that felt unexplored. Like a new pair of shoes waiting in their box, smelling fresh and unused, with the promise of true transformation. She picked up her phone to call Colin.

'I've been meaning to call you, Jade. Now what's this email all about?'

'Hey Colin, I—'

'I'm not happy at all. To send an email on a Friday evening about the following week? It is not professional in the slightest. We've got two big projects on, and you've decided to take a break. Well, that's just not how things work in my business.' He spoke calmly but sternly.

'Well, I'm calling because—'

'You know you're replaceable, right?'

Jade had heard all of this before. The same threat had been hurled at Sophie, Jackson, Lethabo and Jade on many occasions. Colin's forehead would go bright red and the veins in his neck would bulge.

'The thing is, Colin—'

'This is your last, *LAST* warning card, Jade. I cannot be dealing with huge commissions from Netflix or Sky when I'm a man down.'

'Woman down,' Jade hastily answered.

'I beg your pardon?'

'I said woman down. I'm not a man.'

'Yes, well, that's beside the point. I cannot have you taking a break whenever you fancy.'

'With all due respect I haven't had a break in over six

months. If you want a team that is strong and able to deal with such an intense workload then I believe we all need adequate time to recharge and recuperate.'

She smiled, shocked at her own forthcoming speech.

'Do you see me taking time off to recharge and recuperate?' Colin argued.

'No, but that is very much your decision. If you did, and maybe you should, we could easily keep things rolling while you're away. Everybody needs time out. Time to be idle. Time to have fun.' She thought back to her chat with Belinda in the kitchen. 'When did you last have fun, Colin?' She gripped the seat beneath her with the tips of her fingers. This new-found confidence was exhilarating and terrifying at the same time. It felt better than sinking into her usual silence, yet totally alien. Her heart pounded in her chest. She was grateful this conversation was on the phone. She didn't have to look into his beady eyes, or at his shining forehead.

'I don't have time for fun.' Colin's words were clipped. Jade could almost hear his pursed lips tightening.

'Well, fun is important. Otherwise, what is the point of all the hard work?' She knew she was convincing herself at the same time as Colin.

'The point is . . . that you work hard,' Colin stuttered.

'Yes, but for what?'

'Well, to . . .' Colin's silence was deafening. 'To pay the bills and to keep this business running,' he continued.

'You're more than paying the bills, Colin. What's the goal? To have a big company for the sake of it? Where's the bit where you reap the rewards and give yourself time out and have fun?'

'I'm too old for fun.' Jade felt his words soften, as if he were accidentally letting the façade slip.

'Come on. You're hardly too old. What is fun to you?'

'Well, I like gardening sometimes.' Colin's voice began to soften further. The harsh edges dissipating.

'Well, do more of that. What else really floats your boat?'

'Well, I'm not too sure any more.' He sounded genuinely taken aback by this line of questioning.

'You need to go and find out what makes you happy.'

'Well, yes . . . *but*, back to you and work, Jade.'

'You haven't let me finish. I'll be in on Monday. My trip has been cut short, so I'll be back at the warehouse as usual.'

'Oh.' Silence.

'OK, so no stress. You don't need to sack me. I'll be there Monday.'

'Well, OK. Good stuff. I've got some jobs I need you to crack on with.' The hard edges of his voice returned.

'Colin, from now on I would prefer to stick to the designated work for the projects we are running. I'm not up for dog walks and dry-cleaning pick-ups any more.' Jade squeezed her hands tightly as if to hold her confidence in place. She squeezed harder waiting for his response.

'Right. Well. I'll find someone else to do it if you can't be bothered.'

She let a wave of anger coarse through her, then exhaled.

'OK. See you Monday.'

She hung up. Rain lashed against the train window, streaks blocking Jade's view of the fields as the train sped by. She relaxed back into her seat. She felt grown up, which was a jarring admission at the age of thirty-two. It had been a mature transaction on her part. She had said what she wanted and nothing bad had happened. She felt proud of herself.

Picking her phone back up, she punched words onto the screen, wanting to act quickly in case the wave of confidence fizzled out.

Lils, I'm going to need help making the floral archway at the wedding on the day. It's too big of a job to do on my own. I propose I bring my workmate Sophie who is highly skilled.] x

She pressed send and sat staring at her screen. Ten seconds later three dots appeared in the chatbox as her sister typed back: She can help you build it beforehand, but she can't be there on the day. It's a no.

Jade typed back, more feverishly this time: Well I can't do it then. It's not humanly possible to build on the day on my own.

Lily's text fired back almost instantly: Oh, ffs. If you really can't work quickly enough, then fine.

Jade laughed at her sister's relentless need to get a dig in.

Another text followed: She cannot stay for the wedding though.

Jade thought about this. It would be so wonderful to have Sophie there at this hideous and triggering event. She said '*Fuck it*' aloud and typed back: If she stays in my room for the ceremony and lunch, can I bring her out for the party bit?

No.

Well you'll have to pay her then. Jade smiled.

OK. If you really are that needy. She can come to the party bit, ONLY the party bit.

Jade punched the air. She drew the rolled-up script she had found in the pub out of her backpack like a sword, then, smoothing it down, she glanced at the words again. She mulled over how she might use this new-found confidence around the restaurant table tonight.

A small smile crawled over Jade's face. One eyebrow slowly rose. Flattening out the curled script, she grabbed a pen from her bag. Without the means to erase anything, she turned to the last few blank pages. Perhaps this was what those naked pages had always been for: completely rewriting the script. Bright white paper stared back at her. She thought back to her childhood, her desk, the Tupperware of pens, the reams of paper to draw on.

Breathing in deeply, the warmth in her chest rose to her cheeks and she smiled again – more broadly this time. Putting the nib of the pen to paper, she began to write with speed. Words poured out of her onto the blank page. She let her brain flatline so feeling could take over. It might not work, just as the previous attempts had so desperately failed to come to fruition.

But also . . . it just might.

26

'That's a bit full-on for dinner, isn't it?' Adam walked into the bedroom in his pants.

Jade stood in front of the mirror in a pink dress she had bought years ago but had always felt too nervous to wear. She knew Adam would hate it – his own style was much more minimal, monochrome, and, as he called it, *classic*. The pink dress had sleeves that were voluminous, billowing from shoulder to elbow. Its waist pinched before the fabric cascaded down to just below her knees in luxurious folds.

'I love it, so I'm wearing it.'

'You look like a stick of candyfloss,' Adam said, pulling his trousers on.

'Good.' Jade shrugged and turned on her heel. She looked in the hall mirror at her face. Usually, she wouldn't linger. A feeling of deep discomfort would set in if she spent too long looking at her big eyes, invisible eyelids and the three clustered moles that sat atop her eyebrow. An ex-boyfriend had told her it looked like a bird had shat on her. Another of the small mental scars that she carried.

It was time to let go of this self-loathing. She was no longer willing to lug other people's words around. Today she looked directly into her own eyes, let her hand skim across her face. One day she knew she would look back at photos of herself at this age and admire the plumpness of her cheeks and the fullness of her bottom lip, the soft skin on her upper arms and thighs. She smiled. Her uneven teeth that she normally concealed in photos gleamed back at her imperfectly. Holding the smile, she closed her lips and made a promise to look at herself in the mirror every day.

'You look great,' she whispered to herself, shocked at her own little voice.

'Who are you talking to?' Adam yelled from the bedroom.

'Myself,' she replied, consciously blunt. These were the very boundaries Jackson had spoken of. She would not let Adam's opinions or slights impact her tonight. She had the strength to hold on to this newly felt confidence for one night, surely?

'Come on then, candyfloss, we'd better go.' Adam's tone was more sneering than affectionate. Jade pulled her shoulders back and let the fabric move around her body.

For the last hour she had been running through her newly written script. As she had stood under the shower, she'd mouthed the words silently. When she was putting her dress on, she had closed her eyes and imagined herself at the dinner table, speaking her written words aloud. She was one step closer to finding out if it was possible. Small flutters of nerves skipped over her chest. Looking back at the mirror in the hallway once more, she smiled at her reflection and closed the door behind her.

*

Steam clung to the windows of Scalini's, the hot breath of conversation emanating from inside. Young wealthy couples looked unfazed by the fine dining in front of them; all loafers, no socks, and designer handbags. A group of older ladies sat with perfectly coiffed hair held in place by excessive amounts of hairspray, red-lacquered lips slapping together as words spilled from their mouths. Families gathered, champagne held aloft. It was a heady mix of conversation, laughter and financial exhibitionism that made Jade's head spin. She breathed in the last of the night's cool air before pushing the heavy door into the restaurant.

The maître d' stood proudly at the front desk. For a moment she felt foolish for wearing the dress. She steadied herself, then smiled and announced that she was there under the name of Shaw – Tony Shaw.

'Why does your dad love it in here so much? It's so hectic and old-fashioned,' Adam said, looking into the bustling restaurant.

'That's *why* he likes it. He loves the theatre of it all. The waiters dressed in white, the photos of celebrities on the walls. He gets a kick out of it.' Jade kept the tone light rather than feeling resentful that Adam was in fact already moaning about getting a free meal in one of London's best restaurants. She was in a good mood. They weaved in and out of diners to reach the long oval table set for the rehearsal meal.

'Oh, darling Birdy. What have you come as? A flamingo?' Lily laughed, her black bob swinging so violently it looked as if it might fly off, her hands smoothing down her own black body-hugging dress. Her angular shoulders looked almost mechanical. 'Look at Birdy, James. Gosh, what a . . . bright colour.'

Jade smiled. 'It's just a dress. Thought I'd give it a spin for your big dinner.' Her hands started to shake. She would not be knocked. Not tonight.

She kissed her sister on the cheek and let her eyes linger on her black hair. Not a single split end. She moved towards James and gave him a brief hug, then moved across to her mum.

'Hi, Mum. You OK?' Jade spoke with genuine empathy. Sue looked anxious, grey hollows under her mascara-laden eyes. Jade knew that she found being around Jacquie difficult, and that she would have spent far too long choosing her outfit for the dinner. Jade hadn't seen the tangerine velvet top and matching wide-leg trousers before, so assumed they were newly bought for tonight. Her mum's hair was worn in a long plait, a thick orange headband pushing strands from her face. A pair of yellow Adidas trainers poked out the ends of her trousers.

'Yes, yes, darling. I'm fine. Gasping for a wine.'

'Well, let's just wait until Dad gets here before we start ordering drinks, eh.' Jade patted the skirt of her dress and sat next to her sister. Adam had already settled down next to James – they were shaking hands at the other end of the table, muttering about football results to break the ice.

'Mum, do this.' Jade rubbed her index finger over her front teeth. 'Lippie.'

Sue copied Jade, curling her lip up and removing a stain of pink from her teeth with her finger. 'Maybe I'll just order one small glass now,' she said. 'Then I can drink it before they even arrive.'

'It's going to be OK. Just take some deep breaths.'

'Deep breaths? How is that going to help once Jacquie starts boasting about their latest holiday?'

'Just pace it, OK?'

Sue rolled her eyes and sat back in her chair, visibly biting the inside of her cheek. Her bangles rattled as she rearranged the heavy beaded necklace that hung from her neck. The yellow beads jolted Jade's mind back to childhood; she was sure her dad had given them to her mum when she was a tiny kid. Maybe this was Sue's small attempt at one-upping Jacquie.

'I saw Belinda yesterday. She sends her love,' Jade said, trying to distract her mum.

'Oh, I must go visit. Life is just too busy. It all whizzes by. Is she OK?'

'She's great. I wish I could have stayed longer but I obviously couldn't miss this.' Jade nodded to Lily with wide eyes. Her mum did not pick up on the sarcasm.

'Where the hell are Tony and thingy? It's 7:35pm, for god's sake.' Sue looked about the restaurant irritably.

'Mum, they're five minutes late. Just try and relax. And please do not call her thingy when she gets here,' Jade said with genuine concern.

'Darling, the worst thing you can say to someone when they are stressed is "relax". I just want a bloody Pinot Grigio, is that too much to ask?'

'Just try and wait. They'll be here any minute, I'm sure.'

Lily turned from James and Adam and leaned her bony elbows on the table. 'Mum, you'll love this new project I'm working on. It's really allowing me to express my artistic side.'

A laugh escaped Jade's mouth. Lily's head spun round with speed, her huge eyes wider than normal, her smile fixed in an over-egged grimace. 'What?' she spat.

'No, no, nothing. Carry on.' Jade looked away from her stare.

'No, what were you laughing about?'

'Well, I guess it's just a new thing for you to have an artistic flare.' Jade emphasised the word 'artistic', barely believing what was coming out of her mouth.

'Erm, I'm *extremely* artistic, Birds.' Each of Lily's very white straight teeth gleamed as she enunciated the word 'extremely'.

'Are you, though?' Jade gently gibed again.

'I've been working on/off in the arts for years, thank you.' Lily reapplied her smile and relaxed back into her usual self-assured patter.

'Well—'

'I'm a – what's the word? – polymath,' Lily said confidently.

'Oh, what an extraordinary word, what does that mean, darling?' Sue asked, parking her anxiety for a minute.

'Jack of all trades,' Jade threw back to her mum.

'Well, it's more . . . *expert in multiple areas*, but yes, jack

241

of all trades works, I suppose.' Lily pushed her shiny black hair behind one ear, revealing large diamond-drop earrings.

'I guess when you're a jack of all trades you don't end up honing one individual skill like I've been able to do in set-building; that's all.' Jade paused, letting the awkwardness bed in. 'That's why I laughed, I guess.' Jade shrugged and leaned back in her chair.

Lily, unnerved, continued as if Jade hadn't spoken, 'Well, anyway, it's a beautiful house in Suffolk. Real potential. I've had several online consultations with the owners now and they're really loving my mood boards.'

'Hello, you delightful lot,' Tony bellowed as he moved towards the table, jacket open and flapping at the edges, belly and chest protruding forwards. 'And fellas.' He nodded and laughed loudly in Adam and James's direction. Tony was a large man both in height and width, and to Jade he seemed even larger this evening, his volume adding to his general hugeness.

'Hey, Daddy,' Lily squealed in a baby voice. She stood up and lurched at her father before anyone else had the chance, her hug lingering and dramatic.

'Lils, darling, you look a million dollars.' Tony brought one large hand up to his chin and scratched at his stubble.

'Oh, sorry we're late,' said Jacquie, looking flustered. 'It's been one hell of a week. Suitcases everywhere as usual. Hello, Sue.' Jacquie's pillar-box-red hair was piled on top of her head and bouncing as she moved. She leaned in towards Sue, who visibly stiffened.

'Jacquie, lovely to see you.' Sue kept her eyes on her own hands rather than looking into Jacquie's eyes.

'Jade, what a lovely dress. You don't normally wear dresses, sweetheart.'

Jade was genuinely relieved for the compliment. 'Thanks, Jacs.' She stood to hug her, but kept her eyes on her mum. If Jade showed Jacquie too much affection Sue's mood would worsen and her drinking would gather speed.

'Well, thank god you're here at last.' Sue directed her words towards Tony and stood up and kissed him on the cheek.

'I'm not in control of London traffic sadly, Sue.' Tony laughed loudly and sat down next to Jacquie, squeezing her thigh in a reassuring way.

'So, drinks.' Sue looked behind her to try and spot one of the white-coated waiters.

'Hold your horses, Sue, I've not even looked at the wine menu.' Tony delivered this line to the whole table.

'Well, I know what I'm having,' she replied, craning her neck the other way to try and get the attention of a waiter.

'Well, shouldn't we just let Tony order a few bottles, rather than glass by glass?' Jacquie forced a smile in Sue's direction. Jade started to tap her feet under the table. The tension was already mounting, and they hadn't even ordered their starters.

Sue pressed her lips together firmly and turned away from Jacquie. Her long plait whipped like a snake behind her.

'They do a lovely red here, don't they, Tony?' Jacquie said breezily.

'I actually prefer white.' Sue's voice rose in volume slightly.

'Two bottles of red and a white for Sue, then we're all good.' Tony slammed the wine list shut.

'I was actually leaning towards a peach bellini, Dad.' Lily pouted at her father.

'Go on, then. Bellini for you, Lils.'

'Negroni for me please, Tony.' Adam raised his hand casually and spoke without fear of asking for what he wanted.

'Bloody hell.' Tony looked over his shoulder and caught the eye of a waiter.

'Toneeeeeeey.' The waiter, his white jacket perfectly matching his snowy hair, raced over and placed his hands on Tony's shoulders. 'And the whole Shaw family. Hello, ciao, welcome. It has been too long, Mr Shaw. Welcome back. What can I get? Olives? Bread? Wine?'

'Carlo, thank you. Yes, yes, all of it please. Booze-wise . . . two bottles of your best red, a bottle of white, one bellini for my bella Lily here, and a negroni for this young man.' He patted Carlo on the back firmly with his large hands. Carlo nodded and made his way towards the kitchen.

'So, not long until the big day, eh. James, you going to look after my princess?' Tony sat back, his legs apart, taking up as much space as possible.

'Of course, Tony. Only a few weeks to go but I think we've got everything sorted.'

'Well, I should bloody hope so. And I hope you've been spending my money wisely.' Tony's bellowing laughter barely distracted from his need to boast about how much money he had parted with. He picked up an olive from a bowl that had been placed next to some fluffy focaccia on the white tablecloth. Popping the olive into his mouth whole, he then deposited the stone like he had just skinned an animal – plucked out by his large fingers without a scrap of olive flesh attached.

Jade caught the tail end of the conversation. She had assumed that her dad had given Lily and James money towards their wedding, but this was the verbal confirmation she needed. She nodded in the direction of her mum, who was explaining to her how her friend Pauline had recently been diagnosed with a prolapsed rectum, and, still focused on her mum's mouth, tuned into Lily and Tony's conversation.

'Your contribution has been really great, Dad, but we need a little help with the honeymoon. Everything just seemed to go up in price from our initial wedding ideas to the time we actually got around to booking everything. Who knew flowers were so expensive?' Lily threw her hands up in faux shock.

'Everybody, dear. Everybody knew that.' Jacquie, unable to help herself, slipped into the sidelines of the conversation.

'So we've had to use our honeymoon budget on all the food and drink, as we really want to ensure everybody has a perfect time,' Lily continued without registering Jacquie's comment. James nodded and remained silent, staring at his wife-to-be.

'How much you need?' Tony plucked another olive stone from his teeth.

'Well, we're off to Capri for just a little break because obviously I hate to leave the girls. Two weeks in the Capri Palace and then maybe a few days in Sorrento to really rest up.'

Jade looked down at her hands in her lap, aware that her mum was still talking at her. Over two weeks sounded like a very long trip away from Saffron and Jemima and a much longer stint than Lily had discussed with her. The rage began to build in her neck. Flaring her nostrils, she drew deep breaths in to keep her anger from rising to the surface. Now was not the time. She sipped water and carried on nodding at her mum.

'Well, this better be your last wedding, Lils. It's turning out to be quite the production.' Tony looked at James and winked.

'Dad, of course. We just want to make some really special memories. James has been such a great stepdad to the girls. It'll be a really lovely break for us to process the wedding day itself and rest after such a busy period.'

'I'll sort it,' Tony said nonchalantly. 'Jacquie, make a note in your phone for me and get Elizabeth to transfer the money to Lily tomorrow.' Tony looked behind him for the waiter as Jacquie unwillingly typed the note into her phone.

'Was your last wedding this expensive, Lily?' Jacquie

asked with a fake smile plastered on her face. Her red lips matched the colour of hair dye she used.

'About the same I think, Jacquie. But do remember, because Jade's wedding to Navi didn't go ahead, Dad did end up saving quite a bit in terms of any family wedding budget.'

Adam's head whipped round with the mention of Navi.

Jade felt her whole body turn ice-cold. How could she bring this up casually in conversation in front of a whole table of people? Tingles ran across her skull; it felt as if she might leave her own body. Inhaling more deeply, she felt all eyes on her. There had never been a family discussion after Jade had walked away from marrying Navi. She had called it off only weeks before the wedding day and no one ever spoke of it again.

It had been a harsh severing of two lives. Jade and Navi's names had once been uttered as one word, their friends intertwined, their families merged. On the day that Jade walked out, their lives instantly fell away from each other, like cooked meat from a bone. She had mentioned her near-marriage to Adam in the early days of their relationship, but it wasn't a topic either of them wanted to bring up again. Jade had always relied on an unspoken agreement that no one mentioned that period of her life. Now, Lily's desperation to validate her need for their dad's money had overridden common sense and decency.

Sue jumped in. 'Let's not talk about that, eh, Lils?' She tried to look sympathetic and nodded at Jade while anxiously repositioning her orange headband.

'Well, I'm just making a point that it was only the venue deposit for Jade's non-starter wedding that was lost, so Dad ended up saving quite a bit of cash in the end.' Lily's obliviousness was written across her face.

Jade continued to take deep breaths and didn't make eye contact with anyone. She would not think about Navi. Not tonight. She let his face crack into fragments in her mind and concentrated on her pink dress and the shred of confidence she still had.

Lily turned back to Tony. 'Well, anyway, thanks Dad. Love you.' She rubbed her hands together and looked at James. Jade felt her teeth clench together. Breathe, breathe, she thought.

'Well, Jade? What do you think Pauline should do? Regarding her . . .' Sue mouthed the words *prolapsed rectum*.

'I don't know, Mum. Just . . . send her some flowers or something?' Jade's voice sounded distant and distracted.

'I don't think flowers will be much use. Anyway, where the hell is that sodding wine? Are they hand-crushing the grapes back there?'

'Sir, red or white?' A slick-haired waiter appeared behind Tony and leaned to his right.

'Red, lovely.'

'Mine's the white,' Sue hollered.

The waiter ignored Sue and moved to Jacquie.

'Red, please.' Jacquie grinned politely; her red lipstick now slightly smeared outside of her lip line.

'White, please.' Sue grabbed the glass from the waiter before he could place it down on the table. She took three large gulps then sighed.

'Shall we order food while the waiter's here?' Jacquie clearly wanted this dinner to be over even more than Jade did. Jade smiled broadly at her stepmum.

'We've barely been here two minutes, Jacquie. I've not even looked yet.' Sue took one large gulp of wine, mouth open like a goldfish, to finish off her drink. 'I would love another wine, though, please.'

'Well, I tell you what, I know what I want so I'll crack on and order.' Jacquie kept her eyes on the waiter. 'We'll just do mains and puds, right? No starters.' Jacquie looked to Tony.

'Alright, Jacs, hold tight, it's Lily's rehearsal dinner. If I can't have three courses on my baby girl's big celebration, then when can I?'

'Well, it's not the *actual* big celebration,' Jacquie said, giving Jade a knowing look. Jade raised her eyebrows in recognition. 'But, anyway, you lot can do starters if you want. I'll just go for a main and a pud. Can I have the sea bass from the Secondi section, please, and I'll order my dessert later.' Jacquie closed her menu with a little too much vigour.

The waiter nodded and scribbled quickly in his note-pad. 'Madam, for you?'

Sue looked up. 'Oh, bloody hell. Well, I'm making a rushed decision here, but I'll have the prawns to start and the pasta Alfredo for my main. Ta. And another glass of white.' She held out her glass.

'I'll go next,' Lily said, her smile bordering on smug. 'I'm vegan at the moment, guys.' Her face beamed around the table.

Jade looked down at the menu which featured every variation of animal product possible. 'Good luck with that.'

'Does the tomato salad feature cheese?' Lily looked wistfully towards the waiter.

'*Feature* cheese? It's not a recording artist.' Jade shook her head, wondering how they were even related. Lily ignored her.

The waiter smiled through the family tension, replying, 'Yes, there is tomato, basil and mozzarella.'

'OK, yes I'll have that,' Lily said cordially.

'Mozzarella is cheese, Lils.' Jade's eyebrows furrowed.

'Well, it's only a little bit in a salad.'

Jade sighed deeply.

'And for my main—'

Jade jumped in, 'Are you going to ask if the turbot has fish in it? Because I'm imagining it does.' The words escaped her mouth before she had time to think them through. She felt a tingle of fun course through her.

'Jade!' Sue scolded, almost as if she were talking to a dog.

'Does the tagliatelle have dairy in it?' Lily continued, undeterred.

'Yes, madam.'

'Oh well, I'll have that anyway please. It is *my* rehearsal dinner after all,' she said, dismissing James's existence altogether. 'Thank you.' She handed the waiter the menu, tilting her head coquettishly.

Jade ordered the tomato pasta, which, ironically, was vegan, and sat waiting for the scripted part of the evening to arrive. Thinking back to the words on the pages she had read on the train from Dorset, she knew it would begin to unfurl before the starters came out. It could be any second. The room seemed to fall quiet as Jade ran through the new part of the script she had penned on the blank pages. Would she have the confidence in the moment to say the words aloud? She felt anxious, as she often did when all her family were together, but a little mischievous too. Everybody was so used to her being very quiet and accommodating, and she was bored of it. She had nothing to lose. She looked up at various family members talking at each other and heard her tummy rumble.

27

'Oh, Daddy, I got you a gift to say thank you for tonight. Just a little something I picked up at Dukes while I was on my holistic hen?' Lily thrust a small package in his direction.

Daddy? She really was pulling out all the stops now she had a free honeymoon in the bag, Jade thought. Blinking slowly, she forced a smile.

'Oh, you little gem. Pour me another red while I open it, Lils.' Tony held his hands out in Lily's direction, his large fingers grappling with the tightly wrapped paper and strips of tape. Within the layers of wrapping and tissue paper sat a brown leather passport cover with 'TMS' stamped in gold at the bottom.

'Oh, lovely, darling. Very classy.'

'Did you see your initials at the bottom? I got it in the hotel boutique where they have their own monogramming service. Isn't it gorgeous?' Lily pushed her silky hair behind her ears with both hands.

'What's the M, Tony? What's your middle name?' Adam asked, pretending to care.

'Morris. Tony Morris Shaw. *The* Tony Morris Shaw, that's me.' Tony's laughter boomed as he placed the new passport holder next to his wine on the table.

'Well, it'll be handy come September, as Tony and I

are off to Brazil. It's part work trip, as there are some properties we're going to look at—'

Jade sat bolt upright. Oh god, here we go. She knew the script was imminent, but this felt too soon.

Sue slammed her glass down on the table with a little too much force, her newly refilled wine splashing over the sides. '*We*? Is it a joint business now?' Her bangles clashed together as she spoke.

Jacquie's eyes narrowed to a squint. 'Oh, you know what I mean. *We'll* look, *Tony* will do the business part.'

Sue rolled her eyes to the ceiling. Jade felt the temperature drop.

'Then we're off to stay at an eco-lodge an hour outside of Rio. We're trying to learn as much as we can about sustainable living as it's a smart business move to convert as many of our, sorry, *Tony's* properties going forward.' Jacquie fake-smiled in Sue's direction.

Jade looked across and noticed her sister listening with an exaggerated smile that barely masked her jealousy.

Sue swilled her wine around the glass then swallowed two mouthfuls in one. 'Sounds lovely,' she said, slurring slightly. Jade could feel her mum's anger in each syllable, the table almost vibrating.

'Oh, that sounds fab,' Lily blurted out. 'I once stayed at the Fasano Hotel in Rio. It was divine. I was working on a project there in my days as a party organiser. The manager is called Fabian and is quite literally FAB. You must pop in.'

'Oh, darling, you did know how to put on a great

party,' Sue said loudly, as if to show Jacquie how supportive she was towards her daughters. 'You really were the best event organiser out there.' She had nearly finished her second wine. She looked over her shoulder for the waiter.

'Yeah, Lils, we've been there,' Tony said. 'Think I met Fabian when we were over for the carnival one February.' He spoke casually, as if visiting Rio was an everyday affair. 'We've got a lot of work to do out there, though. Not too much of a holiday, Jacs. Got to keep working hard to expand the portfolio. These properties won't buy themselves.' Tony looked directly into Jade's eyes.

Jade picked the skin on her thumbs. *Do not react. Do not react.* She sat patiently waiting for her moment.

'I've heard the scene is pretty good out there at the moment, fashion-wise. I might have to swing by at some point and do a recce.' Adam swigged from his negroni and tried to match Tony's nonchalant tone.

'You don't really swing by, matey. It's a long old flight and not a cheap one. If you're going to be supporting my daughter here you might want to recce nearer to home.' Tony chuckled, making light of his disparaging comment.

'With all due respect, Tony, all businesses have to start out struggling somewhat, with optimistic, confident projections for the future. Putting in the work now means big rewards down the line.' Adam ran his fingers through his hair, the blonde sections separating from the darker shades beneath.

Jade was starting to actually enjoy watching this scene

unfold. It all seemed so ludicrous. One drink in, and everyone was allowing their worst traits to rise to the surface. She remained poker-faced and silent.

'Been there, matey,' Tony replied, 'got the T-shirt. But let me tell you, I wasn't dashing off to Rio in the early days. I was working twelve- to fifteen-hour days. Rio comes later—'

Adam trampled over his last words: 'Times have changed, Tony.'

Tony ignored him and looked over his large shoulder. 'Another bottle, please.'

Jade looked directly at her sister, remembering that she was about to start boasting about her interiors. Two seconds later, Lily looked up at their dad with purpose.

'My interiors business is really taking off, talking of business, Dad. I've had tons of bookings for online consultations and a few prospective clients wanting full renovations.'

'Lovely, darling, well done.' Tony was dismissive, much more interested in his newly poured wine.

'It's a lot of work but it's really taking off.'

Jade sat studying her sister – this creature who shared the same blood, arched eyebrows and foot size, yet was her opposite in every other way. She took in her sister's smooth skin, her barely-there make-up that would have taken her hours, her thin veiny arms and shellac-coated nails.

Jacquie cut through Jade's thoughts.

'Oh, how brilliant. You'll have to help us do a few of our properties up.'

Sue gulped down the last sip of her third glass. '*Tony's* properties up.'

'What's your point, Sue? I've been with Tony for twelve years now. It's really none of your business.'

Jade's eyes widened. She knew what was coming but it was still a shock to see her mum and Jacquie having it out in front of everyone. Two women so familiar to her but so unfamiliar as a pair.

'Mum, maybe make that your last glass of wine,' Lily bellowed from across the table. Jade placed her arm lightly on her mum's shoulder.

'Yes, if you could, Sue. You've already done a whole bottle and we're only on our starters,' Jacquie added.

Jade's eyes moved from one woman to the other like following a ball in a game of tennis. Mum, stepmum, mum, stepmum.

'Go easy on her, guys. It can't be easy for Sue,' Adam chimed in. Jade had almost forgotten this moment when her boyfriend decided it was appropriate to get involved.

'Pipe down, matey,' Tony said. 'Leave this one to the adults.'

Jade used every inch of willpower not to smile.

'I'm thirty-three, Tony.' Adam looked like a little boy at the dinner table.

Wanker, thought Jade.

'This is all getting unnecessarily tense. Aren't we meant to be celebrating Lily and James tonight, guys?' Jacquie straightened her hair.

'Yes, yes we are.' Lily bounced her fist delicately on the table, half diva, half toddler.

'We are celebrating you, Lils. Raise a glass for my princess and James.' Tony thrust his glass high into the air, red wine lapping over the sides and onto the white tablecloth. Adam raised his negroni. Everyone else remained still as statues.

'Can we slow down on the wine, though, everyone? This is clearly not a cheap restaurant so to have brazenly drunk a whole bottle already is thoughtless, Sue.' Jacquie's pent-up anger had started to rise out of her.

'Well, it's also *clearly* not your money, Jacquie, so it shouldn't bother you too much.' Sue was really slurring now. Jade kept her eyes fixed on the red spills of wine on the tablecloth that were starting to spread into bigger, fainter blotches.

'Well, you would know, Sue. That lovely cottage you live in didn't buy itself, did it?' Jacquie stuck her chin out as she spoke. Jade noticed a couple on a nearby table glance over their shoulders to watch.

'No, it didn't. That lovely cottage is what you get after putting up with *that* for twenty years.' Sue's right hand, clutching her glass, jutted out in Tony's direction, splattering wine all over the front of Jade's dress. Jade leapt back and looked down at her damp lap. This was really getting out of hand. More diners had started to turn their heads to see the drama, attempting to not look too obvious. Lily waded in, trying to take the higher ground.

'Mum, Dad's work ethic, which I've been lucky enough to inherit, has paid off in your favour.' Lily pushed her shoulders back so her sharp collarbones protruded. One of her drop earrings was illuminated momentarily in the overhead lighting.

'Jacquie has got a point though,' James suddenly said. 'Do you think you have a drink problem, Sue?' James's first contribution felt jarring to Jade. A new voice in the drama.

'James, you've been part of this family for all of two minutes, I don't think you should be getting involved here.' Adam placed a patronising hand on James's left shoulder. James stared down at Adam's hand without moving.

'This is a joke. I worked so hard trying to organise a wonderful dinner for Lily, and look at you all. It's embarrassing.' Jacquie, on the verge of tears, flung her arms about like a rag doll.

Jade counted the two long seconds of silence in her head before standing on her shaky legs. She heard her own voice leave her mouth. It was calm, crystal clear, measured.

'ALL OF YOU, JUST SHUT THE FUCK UP.'

The whole restaurant fell silent. Time froze; she was on her feet but weightless, suspended in air. Her hands spread out on the table, her arms rigidly keeping her upright. Each family member sat looking up at Jade's face with wide eyes, unable to process what was happening. The restaurant began to chatter again in whispers. Jade felt the adrenaline course through her body, cool white cortisol running up her spine. She looked at her mum.

'Mum, you need to stop drinking. You're a wonderful

person, I love you, but under the influence of alcohol you're not your best.'

Lily stood up. Jade put her hands on her sister's shoulders and pushed her back down. 'Lily, you are a first-class piss-taker. You've managed to get Dad to pay for most of your wedding *and* now a honeymoon. You're clueless. You've barely worked a day in your life, jumping from job to job. You seriously haven't got a clue.'

Lily's bottom jaw jutted out in shock. Before she had a chance to retort, Jade moved on to the next family member, her head turning slowly and precisely like an owl. 'James, you've been brainwashed by my sister. I'm afraid to say you're fanny-struck, my friend.'

James looked down at his hands in his lap.

Jade turned and fixed her eyes on her dad. 'Dad, please can you stop mentioning how lucky I am to live in one of your many properties? Have you forgotten that I pay you full rent? All while Lily continues to raid your bank account. If you want me out of there, can you please be clear about it and just say.'

Jade turned to Jacquie. 'Jacquie, you've been a wonderful stepmum to me over the years. I'll always be grateful for that.' She quickly glanced towards her mum. 'Just try and be compassionate towards Mum. This isn't easy for her, and I hate being in the middle of you both.'

In slow motion she turned to Adam. His face suggested he assumed he would be spared a grilling; it was relaxed and almost cheerful watching her performance. Jade remained calm and looked directly into his eyes.

'And as for you; we're done. Get your shit out of my flat as soon as possible.'

Adam's face burned red. She watched it happen; his pale skin turn from milk to blood. She realised she had never seen him go red, or even look mildly embarrassed before.

'Have a lovely evening everyone.' Jade tipped her head as if she were wearing a hat. She picked up her bag and for a split second imagined tipping the table over, drinks and olives flying in slow motion. Her fingers twitched, but her arms remained by her sides. She turned on her heel, letting the fabric of her pink dress swirl in a perfect circle as she moved. 'Night, Carlo.' She waved and smiled at the waiters as she pushed through the heavy varnished doors.

She stood outside the restaurant for a moment, letting her face feel the cool air. The street-lamps glowed and the scent of summer moved around her gently. She grinned broadly. There had been no hesitation or effort. She had said the words. Every single one of them.

28

'I think I took the boundary thing a bit far, Jackson.' Jade removed her cycling helmet and hung it on a hook, sweat forming in a small pool on her upper lip.

Jackson, in his usual tight jeans and a Soundgarden T-shirt, was spray-painting giant luminous letters to look like neon lighting. The Verve played on the speakers, as always a little too loud for decent conversation.

'Morning, Jade. Go on . . . ?' Jackson replied, barely audible. He carried on painting, Jade standing back to admire the smooth glide of his paintbrush.

'I kind of annihilated my whole family at dinner last night. I think I took it too far.'

'I guess it's all subjective, Jade.'

'But, I mean, I truly annihilated them.' Jade was desperate to tell Jackson about how she had freely written on the blank pages of the script, how she had poured out everything she had previously kept locked inside for years. How, in that moment on the train journey home from Dorset, she had assumed that her written words would remain on the page and would never actually have life breathed into them. Yet explaining all of this was too weird and too complicated. She would save it for Sophie later.

'I even dumped Adam. He didn't come back to the

flat last night so I'm guessing he stayed at Tommo's or Benny's.'

'Well, I think that was on the cards anyway.' Jackson spoke slowly and steadily.

'Yes, I guess so but, well, I told my sister she was a piss-taker and then told her husband-to-be he was fanny-struck. I actually wanted to use the C-word but I was in a public place.'

'Are either of those statements lies?' Jackson's genuine line of questioning made Jade step back.

'Well, no, not exactly. They're very much my opinion, but I think most would agree they're true.'

'So, you've told some people in your family the truth.' Jackson kept his eyes on the wooden board in front of him.

'Yes. But I did it in a really shitty way.'

'OK, so there's room for improvement. But I'd say don't beat yourself up too much. Sometimes people need to be humbled by the truth.' Jackson's hands moved steadily as he twisted and turned his long paintbrush.

'So did I get boundaries right?'

'Jade, that's not for me to say. If you feel edgy about it, I suggest that next time you do it more privately. The key is to have dealt with your own emotions thoroughly, so when you have that moment of confrontation or discussion your words aren't loaded.' Jackson spoke without judgement, his wisdom quietly leaving his mouth without any emotion woven into it.

'What do you mean by "dealt with your emotions"?'

Jade was genuinely intrigued. She felt childlike asking but knew Jackson wouldn't judge her.

Jackson's brush ran in a perfect straight line from the top of the board to the bottom to form the beginning of a new letter.

'Sorting your emotions out is essentially being aware of them. So, with your sister the emotion is irritation, correct?'

Jade nodded.

'So, you notice the irritation. You understand that it is *your* irritation, that she can't make you feel anything. Nobody can *make* you feel anything. We all have a choice as to how we react to each individual in our lives. So, once you recognise your irritation you separate that from your sister. Then you set a boundary with her calmly, because your main objective is to be irritated by her less. Your intentions are therefore coming from a good place. Your intention is to help her understand what is OK and what is not, giving you a better chance of not being irritated in the future.'

As Jackson spoke, he barely moved his head or neck, keeping steady and still to ensure each letter was perfect and fluid.

'OK, OK, I get it. I absolutely did *not* do that at dinner, but I get it. God, you're good at this.'

Jackson carried on painting bulbous letters without looking in Jade's direction.

Jade rushed to the back room, where Sophie was rolling a cigarette.

'Morning, babes.'

Jade hugged her with force. 'Jackson is so unnervingly quiet at times but my god when he does speak it's prophetic. He's a wise old sage in an indie rocker's slender body.'

'I know, he's like Alex Turner in an ashram. What a gem. I love him. I'm headed out for a fag. Joining?' Sophie walked off towards the sliding door.

Outside, she and Sophie leaned up against the wall by the bins, the warmth of August enveloping their bare arms.

'Soph, last night was wild.' Jade's eyes widened in Sophie's direction.

'Did you go out without me?'

'No. Well yes, but not *out* out. It was Lily's rehearsal dinner.'

'Lily's rehearsal dinner was wild?'

'Well, at the weekend I found one of the creepy fortune-telling scripts in Dorset. The scene was set at the dinner. On the train back to London I scribbled exactly what I wanted to say on the blank pages at the back of the script, and then at the dinner I said the actual words out loud. I didn't think it was going to work, so when I was rewriting the script, I really went for it – and every single word came out of my mouth.' Jade spoke without breathing or pausing between sentences.

'Oh my god, babes, tell me. What happened?' Sophie blew clouds of smoke out of her mouth with excitement.

'Everyone was there. First time Mum and Jacquie had been in a room together in a long while.'

'Oh god.' Sophie touched her lips to the roll-up.

'It was a classic case of everyone drinking from the

get-go to cut through the awkwardness, which subsequently drew out their very worst sides. Lily even brought up Navi. I still can't believe it. She mentioned him *and* the wedding that never happened, so casually. She knows how tough that was, yet she almost sang his name aloud at the table like she was reciting a nursery rhyme. I stayed silent as they all talked at each other, getting more inebriated by the minute.'

'I can't believe she brought that up.' Sophie shook her head.

'I know. Anyway, I haven't even gotten to the wild bit. Soph, before we had even been served our starters I stood up – I'm not even sure how as I hate anyone looking at me – but somehow, I found myself on my feet towering above all of them. I then said exactly what I thought of each of them to their faces. I really went for it. Every word I had written in ink on the blank pages of the script came out of my mouth. I didn't have to think or try, they just slipped out effortlessly.'

Sophie stubbed her roll-up out and immediately started clapping her hands.

'Then I dumped Adam in front of everyone.'

Sophie leaned in and hugged Jade tightly. 'What did they do?' she asked, her face alive with anticipation.

'They just sat there, staring at me. At one point Lily tried to interject but I sort of pushed her back down and continued my rant. It was like some greater force took over. Then I walked out.'

'Holy shit. This is insane. How do you feel about it all now?'

'Relieved, in a way. It's like I got to exorcise years of pent-up anger in two minutes. I have to admit that directly afterwards, stood outside on the street, I felt fucking fantastic. But now I do feel quite edgy. I've thought about it too much. Played it over in my head a hundred times. I'm fighting off the guilt somewhat.'

'Well, that's natural. When you change and don't act in the way that everyone is used to, it always ruffles feathers.'

'I think I did more than ruffle feathers. I skinned them alive.'

'Have you spoken to any of them since?'

'God no. But I've got to see them all in two weeks at Lily's sodding wedding. What am I going to do?'

'Oh, bloody hell. I guess you have to hold your own now and not back down. Don't go in over-apologetic. Have they ever apologised to *you* for *their* behaviour?' Sophie questioned.

'Well, no, Soph, but you know I can't stand having people annoyed with me. And they're not all bad. I'm close with Jacquie – I feel terrible for singling her out. I just hate being between her and my mum.'

'She's an adult, babe. She can take it. At the end of the day Jacquie and your mum should behave better. For your sake.'

'Am I a shitty person, Soph?'

'Jade, are you mad? This is literally the only time you've ever sinned.'

'I once stole a girl's pencil case in geography when I was twelve.'

'We'll let that one go, babe. I think you need to walk into this wedding with your head held high. Think Beyoncé coming off stage at Glastonbury, that's the energy we're talking about.'

'I was going to ask – would you mind coming with me? I have to make this sodding floral archway for Lily on the day. You could help with that, chill in my room during the boring bit, then come out for dancing and shots in the evening?' Jade winced, feeling she had asked too much.

'I'm there. Let's have a proper good dance and make the most of it. And at least Adam won't be there. That's one less person to worry about.' Sophie smiled and squeezed Jade's arm.

'Last night I told him to get his stuff out of the flat today. I'm praying he's there now, packing his clothes into cardboard boxes, so I can go back to an Adam-free zone.' Jade licked her teeth nervously and continued: 'I know him so well, though. He's going to make it hard for me. He won't go down without a fight. I don't think he's actually that bothered about being with me, but his giant ego will prevent an easy exit. I'm just not sure I've got the energy for it.'

'Mate, this moment is crucial. You cannot see him when you're feeling weak, or guilty, or on the verge of "repenting all sins". He'll be able to sniff your vulnerability out like truffles and then he'll go for the jugular. He'll pile on more guilt and then you'll let him off the hook and tell him he can stay, and we CANNOT have this happen.' Sophie began to roll fresh tobacco in a Rizla.

'You're right. That's *exactly* what I would do, and I really, really don't want him to stick around. I walked out of that restaurant feeling free, which was the second most surprising thing about the night.'

'Text him now. Tell him you expect all of his stuff to be gone by the time you get home.'

'What if he says he can't because he's working?' Jade chewed the side of her cheeks.

'Tell him if he doesn't you'll leave it all out the front of the main doors when you get back from work.' Sophie tucked her roll-up behind her ear.

'He won't believe I'd do that. He knows how uncomfortable I get when other people are put out. He's played on that one for years.'

'Well, it's time for him to learn the hard way. Come on, let's get that text sent.'

Jade and Sophie went back through the sliding door and across to Jade's backpack, tangy fumes hitting their nostrils.

'I'm a grown-arse woman of thirty-two, why am I so bad at this stuff?'

'Jade, it's not an age thing. I'm sure there are eighty-year-olds who don't deal well with this sort of thing.'

Jade looked down, sighed and watched her chest deflate as she did so. Her fingers moved cautiously over the keys. Then she pressed send and threw her phone back in her bag.

'Well done, babe.' Sophie hugged her tightly then held her hand. Lenny Kravitz's 'It Ain't Over 'til It's Over' blared from the speakers. Sophie pointed upwards as if the song sat above their heads. 'A sign!' Jade laughed and squeezed Sophie's hand. 'You've got to stick to this now, J. God help the poor bugger he ends up living with next.' Sophie shook her head.

Jade laughed again as they both went to the shelves to pull out the paints they needed to help Jackson.

'He's not your problem any more, Jade.'

Jade let that statement sink in and felt a tiny bit lighter.

29

The Chubb lock to the flat was already unlocked. Jade rested her head on her front door. She would have to face the inevitable.

As she expected, Adam was in the kitchen drinking a cup of tea, his phone and keys on the side and his shoes in the hallway.

'Why are you here? I presume to take your stuff?' Jade spoke in a controlled manner, trying not to let her fear show in any way.

'Jade, come on, you can't kick me out straight away, especially after humiliating me in front of not only your whole family but also the whole of Chelsea. Where do you expect me to go?'

Although his words were desperate, Adam's outward expression and cadence seemed as nonchalant as ever. Jade stood in a puddle of her own silence.

'I'm having a shower. It's been a long day.' Adam put his mug down and made his way to the bathroom.

Sentences were compiling in her head, but the words were all in the wrong order. Feeling herself teetering on the edge of going back on every word spoken at the rehearsal dinner, she walked into the kitchen and leaned against the worktop. The clock ticked loudly in the quiet, the clunk of each hand making her heart race quicker. She had the duration of Adam's shower to work out what to say to ensure his final exit from the flat. Luckily he had always had long showers, sometimes so much so that she would be left with tepid or bone-chilling water.

A flash of light on the opposite worktop broke her rumination. Adam's phone gently vibrated as a new message lit up the screen.

JC USA

JC? JC? Staring at the illuminated screen, Jade ran through all of Adam's friends beginning with J: Joe from university, Jamie who he had recently hired to help with Good2's social media, Jaws, his infrequently seen personal trainer. Then the USA part landed heavily: JaneyC from Los Angeles, the woman perched on Adam's lap in the photo with the smooth long legs, thick glossy hair, and white symmetrical teeth. Jade felt her hands trembling as she held Adam's phone. Since finding the photo of them snuggled together, limbs entangled like one never-ending person, Jade had tried to block any images of Janey from her mind. She poked her head around the kitchen door to check Adam was still in the shower, even though she could hear the water running. She knew Adam's phone passcode, so typed it in. Clicking on the message, she felt her breathing quicken.

See you tomorrow, and then a smiley emoji with one winking eye followed by a love heart. She held her breath. Reread the words again.

See you tomorrow? He had been technically single for less than twenty-four hours. She wondered if he had

271

planned this before she had officially ended their relationship, or if he had invited her to London the minute he knew he was free. She could picture him now, sitting at the table at Scalini's, sending Janey winky emojis seconds after her departure from the restaurant. If anything, this was the confirmation she needed to sever all ties and start again.

Any doubt in her mind quickly turned to absolute clarity. She bit down on her bottom lip then ran into her bedroom. All of her trainers were in a large plastic container in her wardrobe. She had used it to move all her shoes from her shared house with Navi after their break-up and then never bothered to take them out of it. She emptied the trainers onto the floor, then opened the chest of drawers where Adam kept his pants and socks and frantically started piling them into the box. Next, his shirts from the wardrobe, her hands trembling as she gripped the hangers tightly. Then his jackets from the hallway coat-hooks. She grabbed his shoes by the door and piled them on top of his belongings, along with his phone from the kitchen. Spotting the espadrilles from Los Angeles behind a couple of umbrellas in the hallway, she grabbed those too and placed them on top of the mountain of belongings. She opened the door with one hand, balancing the container in the other arm. Leaving the door on the latch, she waddled down the stairs as quickly as she could and placed the box outside the main doors to the flats. Her chest heaved as she ran back up the flight of stairs, hoping to make it before Adam got out of the shower. Grabbing his set of keys, she flung them into the fridge, the first place she could think of and hopefully the last place he would look.

The shower stopped abruptly, the noise of the water replaced by the sound of Adam padding across the floor and into the bedroom, humming a song Jade didn't recognise.

She waited. The humming stopped. Silence. A drawer in the bedroom was opened. Statue-still, Jade could hear the wood sliding against wood and the brass handle rattle.

'Where the fuck is all my stuff?'

Jade's mouth opened before she could think what to say. 'Outside on the street in a plastic container.' Her jaw tensed and she closed her eyes as she held her nerve.

'What the fuck?'

'Yup, you'd better go get it before someone thinks it's a charity box left out for people to help themselves from.' She hid round the corner in the kitchen, not wanting to view his reaction.

'Jade, stop dicking about, and go and get it.'

'Your phone is out there too,' she added.

'My phone? Jade, what the hell!'

'As I said, you'd better go get it quick.'

Adam bolted out the door with his towel around his waist, hair drenched and dripping down his back.

She waited for him to leave the flat then slammed the door firmly shut behind him. Creeping to the window in the front room, she peered out to see him checking through the box and retrieving his phone. She watched as he heaved the overflowing box onto his hip with one hand, the other desperately grabbing at his towel so it didn't slip as he moved back towards the doors. His footsteps up the stairs were irregular and heavy. Jade waited nervously for him to reach the front door. A loud thump with his fist made her flinch.

'Jade, let me in.'

'Nope, sorry. I've taken back possession of your keys.' Her voice wobbled a little.

'Jade, seriously, I haven't got any clothes on.' She could hear his attempt at kindness. Each word soft and peppered with light laughter.

'You'd better put some on then. There are tons in the box.' She kept her back flat to the cool wall.

'Jade, open up.' The niceness was slipping.

Jade remained silent.

'Jade. Seriously.'

She clenched her jaw more tightly and sucked in her cheeks.

'Jade!'

Jade counted. A pause of five seconds.

'*Jade!*' A fist slammed on the door.

Six, seven, eight, nine. She breathed deeply, the steady counting keeping her focused and calm. She could hear faint talking outside of the flat. Still holding her breath, she moved closer to the front door and could just make out the edges of a conversation between Adam and her neighbour Geraldine. She remained statue-still until the conversation dissipated, and she heard Adam stomp back down the stairs. Back in the front room, her hands shook as she knelt down, shuffled to the edge of the balcony and peered over the railings to the street below. Now dressed in a crumpled T-shirt and shorts, Adam lumbered down the hill carrying his box of belongings. The smaller he appeared in the distance, the slower Jade's heart thumped. It was then that she noticed he was wearing the espadrilles.

30

'What's that smirk on your face?' In the street outside the warehouse, Sophie and Jade were walking towards each other, Jade pushing her bike along the pavement and Sophie taking the last drags of a small stub of cigarette. The morning sun sat low in the sky and was illuminating one half of Sophie's face, making her skin glow amber.

'What smirk?' Jade took her cycling helmet off and let it swing from her finger.

'Your chirpiness doesn't just look like "The sun's come out at last" chirpiness,' Sophie said, squinting towards Jade.

Chaining up her bike, Jade looked up into Sophie's light blue eyes, yesterday's eyeliner smudged beneath each one. 'I like your cycling shorts, Soph.'

Sophie curtsied, her purple shorts wrapped around her pale legs like a second skin.

'I did it, Soph. I bloody did it. I held my nerve. I didn't catch the guilt. Long story, but when I got back to the flat last night, Adam was in the kitchen drinking a cup of tea.'

'Unsurprising. What a knob.'

'When he went off for a shower, I boxed up his stuff and chucked it out on the street. I kept his keys and refused to let him back in. I had to white-knuckle the first two minutes of him shouting for me to open the door, but somehow I held my nerve for long enough and he left.'

Sophie lurched towards Jade and wrapped her freckled arms around her torso. 'Ahh, I'm so proud of you! In a really non-patronising way, I'm so, so proud of you.'

'I'm proud of me too. Old Jade couldn't have done it.'

'Yeeeeeeess!'

'He might have been cheating on me. I saw a text on his phone from a girl he was with in LA.'

Sophie scrunched up her face. 'What a loser.'

'To be honest, it was a good catalyst to chucking him out.'

'Good. He doesn't deserve you, babe,' Sophie said vehemently.

'Thanks, Soph. But I do feel a bit edgy.'

'Well, that's natural. It's still fresh.'

'It's definitely the right thing to have done, but I do feel a bit scared if I'm honest.' Jade leaned on the wall of the warehouse, letting the sun warm her face.

'Scary is good. Remember, it's so much easier to stay stuck, babe. Even though you knew you weren't happy with Adam it was easier to stay with him. Leaving him *is* the right thing, but it's also initially the harder thing too.'

'Why is the right thing usually the harder thing?' Jade almost whispered.

Sophie shook her head and shrugged. 'Guess it's how we grow. We can't grow when we're stuck.'

277

'I was so stuck.'

'But now you're not.' Sophie winked. 'You're totally unstuck. It's normal to be feeling a bit wobbly. Think about it, when you're stuck, you're in a cycle of going through the motions. You know how it all works and there's a safety in that.'

'Yup. I guess I felt safe in the unhappiness. I was choosing to be in an unhappy relationship as I felt I knew my place in it.'

'That's it.' Sophie nodded and smiled. 'But now you're free and choosing to be happy, and that is scary because it's new.'

Jade smiled back. 'How are you today, Soph? Didn't you have a date last night?'

'Oh, mate,' she laughed. 'He was definitely much older than he stated on the app, and painfully shy. I felt like I was interviewing him. The low point was when, out of desperation, I asked him what his death-row meal would be to fill the silence.'

'Oh god. Is this what I have to come? Quiet old men on dating apps?'

'The worst bit was that he said *an omelette*. Whose death-row meal is an omelette?'

'Oh, he is definitely not the one.'

'Come on, let's get a cuppa.' Sophie and Jade walked arm-in-arm through the sliding door.

'Oh, roll in when you like. Me and Jackson have only been working away on these trees for twenty minutes on our own.' Lethabo's purple cargo trousers flapped as he walked to the trestle table, gesturing towards a half-painted snow-covered papier-mâché tree, complete with hand-cut white paper leaves.

'I can't believe we're working on Christmas projects already. I can't bring myself to think about Christmas, I've not even worn a bikini yet this year,' Sophie protested. 'Anyway, Thabs, I've actually been here for fifteen minutes; I was just catching up with Jade out the front.'

'You can catch up literally all day. And babes, as far as we're concerned today it *is* Christmas. We've got thirty-two of these babies to make for the winter scene at Liberty's and we've got to do it quick as they have a photoshoot next week. Shall I put Mariah on?' Lethabo spun a full 360, his purple Doc Martens squeaking on the concrete floor as he turned to the speakers.

'I don't think I can handle Christmas music too,' Sophie squirmed.

Jackson waved his hand subtly in the air.

'Morning, Jackson,' Sophie and Jade chimed in unison.

'OK, if you don't want Queen Mariah, what am I putting on? Do we fancy chill or party?' Lethabo moved towards his phone that was plugged into the speakers.

'Can we have chilled music please, Thabs?' Jade's voice was softer than she expected, suddenly wiped out from the last twenty-four hours.

'Are we thinking Ludovico Einaudi vibes? Or nineties Morcheeba? Maybe Fleet Foxes?'

'Ludovico, if that's OK with everyone else. I don't want words today.' Jade spoke without realising what she was saying. Recently everything had been about words.

'No words it is.' Lethabo hit play on his phone and all

four fell into a rhythmic flow of painting and cutting and sticking and smoothing, piano notes filling the space around them. Lethabo and Sophie chatted quietly while working, filling each other in on documentaries they had recently watched, as well as the latest on Lethabo's new boyfriend. Meanwhile Jackson and Jade sat comfortably in silence, the brief slicing noise of scissors breaking up the space between them.

'I think I'm starting to understand boundaries.' Jade's voice severed the silence around them. 'I mean properly this time.'

Jackson remained fixated on one small white leaf he was attaching to a nearby papier-mâché tree, his lack of response a cue for Jade to continue.

'So, last night I set a boundary with my now ex-boyfriend and stuck to it.'

Jackson's fingers worked quickly as he glued and carefully fixed a second leaf to a nearby snow-covered branch.

'I told him to leave the flat for good. I put his belongings in a box on the street and kept his keys. So, he's gone. I actually did it.' She kept her voice low.

Jackson, without looking up, said, 'Abracadabra.'

Jade stopped painting and furrowed her eyebrows. 'Er, alright, Paul Daniels,' she said, looking at him quizzically.

'Do you know what it means?' Jackson remained focused on the paper tree.

'Well, yes. Obviously.'

Jackson nodded at her, signalling for her to continue.

'Well, it's the end of a magic trick where there's some sort of mystical reveal.'

'No, I mean the *real* meaning?'

'Clearly not.' Jade was wondering where all of this was leading and what the relevance was.

'It comes from the Aramaic phrase "Avra Kehdabra". It means "I will create as I speak",' Jackson said.

Jade repeated the meaning in her head.

'Do you get it? You have to speak out loud what you want to bring into your reality.'

Jade smiled. 'Rewind . . . what does Aramaic mean?'

'Don't get distracted by semantics.'

Jade laughed and held her arm out as if she were wafting a wand. 'Abracadabra!'

I have changed my mind. I now want all foliage on the wedding arch. Ferns, ivy etc. Bridesmaid dress will be posted out to you this week.

Jade flicked her eyes away from her sister's text message and surveyed the kitchen worktops, as clean and uncluttered as she had left them the night before. Adam's absence had left delicious space rather than a huge hole. She realised she had missed the feeling of space much more than she now missed him. She leaned back on the kitchen counter and re-read the text. The first correspondence Jade had had with Lily for over a week was as emotionless and dismissive as Jade had expected. No 'Hello', no 'How are you?', not even a 'How dare you?' with regards to Jade's restaurant explosion. Jade knew she needed to pick and choose her battles wisely here. As much as she didn't want to change the floral wedding arch that she had already started work on, there was no room for contesting this.

'I can do this. I can do this,' she muttered. She exhaled deeply as she typed out the reply: *Sure. Will order in. I'll make sure it looks great. On another note, I can't have the girls while you're on your honeymoon now. Sorry.*

Jade stopped and re-read what she had typed. She rewrote it, deleting the word 'sorry' and keeping things short, precise, simple: *Sure. Will order in now. On another note,*

I can't have the girls while you're on your honeymoon. Maybe ask Mum instead. X

She pressed send and felt hot adrenaline race through her chest and up to her cheeks. Her phone rang immediately, filling her kitchen with a loud trill. The sound seemed to bounce off every surface as it rang and rang. Jade stared at her sister's name illuminated on her phone screen and let it ring out. If she was attacked verbally by her sister now, she might feel guilty and acquiesce. Lily called immediately again. Jade's finger hovered over the answer button, but it remained there.

There were five days to go until the wedding, when she would have to see her mum, dad, Jacquie, James and her sister for the first time since the rehearsal dinner. The thought of doing so without a partner by her side, exposed with nowhere to hide, made her feel light-headed. The weather clock in the kitchen showed grey clouds as the hands hovered over the twelve and seven.

Watching her coffee whirlpool as she stirred her spoon slowly, Jade imagined five disgruntled faces staring back at her. And not only did she feel anxious about seeing her family, but also about enduring a wedding. She had managed to avoid them since her break-up with Navi. An old school friend had invited her to one the previous summer but fortunately she had been in Barcelona with Sophie and Lethabo, working at a festival painting large sea creatures onto the front of a DJ booth. She knew it would not be possible to attend a wedding and not think of herself carrying out the exact actions of the bride. How could she not picture Navi at the top

283

of the aisle, his thick black hair parted to one side, his brown eyes framed by thick lashes moist with emotion? She had played out their imaginary wedding so many times in her head since cancelling it. The pain still felt fresh and sharp. She knew she had made the right decision, but the guilt, embarrassment and shame still lived alongside her.

Looking back, she couldn't pinpoint where the cracks had started. It was a gradual erosion that left her confused and doubting her every move. After four years together, Navi's proposal wasn't necessarily a shock, but she certainly didn't feel ready. As his family started to compile long lists of relatives that would need to be invited to the wedding and get flights from various parts of the world, she had felt herself spiral in panic. It felt too real, too soon, too permanent. Looking back, she knew she should have called it off sooner, but everything moved so quickly. Not wanting to disappoint Navi or his family became her reason to stay. He was a good person and she loved him, but the feeling in her gut that told her to walk just got stronger the nearer the wedding loomed.

She swallowed down a lump in her throat, recalling memories that had been stuffed down deep for years. A mental image took form as she glugged down another mouthful of bitter coffee; a sharp-focused photograph imprinted on her mind. She had dared to try her wedding dress on. It felt necessary, as if she needed to say goodbye to it before she put it up for sale on Lily's eBay account. With absolute lucidity she could conjure up the scene now: the dress cascading from her waist down to the floor as she sat on her mum's bed, catching the tears on her palm before they fell and hit the delicate fabric. It was a simple dress; one that draped across her shoulders in an attempt to minimise how broad they felt, and dropped from her waist in neat, uniform folds. She hadn't wanted lace, or beaded detail, just something that felt vastly different from her usual paint-splattered clothes. Two suitcases of her belongings had sat next to the bed, her life bundled up and stuffed inside. The dress was beautiful, but it had felt cumbersome on her body, like she was playing dress-up.

She had told Navi three weeks before the wedding. She had stood in front of him right by the front door to the flat they shared in Ealing. She had said the words that had been chasing her for months. The words were soft, without anger or spite. There was nothing to be angry about. He had simply nodded and looked at the floor. Maybe he had known too. In that moment, she had wanted to hug him and tell him he was wonderful, but that marriage didn't feel right. She had wanted to say it was her, not him. But that was a cliché, and she knew she needed to shoulder the pain without gaining comfort from him. She could recall the aching that she felt in her body; her back throbbed, her head pulsed. From this moment on guilt lingered in the wings, waiting to attach itself to anything it could. It felt as if pleasure would always be followed by the sting of guilt.

Swigging down the remains of her coffee, along with shards of kettle limescale from the bottom of her cup, Jade let the images from her past shatter into tiny shards.

How much joy had she missed playing by these self-devised rules? Each footstep towards the shower felt as if she was walking further from her past. In that moment she decided it was time to move on and set herself free: free from her childhood, from the guilt, from Lily's manipulation, from keeping herself small and quiet.

The first blast of ice-cold water stung Jade's back and forced her shoulders up to her ears until the water gradually warmed. Letting it run over her face with her eyes open, words raced around her head. Unspoken conversations with her mum and unuttered words for her dad. They would all need to be said aloud at some point. But first there would be apologies.

'Hello?' A meek voice answered, sounding too far from the mouthpiece.

'Morning, Mum.'

'Bit early, darling,' Sue croaked.

'Sorry. I just wanted to apologise. I know you probably don't want to talk to me, but I wanted to say sorry for my, er, outburst at dinner the other week. I know it wasn't OK.'

'Well, I am a little bruised by it all . . .'

'I went about it the wrong way, but I really, really want you to be happy and I don't think drink is helping with that.'

The line went very quiet. She could hear the shuffle of bed sheets fill the silence as her mum lifted herself to sit upright in bed. The chasm between her words and her mum's response increased with each passing second.

Jade tapped her foot on the floor, willing her to say something.

'Well, I did love what you said to Jacquie.'

'Ha, I'm sure you did,' Jade said, smiling. 'Look, I know it's been hard for you, and I can see how Jacquie rubs you up the wrong way, but I often feel so caught in the middle of the crossfire. You're my mum and I will always love you, but I also have a relationship with Jacquie. I know that's painful for you, but I don't think that the—' Jade pushed both feet into the floor, bracing herself to say the words she had kept inside for so many years '—the drinking is doing you any good.'

More silence. Jade ran her tongue along her teeth, feeling each curve and her twisted incisor.

Sue's voice cut through, ignoring Jade's statement. 'I do think you've made the right decision about Adam too. I worry about you being single but I'm not sure he was a good egg.' Sue cleared her throat at the end of her sentence.

'It's the right decision for me. And there's nothing to worry about. Do you think I can only be happy if I'm with someone?'

'Well . . .' Jade could hear sadness in Sue's voice. 'I just don't want you to end up like me.'

Jade's slight irritation turned to heartbreak in less than a second. 'Mum. You're doing alright. Don't be down on yourself.'

'Jade, it's hard being single at my age. I long for companionship.'

'There's still time. For you and me.'

'Oh, I don't know. I've sort of given up.'

'Mum, you're a catch. You're gorgeous and funny and smart.' Jade knew her mum would be rolling her eyes as she listened. 'Can I give you some advice?' Jade tentatively murmured.

'I'm a bit past advice,' Sue's voice croaked.

'I think you need to properly move on from Dad. I know it's not easy, but I think you've got to stop obsessing about Dad and Jacquie and believe that you can find great companionship with someone else.'

'I don't know.' Sue audibly slumped.

'But look, I understand,' Jade said softly. 'I know it's tough, but I'm serious about the drinking, Mum. If you want help, and I mean proper help, I'm here. I know people who have been through the same. I've also been doing a little bit of research online and there are loads of support groups for this kind of thing.'

'I'm not going to a church hall to sit and chat about my . . . problems. I'm too old and I don't have the energy.'

'OK. I get it. In your own time. Just know I'm here for you.'

In the pocket of silence that followed Jade could imagine her mum's lips tightening. She heard a clatter of bangles and pictured Sue straightening out her pyjama top.

'OK, Mum. Well, see you at the wedding.'

'Yup, see you there. Bye bye, darling.' Sue's tone softened as she ended the call with a quota of audible relief.

Jade hung up and smiled. She wasn't spun out by guilt or twitchy with edginess. A swell of pride moved through her, so unfamiliar it felt as if she were breathing under-water. As she brushed her teeth and washed her face she stared at her own reflection in the mirror. The face staring back looked different, lighter perhaps. Words that had been trapped in her head with no place to go had finally been released. Bouncing out of the flat to work, she felt the most optimistic she had in years.

32

The sound of the large wooden door sliding along its metal tracks was the only disturbance to the morning birdsong. Jade felt a hum of excitement as she scanned the warehouse for Jackson. Over the last couple of weeks, she had been using her newly quiet evenings after work to paint a small canvas – dark blue swirls that merged with turquoise in thick acrylic paint applied with a pallet knife to recreate the sea at Lulworth Cove. Black ink tattooed the back of the artwork with a note: *Thank you. You have no idea how much your words have helped me. Jade.* Now, red-checked cloth covered the canvas in a furoshiki bundle in Jade's hands.

'Morning, gang.' Jade strode further into the warehouse, a thin, light blue T-shirt beneath her usual paint-covered dungarees.

'Someone's got a spring in their step,' Lethabo said, looking her up and down. Sheryl Crow blasted from the nearby speakers.

'Are you now matching the tunes to your outfits, Thabs?' Jade looked down at his red cowboy boots and nodded towards the speakers.

'I like uniformity, babes. You know that about me. Everything has a look and a feel.'

'Hey, mate. Popping out for a fag. You coming?'

Sophie's giant tie-dye T-shirt worn as a dress swung as she walked towards the door.

'No, Soph. I'm going to get back to these sodding snowy trees as the Liberty's deadline is looming. Where's Jackson?' Jade asked, looking around the warehouse.

Lethabo spun round in a precise half-pirouette, his cowboy boots scuffing the concrete floor. 'Didn't he tell you?'

Jade lifted one eyebrow. 'Tell me what?'

'He's left,' Sophie shouted over her shoulder from the door, a cloud of hazy smoke around her.

'Left? What do you mean? Popped out?' Jade asked, confused.

'No, he's left-left.' Lethabo turned the speakers down so he wasn't fighting to speak over the music.

'He didn't call me. I don't get it. Where has he gone?' Jade felt a small stream of panic flowing through her nervous system.

'He said he wants to concentrate more on his graphic-design work so he's off interning somewhere else, then he said he might go to New York for a year.' Sophie stood half in the warehouse, half out, blowing the smoke in the direction of the street.

'What? He didn't tell me.' Jade looked at the floor.

'I wouldn't worry, he's a man of few words. I wouldn't take it personally,' Sophie said, shrugging her shoulders.

Jade felt spun out.

'There's a new girl starting next week called Shannon. Apparently, she's very skilled at spray-painting and good with wood too.'

'OK,' Jade nodded, trying to conceal her level of upset. She slumped to the floor and picked up a roll of gaffer tape. Her phone chimed, snapping her out of the thousand questions flooding her head.

I've changed mind. Don't want foliage. Back to original plan of roses for wedding archway. And we'll discuss Saffron and Jemima's stay for my honeymoon later.

'For fuck's sake.' Jade pushed her phone into the front pocket of her dungarees and sighed with such force she could smell the coffee on her own breath. Breathe, just breathe, she thought. Lily was inevitably going to push back on the girls' stay. And it was almost comically unsurprising that she would change the design of the archway multiple times before the wedding. Jade got her phone back out, cancelled the order of faux foliage and bulk-ordered silk roses – picking out the cheapest ones, knowing her sister had no intention of paying her back. After the first steps towards an honest conversation with her mum, she knew she needed to do the same with Lily. It would require solid, rehearsed patter, a clear and confident delivery, the vigilance of an FBI agent. Lily was the queen of game-playing, so it wouldn't be straightforward. Changing their dynamic required the unravelling of years of pain and dysfunction. Where would she even start? she wondered. Thinking back to her last conversation with Jackson, she whispered: 'Abracadabra.'

33

Jade skimmed her right hand clumsily across her bedside cabinet, hoping to locate her phone without opening her eyes: 6:10am. She pressed snooze and turned onto her back. Sunlight streamed in plumes of bright white through the gap in the curtains. The outlines of a dream faded from her memory; her brain was unable to hold on to the details, but it had left her on high alert. Was she being chased? Was it a man with some sort of animal head? Or a rhino charging, or perhaps it could have been Lily? Faces and shapes morphed as she woke up to the day. She stretched her body out, arms above her head, and released a yawn. As her bedroom came into focus, she was met with the realisation that the wedding day had arrived. Moving on to her side, she attempted to open her eyes properly. It was time to rip the plaster off. She had been fearing this day for months. Years, if she was honest with herself. The first wedding since she called off hers with Navi.

The first thing Jade's eyes landed on was the brown bridesmaid's dress hanging on the wardrobe door. She grimaced and heaved her body out of the softness of her duvet. Pulling back the curtains, she snapped her head back as the light made her squint.

The sky was split exactly in two. One half was a

summer's day, light and bright where the sun hung low on the horizon; the other was an ominous dark grey with large cumulus clouds encroaching like looming mountains. It reminded her of the shortbread biscuits her nan used to give her: one half buttery yellow, the other dipped in dark chocolate.

'Oh dear,' Jade muttered, her eyes to the sky. She imagined the tantrum her sister would already be having. Lily would more than likely be blaming James for the rainclouds or taking out her upset on any unsuspecting bystanders. After a quick shower, Jade towel-dried her hair and pulled on some tracksuit bottoms just as she heard her cab pull up outside. Looking at the large holdall slung over her shoulder, she ran through a mental checklist. Brown dress, bra, bridesmaid's shoes that looked horrifically uncomfortable. Dashing out the door, she grabbed a rectangular package she had left in the hallway the night before. A small tag hanging from a blue silk ribbon read, *Dear Mr Merry, Happy Birthday, love Jade.*

Quietly tiptoeing across the hallway, she laid the wrapped watercolour paints down outside his door and skipped down the stairs.

It was a little after seven when Jade arrived at the Wellington Hotel in deepest Surrey, the dark grey rolls of cloud now covering three-quarters of the sky. She could sense her sister's stress levels rising telepathically. The marquee in the grounds of the hotel was set for the ceremony: chairs in neat, seemingly never-ending rows, each with a brown ribbon tied to its back. Jade raised an eye-brow and said '*Vogue*' to no one. Lanterns lined the aisle, large clusters of peonies peered over the top of glass bowls, and strings of festoon lighting hung like dew-laden spiderwebs. A quiet scene of perfection before the imminent crowd of wedding guests arrived. The dais where the celebrant would stand and conduct the service sat in front of Jade's half-finished archway. Big Brush's courier had dropped it at the venue the day before in his van, a freebie as he was passing that area anyway. Jade had bought him a breakfast bagel and piping-hot coffee on the Friday to say thanks. More tiny details that Lily would never care to ask Jade about.

Rolling her sweatshirt sleeves up, she removed her Ugg boots and started pinning individual silk roses to the foliage she had started making at the warehouse earlier that week. Jade wondered why people spent so much time and money on details at weddings that nobody would notice and certainly wouldn't remember. The hours of work that she had put into the archway would undoubtedly fade into a background of chatter, cooing and drunken dancing. She plodded on constructing the wire frame, then pinning each rose to face out to the seating area. As her fingers pinched at the petals, she noticed that her nails were bitten down and bright blue dye stained the outlines of her cuticles. She could already envisage Lily's flared nostrils and down-turned mouth at the sight of her hands.

A light patter overhead lifted Jade's eyes to the roof of the marquee.

'Oh dear, oh dear,' Jade whispered to herself.

A generator whirred outside the catering tent, where Jade had a clear view of a team in pristine white jackets preparing the lunch that would be held in a second, neighbouring marquee. Jade carried on pinning roses as she watched them work quickly and efficiently. Her eyes moved from white jacket to white jacket as their hands moved quickly over empty plates and trays of prepared food – and then stopped on a head of brown wavy hair, moving from side to side as the body beneath it danced, the man's movements standing out amongst the mechanical flow of those around him. The notes of a familiar song floated through the rain-scattered air, sporadic gusts of wind stealing parts of the melody, delivering a patchy song she couldn't quite decipher. Jade kept her eyes on him, watching his tall body move, her fingers still clumsily attempting to pin roses to the archway. Everyone else in the tent seemed to be cast in shadows, his body instead spotlit by the overhead lighting.

His head tilted upwards in slow motion, as if he could sense Jade's stare. She jumped back, his unexpected glance catching her off-guard. Pretending to rummage around in her plastic box of fake roses, she muttered '*Shit*' to herself.

Desperate to look back and study the eyes that had met hers, but too embarrassed to turn in his direction, Jade tried to recall every detail. The wavy hair that moved as if it had a life of its own, a full bottom lip, maybe a dimple in one cheek? She needed to see him again. A shiver of anticipation raced down her spine. She bit her front teeth into her lip and tried not to smile. Just pin the roses, Jade, she thought, just keep pinning. Her unkempt, bed-ruffled appearance suddenly felt illuminated. She ran her palms over her head to tame the stray clumps of long hair that were yet to be brushed.

After two more minutes of fastidiously concentrating on a job that didn't require that much concentration, she turned her body slightly, and then her eyes, to catch another glimpse. Three women now stood huddled over a tray of what looked like meringues. A piping bag was passed between them. She let her eyes dart to the right then left. But he was nowhere to be seen. Feeling a little desperate, she now looked without inhibition and peered past the caterers to the back of the marquee. Nothing. No one.

'Morning, mate.' Sophie strode into the marquee, her hoodie draped over her head to protect her from the rain. 'Lily isn't going to be happy it's pissing down, is she?'

Jade lunged at Sophie and squeezed her shoulders. 'Soph, oh my god. I'm in love.'

'What? With who?' Sophie took the hoodie from her head and shook out her ruffled bob. 'Can I smoke in here by the way? It's practically outside.' Sophie held her Rizla aloft.

'Yup, go for it,' Jade said, not entirely registering Sophie's request. She craned her neck to see into the catering tent. 'There was a man over there.' She nodded in the direction of the caterers. 'It was like he was illuminated from above. Like angels were shining torches down on him.'

'What you on about?'

'He was all lit up. Almost shining.'

'Shining?' Sophie laughed.

'He had wavy dark hair. Super tall too.' Jade spoke quickly.

'Well, that's motivation for the day ahead.' Sophie winked at Jade. She picked up a silk rose and studied it, then turned down the corners of her mouth.

'I know, they're naff. I got the cheapest faux roses I could find. Let's just finish pinning them on so we can go find Mr Wavy Hair.' Jade frantically grabbed at a bunch of roses and arranged pins between her teeth.

Sprinting to the hotel to avoid the now pelting rain, Jade and Sophie asked the receptionist where the brides-maids were getting ready. The lift cranked into action as Sophie licked a finger and attempted to remove black smudges of make-up from under her blue eyes in the mirrored wall.

'I could murder a gin and tonic right now,' Jade said.

'It's 8:30am, babe. Pace yourself,' Sophie laughed.

'No, I know. I just want something to take the edge off. Not only have I got to endure Lily thinking she's Kate Middleton all day but I'm scared of sinking into a low mood by simply being at a wedding. I've been trying to fight off some pretty vivid mental images of Navi this week.'

'That's natural, babe.' Sophie put her hand on Jade's shoulder.

'I'm also unnerved that I haven't found a script this week.

I mean, part of me is incredibly relieved but, come on, it's Lily's wedding, my mum *and* Jacquie are here, there's bound to be some drama, and I weirdly miss knowing what's going to happen.' The realisation hit her as she spoke.

The lift doors pinged open. Two middle-aged men stood square to the door grasping tennis rackets like swords. They made way for Jade and Sophie to exit the lift.

'Soph, I'm room 303.' She handed Sophie the room key. 'Go have a bath, make a cuppa, and watch *Schitt's Creek* or *Below Deck* or something, and I'll pop back and see you whenever I get a moment to escape, OK?'

'You'd better dash back and update me on Wavy Hair if you see him. I want all the goss. I'll be peering out of the window to spy on you, Jadey.'

'Love you, Soph. Wish me luck: on all counts. I'm off to find the other bridesmaids.' Jade opened her mouth in a silent howl.

'Hellooo.' Jade gingerly pushed the door to room 325. Being greeted by a room of her sister's closest friends was simultaneously comforting and terrifying.

'Birdy! Hello, little one,' cooed Sarita, who was Lily's oldest mate. Jade felt riled immediately – already reminded of her childlike status amongst these women.

'Hey. You all look lovely.' Jade offered a platitude to ease her nerves.

'I've had about an hour's worth of professional make-up, which helps.' Sarita pointed to the slick of shading on her cheekbone that shimmered like manuka honey. 'We're going to look like nineties supermodels by the time we've got our dresses on.' Jade looked over to the brown brides-maids' dresses that hung lifelessly on the wardrobe door. 'You know brown is *Vogue*'s colour of the wedding season? Lily is always so on point with these details,' Sarita beamed.

'Guess so. It's a bit skimpier than I would normally wear,' Jade replied as she peered out of the large bay window that overlooked the hotel grounds and the mar-quee, hoping to catch a glimpse of the tall stranger.

'You'll look cracking, Jade.' Sarita ran a hand down the side of her own tiny waist. Jade knew her words were for sympathy rather than a genuine compliment. One of Sarita's elegant legs protruded from the side of her dressing gown and Jade let her eyes linger on it. Her smooth unblemished skin made Jade reach down and touch her own legs, which she'd forgotten to shave. She hung her own bridesmaid's dress on the wardrobe next to the others. It had been tight when she tried it on. She knew it would be. Her sister had sent a size 10, knowing that Jade wore a size 12, and told her there was no time for modifications.

'Birdy, meet Eve. She's going to be doing your make-up.' Another of Lily's friends, Cathy, steered Jade to a seat where a woman stood in front of a dressing table littered with make-up palettes and lines of brushes.

Jade half smiled at Eve, who had dark arched eye-brows, lipliner that ran outside her mouth, and platinum hair extensions that reached her waist in straight sheets. 'I don't normally wear that much make-up. So just a bit of mascara for me, please,' Jade said politely.

Eve laughed, her giant bright pink lips stretching as she spoke, smudges of cerise caught on the edges of her large teeth. 'Well, there's a brief I'm working to, doll.' She patted Jade on the back with too much force.

'What's the brief, out of interest?'

'That's not for you to concern yourself with, love. Let's crack on.' Eve held a sponge caked in foundation close to Jade's face.

As Jade closed her eyes and felt Eve's fingers massaging foundation into her skin, she thought back on the last couple of weeks. So much had changed. Adam hadn't made contact once. She imagined him cosied up to Janey with her caramel legs wrapped around his torso. She wondered if he missed her at all. She felt numb when thinking of him – and the numbness felt like a relief. The wear and tear of their relationship over the last year had made the transition to being single almost painless. The heartache was so minimal she could barely sense where it was located.

Jackson had left too. Maybe she had gotten a little too reliant on his reassurance. Now a small notebook lay by her bed, and she had started to write down the fragments of his advice she could recall.

'Open your eyes but look down and to the left for me, lovely.' Eve's Yorkshire twang brought Jade out of her thoughts. 'Now the other side. Now open your lips as if you're blowing a bubble.' Eve demonstrated, pouting her lips like a goldfish. Jade half-heartedly copied. 'That's it,' Eve cooed.

Jade blinked; her eyelashes felt heavy.

'Right, that's you done, chicken.' Eve slapped Jade on the back again as she rose from the make-up chair.

'Thanks.' Jade moved to the bathroom tentatively. Once the door was shut firmly behind her, she peered at her face in the mirror. Large dark-rimmed eyes stared back. Brown streaks formed cheekbones that Jade didn't have, and her lips looked almost twice the size. Jade shook her head at her own reflection.

Grabbing a roll of toilet paper, she wiped her cheeks to remove the bronzer, but the eye make-up wouldn't budge. Bending down, she opened the cupboard under the sink to see if there was any moisturiser or bath products that could help her dial it down. Her hands fumbled past rolls of toilet paper and a hairdryer in a cloth bag. It was right at the back of the shelf under the sink that her fingertips touched the sharp edges of a pile of paper. Her hand froze before her brain had time to catch up with her senses. Pulling her hands away quickly, she shook them out like they were wet and breathed in deeply. Peering into the dim shelves, she reached to the back for a second time. Gently pulling the script from its hiding place, she braced herself for who or what was printed on its pages.

34

'You going to be long in there, bathroom hogger?' A loud Irish voice boomed through the heavy bathroom door. Sinead, Lily's friend since secondary school and always a little too loud and a little too blunt, thumped on the door.

'Yup, OK.' Jade stood up sharply and folded the script in half without a chance to scan its contents. 'Coming. Sorry.' Jade felt like a child again having her sister's friends around. She needed to tap into the mature confidence she had felt the last couple of weeks. She unlocked the door.

'Sinead.' Jade nodded towards her. Sinead smiled broadly, lips glistening with a layer of gloss and her face framed by long tendrils of coiled brunette hair.

'I just want to check my make-up in the mirror, Birdy. I told her to go full Kardashian on me.'

Jade smiled, her eyes involuntarily widening at the large flicks of black above Sinead's eyelashes, the heavy lipliner that sat atop the bow of her lip and the dark brown contoured cheeks in her round face.

'I'm sweating in this dressing gown. Can you pop a window open in there?'

'Yup. You look . . . lovely, Sinead.' Jade swallowed and moved away swiftly, keeping the script held tightly to her waist. Stuffing it in her bag, she wondered how and when she would safely be able to look at it properly. Catching a glimpse of herself in the dressing-table mirror, she flinched, seeing the eye make-up she had failed to remove.

'Right, come on, ladies. Let's crack open a bottle.' Sarita was waving a large bottle of champagne in the air with her right hand. Her delicate wrist looked like it might snap under the weight.

'Shouldn't we check on Lily first?' said Cathy, whose skin was gleaming with perspiration, strands of blonde hair stuck to her forehead. The stress and nerves of attending to Lily were starting to show.

'Nah, she won't want us all fussing around her. She'll be wanting to get in the zone peacefully.' Sarita put the bottle between her thighs and pulled at the cork. It exploded from the bottle at the same time as the door of the hotel suite burst open. The combination of sounds made Jade jolt.

'For fuck's sake. I have one shoe. ONE.' Lily was standing in the doorway, both hands pressed into its frame. 'Who was in charge of bringing my dress and shoes from the house?' Her face tightened with anger as if her skin were being stretched.

'Er, you were, I think, Lils,' Cathy said with trepidation.

Lily ignored Cathy. 'One shoe. One! What the hell am I supposed to do with one shoe.'

'Where do you think it is, Lils?' Cathy said with care, her voice cracking with fear.

'I don't know, Cathy, otherwise I would have it.' Lily's usual coquettish mannerisms slipped quickly.

'Could someone go back to the house and look for it?' Cathy asked cautiously.

'Yes, Cathy. *You* can. Off you pop. The ceremony starts in just over two hours, so you'd better get a bloody move on.' She waved Cathy out of the room, taking on the persona of the Queen of Hearts.

'*Off with their heads*,' Jade whispered to herself.

'What, Birdy? What did you say?' Lily's head whipped to her.

'Nothing. Hope you find the shoe, Cathy,' Jade bellowed out to the hallway as Cathy put her raincoat over the top of her dressing gown and marched with purpose down the hotel hallway. Lily swivelled out and slammed the door behind her.

'Flippin' heck,' Sarita mouthed. 'Right, anyway, let's crack on.' She poured a generous glass of champagne for herself then nodded to Sinead for her glass.

Jade discreetly picked up her bag and slowly walked sideways to the door, her exit completely unnoticed. Tiptoeing past her sister's hotel room, she could hear muffled yet audible shouting from inside – her sister reprimanding the hairdresser for making her curls too big. Jade could hear the edges of Lily's authoritative voice which she brought out when she wasn't getting her own way.

Jade kept her head down and tiptoed across the hallway. Ducking into a laundry cupboard by the lifts, she took the script out of her bag.

[Grounds of the Wellington Hotel, outside a marquee.]

                        LUCA

Luca? Who was Luca? 'Luca, Luca.' Jade let the word roll around her mouth. It felt nice to say out loud.

                        LUCA
        Nice dress.

                        JADE
        It's brown.

                        LUCA
        I know.

                        JADE
        I like . . . your jacket.

                        LUCA
        Ha. Thanks. I'm Luca, by the way.

That was it. The rest of the page was blank. Jade thought back to her morning of pinning silk roses and the stranger in the catering tent. Could he be Luca? Please could *he* be Luca, Jade thought. She stuffed the script back in her bag and returned to the bridesmaids' suite.

Just as she was passing Lily's room, the door swung

open. 'Birdy!' Lily boomed as the door crashed against the wall. Jade jumped back. 'What are you doing? Shouldn't you be creating my floral archway?' Lily's lips stretched into an insincere smile.

Jade felt her nervous system switch to high alert. 'I've done that already,' she snapped back.

'Well, shouldn't you be helping . . . someone . . . do . . . something?'

'Nope.' Jade had assumed her sister would bring up the rehearsal dinner but instead Lily was acting as if nothing had happened. This was an occasional tactic Jade was more than used to: feigned ignorance that expressed Lily's savage disinterest in anything Jade did or said.

'Sorry to interrupt . . .'

A low voice startled them both. A man in navy trousers and a matching waistcoat over a white shirt stood in the hallway, smiling politely.

'Oh, Casper. This is my sister, Jade.' Lily's voice returned to a performative tone as her thunderous face switched instantly to a broad smile.

Jade stuck out her hand and he shook it and briefly looked her way. Jade glanced at his badge, which said 'Manager'.

'I was just wondering if I or any of the other staff members could assist you further this morning? Did your champagne arrive?' He spoke formally as if he were pandering to royalty.

'Oh yes, it did. Thank you, Casper.'

Jade noticed Lily had her flirty voice on. The one

which was higher than usual and slightly squeaky on certain syllables. Jade looked on in fascination.

'Oh good.' Casper lingered in the silence. He was definitely Lily's type, Jade thought – sandy hair, lean, slightly posh-sounding.

'Oh, I wonder if you could make the rain stop,' Lily drawled, then laughed manically.

'Of course. We're on to it.'

'Actually, though, could I get some almonds? Unsalted. No raisins. Just almonds. Thank you, Casper.' Lily let her hair fall over one eye.

Jade grimaced. 'Well,' she sighed, 'I'm going to get out of here. Bridesmaid's duties.' She smiled an exaggerated grin towards her sister. 'Nice to meet you, Casper.'

'Jade!' Lily called down the corridor after her: 'Nails.'

Jade didn't look back.

35

An obnoxious, unexpected thunderclap bellowed overhead. Jade, Sinead and Sarita turned to the window, where raindrops swam down the glass as soot-coloured clouds brewed overhead.

'Shit. Another champs, ladies?' Sarita held her empty glass out.

'Any sign of Cathy? I've texted but not heard back yet.' Sinead looked down at her phone. 'Chelsea and back on a Saturday is a push. Poor Cath.'

'Nope.' Sarita shook her head while sipping on her new drink.

'We need to all head out to the marquee in twenty minutes, so it's going to be tight,' Sinead lamented. 'I'm going to put my frock on.' She grabbed at the brown dress on the wardrobe.

Jade looked down at her own dress that felt taut across her hips, and pulled back her shoulders. She would not let this too-tight, shoulder-exposing dress steal her confidence.

The door burst open again, jolting Jade's nervous system which already felt shot from the morning's dramas. It was her mum, resplendent in blue.

'Gosh, Lily is quite stressed out in there about the weather and the shoe,' Sue said, dramatically mouthing 'shoe' as if Lily might hear. She shut the door behind her and puffed air out of her cheeks. Her plait had a blue scarf intertwined with her hair and she wore blue mascara to match the dress. Jade's eyes traced her mum's silhouette down to her feet, shod in blue chunky-heeled boots with David Bowie-style lightning bolts running up the sides.

'Oh, can I have a champs? I'm gasping.' Sue pointed to Sarita.

'Mum, what did we talk about?' Jade said quietly so the others wouldn't hear.

'If I can't have a drink on my daughter's very rainy, already slightly stressful wedding day, then when can I?' Sue whispered back theatrically. She looked past Jade with a wide, forced smile and happily received a glass from Sarita.

'Oh, ladies, you all look lovely.' Sue scanned the sea of brown dresses, contoured cheekbones and over-styled hair. She looked at Jade. 'Aren't you going to have your make-up done, darling?'

'I've had it done already, Mum,' Jade replied.

'Right, what are we going to do about this shoe situation? Lils is due down in the marquee any minute.' Sue looked at her watch.

'Sue, you're going to have to break it to her that Cathy isn't back and we can't get hold of her. Can you suggest barefoot?' Sarita said squeamishly.

'You could say it's hot in *Vogue* right now,' Jade added with a large grin.

'Oh gosh. OK, give us another glass of bubbles first,

eh?' Sue pushed her glass towards Sarita, then drank it in one. 'Wish me luck.'

The three bridesmaids huddled in silence as loud, muffled voices seeped out from under the door of Lily's suite. 'Shit,' they said in unison, eyes darting to meet each other's.

Jade checked her phone in an attempt to avoid the tension. No new texts, so she opened Instagram on autopilot. Scrolling down, she saw that her sister had posted a photo only three minutes ago: a black and white shot of herself sitting in a silk robe with her back to the camera, her face in profile, dress hanging on a nearby wardrobe door. The caption read *The big day. It already feels like pure magic. #L&Jgethitched.* The usual staged pantomime that depicted Lily's life as a fairy tale. Jade laughed, knowing that beneath that thin veneer of perfection sat a disgruntled and passive-aggressive bride with only one shoe.

Sue burst back through the door, her plaited hair swishing like a separate entity, cheeks red and blotchy. 'The barefoot thing went down badly.' Her stack of silver bangles crashed together as she swept her hair from her eyes.

Silence befell the room. No one moved, or even seemed to breathe.

Sue bit her lip. Time ticked.

'Oh bloody hell. She can have mine. We're the same size. I'll wear my Uggs.' Jade bent down and undid the straps around her ankles.

'Well done, darling. It's the right thing to do.' Sue

thrust her hands out to receive the shoes, still slightly out of breath.

Sarita and Sinead busied themselves looking at their own reflections, pouting and tweaking strands of hair and unruly eyebrows.

Suddenly needing air, Jade opened the large bay window and a cool breeze cut through the humidity of the room. Staring out at the marquee and the winding stream that ran along one side, she could see the tent was quickly filling up with guests. Through the open flap at the back she could see damp coats slung over chairs and make-up compacts clicking open as the masses attempted to salvage tendrils of sodden hair. Umbrellas were strewn haphazardly about the floor as the wedding guests hugged, and kissed the air between their faces. An undulating wave of indecipherable chatter was then broken by a booming voice on a microphone. Jade could just make out James's best man, Michael, speaking to the crowd.

'Ladies and gentlemen, please take your seats. The ceremony is about to begin.'

Hushing and shushing replaced the chatter as a guitar started gently playing a Bon Iver track in the background.

Jade and the other bridesmaids moved quickly from the room to the lift, each of them forensically checking their faces in the mirrored walls. Jade simply stared at her reflection, not recognising herself at all: not the dress hugging her hips, her exposed shoulders, the straps cutting into her armpits, nor the thick lashes curling upwards.

They congregated on the sweeping steps in the foyer, peering out at the dark charcoal sky.

'Come on, girls.' Sue was pulling Saffron and Jemima by the arms towards the door.

'I hate this dress,' Jemima wailed. 'I don't like dresses.'

'Darling, you're just going to have to grin and bear it for a few hours and then you can put your onesie back on.' Sue looked flustered. She pushed her long plait over her shoulder and fiddled with the neckline of her blue chiffon dress.

'Can I have my tablet, Granny? I want to play Roblox.'

'Jammy, what did Granny say? When we get to lunch you can have it. Right now you need to walk down the aisle with Aunty Jade and Mummy in her princess dress.'

'I don't want to,' Jemima moaned with a dramatic, wailing expression.

'Saffy, you can't have your thumb in your mouth. Come on, pop it out.' Sue pulled on Saffron's arm but the thumb didn't budge. 'Granny will give you a bag of sweets if you just go down the bloody aisle, OK?' Sue smiled in the bridesmaids' direction with a look of pain beneath her stretched-out smile.

Jade went over and took the girls' hands. 'Come on, you two monkeys. Let's pretend we're on a catwalk and strut down the aisle.' Saffron laughed and pouted her lips, pulled her thumb out of her mouth, and put her hands on her hips.

A click of tiny heels on marble had all heads turning to the ivory staircase. Lily descended with her head bowed, inky hair falling perfectly over one half of her face. Her body moved slowly and carefully as she hitched up the white diaphanous skirt of her dress, her waist pulled in impossibly small; Jade wondered where her vital organs had been repositioned. Her shoulders moved mechanically, exposed to the chill in the air, her hair gleaming and barely moving as she descended the stairs.

'Lils!' screeched Sarita. 'You look like an angel from actual heaven.'

'Seriously, Lils, you look unreal,' Sinead confirmed. Jade tried to keep her eyes on Sinead's face but felt distracted by her boobs, which were spilling over the top and out the sides of her dress.

Lily paused on the bottom step. 'Why are you wearing Uggs, Jade?' Lily's eyes were wide and horrified, her bottom jaw jutting out.

'You have my shoes on.'

'Yes, but you cannot wear those. For god's sake, couldn't you have gone and found something more suitable? It's like you have two jacket potatoes on your feet.' Lily smoothed down her dress and looked in the large gilt mirror by the main doors, momentarily distracted by her own beauty.

'Well, there wasn't much I could do in the twenty allotted minutes before proceedings, so no.'

Just then Cathy came rushing down the hallway, her hands still fumbling with the straps on her bridesmaid's dress, cheeks puffing and pink, her forehead slick with sweat. 'Didn't. Get. The. Shoe. No. Time,' she said, her words punctuated with huge, desperate gasps. 'Traffic. Jam. OntheM3. Hadtoturnaround.' The words tumbled out of her jittering mouth.

Lily turned, ignoring her breathless friend and instead looked out towards the marquee and the guests sitting patiently. Her audience awaited.

'Where are the umbrellas? Please tell me they're white, or at the very least brown.' Lily directed this to the heavens rather than anyone nearby.

'Er, there are these hotel golf umbrellas.' Jade pointed to a large pot by the door.

'They're yellow. Bright yellow!' Lily looked like a lion scanning for its next meal.

Jade shrugged. 'It's that or getting pissed on.'

Each bridesmaid held a luminous yellow umbrella around Lily, creating a tortoise shell of cover from the heavy rain.

'I'm just not paying this weather any attention. I don't want anyone to mention it again, OK?' Lily ducked, keeping her hair from getting stuck in the spokes of the mass of umbrellas.

The bridesmaids gulped and nodded. Moving slowly, all eyes on Lily's pace and stride, they set off.

36

Bottoms shuffled on seats and chair legs dragged on the floor as all heads spun to see Lily standing at the bottom of the aisle. Sarita, Sinead, Cathy and Jade stood behind her, with Jemima and Saffron in front, Jemima looking miserable, Saffron jumping up and down, ready to strut up the aisle.

Tony moved towards Lily, his eyes glistening with pride. 'My angel. Look at you. Don't worry about the weather . . .' Tony's chest was elevated to the sky in his immaculately tailored navy three-piece suit, gold rings on each finger glinting in the overhead lights. A cuddly gangster ready to hand over his daughter.

'Do. Not. Mention. The. Weather,' Lily said through pursed lips.

Tony nodded and shook his hands out in front of him; his non-verbal apology. Jade could see Jacquie out of the corner of her eye, red hair piled on her head and a large fascinator perched atop like a cherry.

'Ladies, you look divine.' Tony directed his compliments to the bridesmaids yet avoided Jade's eyeline altogether. She breathed out deeply, then felt a rush of excitement as she remembered the stranger from the catering team. The dense fluff of her Ugg boots was making her bare feet sweat. Wiggling her toes amongst the now slightly damp lining, she craned her neck to the left to peer into the smaller marquee next door. Tens of uniformed caterers moved quietly and quickly, efficient ants moving from table to table with purpose. There were ponytails, black hair, a redhead, a shaved head, two blondes, a couple of hairnets covering squashed hair, but no mop of wild brown hair.

The train of people started moving towards the floral arch, Lily and her dad leading the way. It felt like a very visual representation of how their lives played out, with Jade trailing behind in heavy boots. Jade looked from left to right, taking in Lily's and James's friends and family, and smiled awkwardly at anyone who caught her eye. All eyes seemed to dart from her face straight to her feet, where they lingered for a little too long. Each footstep seemed to call more focus to her boots. The attention brought on a visceral discomfort that made her feel hyper-aware of her feet and the brown dress that revealed parts of her back that hadn't seen sunlight in months. Navi's face played on a loop in her mind, like a song that had gotten stuck in her head. She focused on her breathing. It was then that she spotted Belinda and Don in the middle of the congregation and felt an instant wave of relief.

As Lily reached the top of the aisle, James wiped away a tear, his eyes glassy and full of longing as he looked at his future wife. Lily, still disgruntled about the missing shoe and terrible weather, looked detached in comparison – but only Jade would notice. Lily was an expert in hiding her aggression under a coy face and slowly blinking eyelids. Jade had witnessed this cover-up so many times.

The couple stood inches from one another, nodding and smiling, James wiping away more tears as the guests listened to them promise their eternal love. Jade looked over their heads towards the floral archway she had spent hours creating, wondering if her sister had even noticed its existence. She thought about how she could have covered it in spoons, or condoms, and her sister still wouldn't have seen it. Picturing multiple colourful condoms hanging amongst the foliage tuned Jade out of the surrounding words of devotion and the subsequent cheering.

'You may kiss the bride.'

The audience roared and snapped Jade out of her daydream.

'Can I play my computer game now, Granny?' Jemima shouted above the cheers. Sue put her finger to her lips and held Jemima's arm, keeping her firmly in her seat.

The rain had picked up pace, lashing down on the roof of the marquee, making it hard to hear the conversation that followed the ceremony. The wedding photos were due to take place outside, but Lily decided for her hair and dress's sake they would be back in the hotel before lunch was served. As the guests settled into the chairs post-ceremony, caterers flooded in with trays of champagne in elegant flutes. Sue grabbed one and drank it down as she followed the rest of the family members towards the hotel. Jade held her nieces' hands and moved with the throng of relatives, while looking around, trying to catch a glimpse of the stranger. She knew she shouldn't pin every shred of happiness on seeing him, but at this point he was the only thing getting her through the day. She squeezed her nieces' hands tightly. 'You did so well, ladies. You looked incredibly cool strutting down the aisle.'

'I'm bored.' Saffron suctioned her thumb back into her mouth.

'Weddings are weird, Saffy. Lots of waiting around and strange behaviour. If things get super dull, let's go watch a movie in my room, eh?'

'Yes!' both girls chimed in unison.

'Can we go now?' Jemima asked. 'I want to watch *Sing 2* with you again, Aunty Jade.'

'Later, maybe. We have to take some photos now.'

'Of what?' Jemima spat.

'Well, us. The whole family. And James's family.'

'Why?'

'I don't really know, Jam. It's just what happens at weddings.'

'Granny doesn't even like Jacquie. She told me she thinks she's bossy and wears too much perfume,' Jemima said.

'OK, well let's not say that out loud when we're all together.'

'Why?' Jemima asked again.

'Come on, let's just get this over and done with.' Jade guided her nieces towards the hotel.

'OK, immediate family first, please,' announced a photographer with a large bun of silver hair on her head and glasses balancing on the end of her nose. She handed her assistant a lens and motioned for a new one. A sea of brown dresses parted to leave Jade standing on her own, exposed and wide-eyed. She moved tentatively towards her dad and Jacquie in front of the huge fireplace.

'Jacquie, I'm so sorry about what happened at dinner.'

'It's all right, Jadey, I get it. I know things aren't ideal between me and your mum.' Jacquie looked tense as she scanned the room for Sue.

'Well, I should have gone about it all in a more discreet manner, so I'm sorry. I know you've always been there for me and I'm grateful for that.'

'I've tried. I know I haven't always got it right. It's a weird old thing to be a stepmother.'

'I know, especially in our family. But I appreciate you, I truly do. You know what Mum is like. She struggles and that causes tension between you both. I guess what I was trying to say at dinner was that she just doesn't have the capacity to hear about your life with Dad.'

'I'm well aware of that. Look, I don't want to make you feel like you're in the middle of all of this. It's our drama not yours.' She leaned in and gave Jade a hug as Tony approached.

'Hey, Dad.' Jade put her arm on his lightly.

'Hello, Jade. No more outbursts today if that's OK with you.' His eyes looked over her head, his voice dismissive.

Jade went to speak. There were things she needed to say to her dad. Words that she had feared saying before now.

'Nice boots,' James interjected. He was clutching Lily's hand tightly.

'Congratulations, you two,' Jade offered.

Lily looked over with a large fake smile.

Lining up for the family photo, Jade was now so close to her relatives she could hear them breathing. She clenched her teeth. She could hear stomachs rumbling, throats gurgling, large inhalations.

'Can the lady on the end tuck in so we can't see the boots.' The photographer pointed at Jade. She tucked in so not a single part of her face or body could be seen.

'OK, think we've got that. Bride and groom on their own now, please.' The photographer strode towards them both to offer some ideas for poses. The family dispersed from the fireplace, breaking the silence with polite chatter. Jade's body loosened with relief.

Moving towards her dad, who was now chatting to James's dad, she pushed in between them.

'Excuse me, gentlemen.' Jade wondered why she was using such formal language. 'I just wanted to have a quick word with my dad, if that's OK.'

James's dad moved away with a polite smile.

'Sorry I caused a scene at the rehearsal dinner. I know it was a little . . . over the top.'

'Well, we've moved on from it now. Let's make today a celebration of Lily,' Tony said calmly but with sincerity.

Jade paused. 'Like we do every day.' She couldn't help herself, the words forming before she had a chance to think. 'Dad, if you really want me out of the flat just tell me now. You mention how fortunate I am at every opportunity. If you're uncomfortable with me there, can you please just say.'

Tony stepped back, a look of puzzlement on his face that Jade hadn't seen before.

'No, no of course not.' His face softened.

'Well, why do you mention it every time I see you?'

Tony looked at his large hands.

'You've paid for all of this.' Jade gestured to the hotel, the marquee, the trays of champagne floating past in the arms of caterers. 'And the honeymoon. Whereas I pay full rent, Dad. Why do you give me such a hard time?'

'I didn't realise . . .' Tony trailed off.

'I can go and live with Mum in the cottage if that makes life easier for you?' Jade looked deeply into her dad's dark, hooded eyes.

'I guess, you know . . . Lily can be quite dramatic and demanding.' Tony spoke quietly. 'It's very difficult to say no to her.'

'I get that. But why give me a hard time?' Jade held his stare.

'You're capable, Jade. You always have been. You get on with it.'

Jade had never seen her dad look so sheepish.

'Well, at times I've had to be.'

Tony nodded while looking at his feet. 'Look, I love you being in the flat. Makes me proud. You've worked very hard.'

These were words Jade had never heard her dad say before. She felt a lump forming in her throat.

'Stay. OK? I won't mention it again.' Tony pulled her into his chest and hugged her tightly.

Jade smiled gently, her head resting on his chest for the first time since she was a tiny kid. 'I'm going to go check on the girls.'

She moved away with a new lightness in her bones. Once outside, she picked up pace, sprinting across the soggy grass, her hands over her head in an attempt to save her hair from the showers. *He was proud.* She had always hoped he was, but hearing it made all the difference.

Most of the guests had made their way to the large round tables in the neighbouring marquee. As Jade approached the now-empty ceremonial tent, she spotted several catering staff collecting abandoned glasses from the floor. A tall figure was hunched over by Jade's floral archway, hair flopping in his face. As he stood upright, she tried to work out how tall he was. Six foot? Actually, much taller than that. She watched his broad shoulders spread wide as he carried two trays full of empties. She picked up pace to try and shorten the distance between them, her boots squelching in the grass as she neared the opening to the marquee.

'Jadey! Haven't seen you for a while.' A damp pair of lips pressed into her cheek.

'Oh, Uncle Darren, hi.' Darren was as wide as his brother Tony but didn't have the height.

'What you been up to? Still doing your arts and crafts?' He stood back with his hands on his expanding waistline.

'Well, it's not really arts and crafts . . .' She looked over her uncle to see in which direction the stranger had gone.

'Must be a right doss just sticking and painting all day.'

'It doesn't really work like—'

'You wanna do a day's work with me at the car dealership. It's a slog. I love it and I am bloody good at flogging them cars, but that's years of experience for you.'

Jade nodded, glancing back to the marquee desperately.

'Bloody hell, your sister's had more weddings than I've had hot dinners. Shame about the weather.' He looked up to the soot-coloured skies. 'Where's that Aaron fella of yours, then?'

'Adam, he's called Adam. We've . . . broken up, so I'm here on . . . my own . . .' Jade's words became quieter as she tailed off.

'Oh, shame. I quite liked him. Well, we'd better find you another fella soon, eh, what are you now? Pushing forty?'

'I'm thirty-two.'

'Well, time flies, don't it, so better crack on, eh?'

'Right you are, Uncle Darren. I'm getting a bit rained on here so I'm just going to—'

'This food better be decent, I'm starving. They always starve you at a wedding. Bloody ravenous.'

'I've just got to go and check on Lily's girls.' Jade skipped passed her uncle without looking back. As she arrived at the marquee it was completely empty, not a wedding guest or caterer in sight.

'Damn.' Jade ran her fingers through the damp ends of her hair. She could hear the crackle of chatter next door, alcohol now circulating through the guests' bloodstreams – with the awkwardness of the formal ceremony over, ties and lips were loosening. For the first time that day Jade wished she had someone with her. She walked into the bustling marquee alone.

37

A large board on an easel stood at the doorway to the lunch marquee, hand-drawn tables and calligraphy swirls alerting each guest to their lunchtime fate. Jade's head fell as soon as she saw the board. Her sister had seated her next to two people she had never met before, a Harry Tiffin and Luca Crane. She wondered why this was commonplace at weddings. The next two hours would be a torturous affair of making small talk with strangers she had nothing in common with. She felt a new sliver of hatred for her sister. Her eyes ran over the names again. Luca. She was sat next to Luca from the script. She felt instantly deflated, knowing that the wavy-haired stranger was not Luca like she'd hoped.

Feeling overly aware of her facial expressions and movement, she weaved between the backs of chairs and loud wedding guests to reach Table 14. A stubby tree trunk sat in the middle of the table with a small signpost sticking out of the top, the word 'Magenta' written on it in calligraphy. Jade turned to scan the other tables, which all seemingly had other colours assigned; an obvious nod to Lily's interiors website.

'Hi.' Jade nodded at the already full table. As she sat, she looked to her left and right and repeated the nod.

'Hi. I'm Harry, but everyone calls me Biffy.' A broad man who looked like a rugby player sat to her right, his first three shirt buttons undone, legs spread apart, leaving her little room. His light hair was pushed back revealing a red forehead, his square chin jutting out as he grinned.

'Oh, hi, I'm Jade.' Not knowing whether to shake her new neighbour's hand, her arms twitched but remained by her side. She turned to her left. A short man with slicked-down, side-parted black hair looked back at her with large, bulbous eyes. He wore a navy suit and a velvet burgundy bow tie.

'Hello, I'm Luca.' The man reached out his hand and squeezed Jade's a little too hard. Jade's heart sank.

'Hi, I'm Jade. Lily's sister,' she replied meekly. She thought back to the script and waited for him to mention her brown dress, but he didn't.

'Biff, pass the white.' A willowy woman opposite Jade reached her thin arm towards Biffy, her yellow silk dress slipping off her shoulders to reveal elegant, black, angular shoulders. Her accent was clipped and tight, and everything about her looked expensive. Biffy passed the bottle then turned straight back to Jade, who now felt even more of a fish out of water. Her sister had clearly, purposely, put her on a table of people who all knew each other.

'Who's that?' Jade asked quietly.

'Octavia. Extraordinary woman. Millionaire before the age of thirty. Runs her own high-end holiday rental business,' Biffy declared casually.

Jade felt herself shrink further. 'Wow.' She longed for Sophie's company.

'So, you're Lil's little sis?' Biffy said with an eyebrow raised.

'Yup, that's me. How do you know my sister?' Jade pretended to care.

'We met many moons ago out on the King's Road. We were both on that party scene back in the day. These days, Lils often comes to my place in Gloucestershire, or sometimes comes skiing. I have a chalet in Verbier.'

Jade had to use all her effort not to grimace. Her sister's elaborate tales of skiing with this Biffy character over the years had turned into fables that Jade barely believed: the long lunches on the slopes, the all-night partying with B-list celebrities and endless bottles of expensive red wine. Jade thought how he was the perfect friend for Lily: innocuous, wealthy and the proud owner of a ski chalet.

'Oh yes, I think I remember hearing about your ski trips together.' Jade attempted a smile.

Biffy stroked his floppy blonde hair from his red forehead, his boxy hands landing back on his wine glass.

'I'm not one for skiing,' said Luca.

'Oh?' Jade turned her head sharply to the left at this unexpected interjection.

'I'm more of a boat man myself. Your sister has been on my boat here and there over the years. Most memorably we had a splendid trip around the island of Capri. Have you been?' His eyes seemed to bulge from his face the more he spoke.

Jade almost snorted at this question. 'Er, no. No, I haven't been to Capri.'

'Oh well, you must,' said Luca, smiling and taking a small sip of wine.

'Well, I'll be sure to put it on my list,' Jade said, aiming for pleasant sarcasm.

'It's a bit old-school. Lots of old money roaming around. Bit too stiff for me,' said Biffy, Jade's head moving from left to right as each man tried to out-do the other.

'Well, it depends where you go. Anacapri is much quieter and has a certain elegance to it that I have yet to find elsewhere in Europe,' Luca countered, running his pale fingers across his slicked-down hair.

'Yeah, mate, not my cup of tea.' Biffy threw this out with the gusto of someone who has just downed two glasses of wine in quick succession. Jade felt her body tense.

'How do you know my sister?' Jade asked Luca, attempting to break the tension.

'I'm one of James's uni pals. We went to Bristol together.'

'Lovely,' Jade said, unable to find the correct, cordial words to keep the conversation flowing.

'Ladies, gentlemen, and little ones, please be upstanding for the bride and grooooom!' James's best man, Michael, bellowed into the microphone to the masses. Cheers and whoops engulfed the marquee as Lily and James waltzed in amongst the tables. Lily was doing her best coquettish smile, hiding any hint of her ferocious demands from earlier. Jade could always see it in her eyes. Whatever Lily's emotion, even as everyone else fell for her exaggerated laugh, Jade could see it. A cacophony of cheers echoed from the sea of round tables as Lily glided like an ice skater amongst them. Jade clapped slowly with a neutral face.

'She's always been so bloody hot, your sister.' Biffy spoke to Jade but kept his eyes on Lily.

Jade ignored him and pushed her Ugg boots off under the table, allowing her clammy skin to feel fresh air.

Eventually Lily and James reached the head table, positioned on a dais above the others. The applause petered out as bride and groom took their seats between Sue, Tony and Jacquie, and James's family. For a split second Jade saw herself up there with Navi, whose face then morphed into Adam's; intrusive thoughts that made her feel dizzy.

'Your stepmum's not bad either,' Biffy said, leaning in conspiratorially.

Jade smiled, keeping her eyes locked on the head table, her arms and legs wrapped in on themselves like a pretzel, creating as much distance as possible from the men on either side.

Her eyes flicked from the conversation going on around her up to her mum. Sue was drinking her white wine in large gulps, only touching her glass back down to the table for mere seconds. Her head was turned away from Jacquie. Jade's gaze moved across to Lily, and she caught her sister's eye. Lily's stretched, glossy smile turned to a tight-lipped pinch as she nodded towards their mum – an unspoken signal for Jade to rein in their mother's drinking. Jade got up without excusing herself and crept behind the head table, only realising she was barefoot when she arrived at her mum's side.

'Hey, Mum. You OK?' Jade placed her hands lightly on her mum's tense shoulders.

Sue turned abruptly to look at who was crouched by her side.

'Yes, yes. Why?'

Jade kept her voice to a whisper. 'Just checking. Remember, it's only 3pm so don't go too hard on the booze just yet. We've got a whole day to get through and a party this evening.'

Sue turned away from her daughter to face the mass of wedding guests and stared at nothing in particular. 'I'm fine, thank you, darling.' She took a swig of her wine and turned back to Jade. 'I see Lily has kindly put you next to some lovely gentlemen for lunch.' She spoke without a whiff of sarcasm.

'Um, yes. Isn't she kind.' Jade straightened up and sloped back to her table, her bare soles sticking slightly to the floor as she walked. Tipping her weight forward so she could teeter on tiptoes, she watched the catering staff file into the marquee to serve the starters. Where was he? Her eyes moved from head to head like a giant dot-to-dot. Reaching her table, she sat down feeling deflated.

'Oh, bloody good starter. Mackerel pâté, delish. Your sister is one classy lady.' Biffy dug his knife into the pâté and piled it on the toast.

Jade nodded, looking at her plate. She pushed it away and picked up a glass of red wine somebody had filled for her, drank it and shuddered. She let her eyes land on the top table once again and saw her mum talking to Jacquie. Her knee began to bounce up and down nervously.

'So, what do you do, Jade?' Luca leaned on his right elbow so he was uncomfortably close to Jade's face. She could smell his sour breath mixed with a spicy after-shave. Before she answered she wondered why it was such a common initial question when trying to get to know someone; as if job identity was the sum of all existence.

'I design and create sets or installations for films, the-atre and TV shows, and festivals.'

Luca sat back and nodded slowly, raising his dark bushy eyebrows. 'Arty. I like it.'

Jade tried to cover her grimace with a polite smile. 'How about you, Luca?' She kept her eyes on the stem of her wine glass.

'I work for my father. We have an insurance company. Well, when I say we have, *he* has, and I work for him but I'm very much his right-hand man.'

Jade took a minuscule sip of bitter wine. 'Sounds cool.'

A hand reached over Jade's shoulder and took her untouched starter away. She looked up hoping to see *him*, but an older-looking Italian man grinned down at her. 'You finished, madam?'

Jade tried not to look disappointed. 'Yes, yes. Thank you. Just not a mackerel fan.'

Biffy intercepted the conversation as the starters were taken, a blob of pâté still perched on his shiny chin: 'So, Lily tells me you're newly single,' he said, licking his lips.

Jade's jaw tensed. 'For fuck's sake,' she muttered. 'Yes, yes, I am. That's so nice of Lily – to discuss my personal business with strangers.'

Biffy sat back, his legs splayed apart. 'Well, we're not strangers now, are we. What happened? Who dumped who?'

'Well, I'd rather not go into details.'

'Oh, did he dump you? I get it. I know that pain. Brutal.'

'Well, no, actually it was me who dumped him, thanks.' Jade's words spiked with frustration at being cornered.

'Oh well, congratulations. He must have been a right loser.'

Jade couldn't counter his statement, but felt a strange sort of compassion towards Adam that she didn't understand. Perhaps it was a complete stranger making such a harsh judgement. Maybe she missed him a tiny bit.

'Anyway, what do you do?' Jade found herself asking.

'I work in the City.'

Jade instantly switched off. She knew nothing about the City and no one from that world. 'Cool,' she managed.

Biffy leaned into her personal space. 'How about you? Lily mentioned something about arts and crafts.'

A hand reached across Jade and placed her main course in front of her, which gave her time to compose herself and not scream 'IT'S NOT ARTS AND CRAFTS.'

'It's actually art and design at a very high level.' She wondered why she was boasting. 'I design and create TV, theatre and film sets, amongst other things.' She looked down at the gloopy risotto on her plate and then to the lamb shank sat atop a swirl of mashed potato on Biffy's, wondering why she had a different meal to everyone else. Looking at the head table she saw her sister tucking into a chunk of lamb and raised an eyebrow, remembering her recent vegan proclamation.

'So what shows have you designed sets for? Anything I would know?' Biffy levered his knife to tear a large lump of meat off the bone.

'Yup. Lots.'

'Go on, then,' he said through a mouthful of oozing meat.

'Did you see the latest Suranne Jones drama?' Jade asked, wondering why she was bothering to try and impress him.

'What, the one on ITV? Course. I bloody loved it.'

'Well, we did most of that.'

'Did you meet her?' Biffy asked, washing the meat down with a swig of white wine.

'Course. Loads. She's super nice.'

'Is she tall? She looks tall.'

'Suranne? Erm . . . not really. Sort of my height, maybe an inch taller.'

'What did she smell like?'

'*Smell* like? I don't know. I was there to paint the set, not sniff the actors.'

Raised voices broke through their conversation. At first Jade couldn't work out whether she was hearing hysterical laughter or distressed screeches. She looked up to see Jacquie and her mum staring right at each other, hands moving as quickly as their mouths.

'Oh god.' Jade put her knife and fork down, poised to intercept or to stand by and watch this nightmare unfold. Both women stood up, Sue's voice increasing in volume. The room was too loud to make out what was being said, but Jade could hear the heat in each word as the clipped edges of consonants reached her. She rose from her seat.

As Jade moved towards the top table, everything happened quickly. Her mum's arm rose up like a lever, glass in hand. Then a wave of white wine surged out of the glass and covered Jacquie's face. Jade gasped and put her hands to her mouth. Jacquie screamed. The marquee fell quiet.

38

'Come on, Mum. Let's go and take a breather outside.' Jade grabbed her mum's elbow, the clattering of Sue's bangles piercing the silence of the room. 'Jacquie, you OK?' she added, looking desperately at her stepmum. Jacquie nodded and motioned for Jade to remove Sue from the table. 'Come with me. Let's go find a quiet corner.' Jade quickly moved her mum from the table, mortification licking at her cheeks.

A small opening in the marquee led out to some Portaloos with a small, makeshift powder room attached. There were baskets with hand cream, deodorant, and packs of chewing gum, all lit by the lightbulb-lined mirrors.

'Mum, what the hell was that?' Jade looked her straight in the eyes, trying to straddle empathy and sternness.

'Darling, don't be harsh with me. I'm feeling very bruised,' Sue replied, raising her voice above the lashing rain.

'Mum, you just chucked a glass of wine in Jacquie's face.'

'She deserved it!' Sue's words were peppered with drama and self-indulgent sorrow.

'It's not the time or place, Mum. As much as it pains me to say it, today is about Lily.'

'I know, I know. Jacquie just winds me up so much. Today it just felt like I hit a wall. Years of accumulated frustration at her boasting about her life with your dad.'

'Look, I get it. It's hard for you, but what did I say earlier? Drinking away these feelings will not help. I'm going to get you a glass of water and then we need to head back in and you're going to have to apologise to her, OK?'

'I'm not going anywhere near that woman.'

'I'm afraid you are, Mum. You need water. Come on, let's go.'

Jade dragged her mum by the arm as if she were shepherding a petulant child. They made their way back through the masses, who had resumed their chatter and drunken laughter.

'Luckily for you she's not here. She must have gone with Dad back to their room to clean up. So, go back to the top table and drink a large glass of water, OK?' She kissed her mum on the cheek.

Sue nodded and slowly made her way through the tables. Lily ignored her arrival, maintaining a display of complete joy and composure for the benefit of any onlookers.

Jade's plate had been removed, even though it too was untouched. She shook her head and grabbed the bread roll which had been left on the side plate. Biffy was talking to Octavia across the table and Luca was in deep conversation with a man to his left. Jade tore off chunks of bread ferociously, letting the salty butter sit on the roof of her mouth. The sound of the rain increased overhead, the relentless drumbeat interspersed with cracks of thunder. Voices were raised to match the pounding rain. Jade felt engulfed by noise.

An arm reached across Jade for a third time and placed a small meringue nest in front of her, a pile of raspberries and blackberries on top. Jade's teeth twinged. It was as if Lily had chosen all of her least favourite foods on purpose. She picked the berries off and popped them in her mouth before she had properly swallowed the bread, a merger of bland and tart.

Suddenly, a loud yelp at the far end of the marquee had all heads turning. Jade jumped, her nervous system already on edge. The room fell silent once more as the sound of gushing water filled the marquee, splintered by shrieks and screams. A section of the roof hung from its metal frame like a giant flap of skin, the open wound exposing those below to the black sky and pelting rain. James's grandmother jumped up, arms in the air, a long string of pearls swinging with the frantic movement. A lady with a blunt grey bob and large green perspex earrings, who Jade recognised as James's aunty, also sprang to her feet, clumsily falling backwards in an attempt to save herself from the sheets of water. Plates clattered and wine glasses clashed together. Two other ladies stood screeching and flapping their arms like colourful birds as they edged back from the table. Chaos rippled from table to table as wedding guests clambered out of the way, knocking into neighbouring diners. More glasses smashed on the floor, and meringues floated in pools of rainwater and wine like little islands surrounded by sea.

'Oh dear,' was all Jade could manage.

'Bloody hell,' said Biffy, standing and slowly taking a sip from his wine glass. On the top table, Lily stood next to her chair, watching in dismay like a Disney princess, hands over her mouth, her long manicured fingernails hovering just below her nose. It was uncertain whether she felt genuine horror as she was such a good actor; Jade was sure she was mostly grateful that the roof hadn't caved in over her.

A microphone screeched into action. 'Ladies and gentlemen, we have had a slight issue with the marquee, as you can see, so for health and safety reasons we are now all going to make our way over to the main hotel, where the catering staff will serve you coffees and chocolates.'

Sodden family members clung to the arms of the dry and were led out to join the throng that was moving like a herd of buffalo to the main building. Jade was the last one to leave the marquee. Desperate to get away from the noise and drama in the air, she slipped her boots back on and walked past the debris of the obliterated table, her Uggs navigating between broken glasses and plates. Huddling under the lip of the tarpaulined ceiling, she breathed in great gulps of air and let her eyes land on the stream that weaved through the hotel grounds. The chattering mass of guests got quieter until she could only hear the moving water and patter of rain. A small laugh escaped her mouth. What an absolute mess this wedding was turning out to be.

She felt somebody appear to her left.

'Nice dress.'

39

Jade gulped. It was him. This close, she could see that his eyes were light green with flecks of golden-yellow, like the inside of a marble. His hair fell over one eye, and he brushed it back with one hand. His white catering uniform was unbuttoned, revealing a dishevelled navy-blue T-shirt underneath. He looked as relieved as she was that everyone had left for the hotel.

He smiled at Jade, and her legs quivered slightly.

'It's brown.'

The words fell out of her mouth quietly, without effort, the script rising to the surface, bypassing rational thought.

The stranger laughed quietly, almost under his breath. Jade's mind raced back to her table neighbour, Luca, with his slicked-back hair and bow tie. The script had never been wrong or muddled details before. Jade could barely bring herself to look at him. She felt a flush of embarrassment and willed her face not to go red.

'I know,' he said, looking her dress up and down.

She followed his gaze and prayed he would stop at her knees and not notice her feet in their giant, inelegant boots. Her hand reached out a little too stiffly. She felt formal and clumsy, a wooden toy soldier lacking movable joints. She looked at her hand, slightly shaking, and willed it to relax. His hand met hers. A slow handshake that sent electrical waves throughout her whole body.

'I like . . . your jacket,' she said to fill an almost awkward silence as she continued to hold on to his hand for a little too long. He looked down at his catering whites and laughed.

'Ha. Thanks. I'm Luca, by the way.'

Luca. *Luca*. Her cheeks flushed red. The name Luca hadn't sat well with her table-mate earlier. He looked like a Robert or a Simon, maybe a Peter – but not a Luca. *This* was Luca.

'Anyway, I'd better go. I need to serve chocolates to the damp guests in the hotel now. Shitty weather, eh?' He spoke slowly, as if not in a rush at all.

Jade's vocabulary seemed to dissipate in seconds. A silence fell where words should sit. The script had ended, and she had run dry. She nodded and smiled as he dashed off, buttoning up his jacket as he sped away. A huge grin spread across her face as she looked up at the grey sky. She walked out from the shelter of the marquee and let the rain fall on her face. Turning lightly, she walked towards the hotel, her grin remaining firmly in place.

The Fireside Room of the Wellington Hotel was a moving mass of guests, the windows slick with condensation. Cups and saucers clinked, bodies were draped over sofa arms, suited torsos resting up against walls. Clusters of people congregated throughout the room, creating raucous noise. Jade walked in slowly, looking for a quiet spot to sit without drawing too much attention to herself. A small window seat was unoccupied, so she weaved through the crowd and sat down, looking out to the dilapidated marquee. Ten or so hotel staff in anoraks were trying to fix the damaged roof. Ladders wobbled on soft turf, and hands grabbed at the sheets of ripped tarpaulin. In the neighbouring marquee Jade could see another group laying down a dance floor. A DJ deck was being assembled in front of her floral archway and a mirrored bar constructed at the back of the marquee.

'Why are you all on your own, Jadey?' Belinda glided onto the window seat next to Jade, her green silk dress landing a second after her body.

'Belinda!' Jade said with genuine delight. She squeezed her godmother tightly and let her head lie on her shoulder for a short moment. 'I'm just having some time out. I find these things so overwhelming.'

'I know. I'm sure not helped by your mother flinging wine all over Jacquie.' Belinda raised an eyebrow. 'I haven't managed to find her yet to check if she's OK.'

'She'll be OK. She's currently half embarrassed, half intoxicated.' Jade attempted a smile. 'You know, you're the only person who could pull off an entirely green outfit,' she said, changing the subject. Her smile grew as she took in her godmother's emerald-green floor-length dress, matching velvet pumps and clutch bag the colour of moss.

'And you look lovely in . . . what do we call this colour? Mud?' She laughed softly.

Jade looked down at her dress and thick boots and

shook her head slowly. 'I ended things with Adam.' She looked directly into Belinda's eyes for reassurance.

Belinda placed a warm hand over the top of Jade's. 'Well done, my darling. How do you feel about it?'

'I have been fine, but being at a wedding has been slightly triggering; seeing loads of couples together and thinking back to my own failed attempt.'

'Well, that's natural. It's all new, and new usually equals a bit of discomfort, but that doesn't make it wrong.' Belinda shuffled closer. The hum of chatter around them seemed to fade. 'You need to be face up to the sun, remember.' She put her index finger to her chin and tilted her own head to the ceiling. 'A sunflower in all her glory, beaming, with petals outstretched.' Belinda unfurled her arms and stretched them out wide, the arms of her silk dress billowing like wings. Jade exhaled and remembered the fields of flowers in Dorset.

Belinda leaned in further so she was an inch from Jade's face. 'Let's have a shot of something, eh?'

Jade sat bolt upright. 'A shot? It's only 6pm.'

'Darling, I may be old, but with that comes wisdom, and I have a feeling you need to have some fun.' Belinda stood up and shook out the skirt of her dress. 'You must never take life too seriously. Honestly, you get to my age and realise that there is always more room for laughter.'

'Bloody hell. OK. A shot it is.'

'Come on, darling, let's be a pair of sunflowers.' Belinda snaked her arm through Jade's and led her to the bustling bar. 'Two shots of tequila, please,' she bellowed to the nearest barman.

343

'Tequila? Oh god.' Jade turned to look at Belinda's grinning face. Her green eyeshadow sparkled and crinkled in the corners where her smile was setting in.

'It's clean booze, darling. Barely a hangover with tequila.'

The barman handed over two shot glasses full to the brim.

'Here we go, darling. Three, two, one . . . to sunflowers.' Jade and her godmother slugged down the shots of tequila and shuddered. The roof of Jade's mouth contracted.

'I think the sunflower metaphor has been stretched a little, Belinda, but thank you for the shot none the less.'

'Jade, remember, you're free now. Don't look at what's missing in your life, look at what is gained. You have gained free time, autonomy, and more wardrobe space.'

Jade laughed. A wave of intoxication coursed through her head. 'I genuinely can't wait to infiltrate Adam's side of the wardrobe,' she laughed.

'Now look into my eyes. I want you to remember how bloody marvellous you are. You're a shining light, always have been. Don't let anyone tell you otherwise.' Belinda clutched Jade's shoulders, her nails slightly digging into Jade's skin.

'Well, same goes for you, Belinda,' Jade replied, feeling the weight of her godmother's genuine love. 'Could you do me a favour?' The need for her to change the subject felt all-consuming.

'Anything for you.'

'Can you go and find Mum for me, and check on her?

I don't want her falling into a pit of shame over the wine moment. She needs to brush herself off, apologise to Jacquie and enjoy the rest of the wedding. My words usually fall on deaf ears. She might listen to you.' Jade scrunched up her face with the discomfort of delegation.

'Of course. I'll see to it right away. Now you go and have some fun.'

Belinda slunk from the bar with a slightly intoxicated sway. Turning back, she called, 'Jade. Remember. Sunflower!' She stretched her arms out wide and tilted her head to the ceiling.

Jade gave her a double thumbs up.

40

'Jade.' A firm hand pressed into her back.

'Oh, bloody hell, James, you spooked me.' Jade's body jolted upright with the cold touch of James's palm on her bare back.

'Haven't properly spoken to you since your big freak-out at our rehearsal dinner, so thought I should come over and break the ice, so to speak.' James's vowels were soft and his consonants sloppy, the edges loosened by a steady flow of wine.

'Oh well, first up, congratulations on your marriage to my sister . . . brother-in-law,' Jade said with a little too much forced enthusiasm.

'Oh yeah, Mr Fanny-Struck, married to the piss-taker.' James waved to the barman to get him a drink.

'Look, I'm sorry. I was fired up that night.' Jade kept her eyes fixed on the smooth surface of the mahogany bar.

'It's fine. I was more upset that you said Lily is a piss-taker. She works so hard and is really trying to start her business from scratch.'

James took a sip of a newly poured vodka and soda. Jade's brain scrambled to find some sort of happy medium where she didn't ignore the truth yet simultaneously stayed on the right side of civil. 'Well, she's been lucky, I guess. I mean, look around. Lily's new business certainly didn't pay for this wedding.'

'It's OK to be a bit jealous, Jade.' James spoke with a patronising sincerity. The muscles in Jade's jaw tightened and slightly ached.

'You could not be more wrong, James. I love my job, I'm newly single and excited about it, and don't owe my father thousands of pounds for a wedding and honeymoon.' Jade kept her eyes on the bar staff as she spoke. 'Gin and tonic, please,' she motioned to a nearby bartender with a tightly scraped-back bun.

'One does protest too much.' James's speech was beginning to slur.

'Slow down there, Jimmy.' Jade pointed to James's empty glass. 'And no, I'm not protesting at all. I'm simply telling you how it is. As I said, sorry for my outburst at the dinner and . . . congrats on today . . .'

'LADIES AND GENTLEMEN . . .' The best man at the mic broke the mounting tension. 'The dance floor is now ready. So, leave your inhibitions and umbrellas at the door . . . LET'S PARTY!'

Squeals of booze-infused joy rippled through the room as feet shuffled from the bar towards the back doors of the hotel. Jade was carried along in the throng of bodies, her gin and tonic spilling over the sides as enthusiastic guests pushed towards the exit. The rain had stopped, and small areas of blue sky were starting to appear like squares on a patchwork blanket. As the guests moved across the grass to the marquee, Jade could hear the music growing in volume, Wham's 'Club

Tropicana' seeping out into the early evening air. Something about the laughter threaded through the song lyrics and the mass of people linking arms made Jade feel unanchored to reality. The wedding ceremony and lunch had been manageable on her own, and maybe that was because they involved rules and structure: sit here, cheer now, walk this way, eat this, clap now, talk to this person. The rest of the evening would be free from formalities as the intoxication and loud music unravelled even the most uptight. The thought of it quickened her breath and once again brought Adam's face to mind. She wasn't sure she missed him or any of his qualities, but she missed the familiarity of him being there as a barrier to the outside world.

Wedding guests bumped into her shoulders, eager for another drink. The three other bridesmaids had already gathered around a small round table inside the marquee, champagne flutes in hand and heads thrown back in laughter. Jade walked with a little more purpose towards them, relieved to see familiar faces.

'Jade, what happened with your mum and Jacquie earlier? Bloody hell, that livened things up.' Sarita's amber eyes were shining with the recall of it all.

'Oh, god, I know. I told Mum to slow down on the drinking but she can't help herself.' Jade played down her genuine concern.

'Is Jacquie OK?' Cathy leaned in, desperate to know more.

'I haven't seen her. I think she's still hiding in her room. I'm sure she'll be down soon for the party.'

'Well, Jade, you've caught us in the middle of slagging off our husbands if you want to join in,' Sarita said. 'I know you're not married, but feel free to be a spectator.' She swiped a lipgloss wand over her pouting lips.

'Well, I actually broke up with my boyfriend recently, but I'm happy to listen in.'

'Well, you're better off without him, darling,' Sinead said. 'Steve is driving me mad at the moment – look.' She pointed towards the bar. 'I've asked him to go easy so he can deal with the kids tomorrow, but he's propped up at the bar on his sixth pint already.' She shook her head, coils of long brunette hair bouncing with the movement. Jade could see Steve standing with a pint glass in hand, his top two buttons undone and his bald head glinting with a reflection from the large disco ball overhead. 'He'll no doubt try it on with me when we get back to the room later too, and I really cannot be doing with that after such a long day.' Sinead threw the remains of her champagne down her throat.

'Don't get me started on that one, babe.' Sarita puffed out her cheeks. 'Why are men so permanently up for it? Jacob would happily have sex every day, maybe twice a day if I let him.'

'I know,' Cathy chimed in. 'Last week, it had been about six days since Pete and I had done the deed so I thought to myself, I'd better initiate it to break the tension I could feel in the air. When I asked him, he pretended he wasn't that bothered, which is a classic move on his part – he said he wanted to finish his cup of tea first. I went upstairs to brush my teeth and freshen up and by the time I came out of the bathroom he was lying in the bed naked. There is no way he could have finished a cup of tea in that time.'

Both Sarita and Sinead stood with their mouths slightly open. 'Cathy, explain the day six thing to me,' Sarita said with urgency.

'Yes, Cathy, what do you mean by six days?' Sinead echoed.

Cathy stood with her brows furrowed in confusion.

Sarita moved nearer and almost whispered, 'Cathy, *how often are you having sex?*'

Cathy stuttered, 'Well, I mean, maybe twice a week, three times if I've gotten the kids to bed on time.'

'Cath! Seasons change in the time I'm not having sex,' Sarita proclaimed.

'Same. Once a month over here.' Sinead raised her hand. 'You're literally a pornstar, Cathy. How long have you been married?'

'Twelve years.'

'Oh my god, babe. How can you be bothered?' Sinead shook her head and looked back towards Steve at the bar, a third shirt button now undone.

'Really? I thought only a couple of times a week was bad.' Cathy was now laughing heartily, half with relief, half with joy.

'Never let Pete speak to Jacob, OK? He must not know about this,' Sarita demanded with absolute sincerity.

'Yes, Steve cannot hear about this either, Cathy. He has full acceptance of our unspoken arrangement these days. He must never know there is another way.' Sinead pointed her finger accusingly then brought it up to her lips.

'OK, OK. I'll make sure of it.' Cathy swigged her wine with glee.

'I have absolutely no input to this conversation, but it's been an eye-opener.' Jade smiled; her cheeks rosy from laughter.

'See, count yourself lucky that you're not in a long-term relationship,' Sinead said, placing her hands on Jade's shoulders with the authority of an older sibling's mate. 'You're free.' She looked directly into Jade's eyes and winked.

Jade smiled as her mind landed on a mental image of Luca.

41

Bodies moved in irregular rhythms, arms swaying and pointing above the crowd of bobbing heads. The dance floor was starting to fill up, a familiar nineties dance tune filling every corner of the marquee. Jade spotted Lily in the middle of the floor; a space seemed to naturally form around her in the homogenised throng of bodies. The spotlight followed her every move and illuminated her dress, so it looked like sunlight on snow. Lily had changed into a new gown, more relaxed than her wedding dress, its scooped neck revealing her cleavage and a low back showing everyone she didn't need to wear a bra. Jade looked on with fascination. She tilted her head and felt a pang of envy. Not for the wedding, or the eyes on Lily, but for the confidence and comfort her sister felt in her own skin. The silk clung to each angle of Lily's body, her hip bones gliding beneath the fabric. Jade was certain she had not experienced that level of comfort in an outfit that wasn't dungarees. Simultaneously, she wondered how much the second dress had cost their dad.

Two arms draped over her shoulders from behind and a sprout of strawberry-blonde hair tickled her cheek. 'Babe, I'm gasping. I did the whole of series one of *Happy Valley*. I love James Norton but I'm so excited to be out of that hotel room and *so* ready to have a dance.' Jade hugged Sophie with pure relief. Sophie stood grinning in a bright red polka-dot dress and strappy shoes.

'I don't think I've ever seen you in shoes, Soph. I mean, shoe shoes. You look adorable.'

'Thanks, mate. I do scrub up OK, don't I? I had a lush bath in that free-standing tub, too. I had no idea how much I missed baths until today. I cannot wait to have a bathroom big enough for a tub one day. Drink?'

Jade's eyes moved back to her sister snaking across the dance floor. 'Look at her, Sophie. Imagine feeling that good in your own skin.' Jade nodded towards Lily, who was shaking her shiny hair in time with the music.

'I don't believe she is, mate. I think she's used to putting on a show.'

Jade stood, eyes fixed on the white silk flowing like water around Lily's body, the light ricocheting from her hair.

'I'm going to get a beer, want one?' Sophie winked at Jade and scampered off to the bar.

A clunk over the speakers stopped all movement on the dance floor as the best man's voice boomed into the chatter. 'Ladies and gents, due to the earlier erectile dysfunction of the marquee—' Cheers and ooohhh's rose in volume at the innuendo '—we will now be hearing the speeches. First up, please welcome the big man himself, the big T, the Tonestar, the father of the bride, *Tony Shaw*, everyone!'

Tony's swagger parted the crowd, his dark blue suit undone and flapping as he walked towards the low-rise stage. Booming chants of 'Toneeeey, Toneeey' carried him up onto it.

'Enough of the "big", thank you, Micky-boy.' Tony pointed at the best man and winked with an ominous sneer. Michael threw his head back in exaggerated laughter to cover the visible tinge of fear.

'Ladies and gentlemen, thank you for being here today to celebrate the marriage of my princess, Lily . . . and James.' He looked down to the front row, where Lily was coyly blinking her eyelashes slowly, as if being caught on a cinematic close-up.

Jade let her dad's voice fade into background noise and scanned the sea of heads, scattered with fascinators, and the grinning faces turned to the stage.

A flash of white just outside the marquee caught her attention, and she saw Luca heading for the kitchen.

'Excuse me. Thanks. Sorry. Excuse me. Thank you.' Jade weaved through the crowd towards the opening in the marquee. She gulped in fresh air and felt her heartbeat quicken. She looked to the left and right but there was no one in sight. She could hear car doors rhythmically slamming in the car park. The evening guests had started to arrive, fresh-faced and stiffer in posture than the intoxicated day guests, who were standing tight as sardines at the foot of the stage. Women staggered across the gravel of the car park in their teetering heels. In the marquee, the voice on the microphone had switched from Tony's booming tone to the best man. Michael was clearly retelling mortifying tales of James as a teen, or perhaps a reckless university student, as the crowd wailed in a chorus of hysterical laughter. Trying not to feel desperate about Luca, Jade turned slowly back towards the howls of laughter.

The crowd were dispersing as James finished up his manifesto of love for Lily. Jackie Wilson's 'Your Love Keeps Lifting Me Higher' blared from the speakers and feet began to move with varying degrees of rhythm. Jade let her eyes drift across the wave of movement on the dance floor. She spotted Biffy in the centre of the crowd, his shirt half unbuttoned, blonde chest hair springing out in tufts. His arms were aloft, palms facing the ceiling, head thrown back in euphoria, hair slick with sweat on his raspberry forehead. She walked slowly towards the bar in an attempt to look less lost, joining the rows of thirsty guests bustling to the front. She stood inconspicuously and fiddled with her fingers. Looking down at the brown dress, she wished she had remembered to bring a change of clothes for the evening party.

Lifting her head to try and catch a bartender's attention, she spotted a deeply familiar head of hair. The back of this head turned to the side to reveal a profile she knew all too well.

42

'Adam.' Jade whispered his name in an attempt to suppress her shock. He turned round, a confident smile plastered on his face.

'What are *you* doing here?' Jade attempted to look emotionless and concentrated on her breathing.

'Oh, hey Jade, nice to see you too,' Adam snapped sarcastically. 'James invited me to the evening party.'

'Well, didn't you think to tell me, or ask me first?' Jade kept her voice low and quiet.

'Last time I checked, we had broken up, so I don't actually have to tell or *ask* you anything.'

'It's my sister's wedding, Adam. It would have been the decent thing to do.'

'Decent? Since when have you been the arbiter on decency?'

'Oh fuck off, Adam.' Jade waved her hand in the air at a nearby bartender. 'Large gin and tonic, please.'

Adam shook his head and turned back to the woman on his left. He patted her on the shoulder as if to apologise for the interruption. Jade snatched the glass of gin and let the liquid slip down her throat, swallowing her frustration along with her drink. The frantic electronic opening bars of The Source's 'You Got the Love' sparked out of the speakers. The hairs on Jade's arms stood on end. She wasn't sure she had ever danced freely at a wedding. There was one time her late grandad had taken her hand and twirled her round at Lily's first wedding, but she had never had the courage to navigate a dance floor on her own. Sheepishly she moved closer to the edge of where bodies writhed and feet moved. Closing her eyes, she let each bass note and lyric run across her skin, blocking out the other guests nearby. Her head swung to the side as her hips jutted out in the opposite direction, her arms worked their way up her body like a plant unfurling in springtime. Crystal flecks of bright white freckled the faces around her as the giant disco ball cast a spectrum of light over the guests below. Her lungs expanded, her heartbeat thumped, her fingertips tingled with electricity; it felt as if she were exorcising years of suppression, stomping it out as her feet met the floor on the beat of the song. She knew Adam would be watching. A tie made into a lasso swung overhead, Biffy's large hand clutching one end. He moved closer to Jade, his hips pushed forwards. She spun around to face the other side of the marquee, her body now facing the bar, the queue her audience. She opened her eyes and saw Adam still lingering with a drink in hand, his body now inches from the woman he had been chatting to earlier, her large boobs grazing his torso, her fingers stroking her own neck seductively. Jade spun away, straight into Biffy's orbit, sweat now dripping from his forehead as he spun around.

Over undulating waves of heads, Jade spotted a bob the colour of honey, swinging wildly. She moved through the throng of people to her refuge. 'Soph!' she called over the all-consuming music. Sophie was being spun around by a tall flame-haired man, her head thrown back in glee. Jade moved closer, sweating bodies emanating heat at every turn.

She caught Sophie's eye and shouted, 'Adam's here, for fuck's sake.'

Sophie kept spinning, the remnant of a large grin on her face. 'Oh, ignore him, mate. Where's old Wavy Hair? Have you spotted him yet?'

'We spoke for two seconds earlier. I was so shy. I need to track him down again and redeem myself.'

A screech of feedback split the music in two.

'Ladies and gentlemen, please welcome the bride and groom to the floor for the FIRRRSSST DANCE.'

Unsure whether she could handle witnessing any more of her sister's fairy tale, Jade kissed Sophie on the cheek and said, 'I'm going to get some air, babe.'

Sophie nodded and turned back to the towering redhead.

It was 10pm and the light was almost purple. Taking off her Uggs once again, Jade let her bare feet sink into the spongy ground outside the marquee. Swathes of indigo light skimmed the surface of the small stream. The cheering faded as she moved away, Seal's 'Kiss from a Rose' getting quieter as she neared the stream. As she sat down on a log, a flock of ducks flew away with the disturbance; their quacking sounded like laughter.

She peered over her shoulder back towards the cater-er's tent. A blur of activity and tens of white coats. Then he appeared.

Luca was leaning over a table, his hair flopping over his eyes. She ducked a little and hoped the dusky shadows were enough to keep her out of view. It was difficult for Jade to make out what he was doing. Maybe arranging more champagne glasses on a tray. Perhaps sorting out some late-night snacks for the dancing guests. Another silhouette moved in, a smaller figure with a long ponytail who approached Luca and hugged him. He then seemed to bend down and kiss her on the head.

Jade felt her stomach jump. An acidic rush hit her throat. She swallowed it down desperately, recognising the feeling: foolishness. She had been here before. Pinning all of her joy on one outcome, one person. She felt shame course through her body like icicles. Pushing her palms down on her thighs, she rose from the log and walked with purpose towards the marquee. Another stiff drink was needed to flatten out this feeling. A mental image of her mum lingered as she worried she was slowly turning into her. Did everyone turn into their mothers in the end, she wondered. Was it inevitable?

As Jade neared the marquee, loud yelps and gasps could be heard and 'Kiss from a Rose' stopped with a disturbing finality. Jade picked up pace and sprinted towards the centre of the marquee, where several guests were huddled. James staggered backwards, but Lily was nowhere to be seen.

43

'Sinead, what's going on?' Jade spotted the other brides-maids and grabbed at Sinead's upper arm.

'Oh, Birdy. James has had a little too much to drink. The first dance was going ever so well until James picked Lily up, in what I expect was a spontaneous, unplanned move, and spun her around maybe five or six times, and then accidentally let go of her and she hit the deck. Looks like she's split her lip. Do you think we should go in and help her?' Sinead's concern was blurred by booze.

Jade pushed through the crowds and found Lily sitting on the floor, a trickle of raspberry-coloured blood dripping from her lip, splatters of red down the skirt of her silk dress. A Jackson Pollock nightmare.

'Lils! Are you OK?'

'Clearly I'm not. Get me a napkin. Bloody hell.' She pushed Jade's hands away from her arm.

Jade dashed to the nearest table and grabbed a dis-carded napkin, then bent back down to press it against Lily's lip.

'OK, don't make too much fuss. I just need to get to the loo so everybody stops looking at me.'

Lily stood, a weak smile on her face, hand pushed into her mouth, the napkin firmly covering the split. James was slunk down in a chair on the edge of the dance floor, legs splayed and several mates forcing a glass of water to his mouth. Jade stepped back, letting her sister move quickly across the dance floor to the toilets. Usually, Jade would experience a reflex of annoyance having been dismissed by Lily, but instead she saw her pain. Lily had wanted this day to be perfect and it wasn't. For the first time Jade could sense the insecurities that sat deep down beneath the perfect smile, ample bosom, thin upper arms and shiny, shiny hair. She thought back to an article she had read in the paper the week before, explaining how the shell of an egg gets shinier the more rotten it becomes inside. Seeing her sister rush from the dance floor in her silk gown, looking around at the fairy-lit marquee, she could clearly see Lily's attempts to keep the exterior glowing. She wondered how rotten things would have to get for the shell to crack.

As she watched her sister walk away, for the first time in years she felt sorry for her. The dance floor started to fill again, the silence mitigated by Katy Perry's 'Firework'.

'Jade, can I have a word?'

Adam stood blocking her from the dance floor.

'About what?' Jade tried to move backwards away from him.

'I just want a word. Can we go outside where it's not so noisy?' His voice was unusually soft.

'Can we just chat here?' Jade said bluntly, scanning the room for Sophie.

Adam looked around to see who was nearby.

'Look, I came here today . . . because I think we should make another go of it.' He attempted to contort

361

his face into an expression of remorse but it was unfamiliar and he subtly missed the mark.

'What?' Jade's face rippled with confusion.

'I think we're good together,' Adam clarified.

'No you don't.' Jade remained calm. 'I just saw you with a beautiful lady's tits in your face. And that's before we even get to discussing Janey in LA.'

Ignoring Jade's protest, he continued: 'I even spoke to Lily earlier and she agreed that I'm good for you. That I bring out the best in you. She really thinks we should give it another go. She thinks you don't cope well when alone and that I really am a pillar of support. She also made the good point that you're thirty-two now and should really think about settling down. We can't chuck everything we built together away, Jade.' Adam looked deeply into Jade's eyes and smiled with one half of his mouth, a display of pure confidence.

'Adam, my sister has no clue about who or what brings out the best in me,' Jade said calmly, the knowledge that she had nothing to lose allowing her to stand steadily in front of him. 'You're not used to hearing me say no. I had gotten into the habit of placating you, and quite frankly everyone around me, but that has stopped and it's going to take some getting used to for everyone.' Jade took her time, enjoying the sound of each word boldly forming. 'I don't want to put up with your unnecessary trips away, or your put-downs, or your disinterest in anything I do. I am not only saying this aloud for the first time, but I'm also believing it properly for the first time; I deserve better.' She held his gaze, his face twitching with the uncertainty of how to respond. She stepped back one pace from him. 'I deserve better, Adam.' He nodded slowly and looked at the floor.

'Well . . . fuck you, Jade,' he stage-whispered, now unable to contain his childlike anger, which was only millimetres from the surface. Jade stepped back again and waved, her face settled in a confident smile.

'Brown's not your colour, either,' he hurled as she walked quickly away.

She didn't look back.

Walking across the soft lawn, she felt lighter, her bare feet sinking into the sodden turf as she strode towards the hotel.

Warm lights glowed from the wedding suite above. She imagined her sister was touching up her make-up after the split lip, no doubt editing some staged black and white wedding photos for Instagram at the same time. It was the perfect opportunity for Jade to tell her never again to encourage a reconciliation with Adam. She sprinted up the carpeted stairs two at a time, her breath quickening as she neared a confrontation with her sister.

Outside the wedding suite, she placed her left palm flat on the door. It was silent inside, but the lights were on. Twisting the medieval-looking knob, the unlocked door swung open with force and bashed into the wall.

Two faces stared back at her, the loud thump startling them, wide eyes and cheeks flushed with guilt. Jade recognised the man on the bed as Casper, the hotel manager. And the woman whose body he was leaning towards — their faces centimetres apart — was the bride.

44

'OH MY GOD!' Jade stepped into the room and shut the door quickly behind her. Lily pulled the straps of her dress back fully over her shoulders and sat up straight.

'Were you two . . . having it off?' Jade said, and wondered why she had used such an odd turn of phrase, but the shock was enveloping her and making her head spin.

Lily put on a display of fake outrage. 'Of course not.' She smiled, trying to cover up the lies. 'We were discussing the fallen marquee and possible compensation.' The lie came quickly. She spoke with a stern edge to her voice, one Jade had come to know when she was covering up the truth.

The hotel manager buttoned his waistcoat and looked at Lily with confusion.

'Casper here is hoping to help us claim back some of the money from the marquee company, maybe even catering too, as nobody got to eat their meringues,' Lily added, clearly hoping more detail might validate her story. She stood up as if to leave the room.

'On your wedding day? Couldn't it wait?' Jade could feel her heart beating in her chest. 'But Lily, seriously . . . ?' She gestured towards the bed, Lily's low-slung dress straps, her flushed cheeks.

'Right. Party time. Thank you, Casper.' Lily nodded at

the manager as she held the door open for him to leave, completely ignoring Jade. He sloped out, the back of his shirt still untucked from his waistband. Lily calmly smoothed down her dress, which still had specks of red blood dotted on the skirt, and began to tiptoe down the hallway. Jade raced to catch up with her. Halfway down the stairs, she pulled on her sister's shoulder to halt her escape. Portraits of men on horseback stared down at the sisters. 'Lily. What is going on?' Jade spluttered. 'I could feel it in the air. That tension when something is happening that shouldn't.' Lily tried to turn and walk down the stairs, then stopped and looked back over her shoulder at Jade with suddenly sincere eyes.

'Look, Jade. Life isn't perfect. Sometimes situations don't play out as planned. That's life. I wanted the perfect wedding, and it hasn't quite unfurled as imagined . . . OK?' Lily looked down the staircase as if to check for any onlookers.

'But you're in love with James? Or did you just want the big wedding?' A concoction of alcohol and shock made Jade feel dizzy. She clung to the banister.

'Well, of course I wanted the big wedding. And I do love James, but he has really irritated me tonight. Have you seen my lip? It's a mess.' Lily's manicured nail pointed at the dried blood that clung to her lower lip. Jade could see she had tried to cover it with make-up, beige concealer sitting in the grooves of the wound. 'And the . . . *weather.*' Lily spat the word as if it were blasphemy.

'I don't think that's James's fault.'

'Well, it hasn't gone as I had planned. As I wanted.'

'So you thought you would cheat on your brand-new husband with the manager of the hotel you're having the wedding in?' Jade mouthed the words 'cheat' and 'manager' in case the sound travelled in the wrong direction.

'We didn't cheat. OK? It was harmless. A strange, spontaneous moment. Do not tell a soul, OK? Not a soul.' Lily's eyes locked on Jade's. The air between them felt thick and claustrophobic. Jade broke the stare and looked at her bare feet on the patterned carpet runner, remembering she had left her boots outside the marquee. Purple nail varnish, months old, sat in irregular dots in the middle of each nail.

'It's OK for you, Jade. You don't need all this.' She waved her hands at the grandeur of the hotel. 'You don't need to be married to feel OK. You called off your wedding to Navi and proved it to us all. It was . . . brave.'

Jade could see the pain in Lily's face, admitting it.

'You don't really need anyone,' she went on. 'You're lucky, do you realise that?'

The veneer had cracked. Jade wasn't sure she had ever seen her sister's mask drop. Even after her divorce from Saffron and Jemima's dad, or the failed crystal business, or falling out with her friend who ran the events business; she had always managed to keep up the pretence that everything was OK. Jade could see her sister now, the real Lily underneath the performance and lipgloss and shiny black hair. The one that was a bit broken, somewhat of a mess and the one that envied *her*. It had not once occurred to Jade that Lily might want what she had. Perhaps she was the lucky one.

'I just assumed you wanted all this.' Jade's eyebrows furrowed with confusion.

'I *need* it, Jade.'

Jade stood motionless, rooted to the carpet.

Lily walked down the stairs to the foyer. 'Life isn't perfect!' she called again over her shoulder.

45

Flecks of amber sparked from the fire pit outside the hotel entrance, its crackle muffled by the chatter and howling laughter of those huddled around it, shawls on shoulders, honey-coloured whiskey in hands. Jade passed them, unable to appreciate the cosy scene as she unconsciously moved away from the bustle and back towards the quiet of the stream.

Jade was so used to Lily's behaviour that she hadn't stopped to think what was driving it. Jade's life, her past, her whole childhood, totally flipped on its head. Her mind scrolled back to when they were teenagers and every moment of drama Lily courted. Jade wondered whether Lily felt she existed at all without the drama and attention. How had she not seen it before? Lily had needed it, and Jade hadn't. It was that simple. She felt weightless, as if she could float off into the inky sky and touch the stars.

She stood staring at the moving water, now as black as the sky above, her body static and her mind spinning. She wondered whether she should tell James – or maybe her mum – about the hotel manager. She considered locating the sleazeball herself to grab him by the waistcoat and shake some sense into him. What kind of man hits on a woman so freshly married she is still in her wedding dress?

'Hello.'

She turned her head quickly and saw him. 'Oh god, you scared me.' Jade stepped back and a shard of wood dug into the sole of her foot. She winced as subtly as she could and lifted her foot to relieve the pressure.

'Jade, right?'

Jade nodded and willed her cheeks not to blush. 'Luca, right?' She pretended to only just remember his name. Luca nodded. Jade's stomach dropped, remembering him kissing someone else in the tent.

'How's the wedding?' Luca was looking out to the water rather than at Jade.

'It's, um, eventful.' Jade fiddled with the rings on her fingers. 'How has your day been?'

'Pretty full on. It's been long but nothing too stressful.' Luca looked down at the glistening water.

Jade tried to stop her leg from shaking. She pressed her hand down on it with force.

'Have you been very busy this summer with weddings?' Jade took a quick glance at his profile. His hair flopping over his right eye, his full bottom lip, his strong nose.

'Well, no, not really. This isn't my day job, so to speak.' He looked at Jade square-on. 'So whose wedding is it?'

Careful not to slur her words, she enunciated slowly, 'It's my sister's. She's a bit of a nightmare, hence why I'm out here getting some air.'

'Oh, families. I get it. Complex, right?' Luca brushed his hair from his eyes.

'Yup.' Jade desperately wanted to ask who the woman was in the tent. She went mute, unable to work out what the next natural thing to say would be.

'How come you're out here on your own?' Luca faced Jade and didn't blink. Her heartbeat picked up pace as she felt an involuntary swallow move through her throat.

'Er . . . well, I'm at the wedding on my own. I mean, my ex is unfortunately in the marquee, but we are not together, hence the "ex" bit.' Jade knew she was over-sharing but felt unable to stop. 'I'm rolling solo.' She cringed at her choice of words.

'Cool.' The left side of his mouth turned up, but his expression was unrecognisable in the midnight shadows. 'Anyway, I should be getting back to work. We've still got a ton of glasses to pick up—'

'And I'm a little chilly, so I'm going to head back in.' Jade's words clashed with his.

They moved away from the stream at the same time. Jade nodded at him a little too formally and sprinted off towards the marquee. It was nearly 1am and half the wedding guests had now retreated to their rooms or back to their cars, leaving the hardier guests to the dance floor. Biffy was still in the middle, shirt now fully unbuttoned, his belly bursting out as he strutted in circles. Jade spotted Belinda and Don at a table littered with glasses and small clutch bags.

'Belinda.' Jade hugged her tightly.

Belinda sat regally on her chair, her green hat at a tilt. 'Have you started having fun yet?' she enquired.

'Well, it's been eventful.' Jade's eyes widened. 'I still hate this dress. I'm going to burn it in some sort of farewell ceremony tomorrow.'

Belinda laughed heartily. 'I saw Adam earlier. He looked very cosy, shall we say, with another lady.' She raised a grey eyebrow.

'I've dealt with him. I think you'll be proud of me.'

'Face up to the sun, darling, remember.'

'Oh, it is.' Jade smiled and sat down next to her godmother. 'Can I tell you something, Belinda? I keep bumping into this man – and I can't get him out of my head. But I think he has a girlfriend.'

'How do you know?'

'I saw him kiss a woman from a distance in the catering tent.'

'Oh, someone here? Well, did it look friendly or passionate?' Belinda leaned towards Jade, creating their own little space away from the loud music and nearby chatter.

'Hard to tell. I was quite far away.'

'Well, Jade, you know what I'm going to say; you only live once. What do you young people say? YOLO?'

'Ha, yes.'

'Go and get yourself a drink, then walk back to the catering tent and outright ask him. Or give him your number on a slip of paper. I once did that back in the day. I walked right over to this delicious young man I was besotted with and, without speaking, I placed a small piece of paper with my number in his hand. It was ever so sexy.'

'Bloody hell, Belinda,' Jade laughed. 'OK, OK. I'll do it.' Adrenaline pumped around her whole body as she rose from the chair and kissed Belinda on the cheek.

46

The bar was still surrounded by swaying wedding guests, but the rush of adrenaline pushed Jade through the queue. As she waited, she surveyed the scene: bodies pulsating on the dance floor, loose with booze, small groups chatting at tables around the edges of the marquee, some familiar faces, some complete strangers. Not a single member of her family was in sight.

Suddenly a screeching noise tore through the sky, followed by calls from those outside. Jade felt herself being carried by the crowd into the cool night air. An electric-pink streak cut through the black of the sky, then exploded into a dandelion of gold.

'Jadey!' Sophie appeared by her side. 'Bloody love a firework. Tonight is proper magic.' Both Jade and Sophie stood, heads tilted back, eyes on the flecks of sunburst yellow and bright white that fell from the sky. Sophie draped her freckled arm over Jade's shoulder. 'He's called Hayden. The redhead. He's Scottish. I could eat his voice, it is so delicious.' Jade squeezed Sophie's shoulder and leaned her head against hers.

'How bloody gorgeous. I'm so glad you're having a fun night. I love you, Soph.' Jade turned to her friend; splinters of fireworks reflected in Sophie's light eyes.

'And I love you, mate.'

'What do you think this whole weird script thing has been about? Where have they come from? And why?' Jade's gaze followed drips of bright green as they slowly fell from the sky and burned out into black.

'Don't know, mate, I just don't know.' Sophie gripped Jade's arm tightly.

'The last script had Wavy Hair's name on it. I found one this morning while I was getting ready. He's called Luca. I need to go and track him down.'

'What are you waiting for?'

'What if he's not interested? I think I saw him kiss someone earlier.'

Sophie turned to Jade and held her shoulders, her eyes wide and serious. 'Mate, you have nothing to lose. Go! Go and find him – and write your own script, with him in it.'

The fireworks squealed overhead, all eyes turned upwards. The sound faded as Jade felt her heartbeat quicken as if it were outside of her chest. One foot in front of the other – she couldn't turn back now. The food-tent lighting looked clinical in contrast to the fireworks above. Luca was standing on his own, espresso cup in hand. She paused, then spoke. 'Hey. Luca.' He looked up. 'Can I have a word?' It sounded more formal than she had hoped.

He shrugged and put his cup down. 'Sure.'

She felt light-headed. Motioning for him to step outside, she sucked in her cheeks to stop her lip from quivering. Her throat suddenly felt constricted. A small cough to clear it.

'So, I'll just come out with it. Who was the lady you kissed earlier? Is she your girlfriend? Wife, perhaps?' Jade attempted to sound casual and inquisitive rather than desperate.

'Ha. Have you been spying on me?' He raised an eyebrow. She was right about the dimple, which appeared on his left cheek.

'Oh god, no. I was just, er, sitting by the stream earlier and I guess because I had left my phone in my hotel room, I wasn't so distracted so was just sort of looking around, and . . . saw you . . . kissing someone . . . in the food tent.' Jade's mouth ran dry, conscious she was over-explaining.

'I don't remember kissing anyone today. Are you sure it was me?'

Oh god, he was lying. Maybe this stranger couldn't be trusted. Jade's mind raced. 'Well, I saw you. You were doing something over by one of the work-stations and a lady with a ponytail came and hugged you and you . . . kissed her. On the head?'

Luca threw his head back and laughed. 'That's my small Italian mum! It's her catering company. I'm only helping out today as one of her team pulled out yesterday. Trusty son saves the day.' He raised two thumbs in the air and grinned. Simultaneously Jade felt her bones lighten with relief and her face burn.

'Oh.' She laughed along with Luca nervously.

'Birdy, Birdy, darling?' The startling sight of Sue and Jacquie racing towards her was enough to snap her out of the embarrassment.

'Birdy?' Luca looked at Jade curiously. Jade didn't have time to explain.

'Birdy, crisis talks needed,' Sue puffed, her plait a mess of unruly strands.

Luca waved a hand and walked back towards the catering tent. Jade threw her mum a death stare.

'What?' she snapped, her frustration obvious. 'Is everything OK? Also, how come you two are together? Bit of a turnaround from lunch.' She looked incredulously at her mum and stepmum.

'We've put our differences to one side for now,' Jacquie said softly.

'Anyway, darling, we have a scene on our hands,' Sue said, waving her arms around frantically, silver bangles clashing dramatically. 'Sarita has it on good authority that the hotel manager recently entered Lily's hotel room *with* her . . . holding hands. What do we think? What do we do?' Sue wiped her forehead then put her hands on her hips.

Jade tried to clear her mind. Should she mention what she had seen earlier? 'Where is Lily, Mum?' she asked, stalling for time.

'We don't know. Darling, look at my Fitbit. I've done nearly ten thousand steps trying to find her in the last hour.'

'I think we need to find her and ask her outright,' announced Jacquie firmly.

'I think we keep quiet until we work out what has been going on,' Sue said simultaneously, both women loving the drama.

'Wow, Mum, Jacquie. Let's not rush into anything. Let's just work it out together. Where is James?'

'His friends are currently forcing him to drink water and eat a bacon roll in the marquee to sober up. He's in a terrible mess,' Sue exclaimed. 'Do you think he knows? Is that why he got so shit-faced?'

'Makes a change from you, Sue,' Jacquie said smugly.

'Mum, Jacquie. Stop. No more slights and digs.' Jade breathed in deeply. 'You split up and try and find her. In the meantime, I'll try and get to the bottom of all of this. Got it?' Jade looked at her mum and stepmum sternly.

'Got it,' the women chimed in unison.

It was approaching 2am, and the dance floor held only a few couples. Boyz II Men echoed around the emptying marquee as pairs of guests pressed their bodies together and swayed loosely around the floor. Jade's eyes darted from person to person. Sophie's head was tilted to one side, her pink cheek pressed into the tall redhead's chest. There was no sign of Lily or the other brides-maids. Jade dashed in and out of couples slow-dancing, then walked to the exit at the back of the marquee. Dim yellow lights lit the porch of the hotel. As she approached the entrance, a figure walked out of the shadows and placed their hands around her waist.

'Woah.' She turned round quickly.

'Jade! I've been looking for you all night.' Biffy's large hands squeezed her waist.

'Oh god. I'm trying to find Lily.' She pushed his hands away and stepped back from his alcohol-infused breath.

'Better dash.' She smiled and ran into the lobby, leaving Biffy swaying on the lawn in the dark. A dozen guests were slumped on sofas, floppy limbs sprawled, make-up smudged in the dim light. She didn't recognise any of them. After ten minutes of walking the corridors of the hotel she gave up and went back outside in search of a glass of water, her mouth furry and tongue acidic. She wondered what was better, finding her sister to warn her that word was getting around, or leaving her mum and Jacquie to deal with it all. The food tent was now empty. All the catering staff seemed to have left and were more than likely already on the motorway back into town. A cool breeze whispered. Walking aimlessly, she gazed up, locating Orion's belt and the Plough, the only constellations she knew. Silently a finger tapped her shoulder. She jumped back. 'Biffy, for fuck's sake.'

'Biffy?' replied a deep voice.

Jade turned to face Luca, only inches from her face.

47

'Oh god, sorry, I just thought you were . . . I was just looking at the stars and . . .' She petered off, aware that she was headed towards another rambling torrent.

Luca leaned in and pressed his lips against Jade's. He smelled of summer and smoke, of escapism and recklessness. In the shock of feeling him so close, his lips on hers, she froze. He pulled away and looked at her, his face a scramble of sudden uncertainty.

'No, no, it's fine,' she said, leaning her head back in towards his. Her hips melted into his as his hands pulled the base of her back closer. The sky above felt as if it had wrapped its velvet around them both. The music in the marquee had stopped, leaving a silence that allowed Jade to experience every physical sensation without distraction. Liquid ecstasy ran through her veins.

He pulled back. 'The second kiss I've had today.'

She laughed. 'Sorry about earlier. Spying on you,' Jade winced.

Luca smiled. 'Well, I like that you asked me outright if she was my wife. You're pretty outspoken, huh?'

'Well . . . I didn't use to be.' The last three months whizzed through Jade's mind. She changed the subject. 'You and your mum get on well, then?'

'Yup, she's pretty wonderful,' he said. 'It's just me and her so we're really close. Was that your mum who came running up?'

'My mums, plural. The one with the bright red hair is my stepmum. I've sent them off on a wild goose chase, so at least they're occupied. Should stop them from killing each other.'

Luca smiled curiously. Their bodies were only centimetres apart and Jade could feel heat in the space between them. The silence felt palpable.

'Do you live in London, then? With your mum?' Jade asked. The question felt clumsy, but it filled the gap in conversation.

'No, not with Mum. I don't think she'd be happy if her thirty-two-year-old son was still at home. Mum's in Crouch End, I'm in Angel.'

'I'm thirty-two too.' Jade felt instantly juvenile for saying it out loud.

'Are you in London?' Luca asked. Jade sensed his own nervousness for the first time.

'Richmond. So, sort of.'

'Fancy.' Luca raised an eyebrow.

'It's really not. It's a shoebox of a flat. But I love it.'

'Look, I'd better go. I'm back to my actual job tomorrow first thing.'

Jade's whole body deflated. It took mental effort to stay upright. 'Oh, OK.' Butterflies danced around her belly. 'What is your day job?' She attempted to sound breezy, not wanting the conversation to ever end.

'I'm a writer. Scripts, to be precise.'

Jade laughed loudly.

'I know, it sounds pretentious,' he replied hastily.

'No, no, it's not that. I don't think it sounds pretentious at all.'

More silence. Jade ran through sentences in her head that could keep him from leaving.

'Want a lift back home?' Luca tentatively asked.

'Well, yes. OK, then,' she stuttered. 'But I just need to do one thing.' Jade nodded to Luca, a look that said, 'Please stay.'

She leaned in and kissed him again. She had never been this forward, this naturally confident. She turned and ran up towards the hotel.

Sophie was in the foyer, headed towards the stairs, her polka-dot dress slipping from her shoulders. 'We swapped numbers!' Sophie held her phone aloft in celebration. 'Me and the Scot.' Sophie bit her top lip, then threw her arms sloppily around Jade's neck. Jade could smell tobacco, vodka and rose perfume on her friend's neck. She squeezed her tightly.

'I'm getting out of here, Soph. I don't fancy waking up to all this drama with my sister. You OK staying here tonight without me?' Jade winced.

'Sleeping in a massive bed, having room service and another bath tomorrow in that tub? Yup, think I'll cope.'

'Will Shania Twain be OK?'

'I'll text Cassandra downstairs. She can feed her. Now stop worrying about my cat and get out of here. How are you getting back to the flat?'

'Wavy Hair is giving me a lift.' Jade's face broke into a huge smile.

'What a dream. Remember, a kiss in the car is fine but you break off the kiss first to leave him wanting more. Do not invite him up to the flat and do not thank him profusely for the lift. Also text me when you get there so I know you're safe. You deserve this, Jade. Head high, Beyoncé energy. Now go!' Sophie shooed her away. Blowing a kiss in Sophie's direction, Jade made for the stairs.

Her bag was still in the bridesmaids' room. She sprinted up the three flights, willing Luca to still be there when she got back. She burst into the room to find her mum, Jacquie and dad huddled together. Tony's voice boomed around the capacious room as he protested that it was not possible his princess, Lily, had done such a thing. Sue barked back that she would threaten to go legal with the hotel due to the misconduct of the manager.

The jumbled noise of conflicting voices was broken by Jade's entrance. All three heads turned. 'Jade, oh Jade, get in here. We need your help. We have to fix this mess and make sure Lily is alright,' said Sue. Her cheeks were impossibly pink, her lipstick smudged across her chin, desperation in her eyes. Jade grabbed her bag without saying a word, turned and shut the door behind her.

Her thigh muscles twitched as she leapt down, two steps at a time. She could still hear her mum calling after her. She stopped in the foyer, catching a glimpse of herself in the large gilt mirror. Her hair was in straggles, her eye make-up grey smudges, and her mouth was pulling into an involuntary smile. She was happy.

Her phone vibrated from within her bag. Pulling it out hastily, she saw a text from Jackson. He hadn't contacted her since he left. She clicked on his name and saw one word.

Abracadabra!

She laughed out loud and felt her eyes well. As she approached the main doors, an exhausted-looking member of staff was laying out sheets of paper on a side table underneath a grand mirror.

'Want one of these now? It's the activity sheet and schedule for tomorrow. I believe there's lawn games and a post-wedding lunch.' He unenthusiastically waved sheets of paper in Jade's direction. Jade took the top one and walked towards the door. She squinted in the darkness, unable to clearly read the words, yet the font had a remarkable familiarity.

LILY

Birdyyy!

She read the first line of the script then scrunched the sheet of paper into a tiny ball. Blue light danced next to orange, the fire pit still burning bright with not a soul nearby to heat. Jade tightly gripped the scrunched-up paper and tossed it into the flames.

Words burned into dust – only ashes left, that would float freely into the infinite sky. As she watched it burn, the paper coiled and contorted, receiving its fate, until shards and grey flakes crumbled at the flame's feet.

Walking back towards the car park, her heart pounded. She oscillated between euphoric joy that she might see Luca still waiting and a stern pessimism so as not to be too disappointed if he wasn't. She walked around the screen of trees that separated the hotel and the car park. The gravel was painful underfoot, small stones creating imprints on her bare soles. Smoothing her hair down, she rounded the corner to see a figure standing by a car with the passenger door open.

Luca.

48

Holding her arms out to balance herself, she navigated the discomfort of the gravel underfoot. She dared to look up and saw him watching her with the corners of his mouth upturned. His shoulders were broad, his limbs long and forearms muscular. She dug her teeth into her bottom lip. He nodded to the car.

'BIRDYYY. BIRRRDYYY!' A vulture-like screech was tearing through the air from the direction of the marquee. 'BIRDYYY.'

Jade's eyes widened. Lily stood at the edge of the car park, her hands in the air, one shoe on, one off, mascara running in charcoal rivers down her cheeks, a plaster hanging from her lip and splashes of red wine now adding to the blood on her silk gown. Luca looked at Jade with wide, concerned eyes.

'Wait,' she said softly, and put a hand on Luca's shoulder. She dropped her bag and tiptoed back across the painful gravel until she was a metre in front of her sister.

'Birdy, where are you going?' Lily screeched.

'I'm leaving, sis. Are you OK?' Jade kept her voice upbeat.

'OK? Clearly, I am *not* OK. You can't just leave. James is asleep on the garden furniture; everyone has left and barely a single guest said thank you or paid a compliment to the day. My dress is ruined, my face is ruined.' She began to dramatically sob. 'You have to do something.' Lily's voice made Jade flinch.

'Lily,' Jade whispered with gentleness. 'I'm sad for you that today didn't turn out how you wanted. I know you needed it to be perfect, but as you said to me earlier, life doesn't always work out that way. And you know what, that's OK. I would rather see your imperfect side than constantly be met with the—' Jade scrambled to find the right words '—fake side,' she said awkwardly.

'Fake? Are you alluding to my breast surgery?'

'No, no, obviously not. I mean your need to show everyone that your life is perfect. You know it's OK to show people you're struggling. It's OK to show people you have flaws.'

Lily's mouth opened to respond but nothing came out.

'It's alright that this has all been a bit of a mess. I just can't save you,' Jade continued.

Lily stared into Jade's eyes, disbelief and desperation written across her face.

'I love you, sis. It's going to be OK. Go get some sleep.' Jade leaned in and kissed Lily's mascara-stained cheek, then turned away.

She skipped back over the gravel to where Luca was waiting at the open car door. As the engine roared into life, Jefferson Airplane blared out, the haunting vocals of 'Somebody to Love' filling the air.

Jade gazed back at Lily, who was screaming something, her mouth wide, forming words Jade couldn't hear. She smiled and waved as Luca reversed the car, churning up the stones below. A small portion of guilt landed in her stomach, but she knew this was not her problem to solve. As they left the car park, she gave a final look at her sister, standing in a pool of her self-made chaos, then down at the back seat of the car, where something caught her eye. A wad of paper. She leaned on her elbows and peered in more closely. At the top of the page it simply said:

JADE

The rest of the page was entirely blank.

She looked forward at the seemingly endless road ahead, then caught a glimpse of her own reflection in the rear-view mirror, and winked.

Acknowledgements

Writing this book has been the greatest creative joy of my life. Every time I've opened my laptop, I've jubilantly waltzed into Jade's world, excited to see where she would end up. I'm fascinated by the roles we all play in families and social settings and the moments where we lose our voices altogether, so I have many people to thank who have, over the years, helped me to realise my own voice.

I would like to start by thanking my friend Clare, who gave me a huge push to start writing this book. The idea for *Scripted* landed in my head while I was out running one day, and at first I wasn't sure what to do with it. Was it a TV show? A metaphor that I could use in a podcast? Or a work of fiction? When telling Clare, a fellow writer, the outline of the story, she questioned my hesitance to write it as a novel. I admitted I was nervous, having never done it. Her response was: 'Just open your bloody laptop tomorrow and start.' So I did, and I'm forever grateful she gave me the push I needed.

Lily was by far the most fun character in this book to play around with, largely because she is such a novelty to me. My brother Jamie is the antithesis of Lily and her outrageous antics. His cool, calm demeanour has always been a salve and his uncomplicated view on life has often helped me swing back from worry. Growing up with such a lovely brother allowed me to deeply explore what the opposite would be like within the pages of this book. Thank god you're not like Lily.

Thanks to my cousin Shannon, whose real-life job is set and installation design. Poring over Shannon's Instagram page was a huge inspiration to bring this colourful job to life. Although she doesn't have a boss like Colin, she certainly lives and breathes art and design like Jade. I always love hearing what exciting and adventurous jobs she's working on and was thrilled she was happy for me to use her artistic flare as the foundation of this book.

Throughout the writing of this book, I found myself having the right conversations at exactly the right time, and that was certainly the case when Jo Bowlby taught me the true meaning of the word 'Abracadabra'. Thanks for that critical gem of information, Jo. Your wisdom has helped me so much over the years.

Amanda Harris, my literary agent, has long supported my writing and I'm grateful she didn't dissuade me from having a go at fiction. I kept the book as a dreamy little secret for around 40,000 words, then thought I'd better show Amanda in case it was terrible. As usual, she cheered me on from the sidelines and offered valuable advice when needed. I'm so grateful for her thoughtful words and gentle lines of questioning that never fail to get me to write better and brighter.

Thank you to Clio at Michael Joseph. I'm not sure where to start. Some time ago in a brightly lit office I mumbled my way through the outlines of this book, hoping that I was making sense. Clio understood my vision and passion for this story from the start. Her enthusiasm for Jade's world was solid from day one and she never stopped asking me interesting questions about Jade's childhood, her thoughts, and her reasons for losing her confidence. Without this level of support and understanding there is no way this book would be what it is today. Thank you for believing in *Scripted*, Clio. I'm forever grateful.

Thank you to the whole Michael Joseph family for welcoming me into the fold. I'm so lucky to have such an incredible team around me and this book.

Thanks to Eugenie for your eagle-eyed editing. You pushed me to think things through much more thoroughly and helped me to tighten this book up and make it the best it can be. I'm grateful for your expertise and vigilance.

Lee Motley, huge thanks for creating the most brilliant cover. It has brought Jade to life so beautifully without giving too much away. It was a genius idea to have a peek of one of the scripts on the cover, alluding to the adventure she is about to go on. I'm so grateful for your ingenuity and for the final piece in the *Scripted* puzzle.

Sarah White and Matt Page at YMU, thank you for scheduling in time for this project. You both understood how much this book meant to me and helped me find the space and pockets of time to dive into the writing process. You're both angels from management heaven.

Behind every shattered writer there is a partner making tea, and that is certainly the case when it comes to Jesse. Thanks to my brilliant husband for being generous with his time so I could put time into this book and finish up on edits in moments when our house felt like a zoo. Love you, J.

My children have so far been mainly unimpressed by my work credentials but with this book have been intrigued by the storyline and 'what happens next'. It's been a joy to explain snippets of the story and see their eyes light up. It might not be appropriate reading material for you yet, Honey and Rex, but maybe one day you'll enjoy it. Thank you for being my biggest inspiration.

Mum and Dad, thank you for always supporting my creative endeavours. I'm not sure how I ended up writing multiple books, but I'm so grateful that my twisty and turny path got me here. Without your unwavering support it would have been a lot harder.

Lastly I would like to thank you for reading this book. Jade's story has brought me so much joy, which I can only hope you feel too. I'm grateful that you decided to take a chance on this story, and I hope if you haven't quite found your voice yet, that Jade can give you a much-needed nudge to do so. It's very much time for you to write your own script.